FORGET ME NAT

MARIA SCRIVAN

graphix
An Imprint of
SCHOLASTIC

For my parents
(the most loving people I know)

Library of Congress Control Number: 2019947168

ISBN 978-1-338-53825-0 (hardcover)
ISBN 978-1-338-53824-3 (paperback)

10 9 8 7 6 5 4 3 2 1   20 21 22 23 24

Printed in China 62
First edition, September 2020
Edited by Megan Peace
Book design by Phil Falco
Publisher: David Saylor

CONTENTS

Crush	1
You + Me = We	11
Love Songs	23
Falling for You	35
Campaign	51
Brace Yourself	77
The Day before Valentine's Day	93
Stuck on You	99
The Dance	107
Sour Grapes (And Everything Else)	121
Practice	137
Promises	147
Friends	161
Vote	169
Rubber Band	179
Election Results	185
Promises Too	195
Yearbook	209
The Outtakes	223

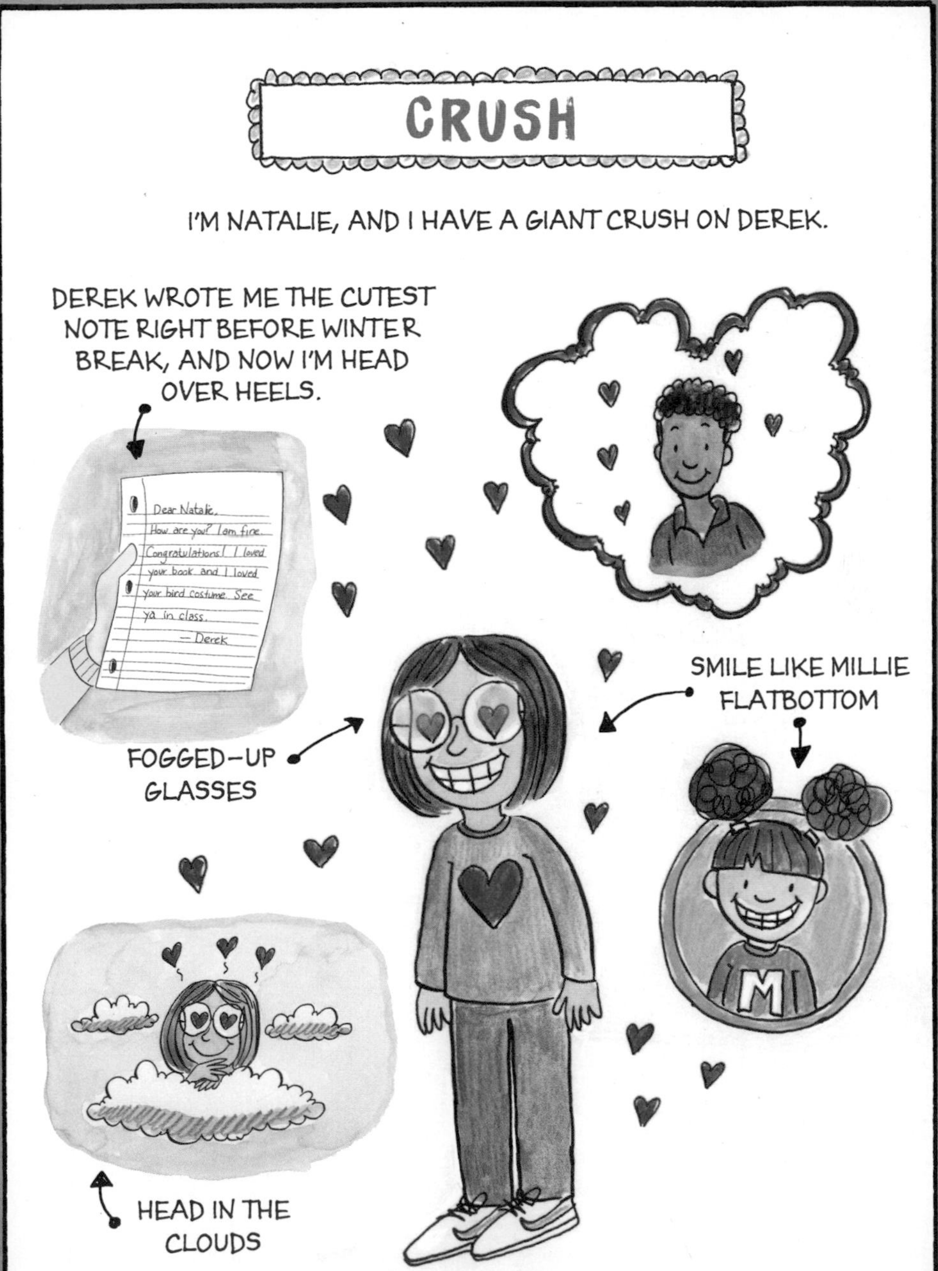
CRUSH
I'M NATALIE, AND I HAVE A GIANT CRUSH ON DEREK.
DEREK WROTE ME THE CUTEST NOTE RIGHT BEFORE WINTER BREAK, AND NOW I'M HEAD OVER HEELS.
Dear Natalie,
How are you? I am fine.
Congratulations! I loved your book and I loved your bird costume. See ya in class.
— Derek
FOGGED-UP GLASSES
SMILE LIKE MILLIE FLATBOTTOM
M
HEAD IN THE CLOUDS

DEREK IS ALL I THINK ABOUT.

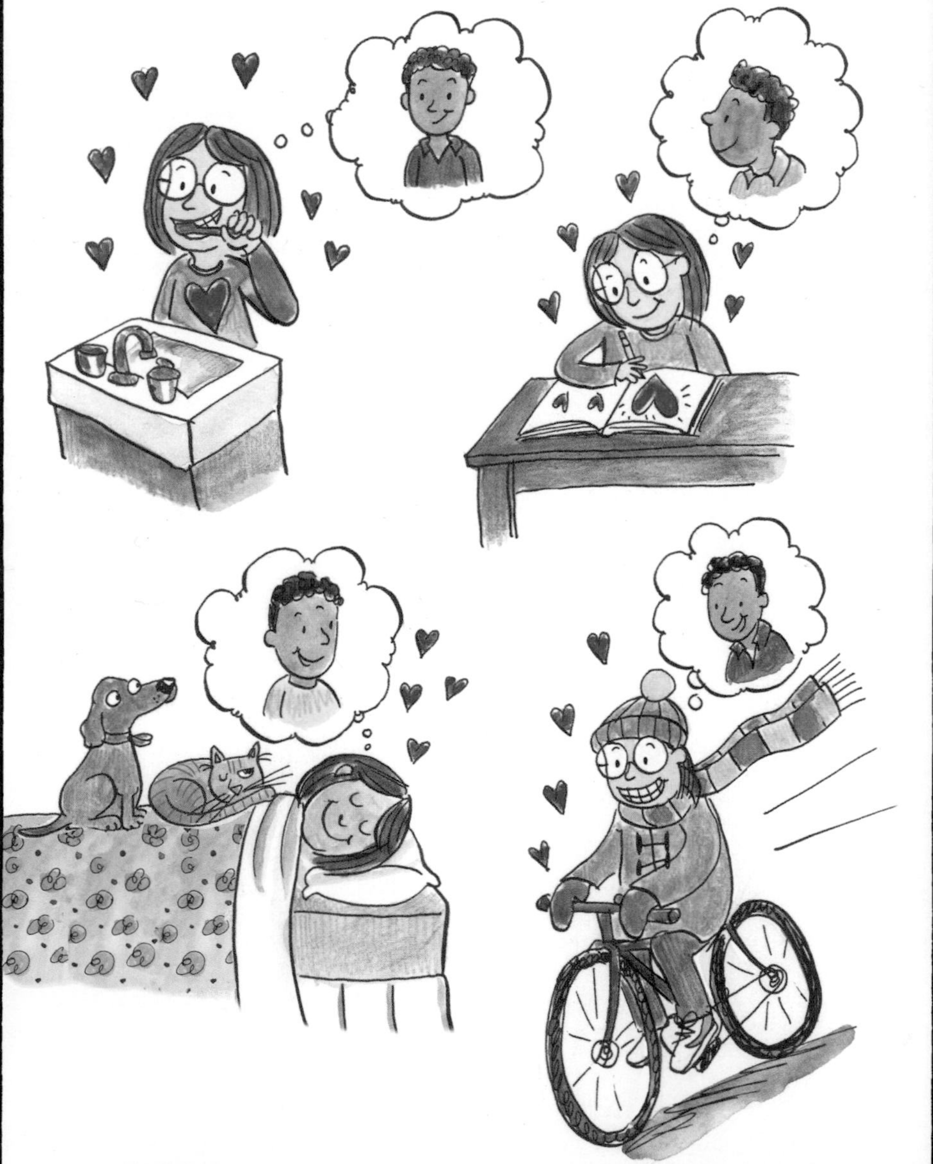

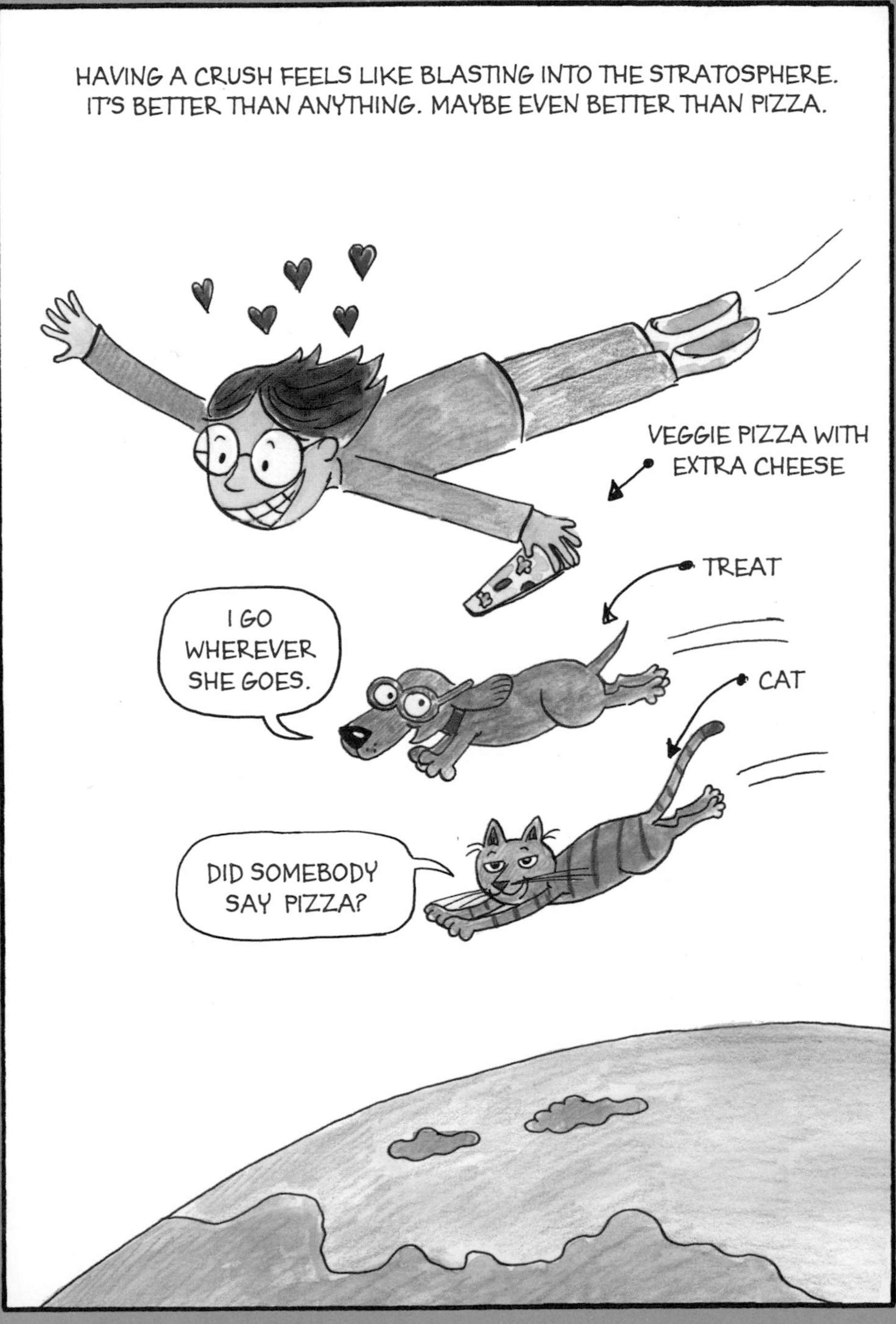
HAVING A CRUSH FEELS LIKE BLASTING INTO THE STRATOSPHERE. IT'S BETTER THAN ANYTHING. MAYBE EVEN BETTER THAN PIZZA.
VEGGIE PIZZA WITH EXTRA CHEESE
TREAT
I GO WHEREVER SHE GOES.
CAT
DID SOMEBODY SAY PIZZA?

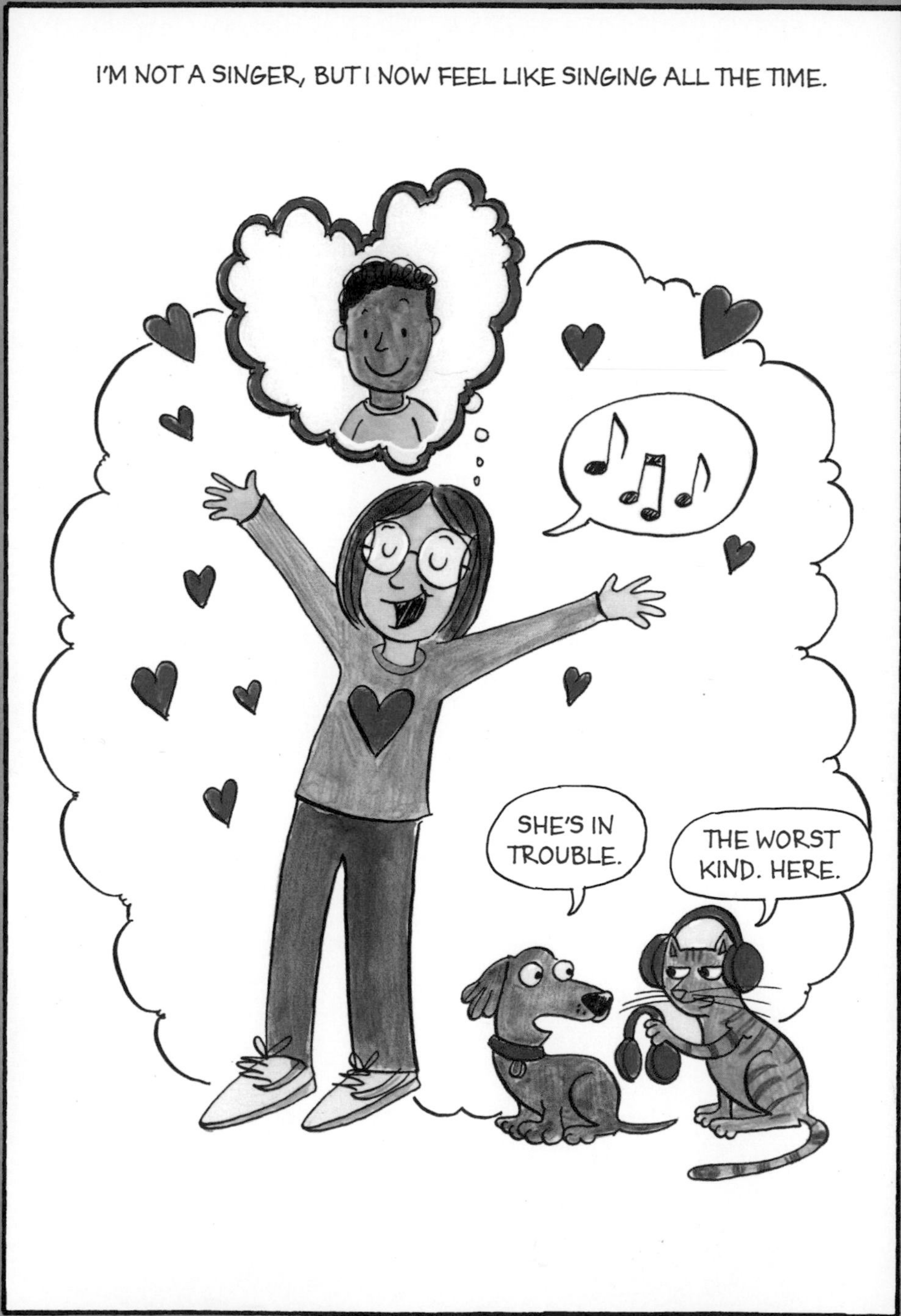
I'M NOT A SINGER, BUT I NOW FEEL LIKE SINGING ALL THE TIME.
SHE'S IN TROUBLE.
THE WORST KIND. HERE.

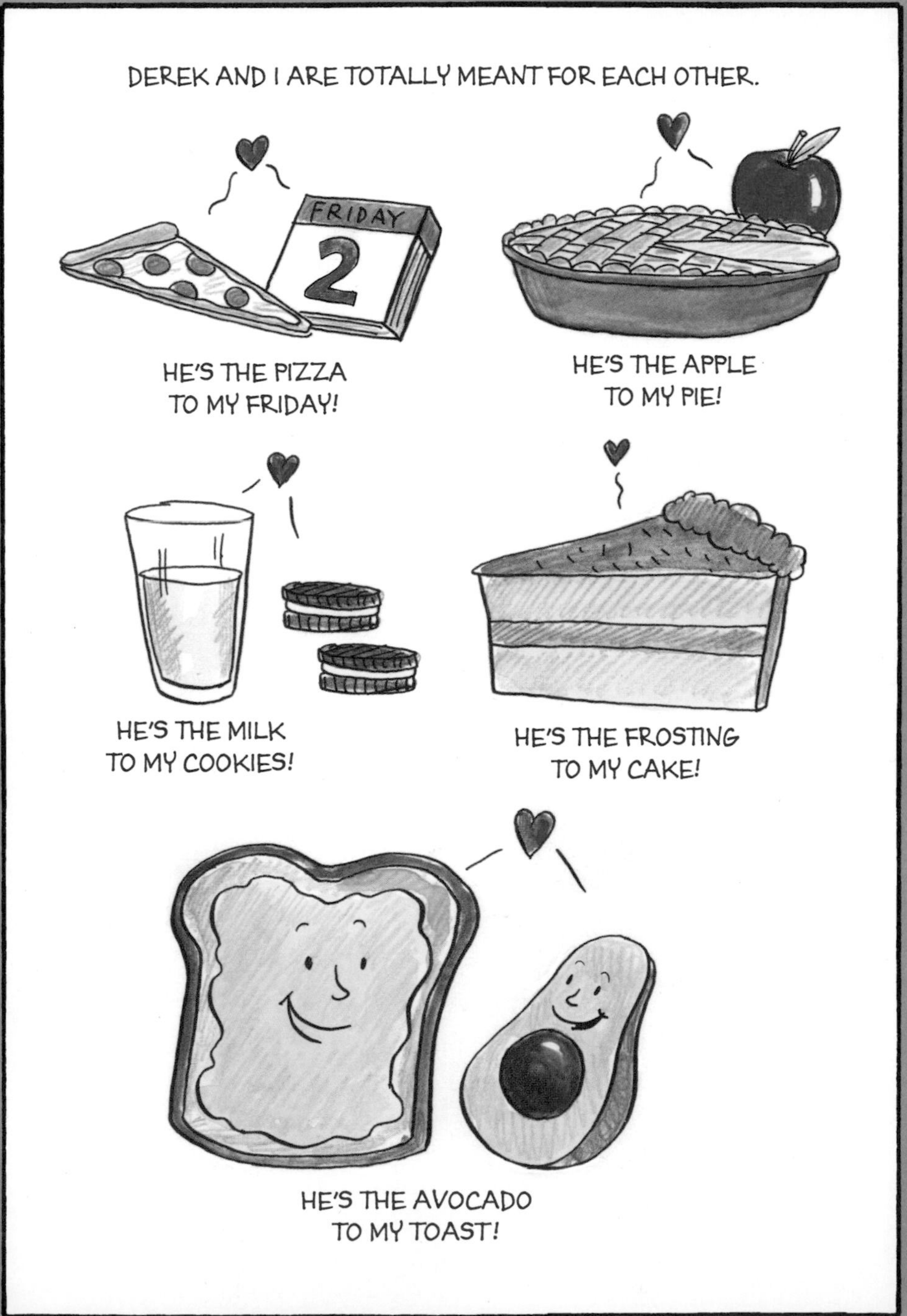

DEREK AND I ARE TOTALLY MEANT FOR EACH OTHER.
FRIDAY
2
HE'S THE PIZZA TO MY FRIDAY!
HE'S THE APPLE TO MY PIE!
HE'S THE MILK TO MY COOKIES!
HE'S THE FROSTING TO MY CAKE!
HE'S THE AVOCADO TO MY TOAST!

HOW TO TELL IF YOU AND YOUR CRUSH ARE MEANT TO BE:

IF YOU THROW A PIECE OF CRUMPLED PAPER INTO THE TRASH AND GET IT IN ON THE FIRST TRY, IT'S MEANT TO BE.

IF YOU PICK OUT THE COLOR CANDY YOU CALLED IN ADVANCE, IT'S MEANT TO BE.

IF YOU CONSULT A MAGIC 8–BALL AND ALL SIGNS POINT TO YES, IT'S MEANT TO BE.

IF YOU READ THEIR HOROSCOPE AND IT SAYS SO, IT'S MEANT TO BE.

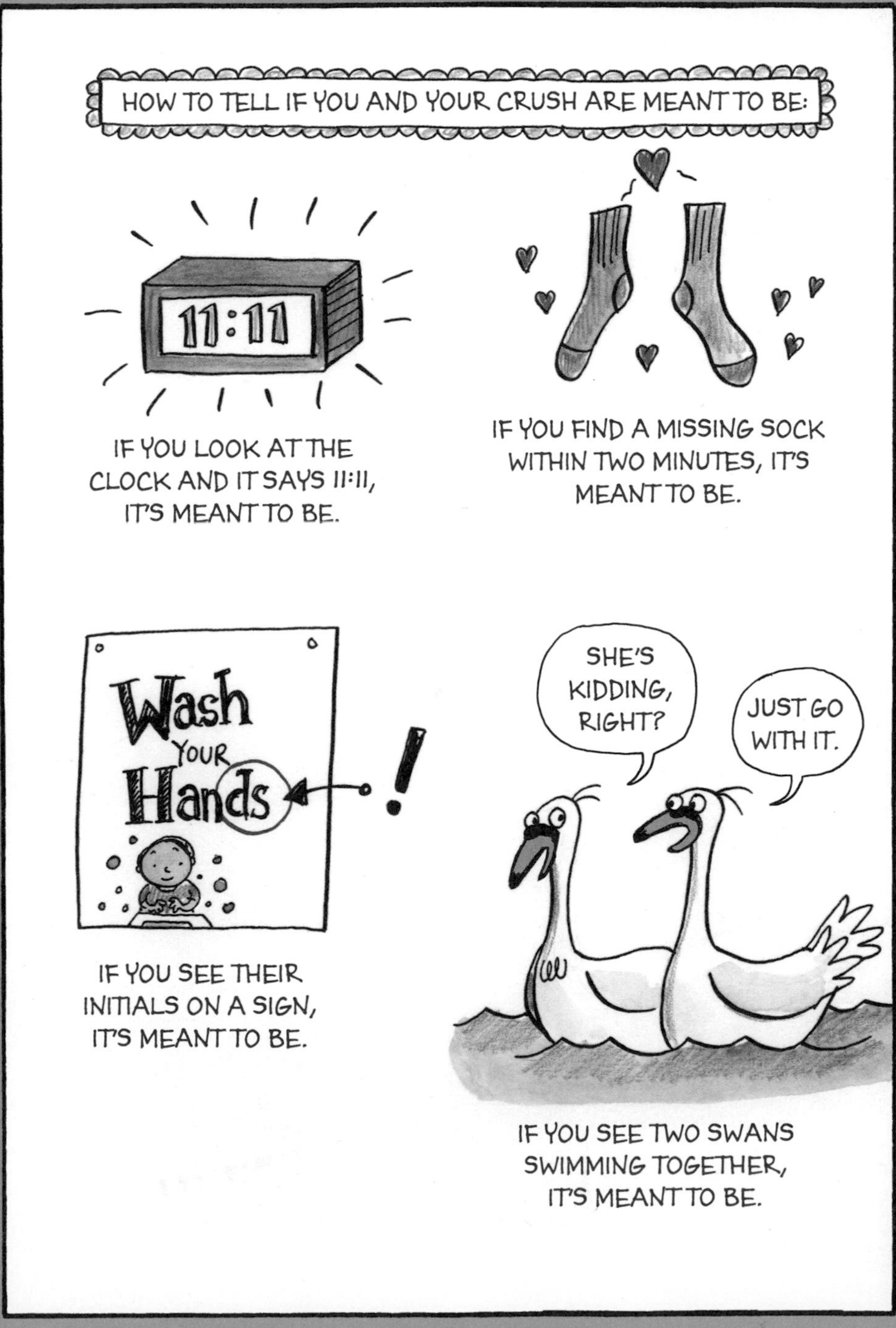
HOW TO TELL IF YOU AND YOUR CRUSH ARE MEANT TO BE:
11:11
IF YOU LOOK AT THE CLOCK AND IT SAYS 11:11, IT'S MEANT TO BE.
IF YOU FIND A MISSING SOCK WITHIN TWO MINUTES, IT'S MEANT TO BE.
Wash Your Hands
!
IF YOU SEE THEIR INITIALS ON A SIGN, IT'S MEANT TO BE.
SHE'S KIDDING, RIGHT?
JUST GO WITH IT.
IF YOU SEE TWO SWANS SWIMMING TOGETHER, IT'S MEANT TO BE.

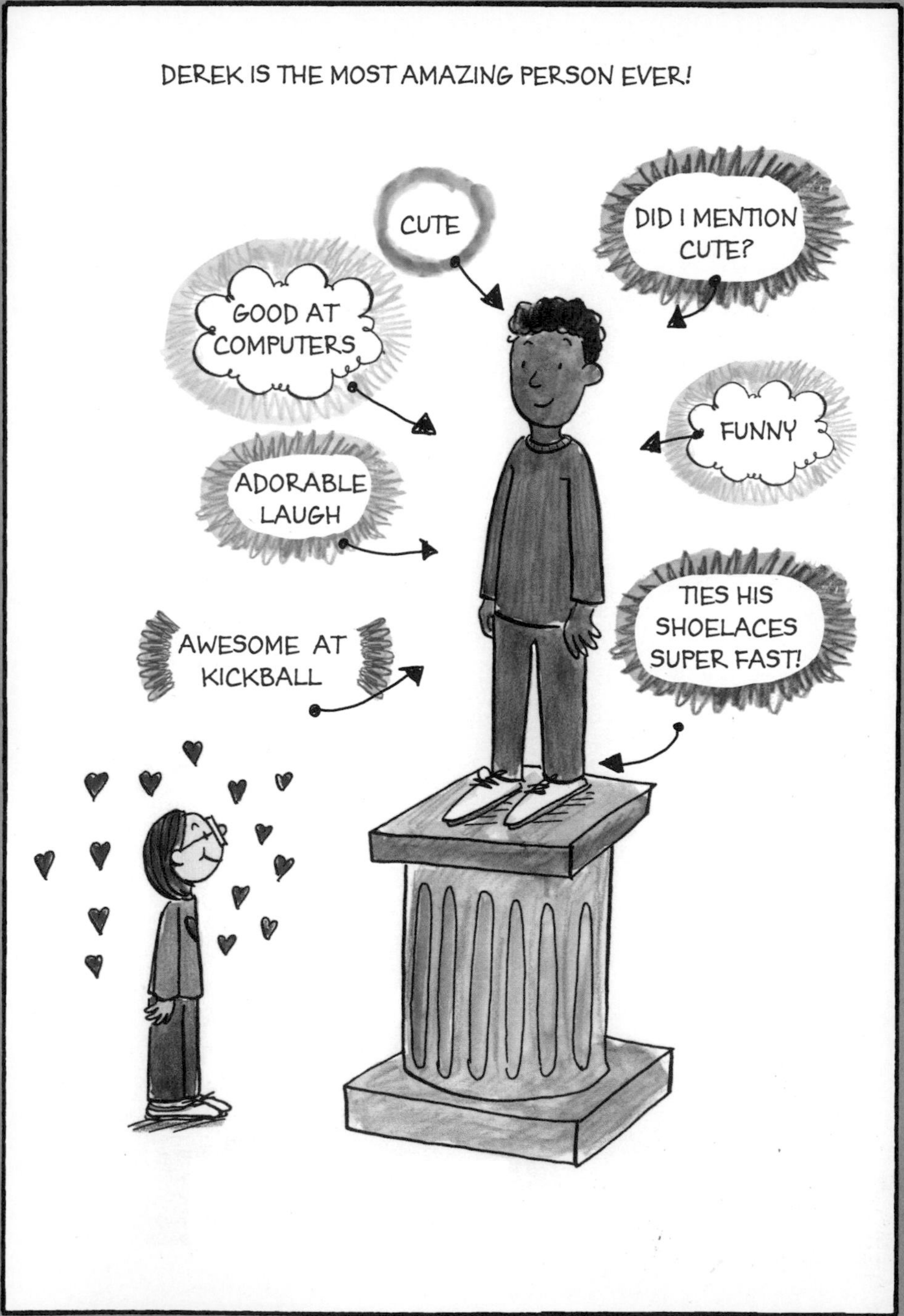
DEREK IS THE MOST AMAZING PERSON EVER!
CUTE
DID I MENTION CUTE?
GOOD AT COMPUTERS
FUNNY
ADORABLE LAUGH
TIES HIS SHOELACES SUPER FAST!
AWESOME AT KICKBALL

WINTER BREAK WAS GREAT, BUT I COULDN'T WAIT TO GET BACK TO SCHOOL TO SEE DEREK.

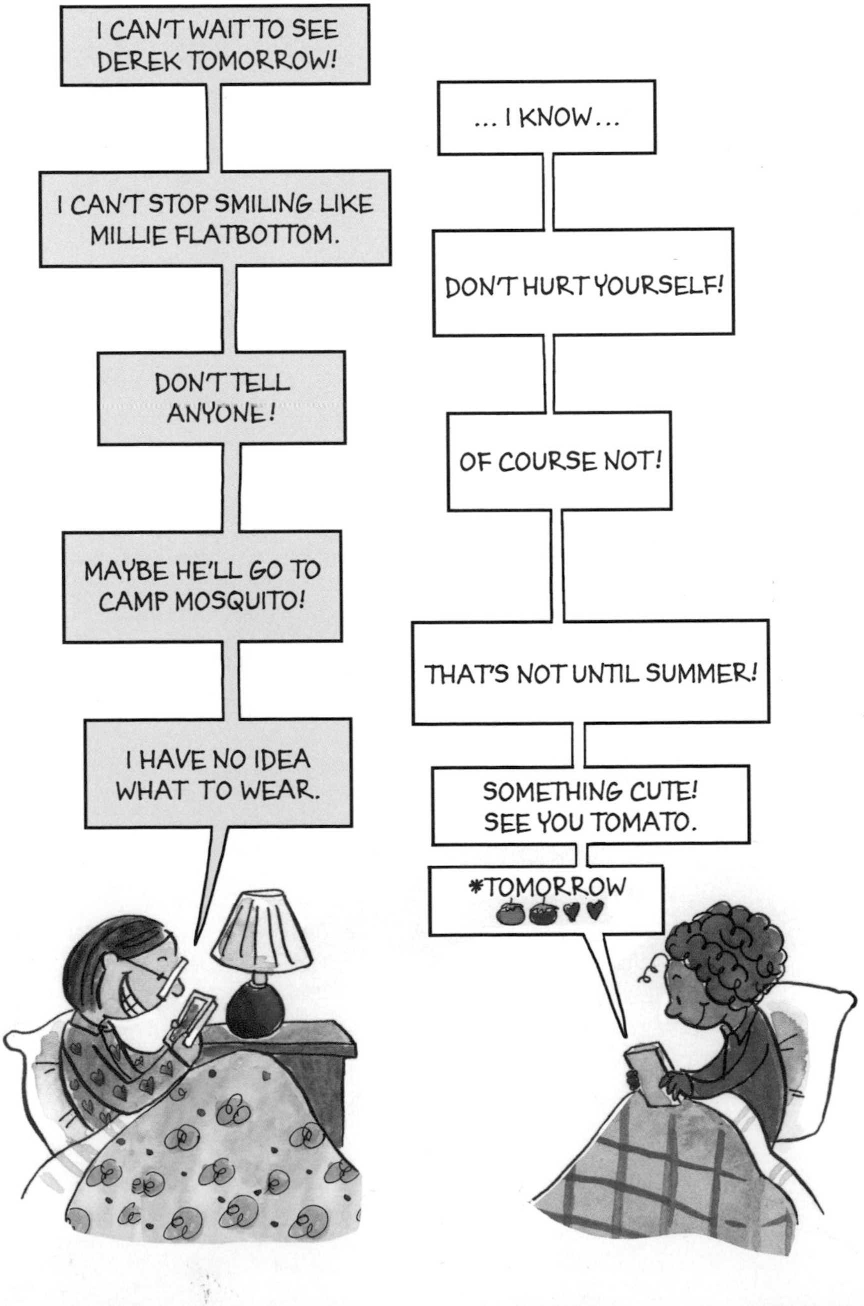

I CAN'T WAIT TO SEE DEREK TOMORROW!
... I KNOW...
I CAN'T STOP SMILING LIKE MILLIE FLATBOTTOM.
DON'T HURT YOURSELF!
DON'T TELL ANYONE!
OF COURSE NOT!
MAYBE HE'LL GO TO CAMP MOSQUITO!
THAT'S NOT UNTIL SUMMER!
I HAVE NO IDEA WHAT TO WEAR.
SOMETHING CUTE! SEE YOU TOMATO.
*TOMORROW

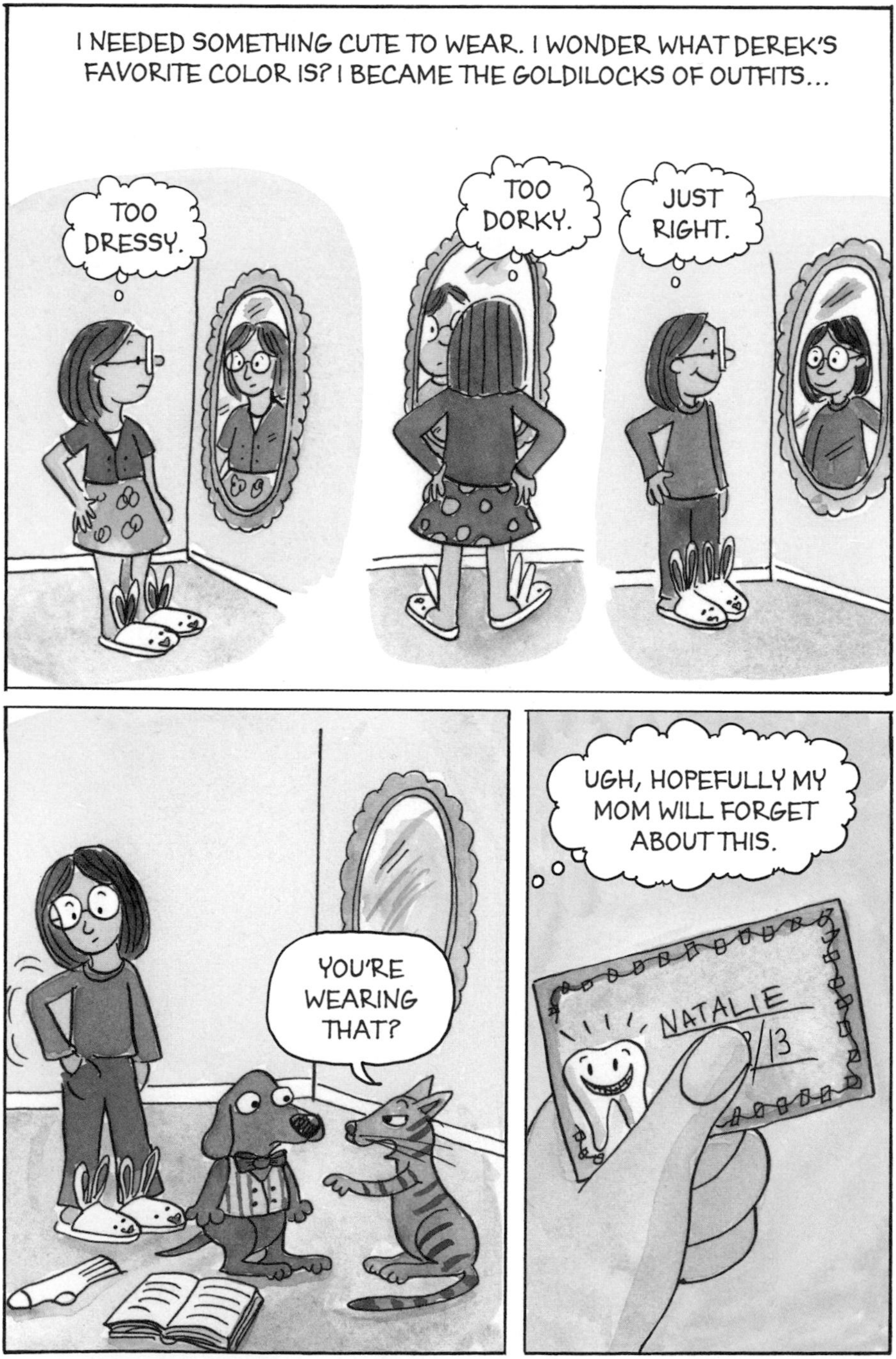
I NEEDED SOMETHING CUTE TO WEAR. I WONDER WHAT DEREK'S FAVORITE COLOR IS? I BECAME THE GOLDILOCKS OF OUTFITS...
TOO DRESSY.
TOO DORKY.
JUST RIGHT.
YOU'RE WEARING THAT?
UGH, HOPEFULLY MY MOM WILL FORGET ABOUT THIS.
NATALIE

CHAPTER 1
YOU + ME = WE

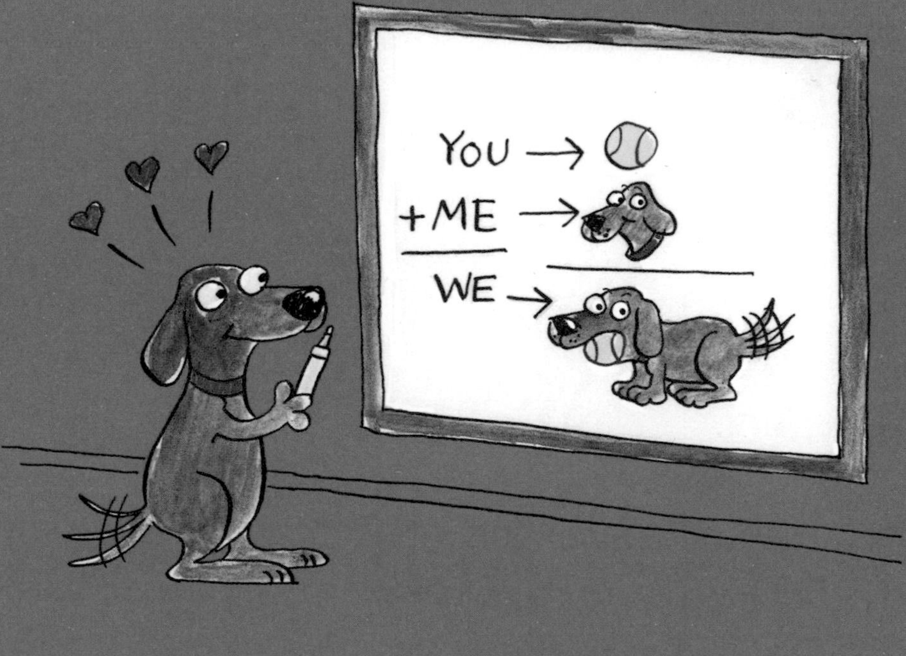

YOU →
+ME →
WE →

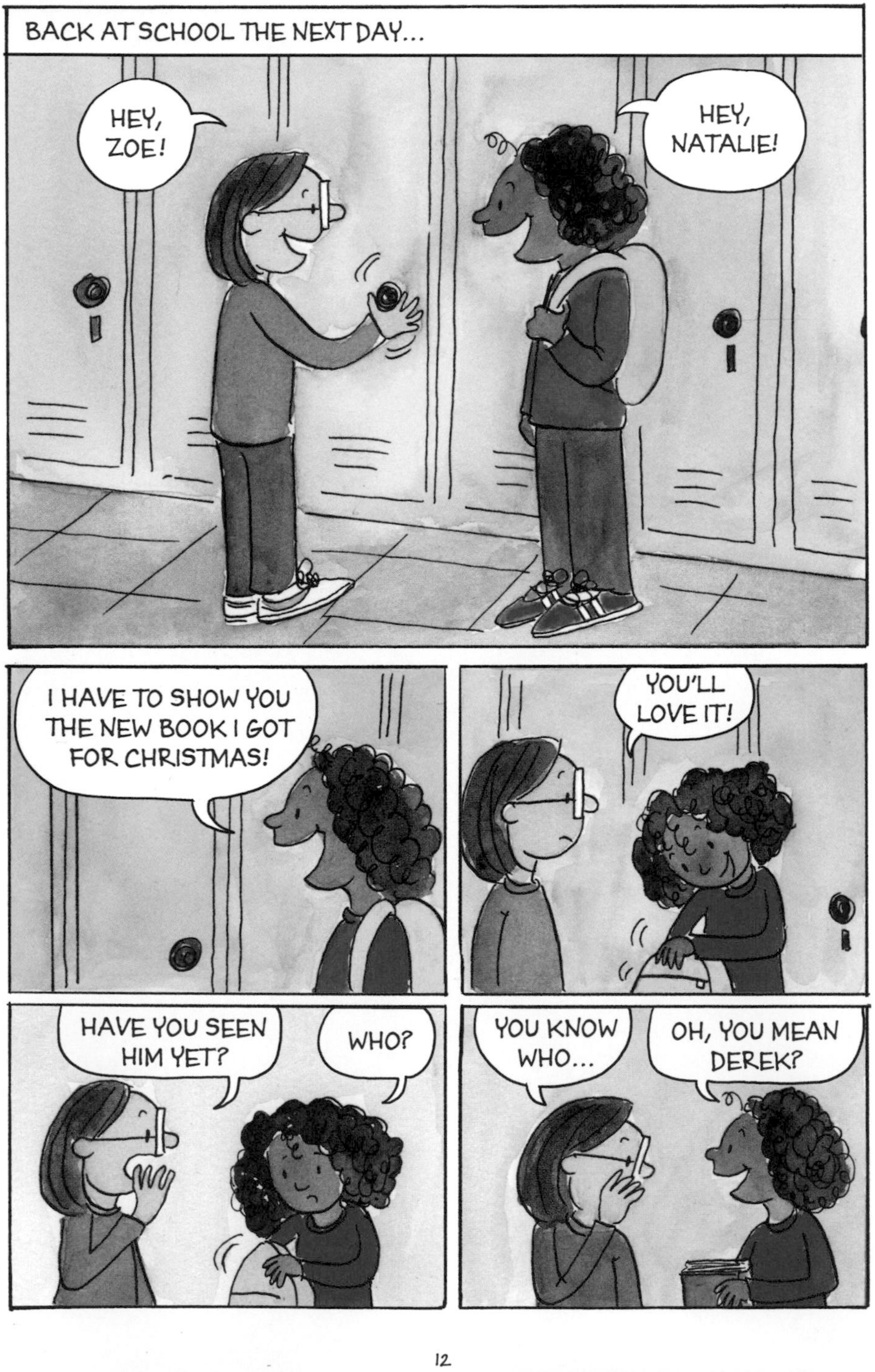
BACK AT SCHOOL THE NEXT DAY...
HEY, ZOE!
HEY, NATALIE!
I HAVE TO SHOW YOU THE NEW BOOK I GOT FOR CHRISTMAS!
YOU'LL LOVE IT!
HAVE YOU SEEN HIM YET?
WHO?
YOU KNOW WHO...
OH, YOU MEAN DEREK?

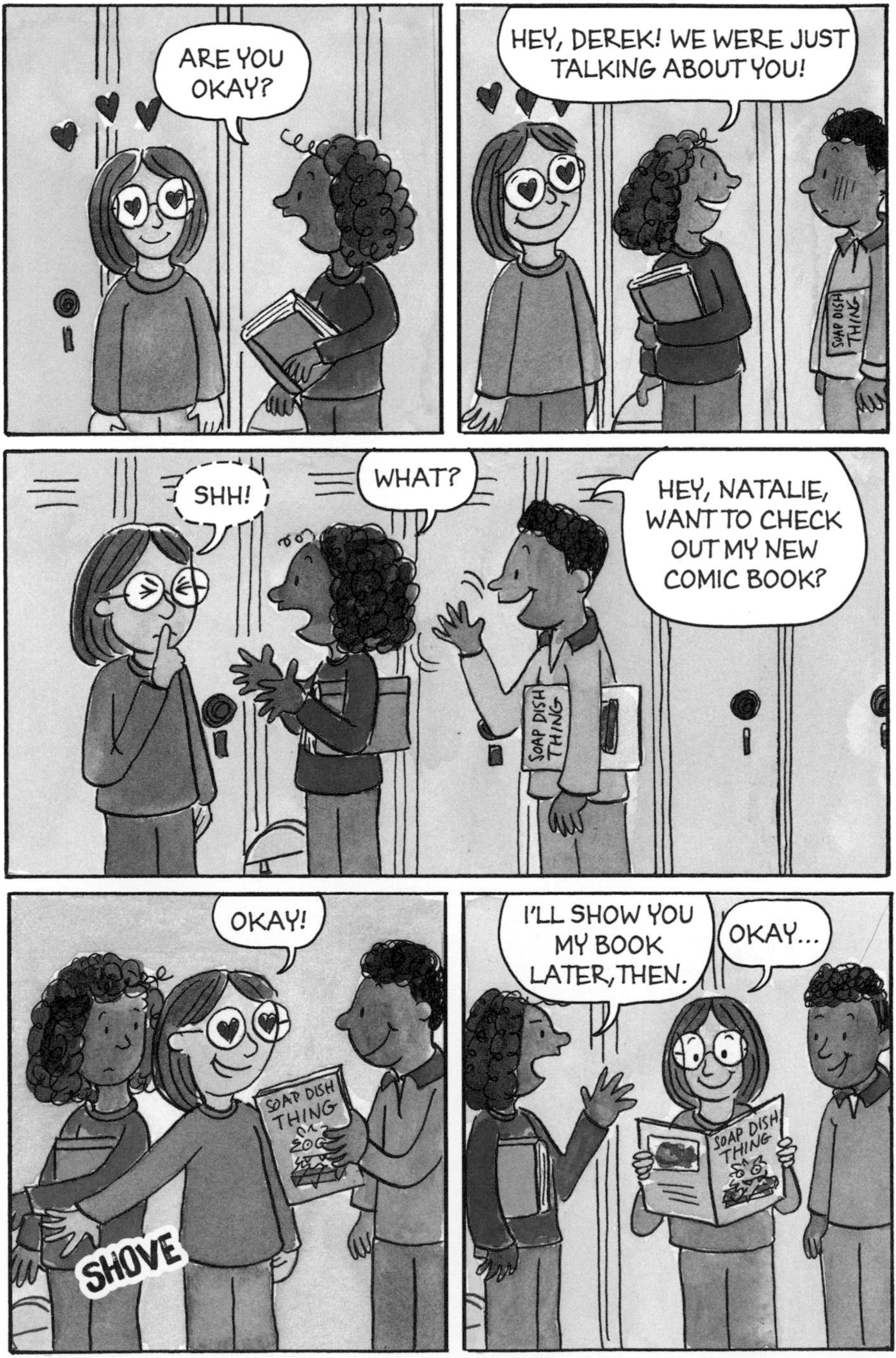
ARE YOU OKAY?
HEY, DEREK! WE WERE JUST TALKING ABOUT YOU!
SOAP DISH THING
SHH!
WHAT?
HEY, NATALIE, WANT TO CHECK OUT MY NEW COMIC BOOK?
SOAP DISH THING
OKAY!
SOAP DISH THING
SHOVE
I'LL SHOW YOU MY BOOK LATER, THEN.
OKAY...
SOAP DISH THING

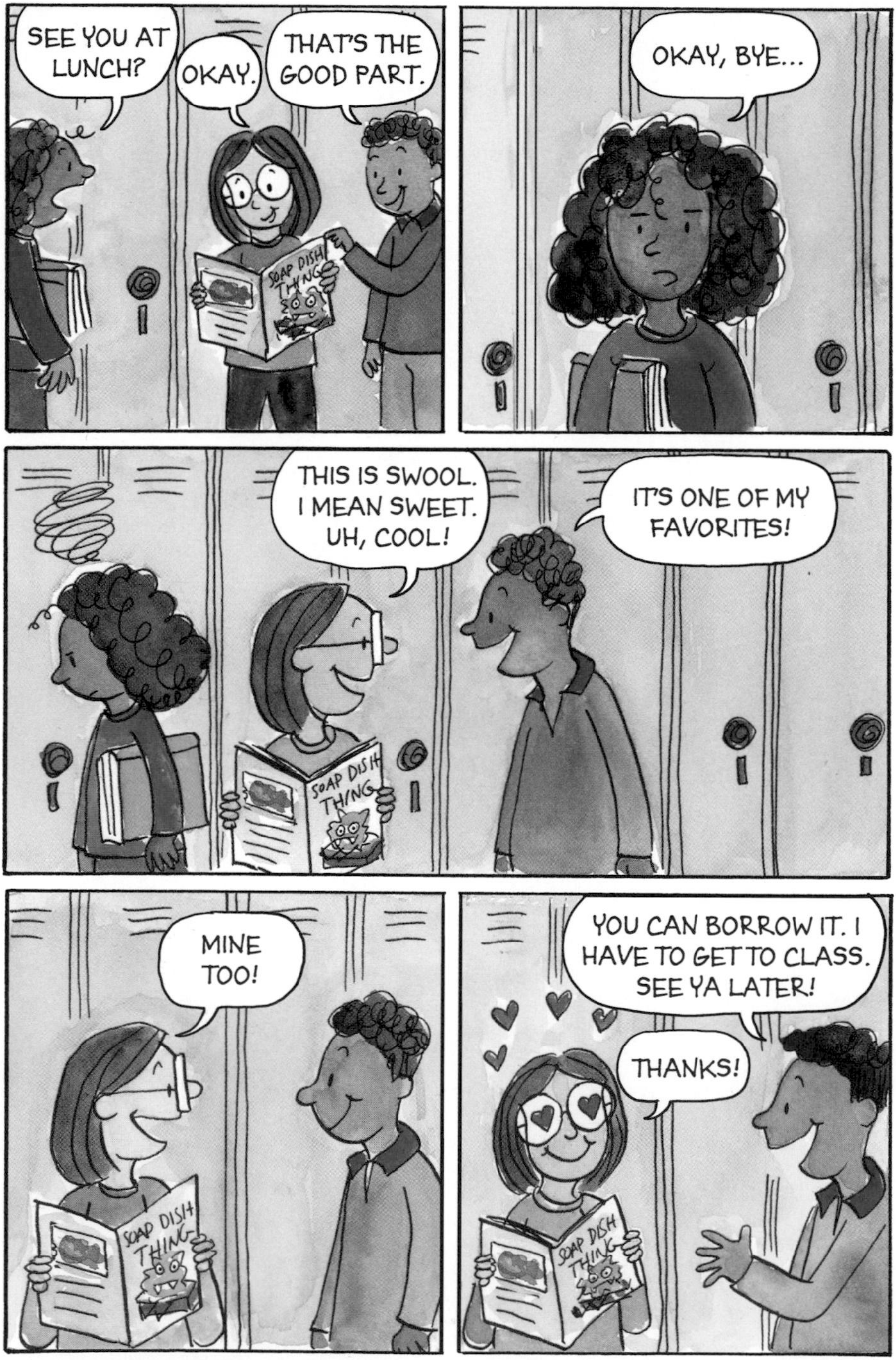
SEE YOU AT LUNCH?
OKAY.
THAT'S THE GOOD PART.
OKAY, BYE...
THIS IS SWOOL. I MEAN SWEET. UH, COOL!
IT'S ONE OF MY FAVORITES!
SOAP DISH THING
MINE TOO!
YOU CAN BORROW IT. I HAVE TO GET TO CLASS. SEE YA LATER!
THANKS!

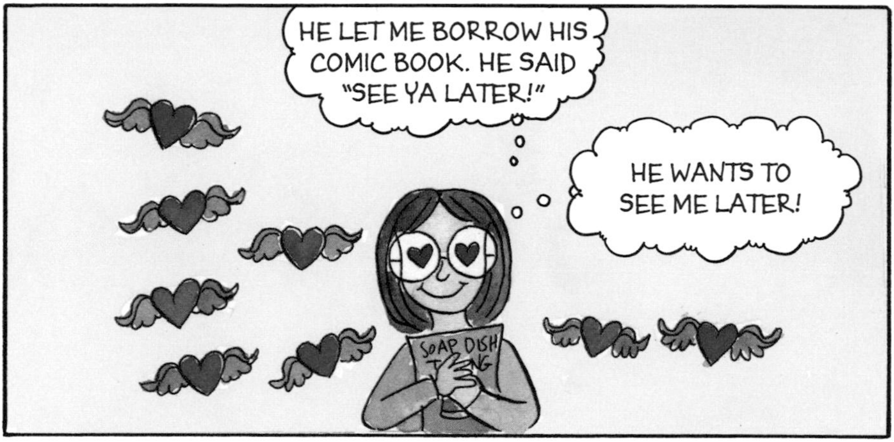
HE LET ME BORROW HIS COMIC BOOK. HE SAID "SEE YA LATER!"
HE WANTS TO SEE ME LATER!
SOAP DISH THING

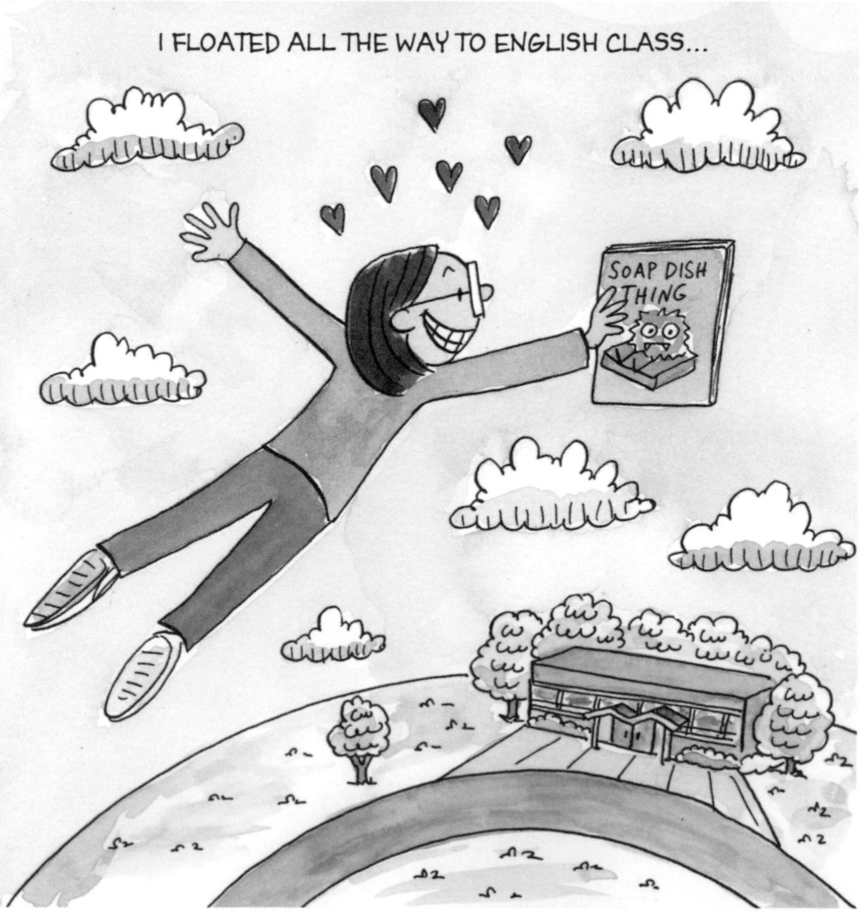
I FLOATED ALL THE WAY TO ENGLISH CLASS...
SOAP DISH THING

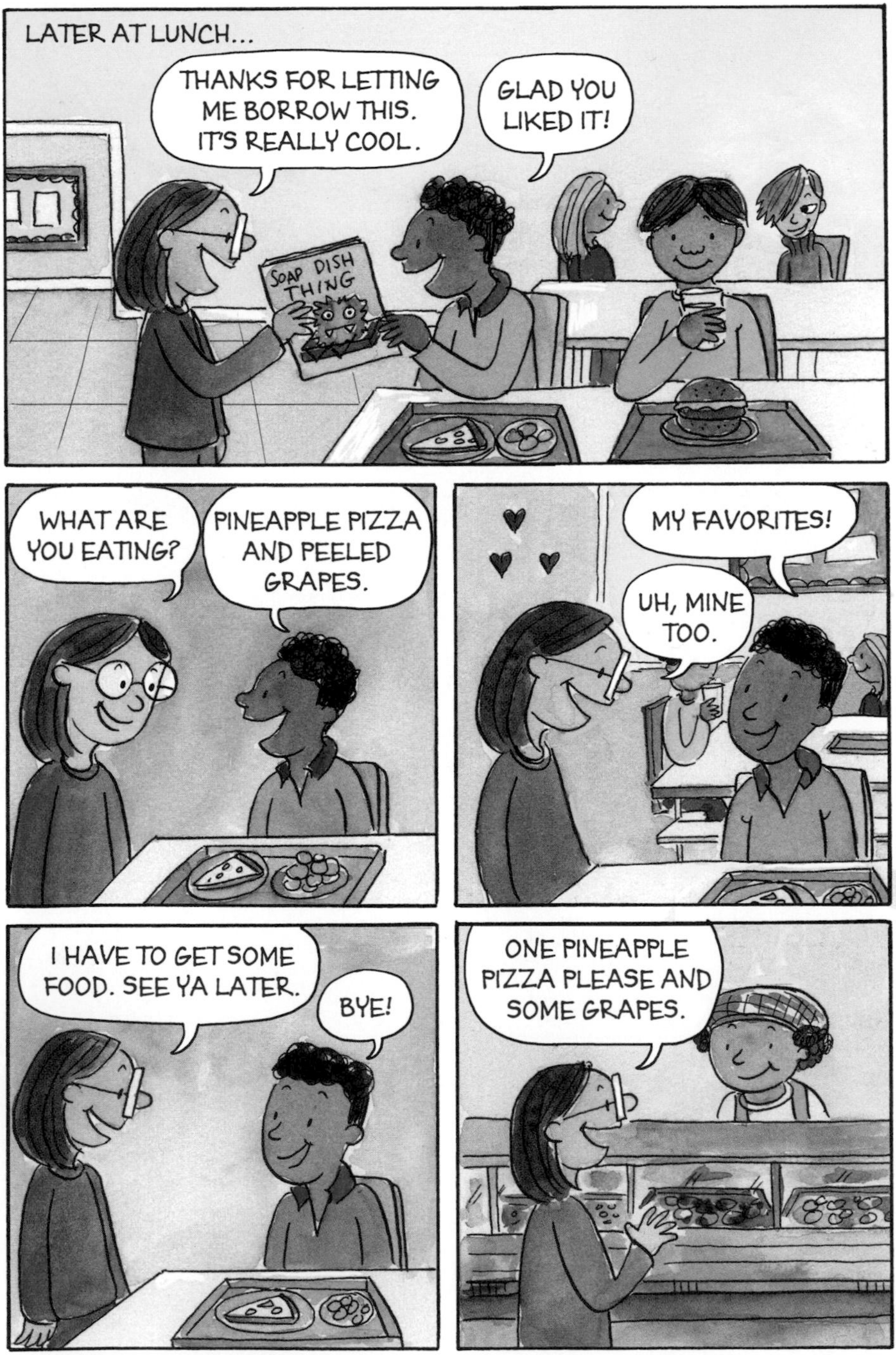

LATER AT LUNCH...
THANKS FOR LETTING ME BORROW THIS. IT'S REALLY COOL.
GLAD YOU LIKED IT!
SOAP DISH THING
WHAT ARE YOU EATING?
PINEAPPLE PIZZA AND PEELED GRAPES.
MY FAVORITES!
UH, MINE TOO.
I HAVE TO GET SOME FOOD. SEE YA LATER.
BYE!
ONE PINEAPPLE PIZZA PLEASE AND SOME GRAPES.

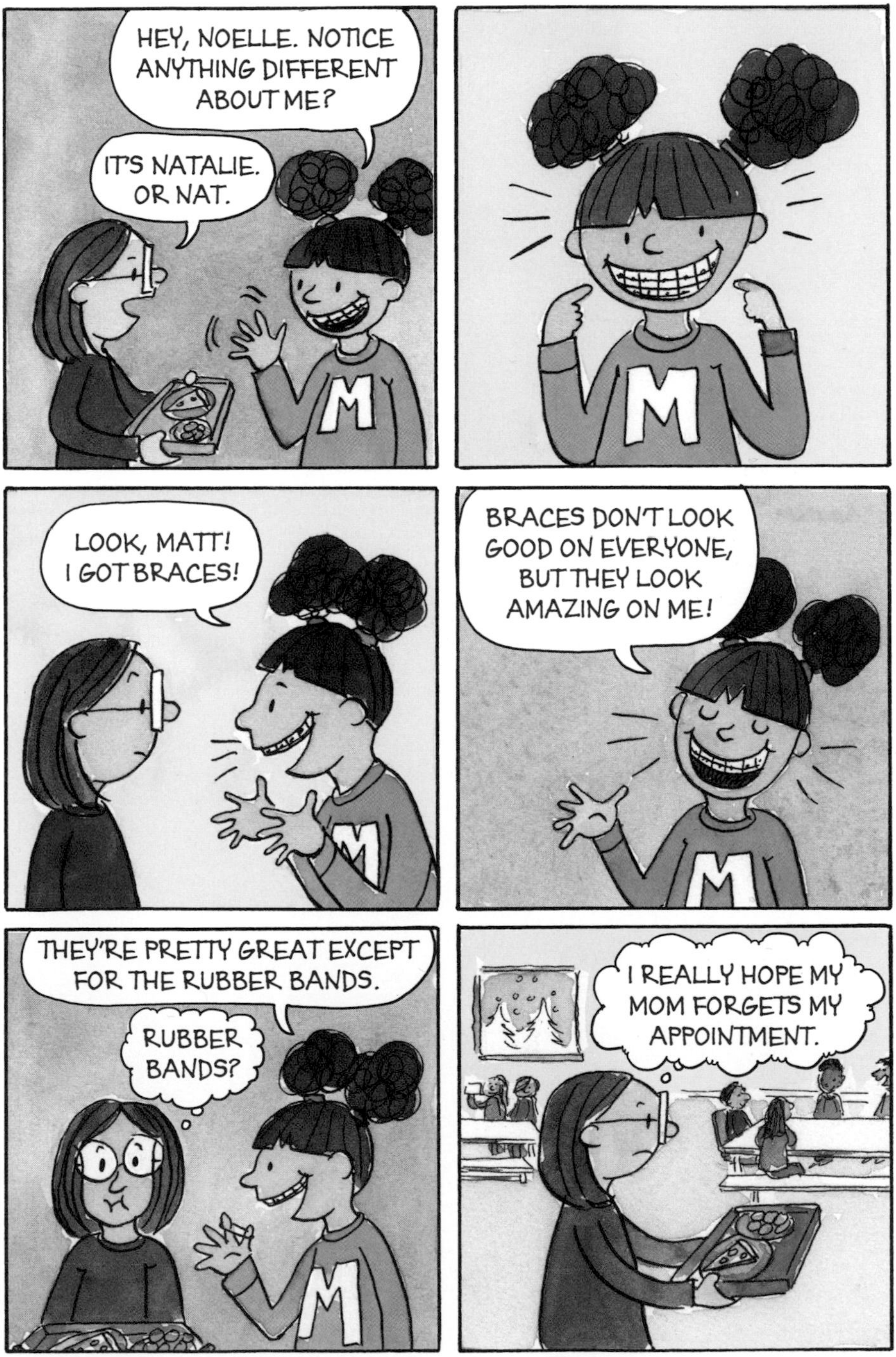
HEY, NOELLE. NOTICE ANYTHING DIFFERENT ABOUT ME?
IT'S NATALIE. OR NAT.
LOOK, MATT! I GOT BRACES!
BRACES DON'T LOOK GOOD ON EVERYONE, BUT THEY LOOK AMAZING ON ME!
THEY'RE PRETTY GREAT EXCEPT FOR THE RUBBER BANDS.
RUBBER BANDS?
I REALLY HOPE MY MOM FORGETS MY APPOINTMENT.

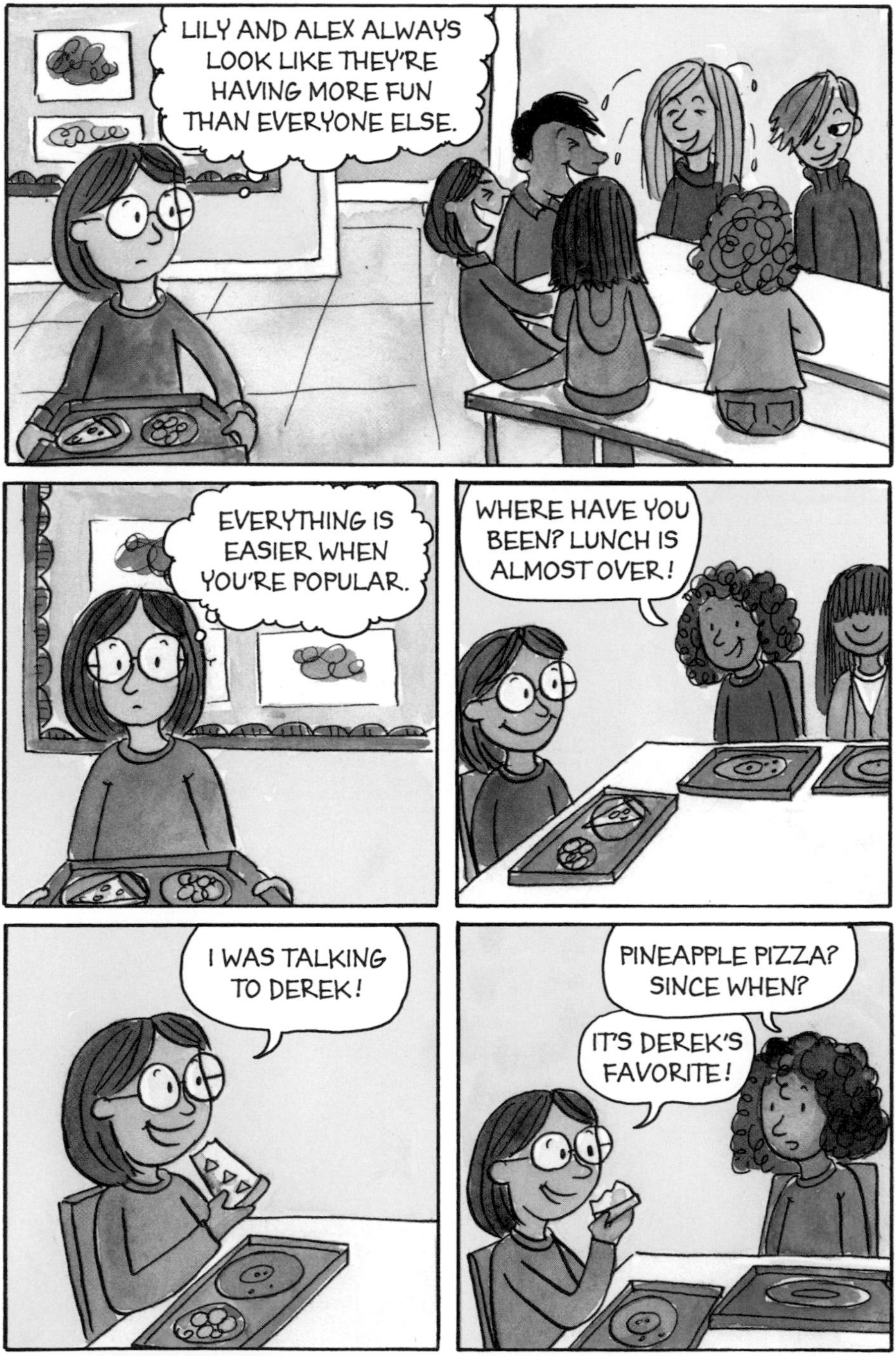
LILY AND ALEX ALWAYS LOOK LIKE THEY'RE HAVING MORE FUN THAN EVERYONE ELSE.
EVERYTHING IS EASIER WHEN YOU'RE POPULAR.
WHERE HAVE YOU BEEN? LUNCH IS ALMOST OVER!
I WAS TALKING TO DEREK!
PINEAPPLE PIZZA? SINCE WHEN?
IT'S DEREK'S FAVORITE!

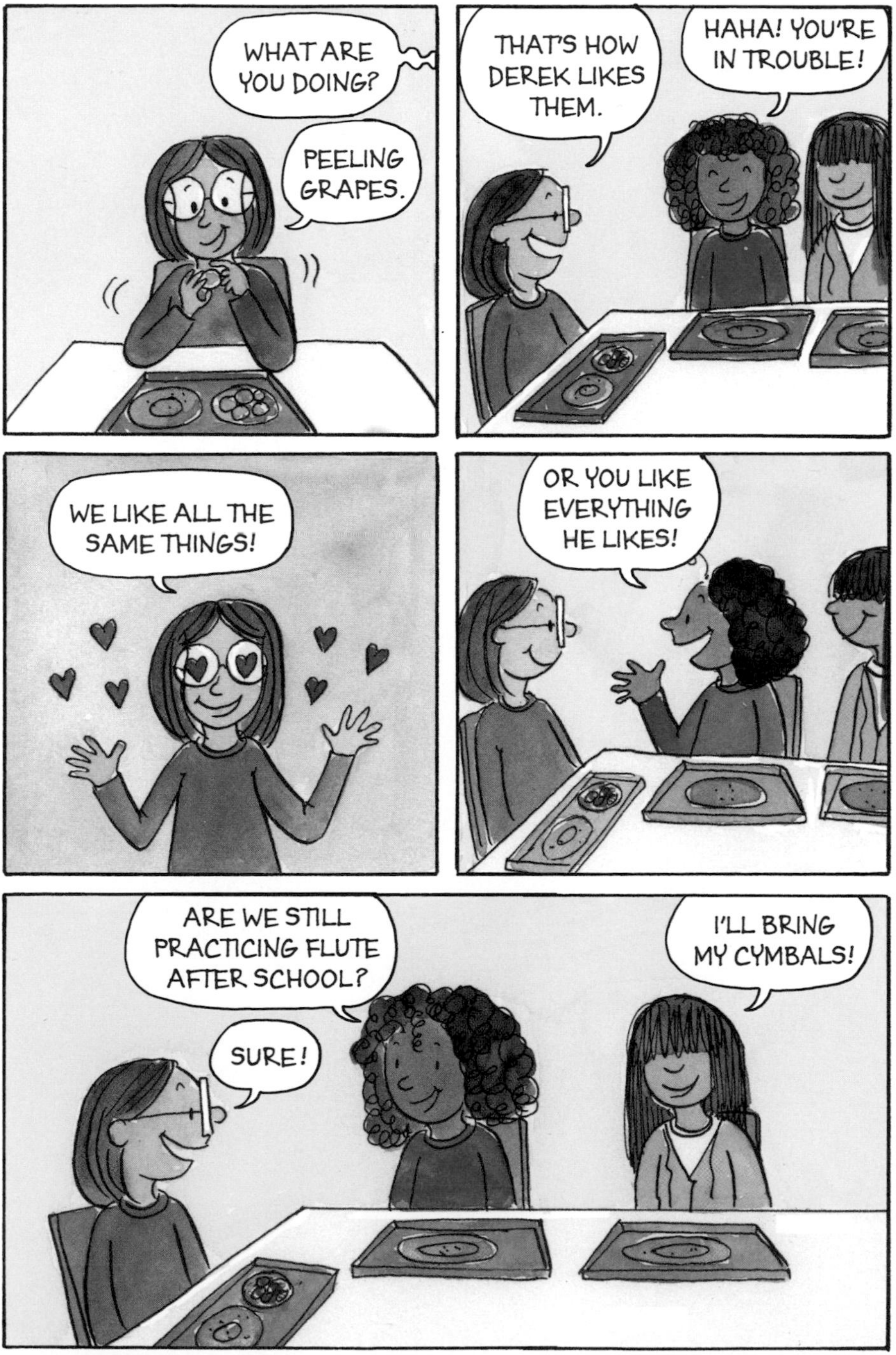
WHAT ARE YOU DOING?
PEELING GRAPES.
THAT'S HOW DEREK LIKES THEM.
HAHA! YOU'RE IN TROUBLE!
WE LIKE ALL THE SAME THINGS!
OR YOU LIKE EVERYTHING HE LIKES!
ARE WE STILL PRACTICING FLUTE AFTER SCHOOL?
SURE!
I'LL BRING MY CYMBALS!

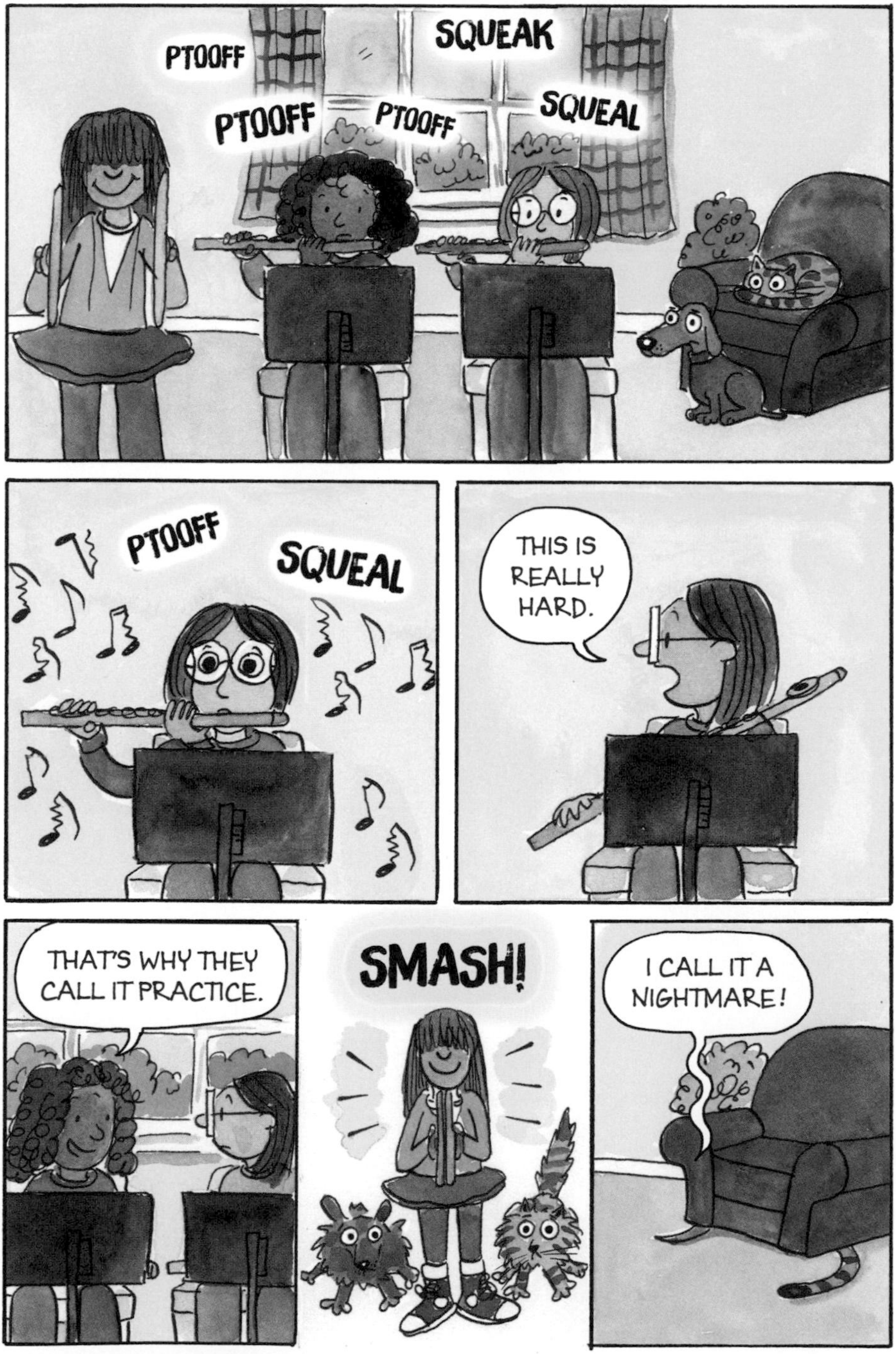

PTOOFF
SQUEAK
PTOOFF
PTOOFF
SQUEAL
PTOOFF
SQUEAL
THIS IS REALLY HARD.
THAT'S WHY THEY CALL IT PRACTICE.
SMASH!
I CALL IT A NIGHTMARE!

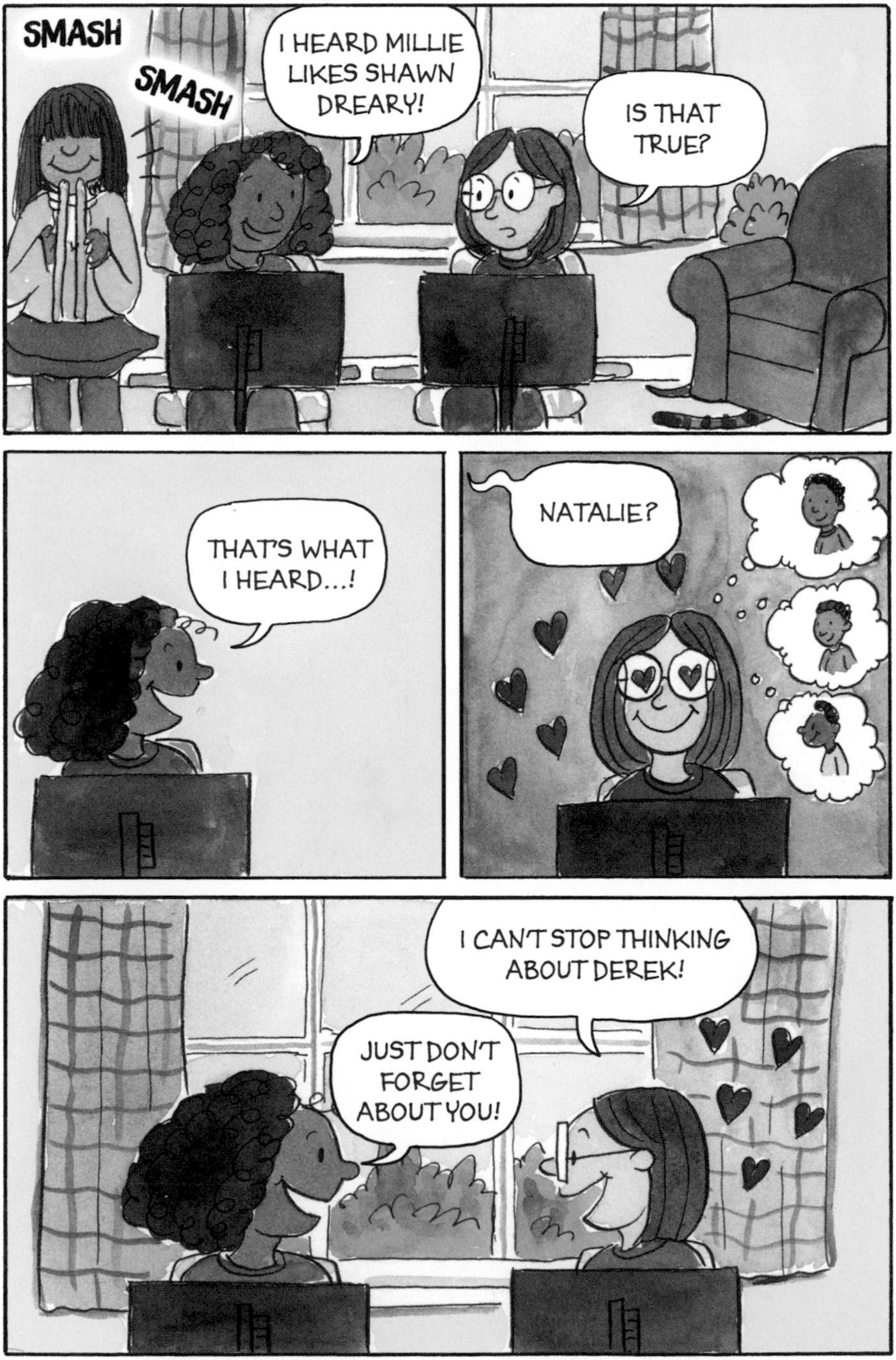
SMASH
SMASH
I HEARD MILLIE LIKES SHAWN DREARY!
IS THAT TRUE?
THAT'S WHAT I HEARD...!
NATALIE?
I CAN'T STOP THINKING ABOUT DEREK!
JUST DON'T FORGET ABOUT YOU!

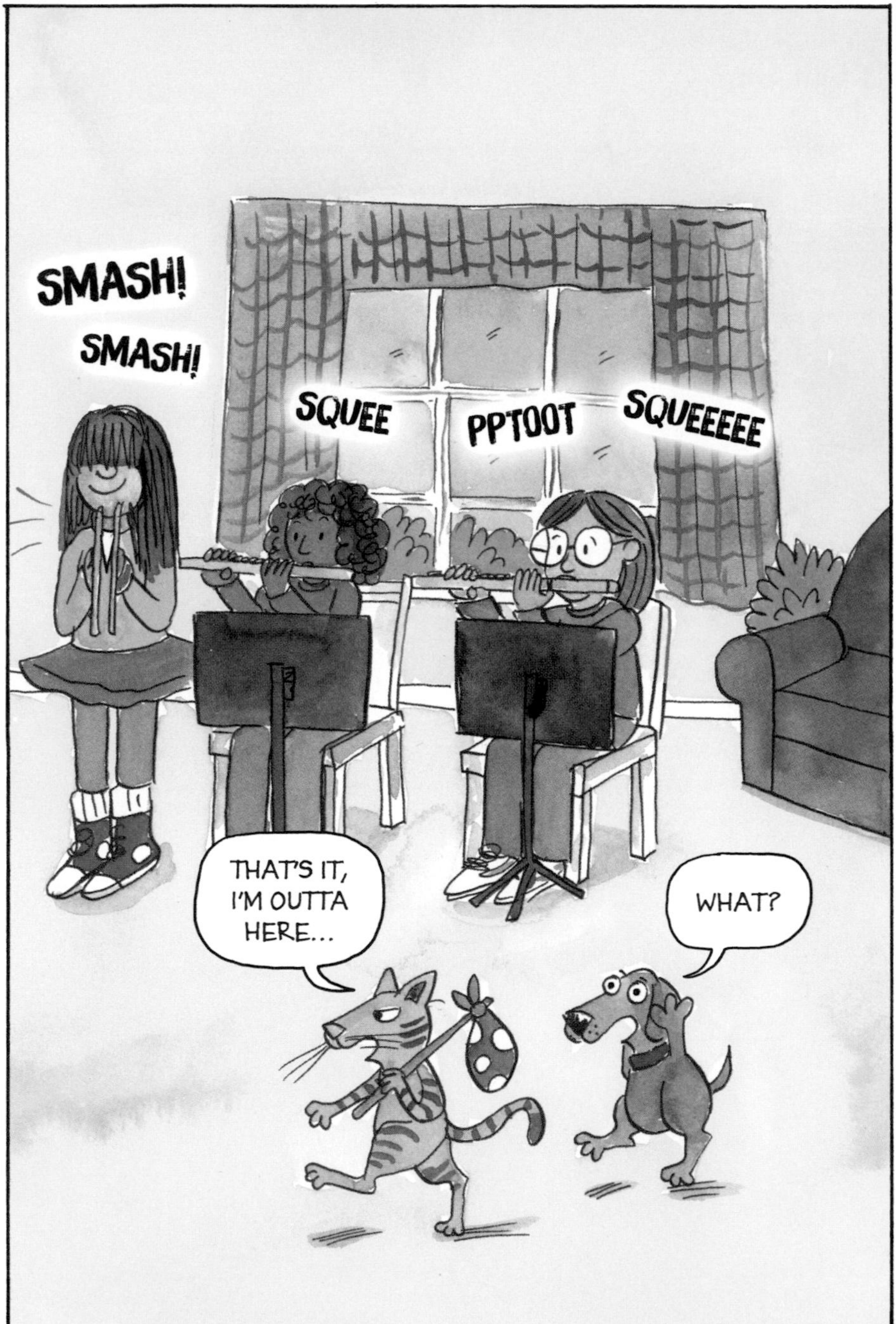
SMASH!
SMASH!
SQUEE
PPTOOT
SQUEEEEE
THAT'S IT, I'M OUTTA HERE...
WHAT?

CHAPTER 2
LOVE SONGS

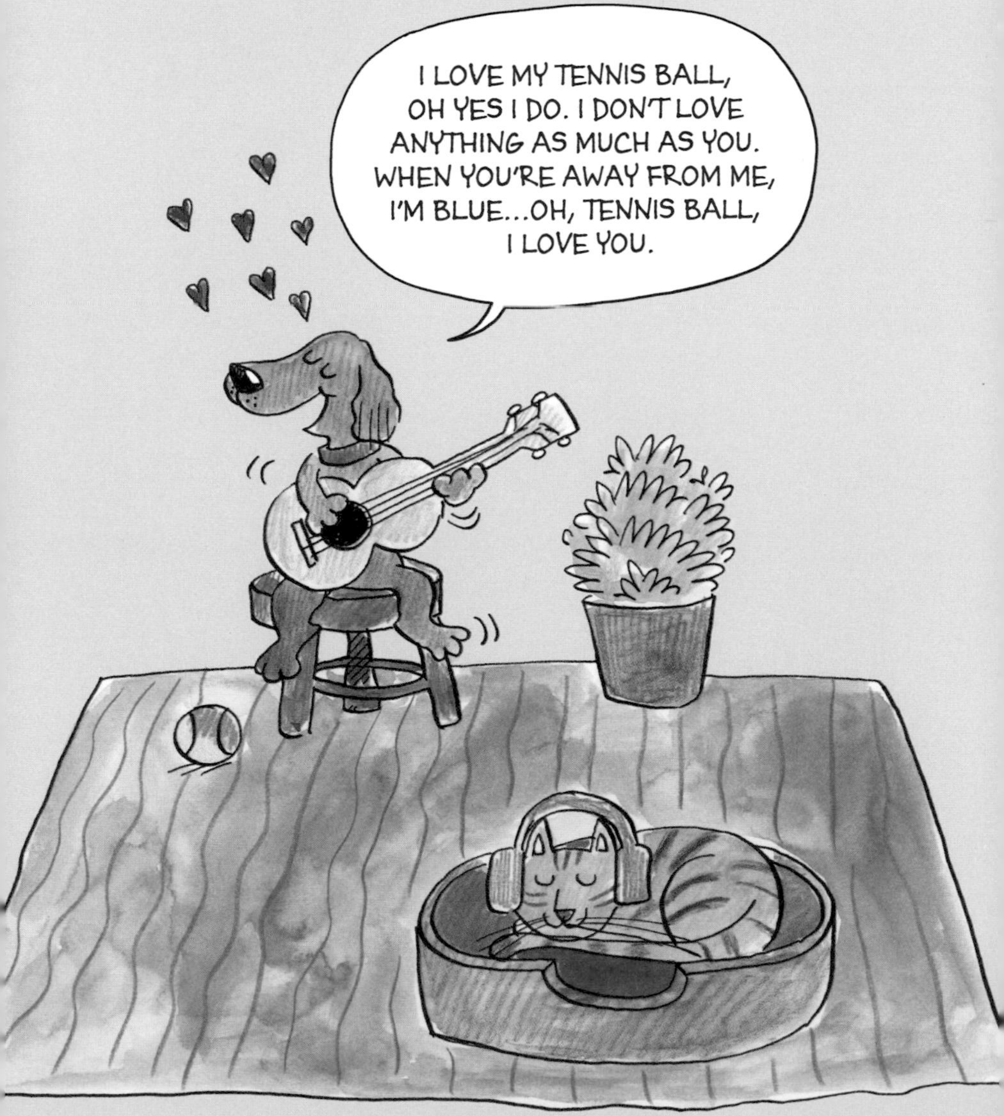
I LOVE MY TENNIS BALL, OH YES I DO. I DON'T LOVE ANYTHING AS MUCH AS YOU. WHEN YOU'RE AWAY FROM ME, I'M BLUE...OH, TENNIS BALL, I LOVE YOU.

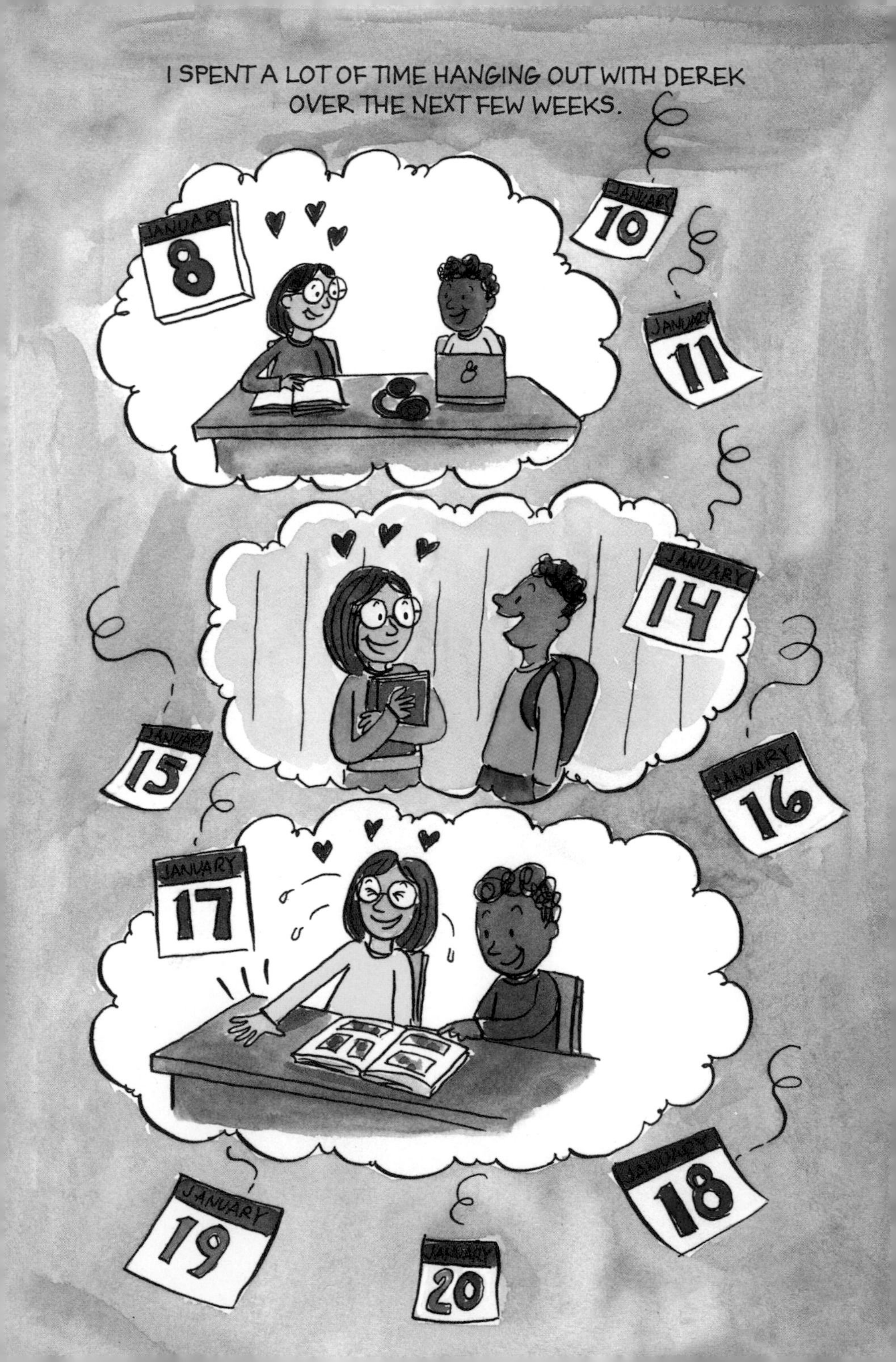
I SPENT A LOT OF TIME HANGING OUT WITH DEREK OVER THE NEXT FEW WEEKS.
JANUARY 8
JANUARY 10
JANUARY 11
JANUARY 14
JANUARY 15
JANUARY 16
JANUARY 17
JANUARY 18
JANUARY 19
JANUARY 20

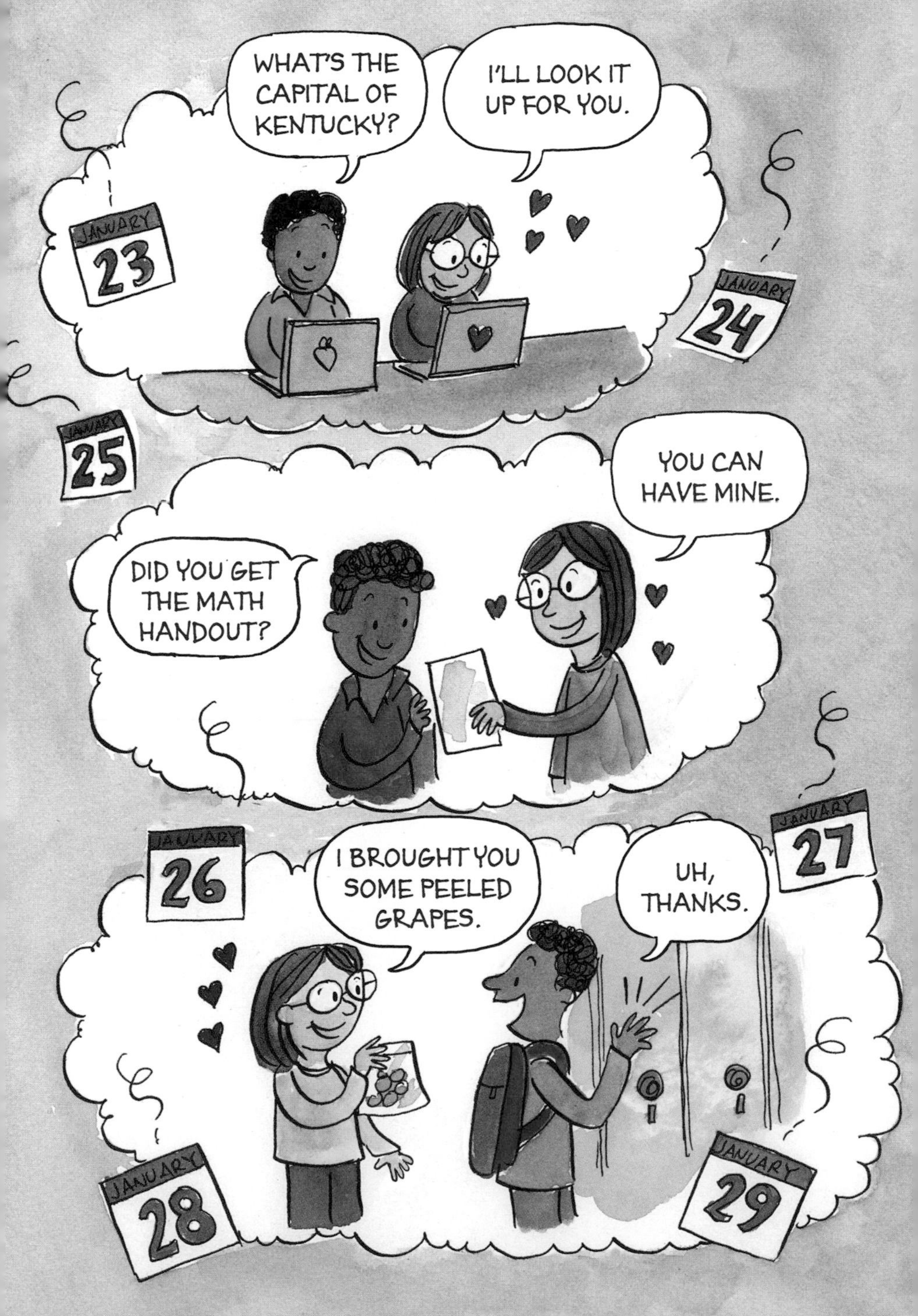
WHAT'S THE CAPITAL OF KENTUCKY?
I'LL LOOK IT UP FOR YOU.
JANUARY 23
JANUARY 24
JANUARY 25
YOU CAN HAVE MINE.
DID YOU GET THE MATH HANDOUT?
JANUARY 26
I BROUGHT YOU SOME PEELED GRAPES.
UH, THANKS.
JANUARY 27
JANUARY 28
JANUARY 29

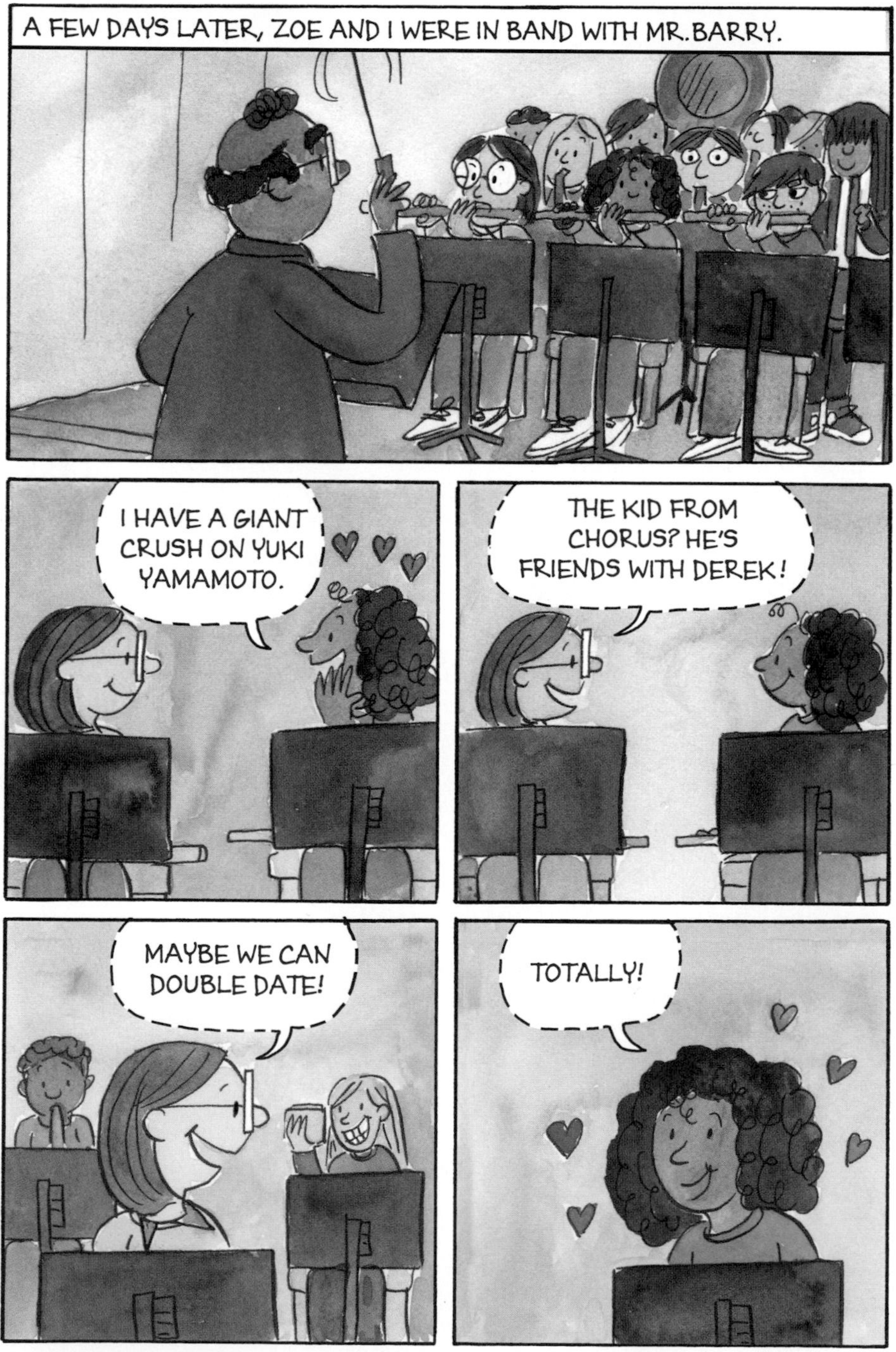
A FEW DAYS LATER, ZOE AND I WERE IN BAND WITH MR. BARRY.
I HAVE A GIANT CRUSH ON YUKI YAMAMOTO.
THE KID FROM CHORUS? HE'S FRIENDS WITH DEREK!
MAYBE WE CAN DOUBLE DATE!
TOTALLY!

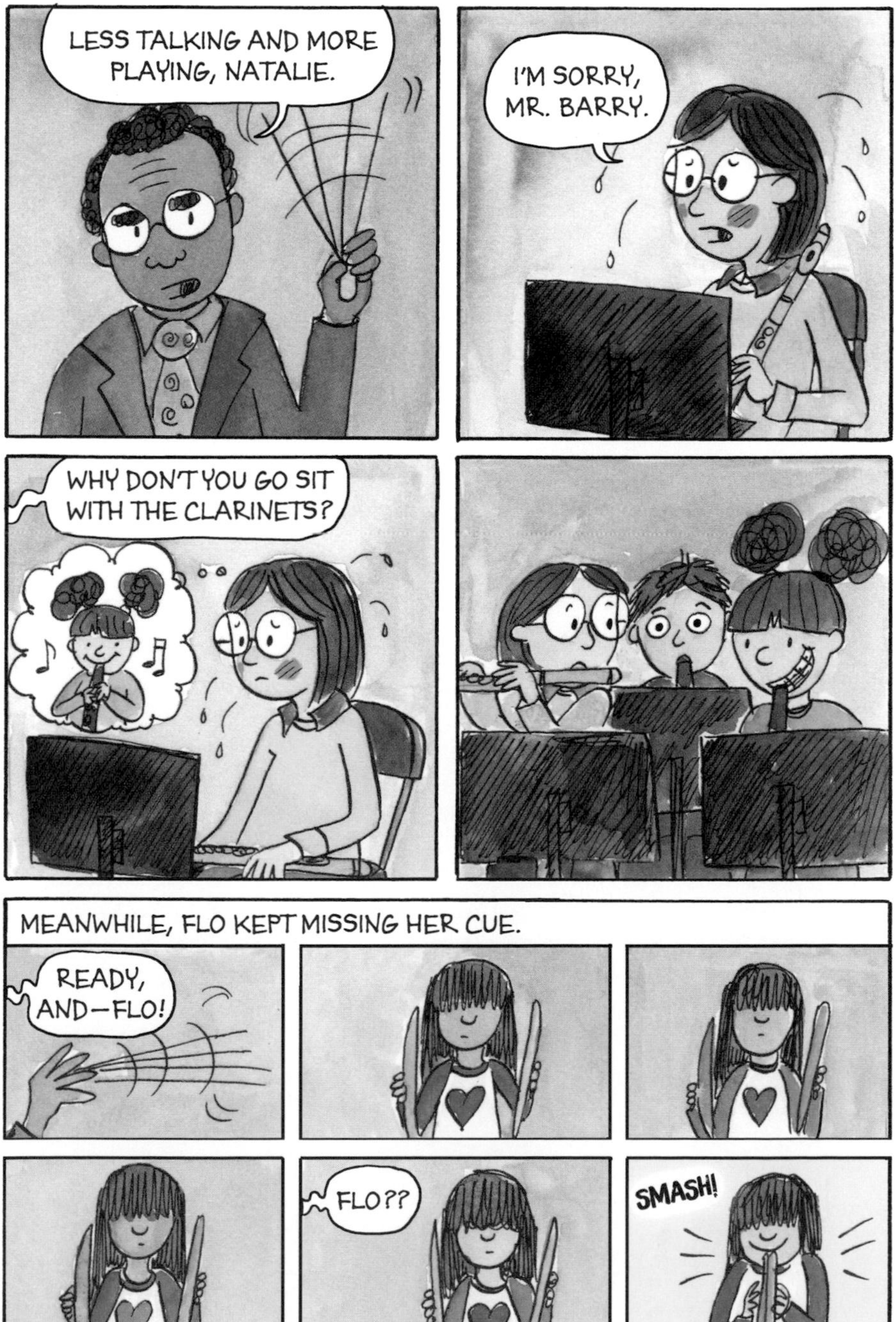
LESS TALKING AND MORE PLAYING, NATALIE.
I'M SORRY, MR. BARRY.
WHY DON'T YOU GO SIT WITH THE CLARINETS?
MEANWHILE, FLO KEPT MISSING HER CUE.
READY, AND—FLO!
FLO??
SMASH!

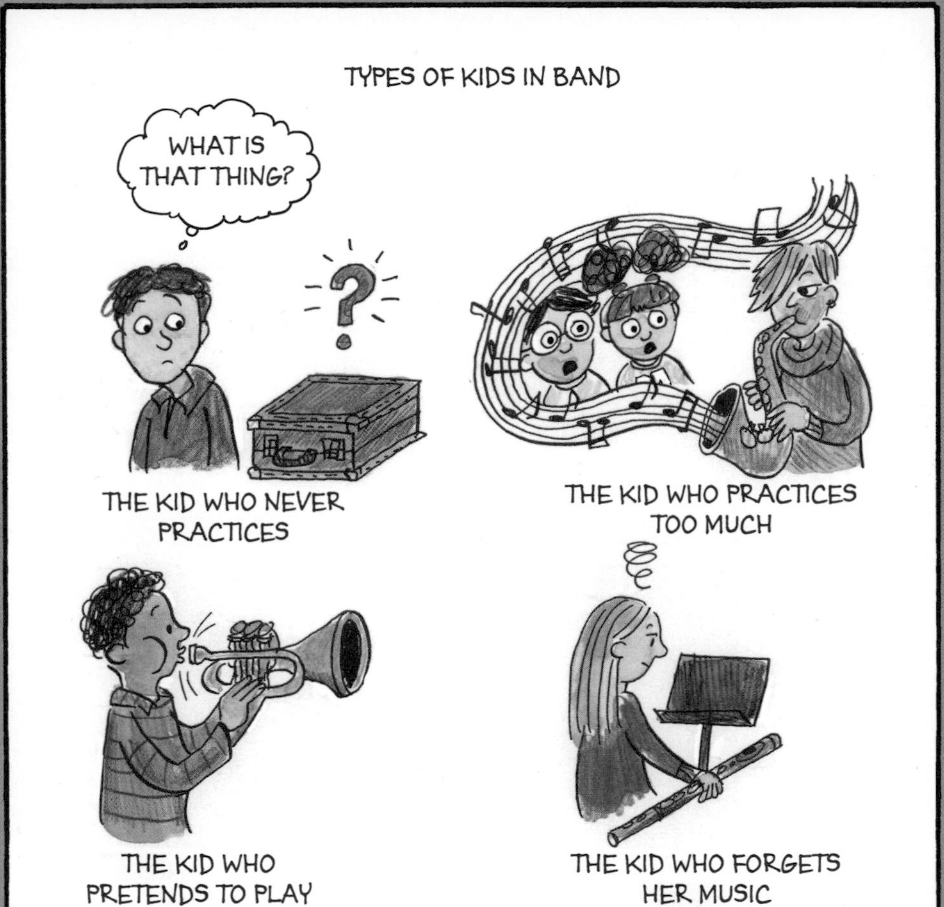
TYPES OF KIDS IN BAND
WHAT IS THAT THING?
THE KID WHO NEVER PRACTICES
THE KID WHO PRACTICES TOO MUCH
THE KID WHO PRETENDS TO PLAY
THE KID WHO FORGETS HER MUSIC
THE KID WHO NEVER CLEANS HER INSTRUMENT
THE KID WHO TALKS TOO MUCH

ZOE HAS A GIANT CRUSH ON YUKI YAMAMOTO.

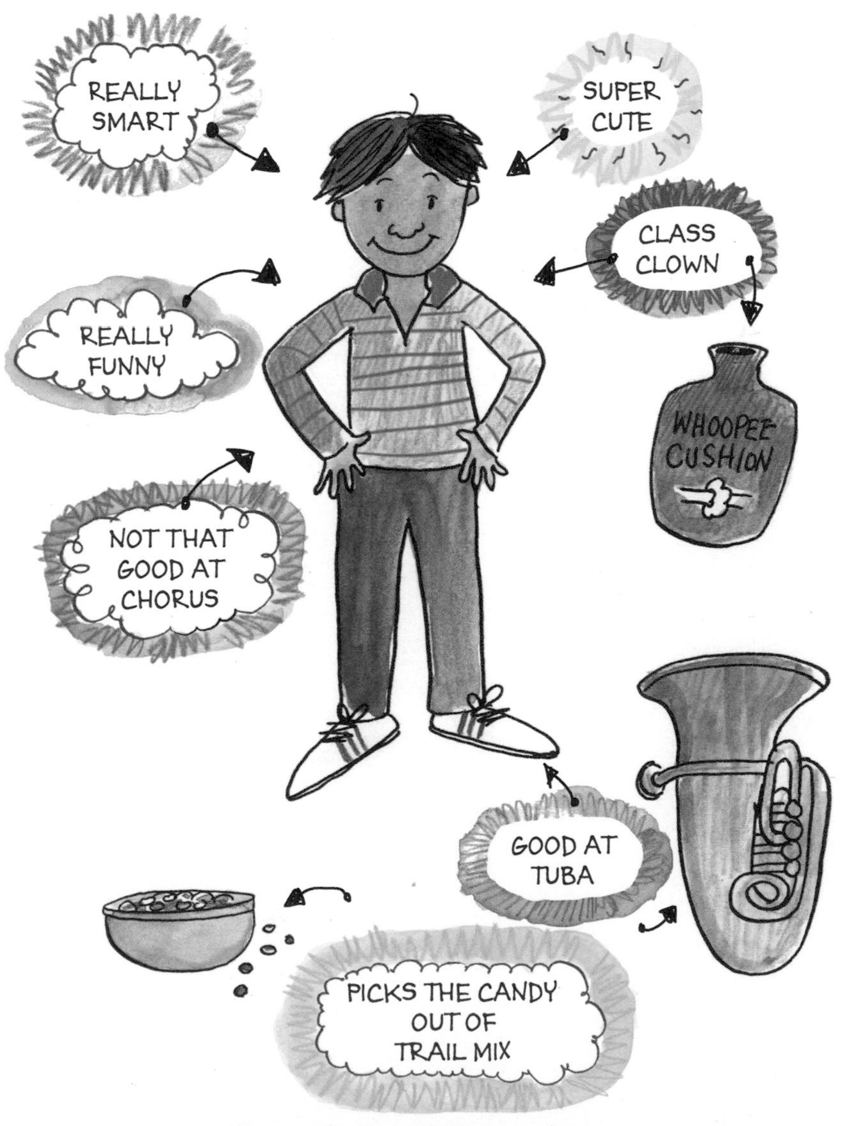
REALLY SMART
SUPER CUTE
CLASS CLOWN
REALLY FUNNY
WHOOPEE CUSHION
NOT THAT GOOD AT CHORUS
GOOD AT TUBA
PICKS THE CANDY OUT OF TRAIL MIX

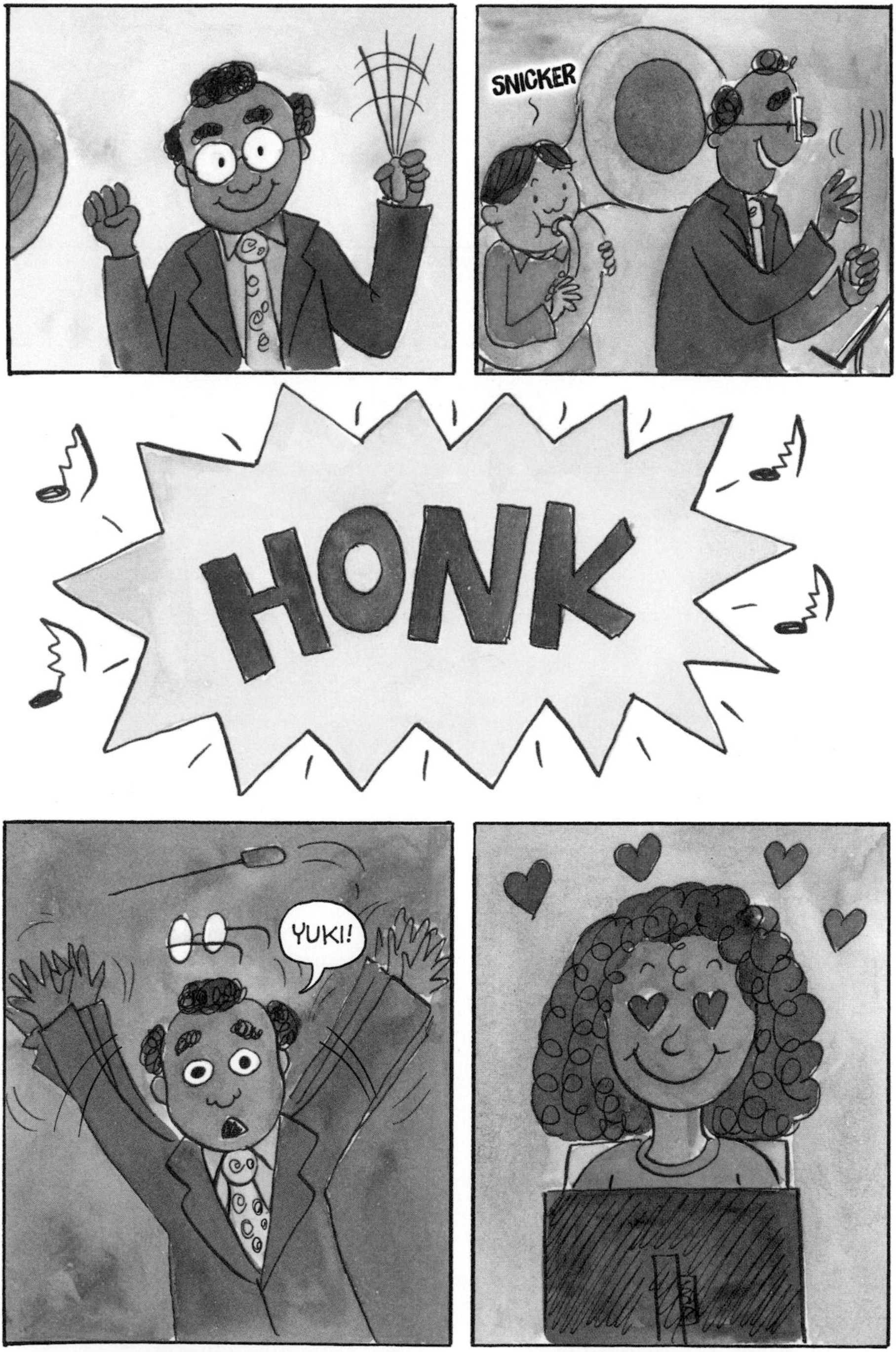
SNICKER
HONK
YUKI!

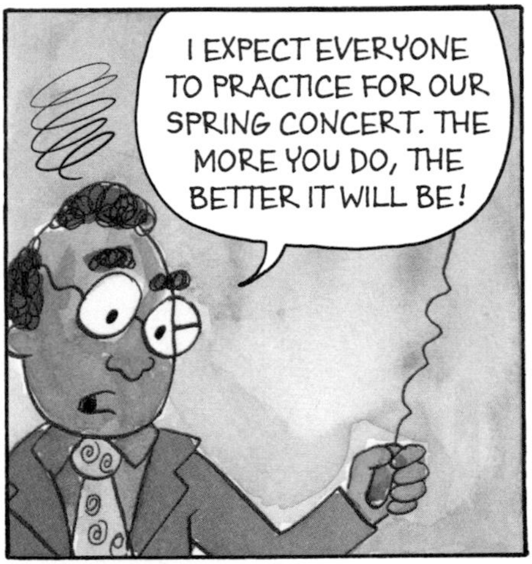
I EXPECT EVERYONE TO PRACTICE FOR OUR SPRING CONCERT. THE MORE YOU DO, THE BETTER IT WILL BE!

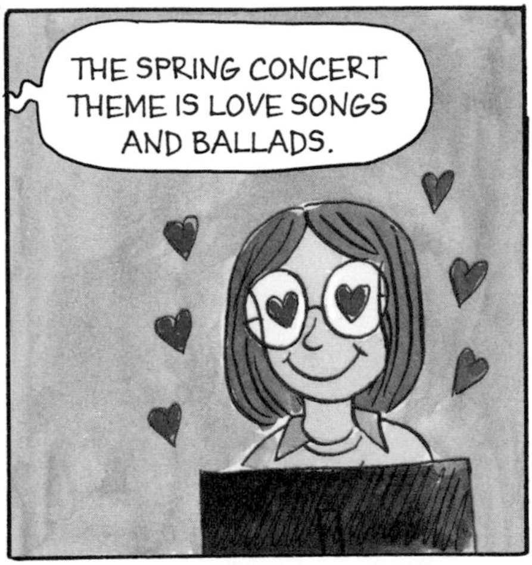
THE SPRING CONCERT THEME IS LOVE SONGS AND BALLADS.

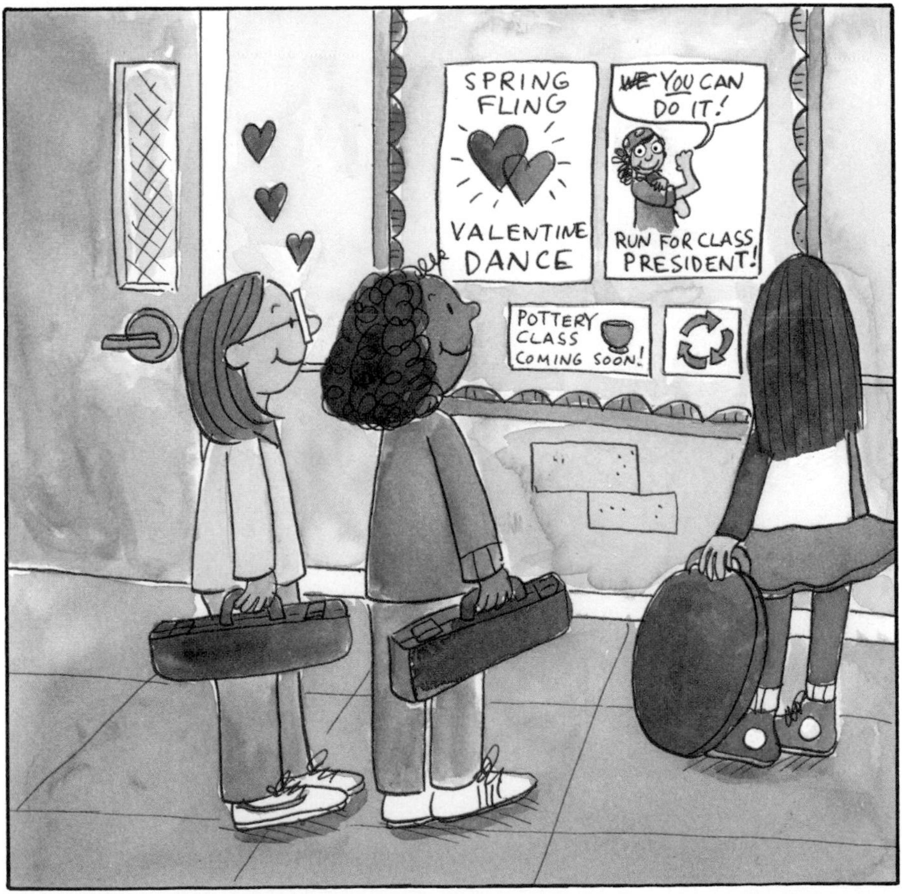
SPRING FLING
VALENTINE DANCE
~~WE~~ YOU CAN DO IT!
RUN FOR CLASS PRESIDENT!
POTTERY CLASS COMING SOON!

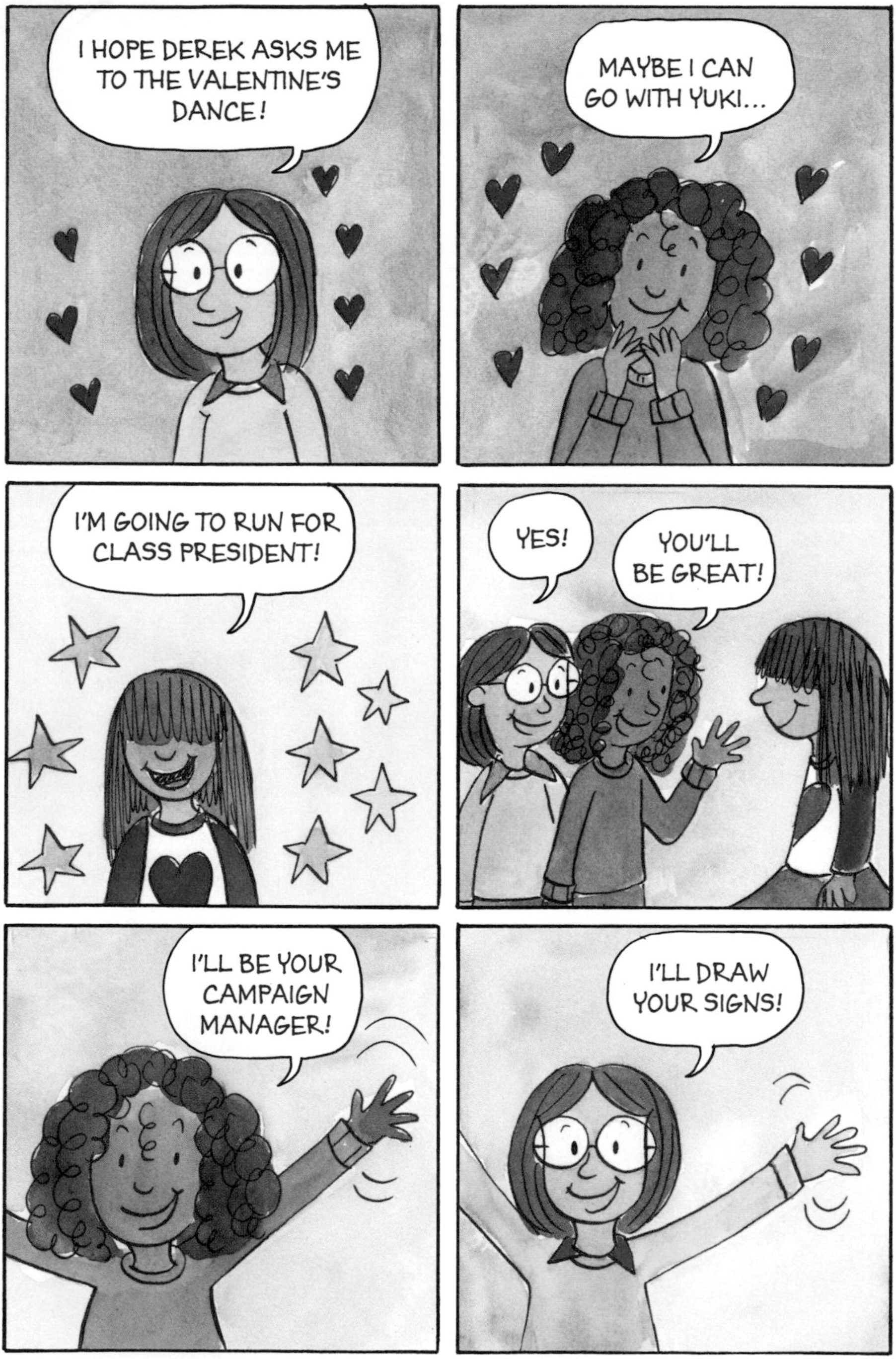
I HOPE DEREK ASKS ME TO THE VALENTINE'S DANCE!
MAYBE I CAN GO WITH YUKI...
I'M GOING TO RUN FOR CLASS PRESIDENT!
YES!
YOU'LL BE GREAT!
I'LL BE YOUR CAMPAIGN MANAGER!
I'LL DRAW YOUR SIGNS!

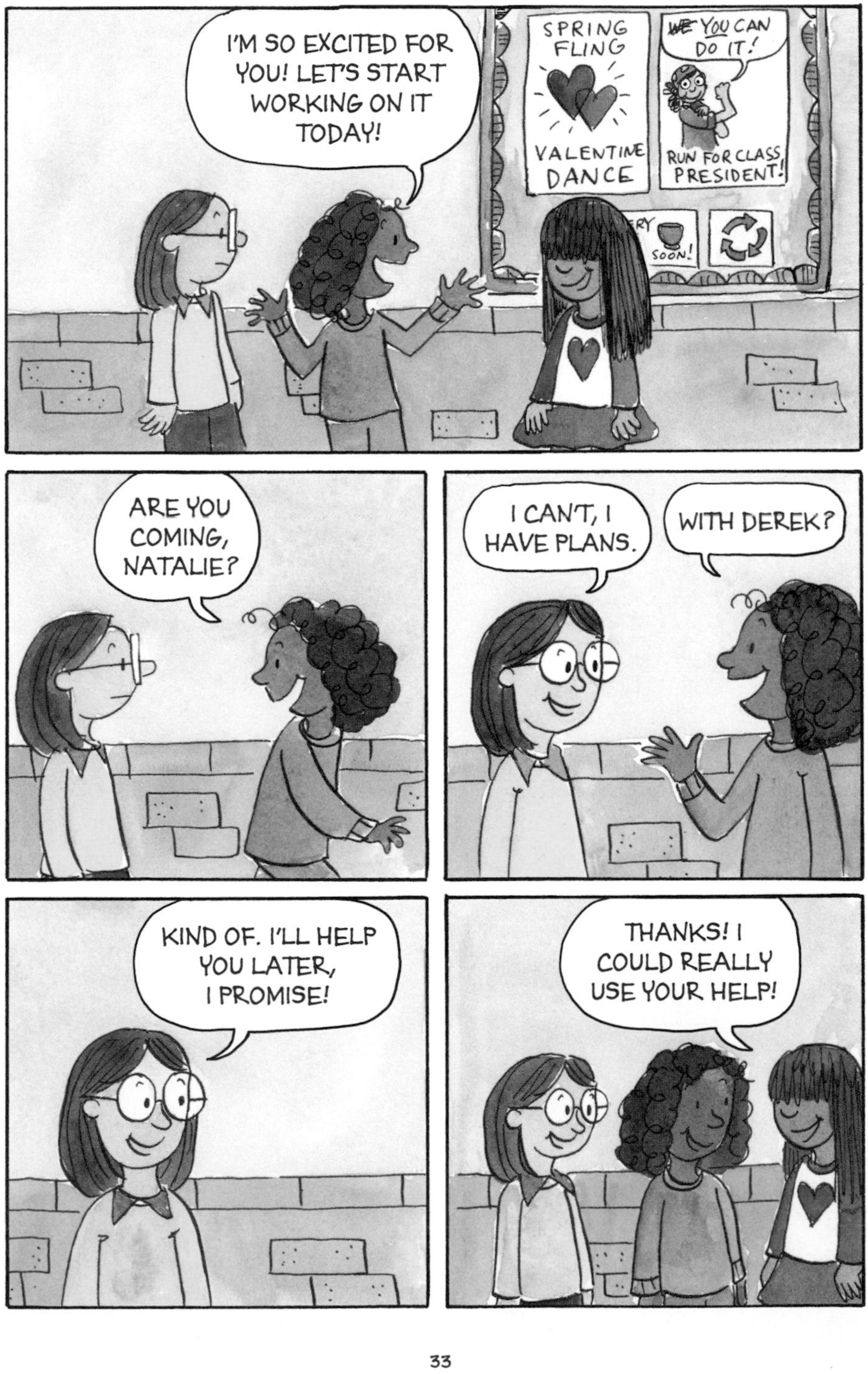
I'M SO EXCITED FOR YOU! LET'S START WORKING ON IT TODAY!
SPRING FLING
VALENTINE DANCE
~~WE~~ YOU CAN DO IT!
RUN FOR CLASS PRESIDENT!
ARE YOU COMING, NATALIE?
I CAN'T, I HAVE PLANS.
WITH DEREK?
KIND OF. I'LL HELP YOU LATER, I PROMISE!
THANKS! I COULD REALLY USE YOUR HELP!

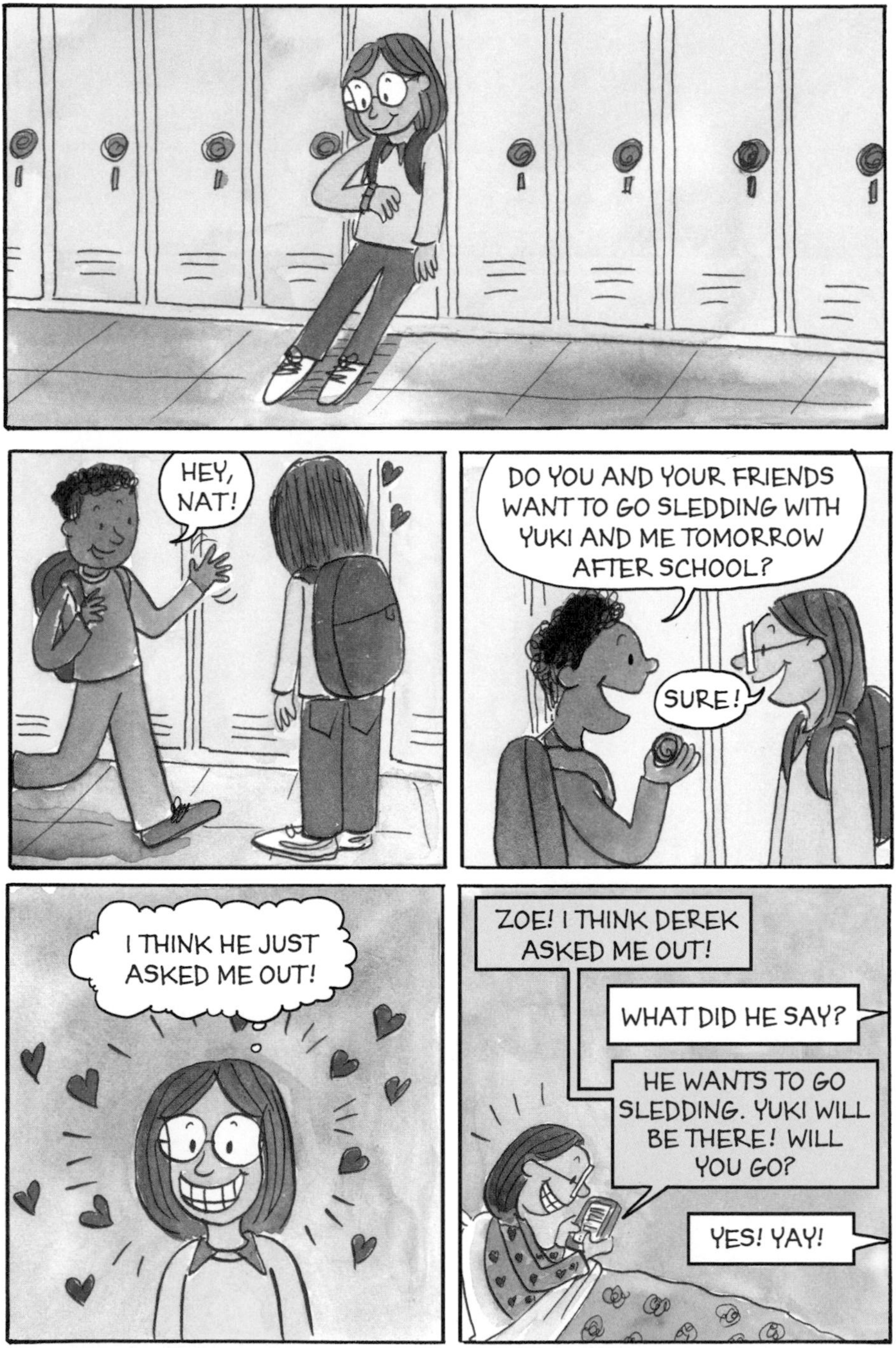
HEY, NAT!
DO YOU AND YOUR FRIENDS WANT TO GO SLEDDING WITH YUKI AND ME TOMORROW AFTER SCHOOL?
SURE!
I THINK HE JUST ASKED ME OUT!
ZOE! I THINK DEREK ASKED ME OUT!
WHAT DID HE SAY?
HE WANTS TO GO SLEDDING. YUKI WILL BE THERE! WILL YOU GO?
YES! YAY!

CHAPTER 3
FALLING FOR YOU

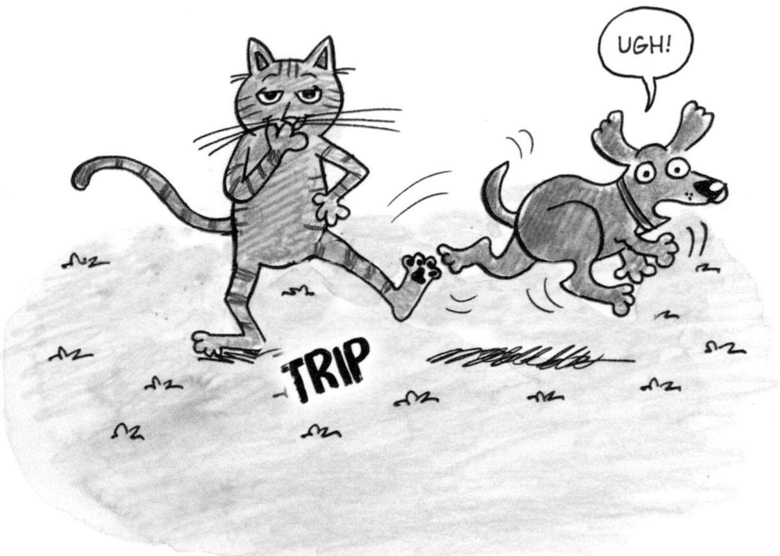
UGH!
TRIP

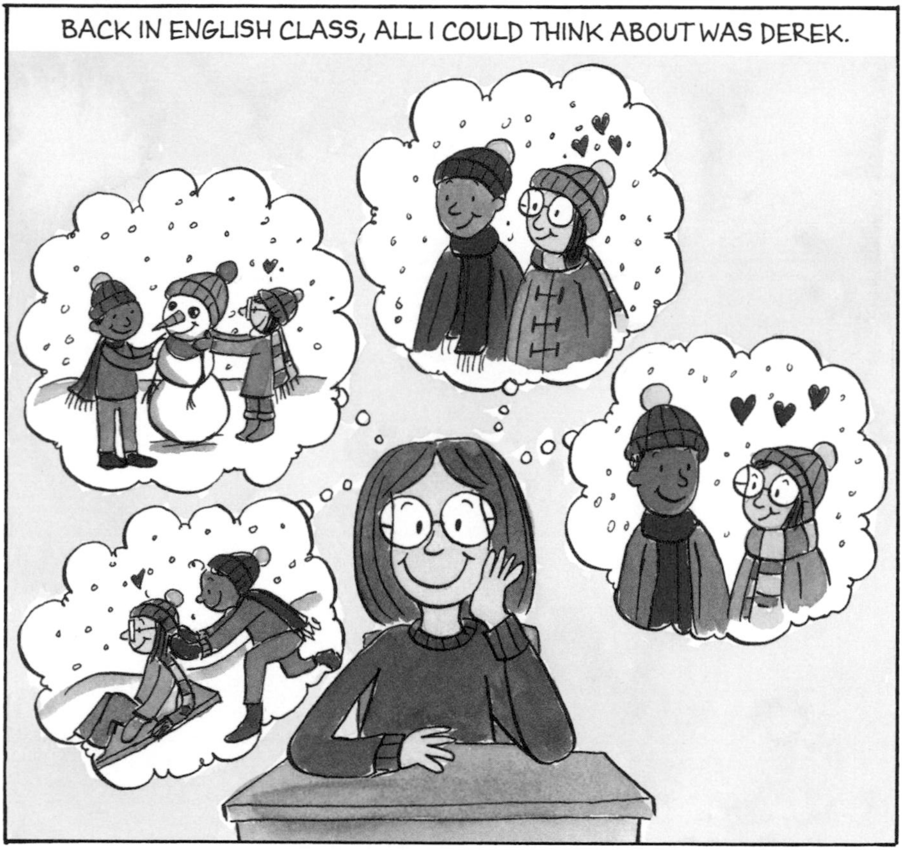
BACK IN ENGLISH CLASS, ALL I COULD THINK ABOUT WAS DEREK.

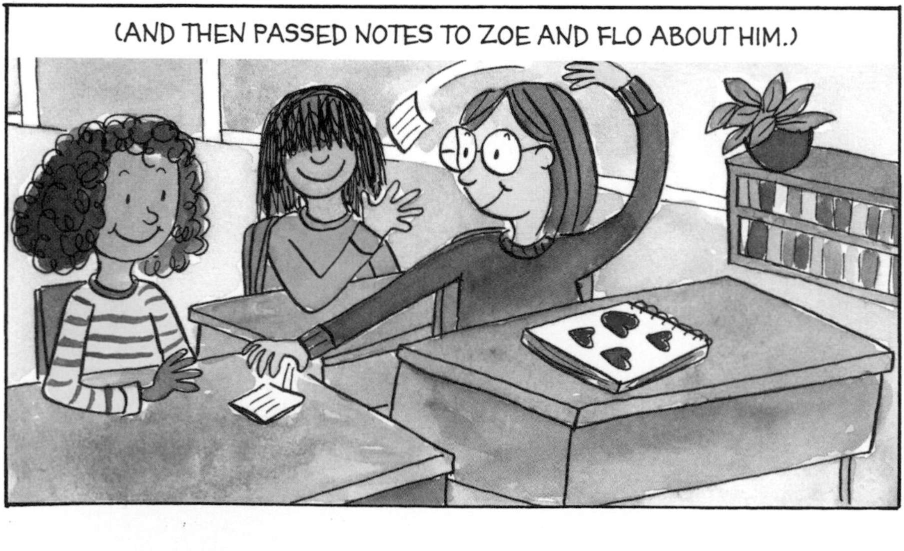
(AND THEN PASSED NOTES TO ZOE AND FLO ABOUT HIM.)

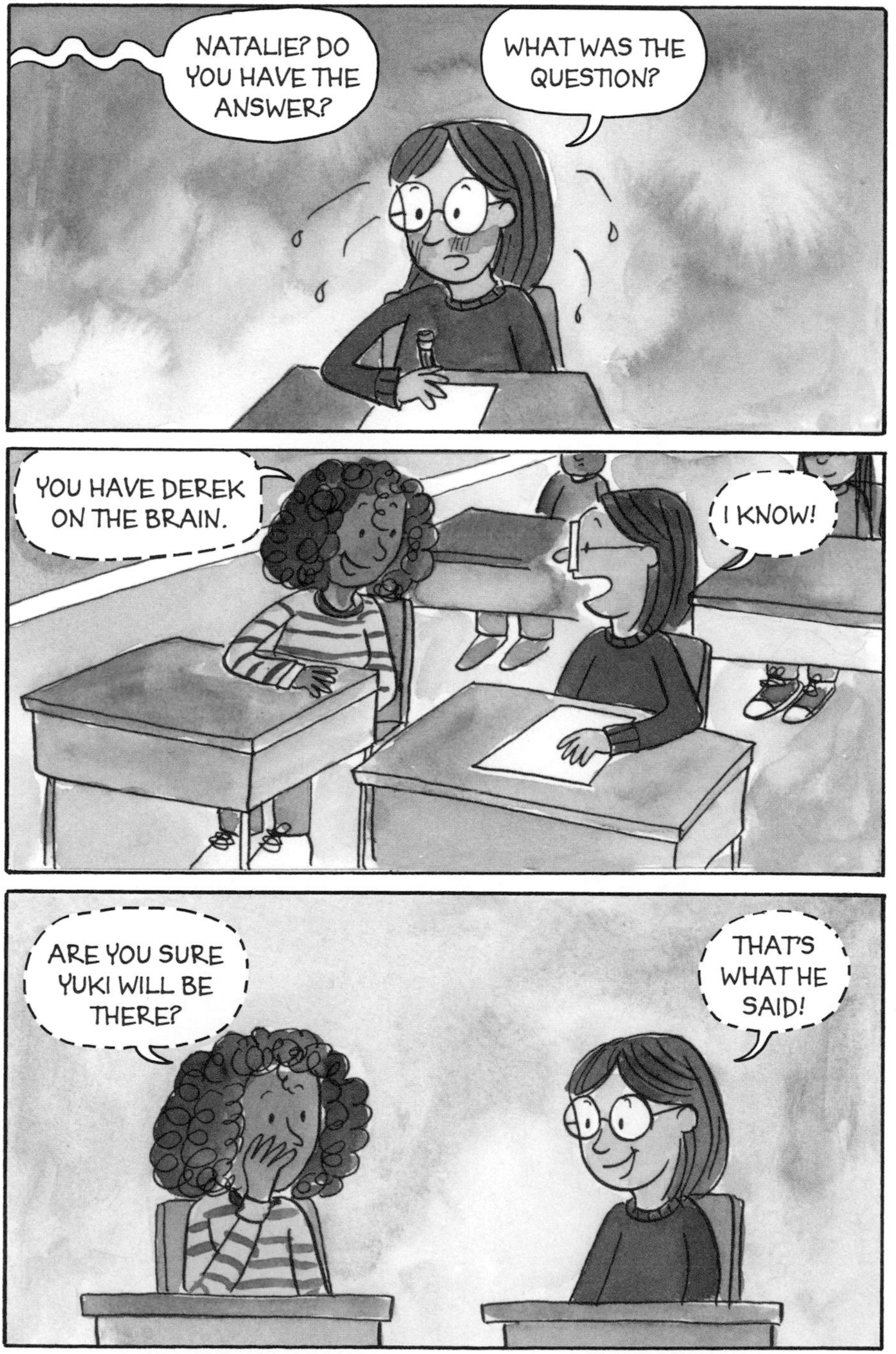
NATALIE? DO YOU HAVE THE ANSWER?
WHAT WAS THE QUESTION?
YOU HAVE DEREK ON THE BRAIN.
I KNOW!
ARE YOU SURE YUKI WILL BE THERE?
THAT'S WHAT HE SAID!

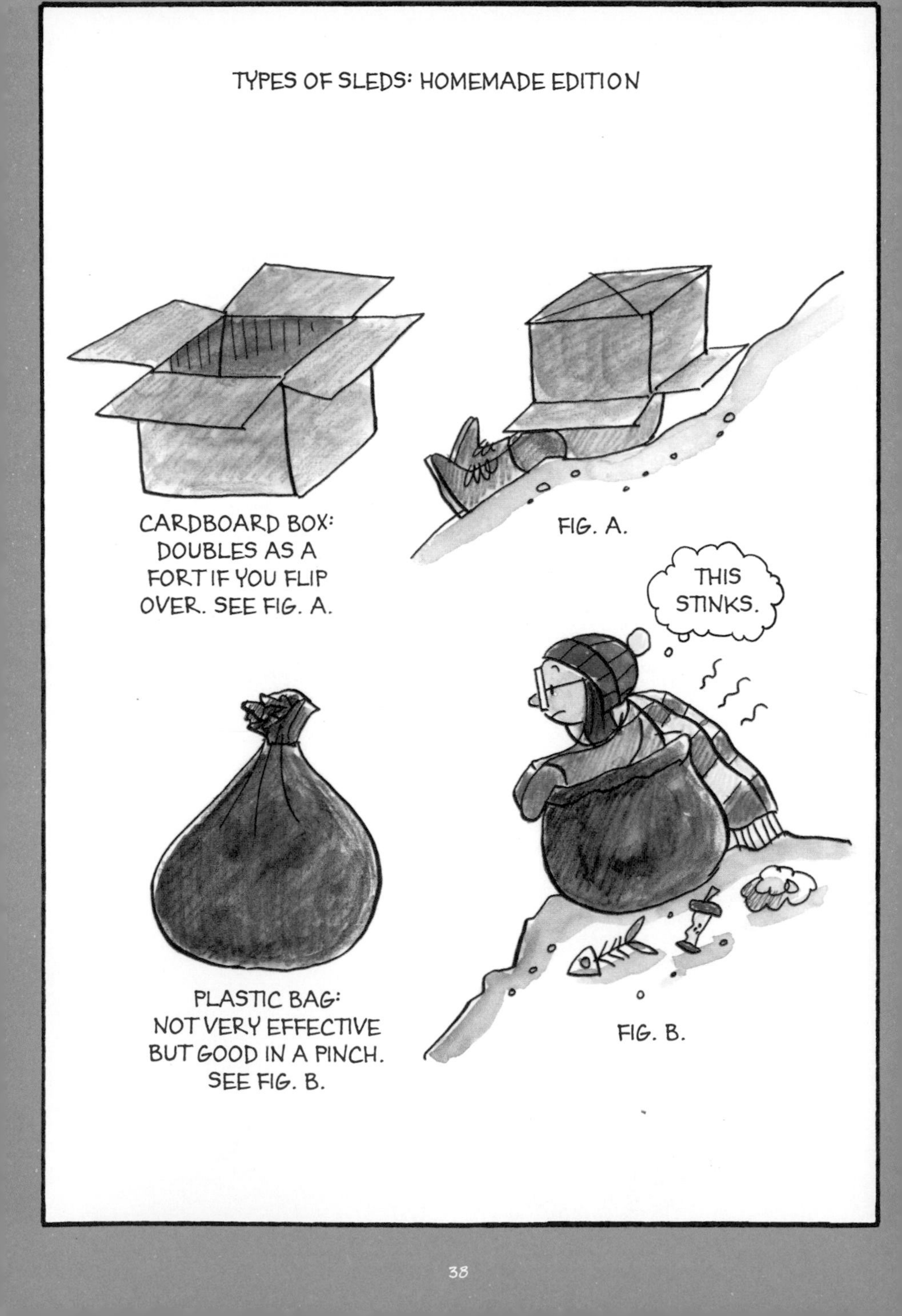
TYPES OF SLEDS: HOMEMADE EDITION
CARDBOARD BOX: DOUBLES AS A FORT IF YOU FLIP OVER. SEE FIG. A.
FIG. A.
THIS STINKS.
PLASTIC BAG: NOT VERY EFFECTIVE BUT GOOD IN A PINCH. SEE FIG. B.
FIG. B.

TYPES OF SLEDS: STORE-BOUGHT EDITION

FIG. C.

FLYING SAUCER:
GOOD IF YOU WANT TO GO
REALLY FAST, BAD IF YOU
WANT TO FACE FOWARD.
SEE FIG. C.

FIG. D.

WOODEN SLED:
GREAT ON ICE, LOUSY
ON DEEP SNOW.
SEE FIG. D.

FIG. E.

TOBOGGAN:
BEST USED IF YOU WANT TO
SIT NEXT TO YOUR CRUSH.
SEE FIG. E.

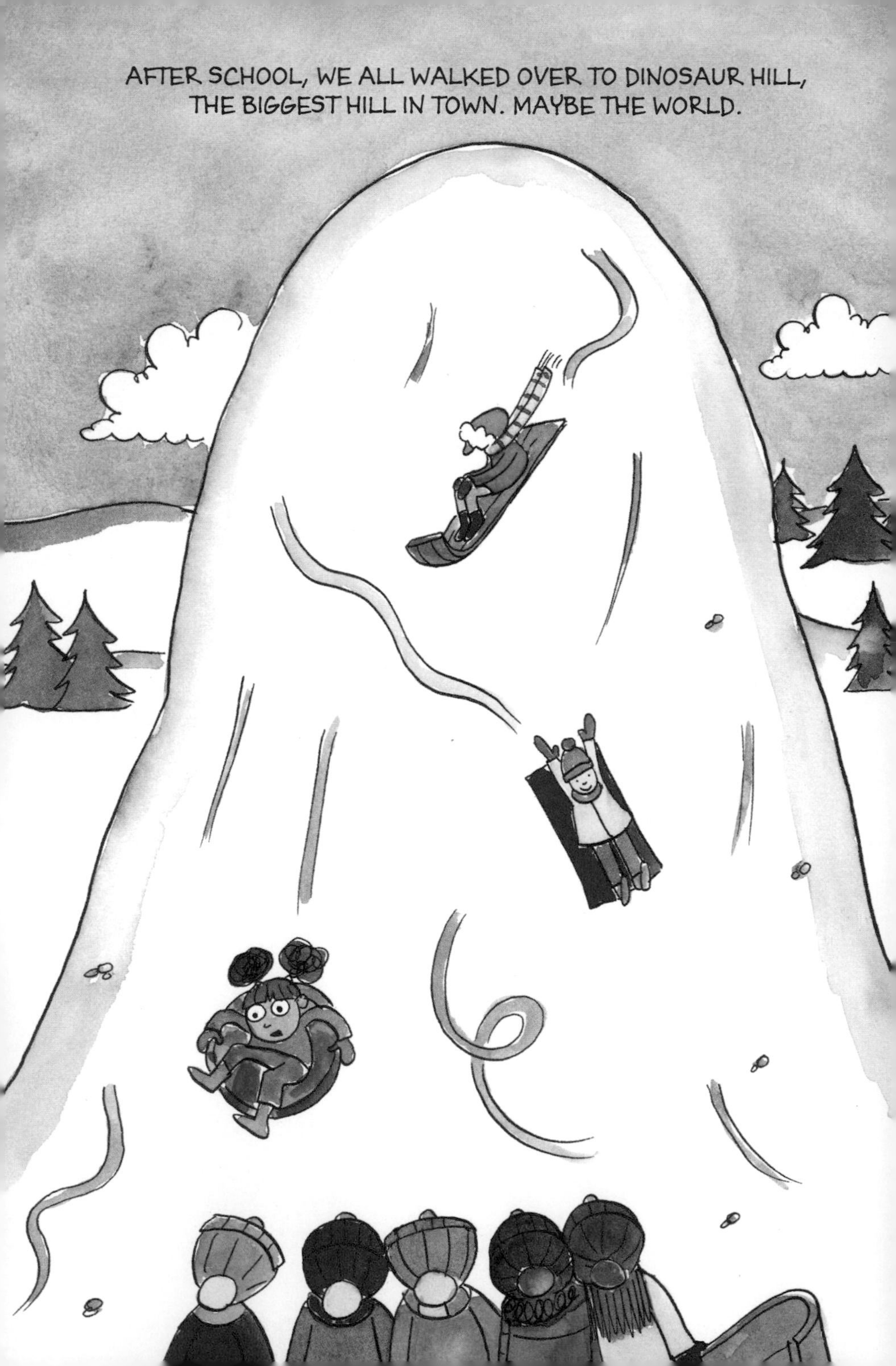
AFTER SCHOOL, WE ALL WALKED OVER TO DINOSAUR HILL,
THE BIGGEST HILL IN TOWN. MAYBE THE WORLD.

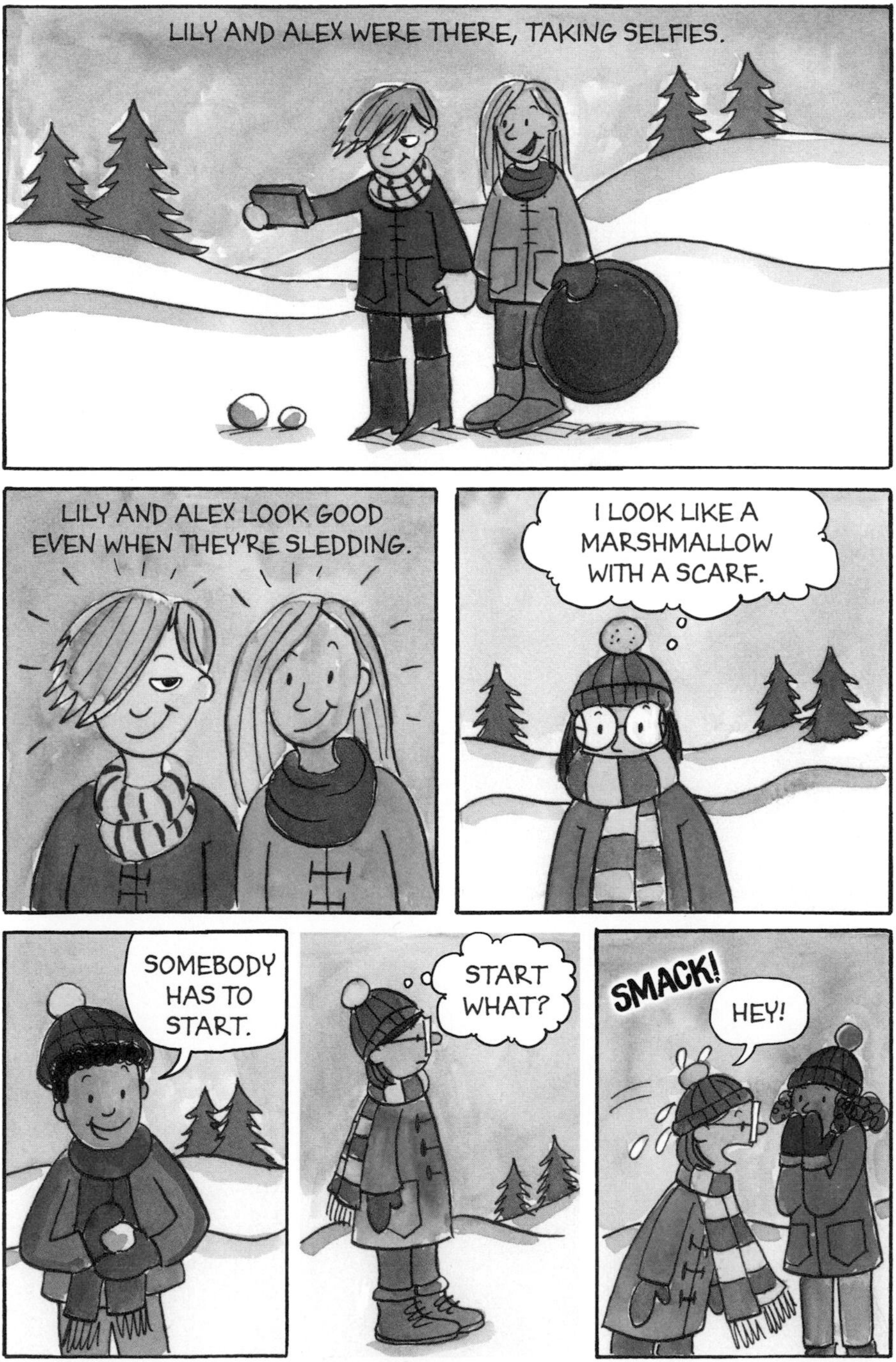
LILY AND ALEX WERE THERE, TAKING SELFIES.
LILY AND ALEX LOOK GOOD EVEN WHEN THEY'RE SLEDDING.
I LOOK LIKE A MARSHMALLOW WITH A SCARF.
SOMEBODY HAS TO START.
START WHAT?
SMACK!
HEY!

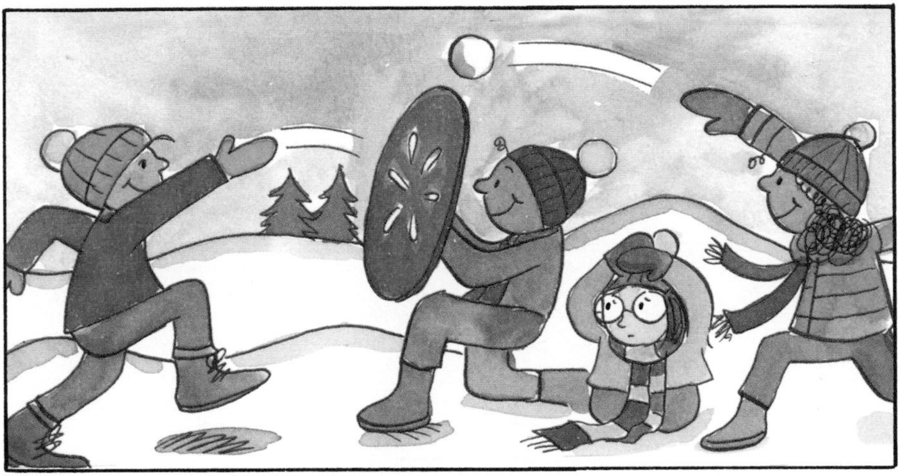

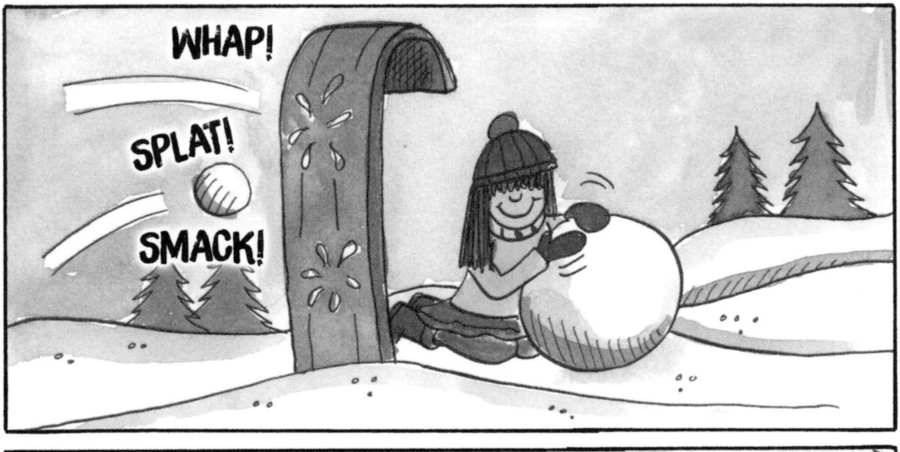
WHAP!
SPLAT!
SMACK!

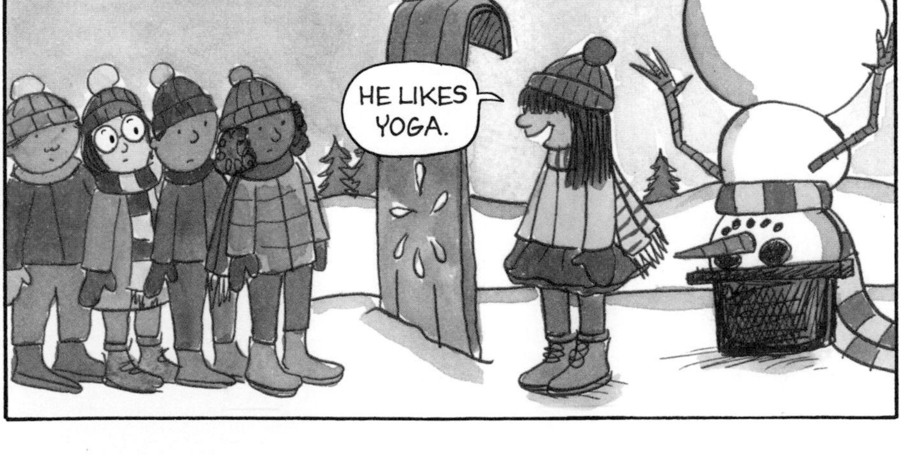
HE LIKES YOGA.

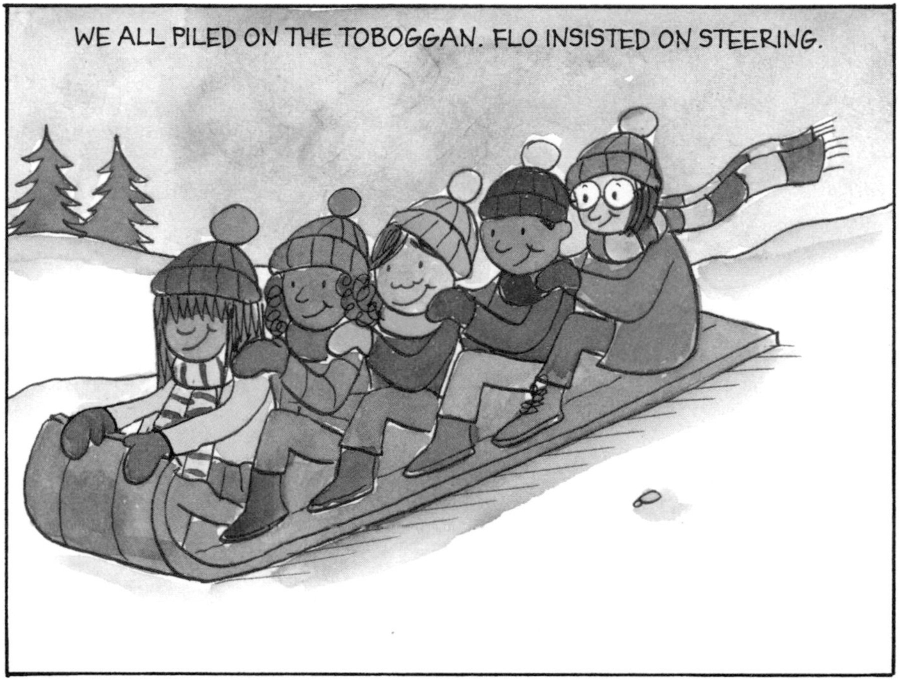
WE ALL PILED ON THE TOBOGGAN. FLO INSISTED ON STEERING.

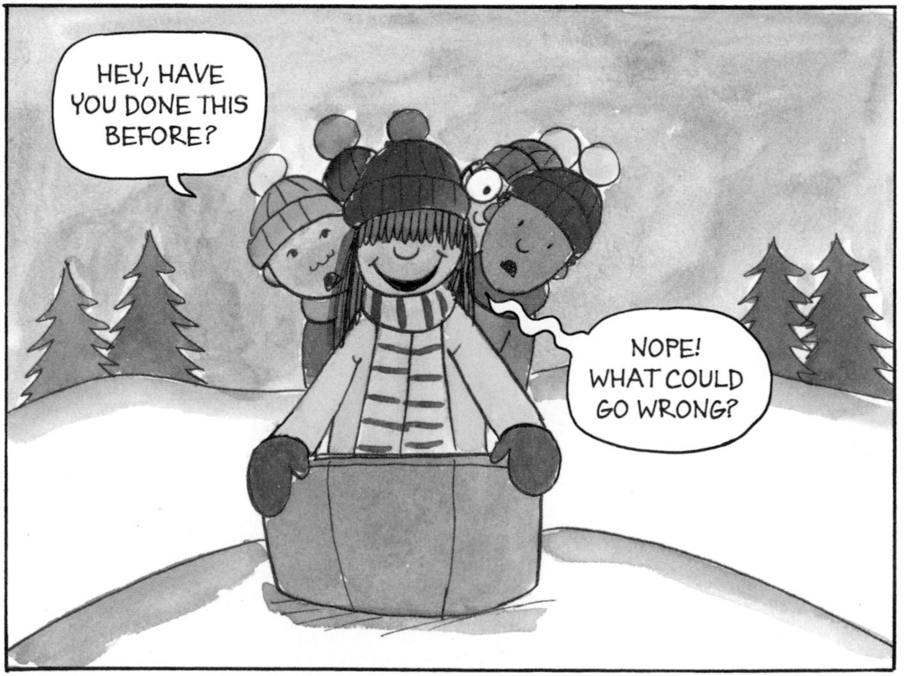
HEY, HAVE YOU DONE THIS BEFORE?
NOPE! WHAT COULD GO WRONG?

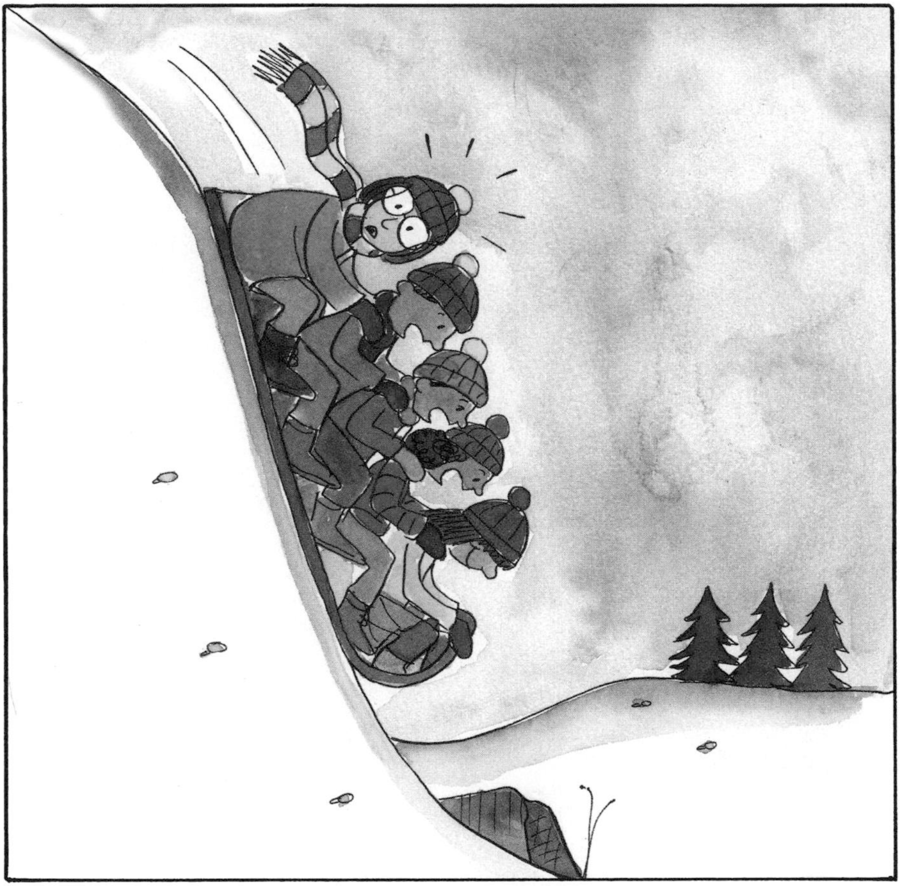

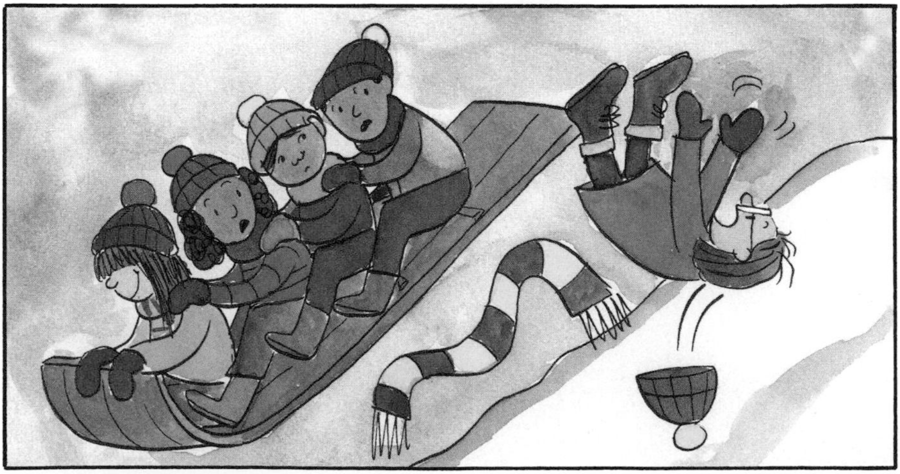

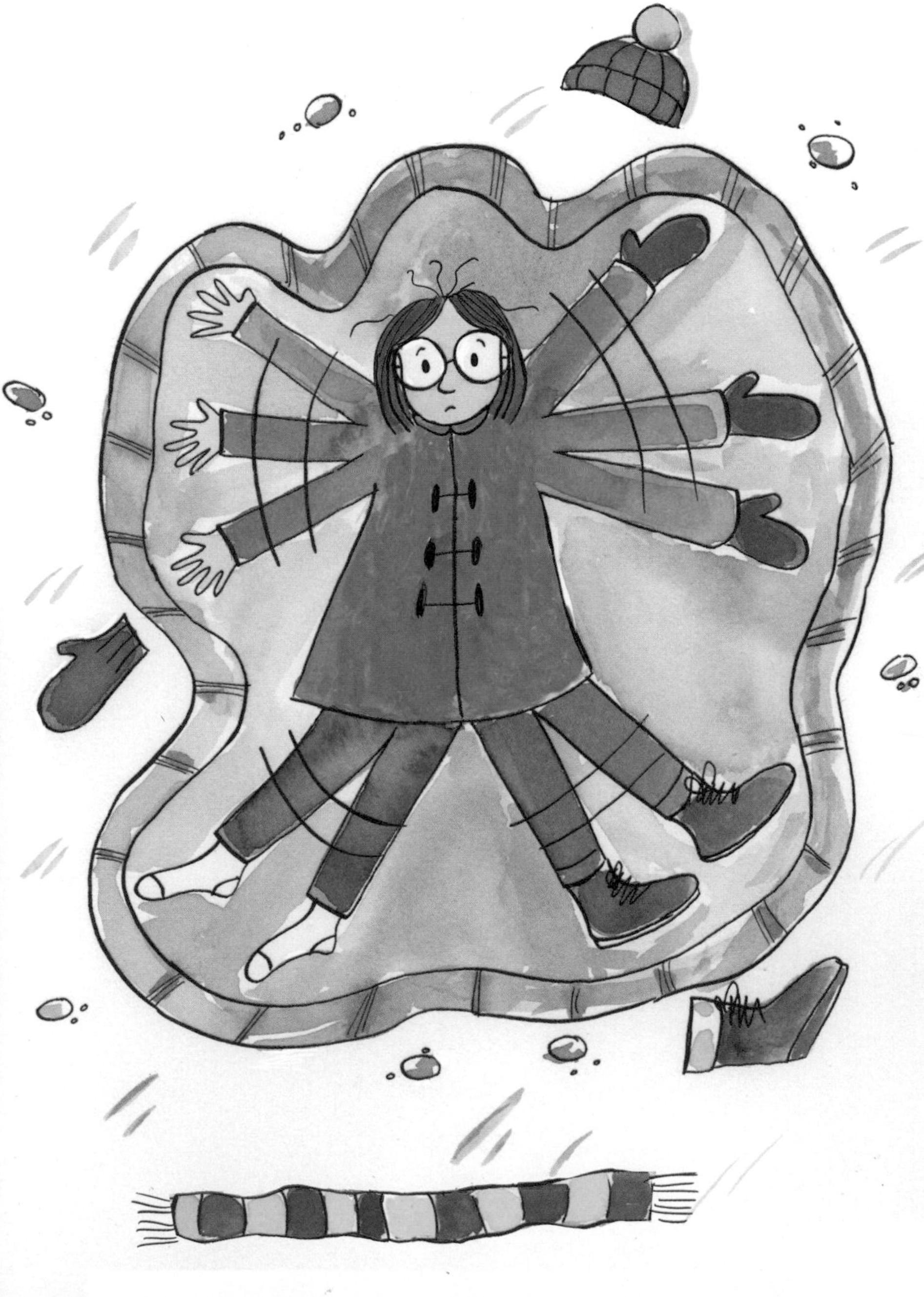

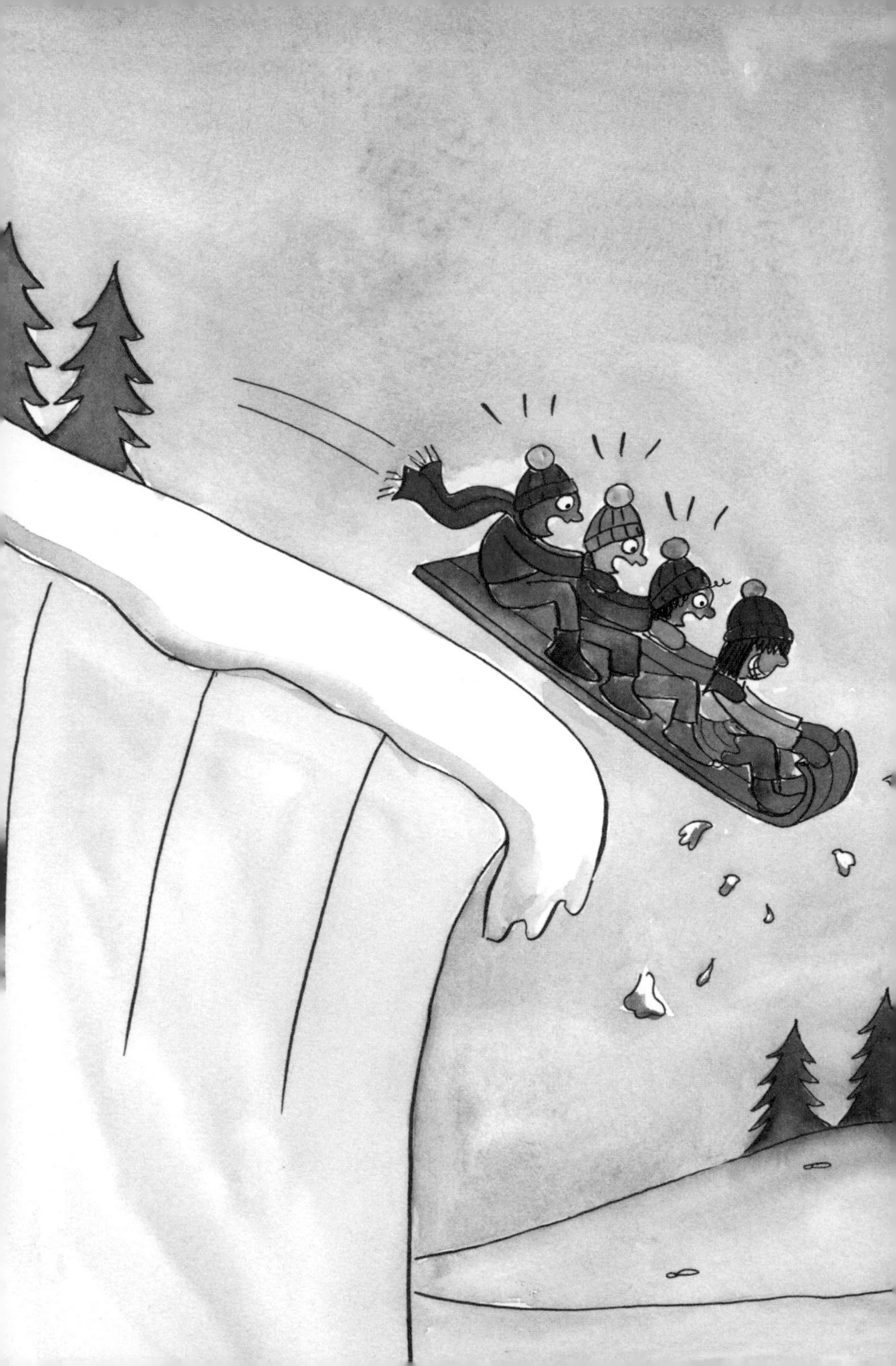

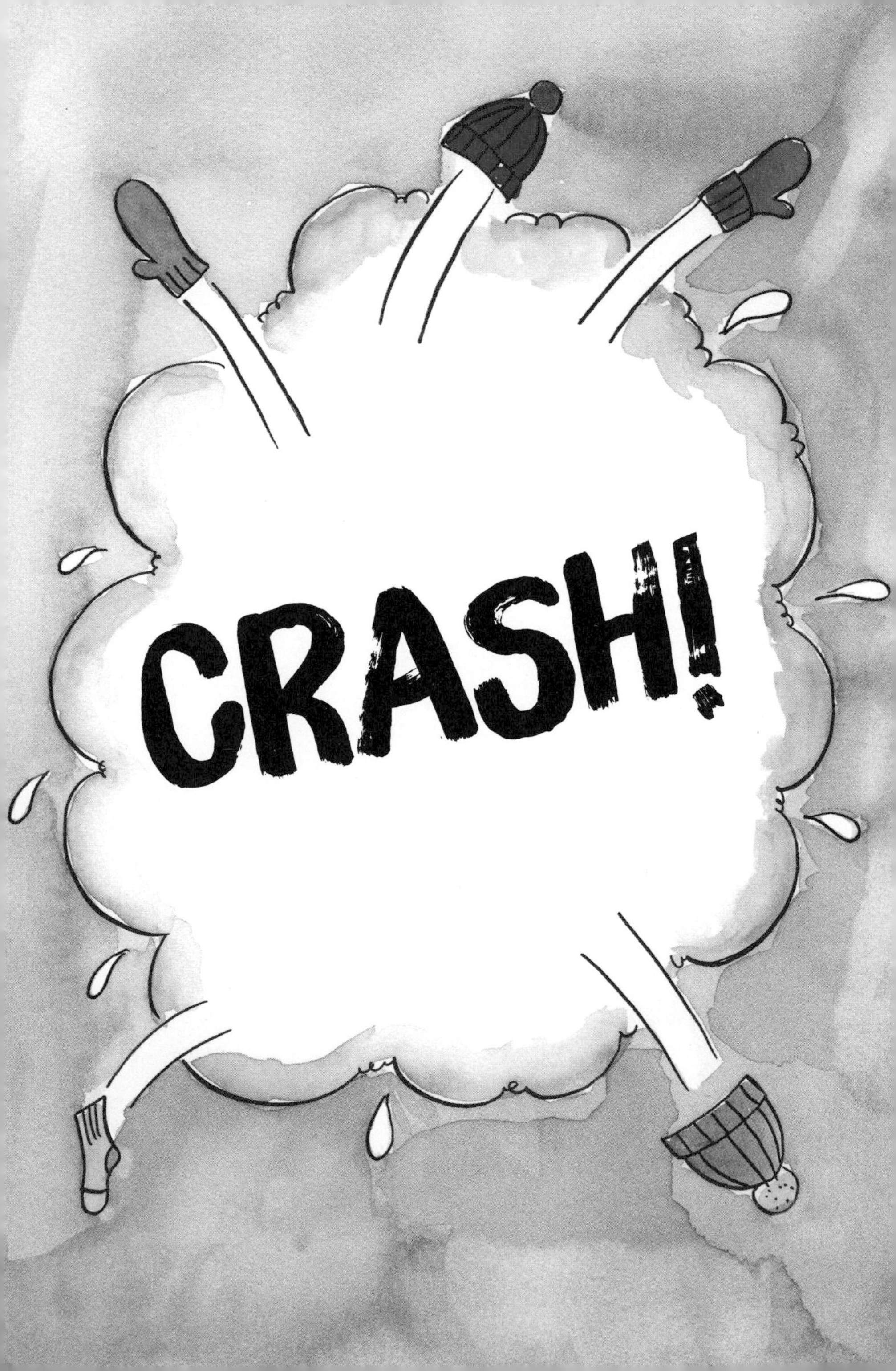
CRASH!

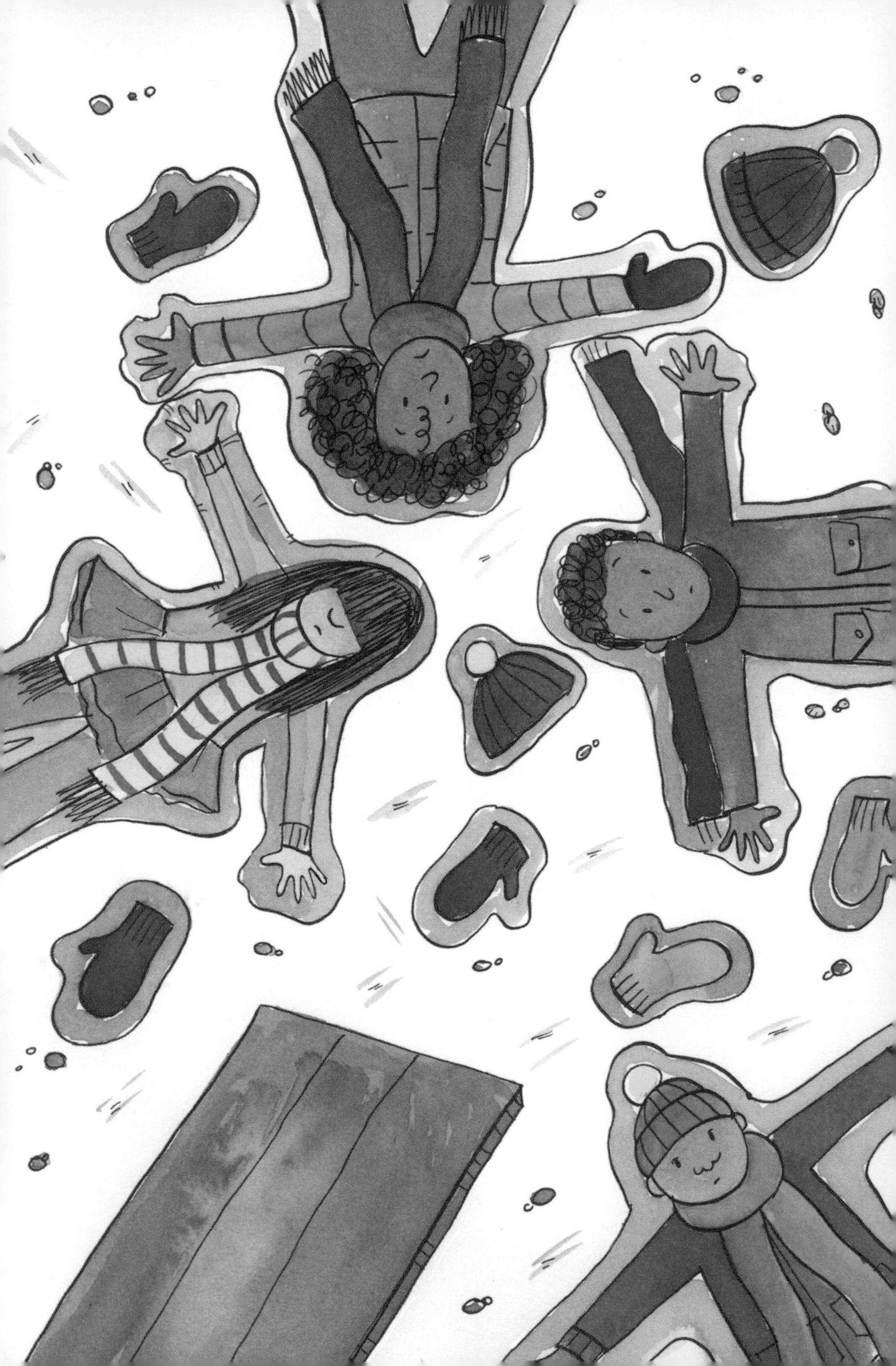

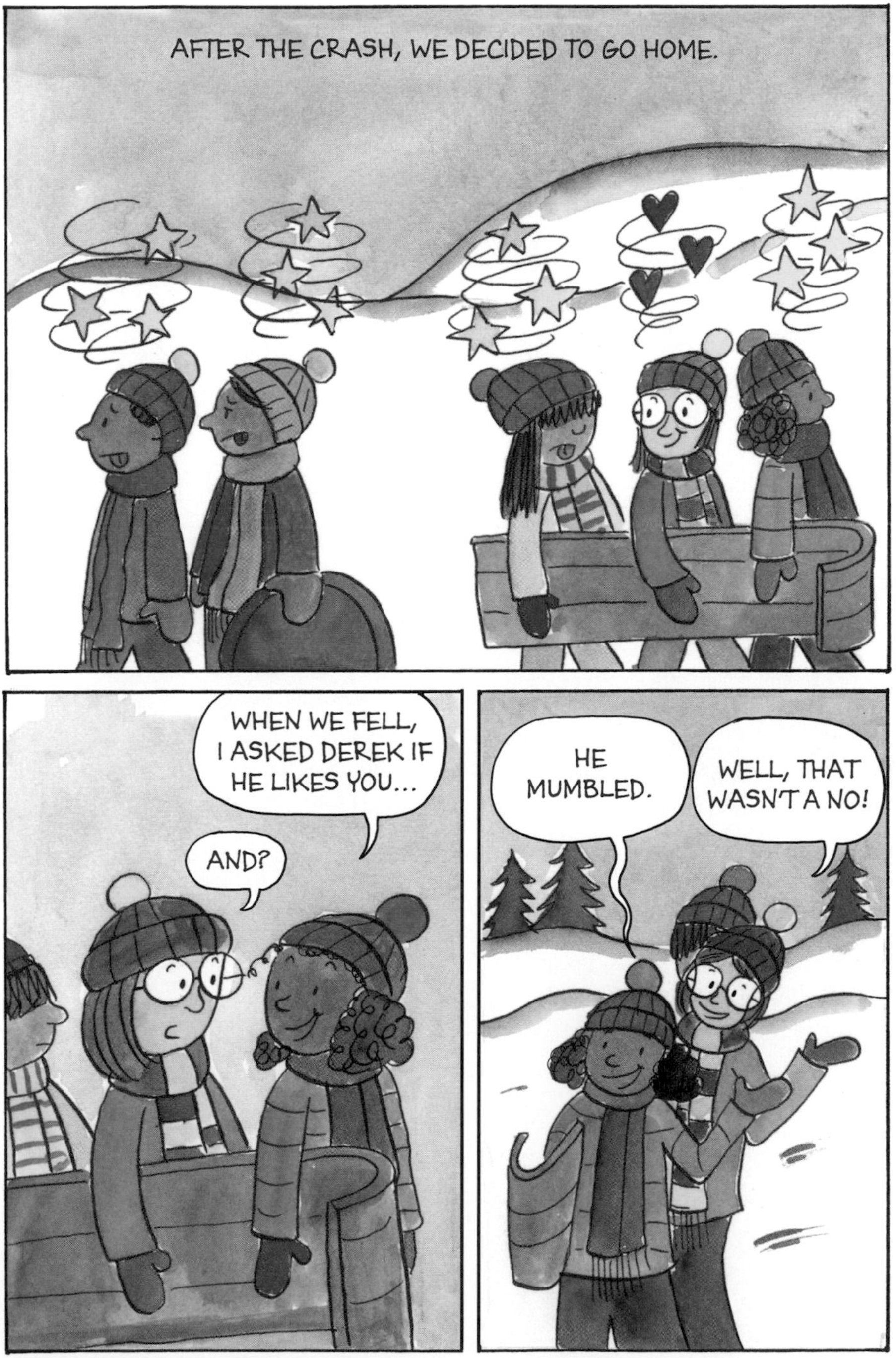
AFTER THE CRASH, WE DECIDED TO GO HOME.
WHEN WE FELL, I ASKED DEREK IF HE LIKES YOU...
AND?
HE MUMBLED.
WELL, THAT WASN'T A NO!

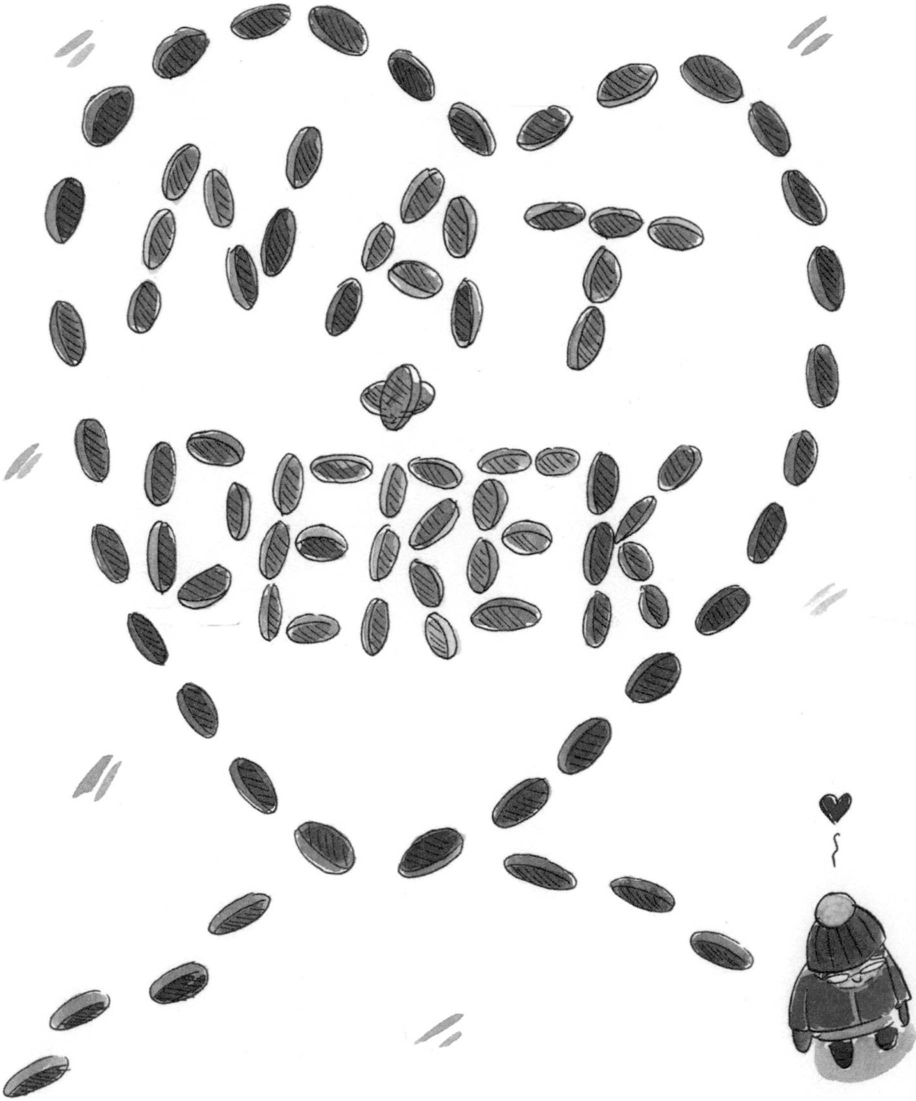
NAT + DEREK

CHAPTER 4
CAMPAIGN

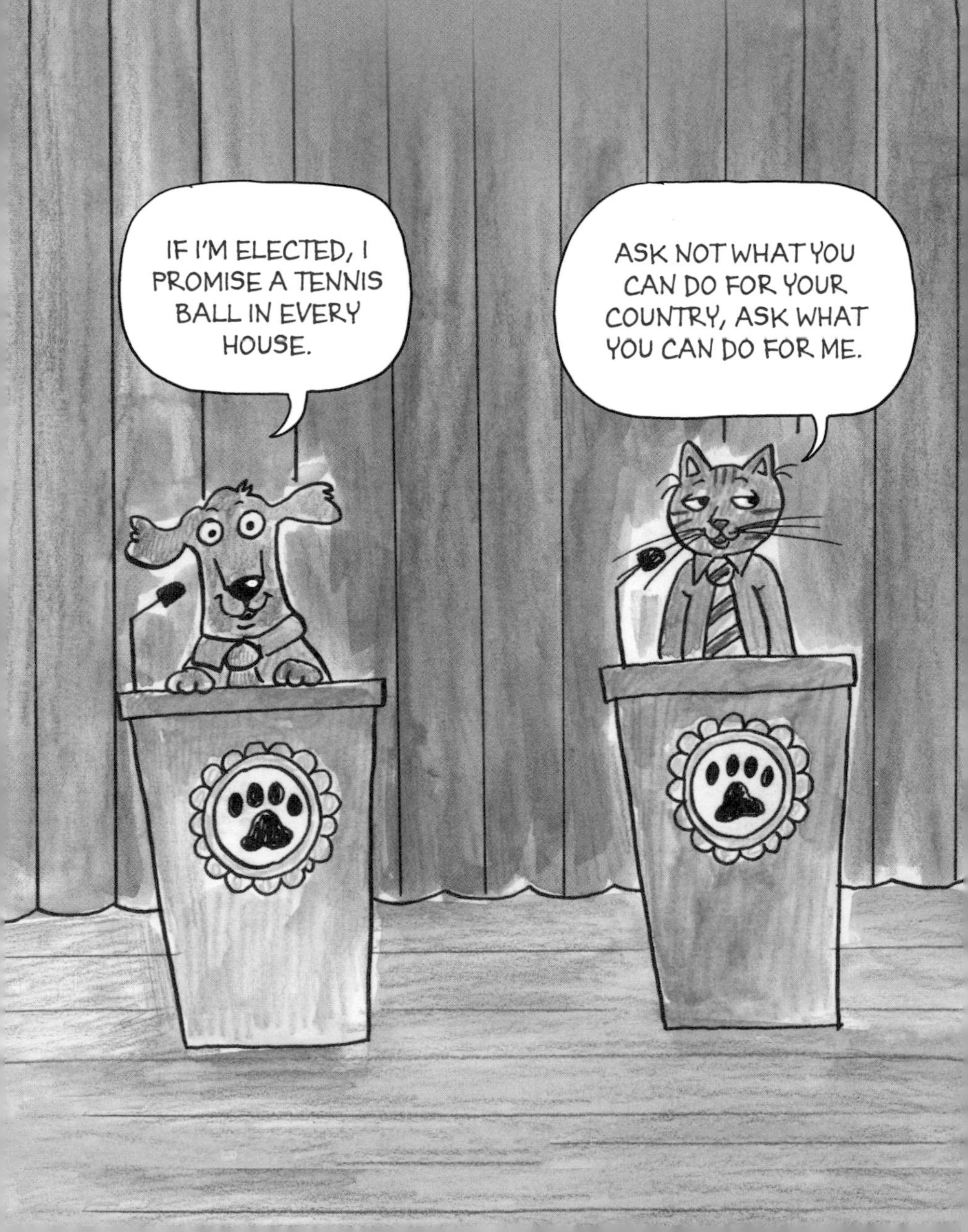
IF I'M ELECTED, I PROMISE A TENNIS BALL IN EVERY HOUSE.
ASK NOT WHAT YOU CAN DO FOR YOUR COUNTRY, ASK WHAT YOU CAN DO FOR ME.

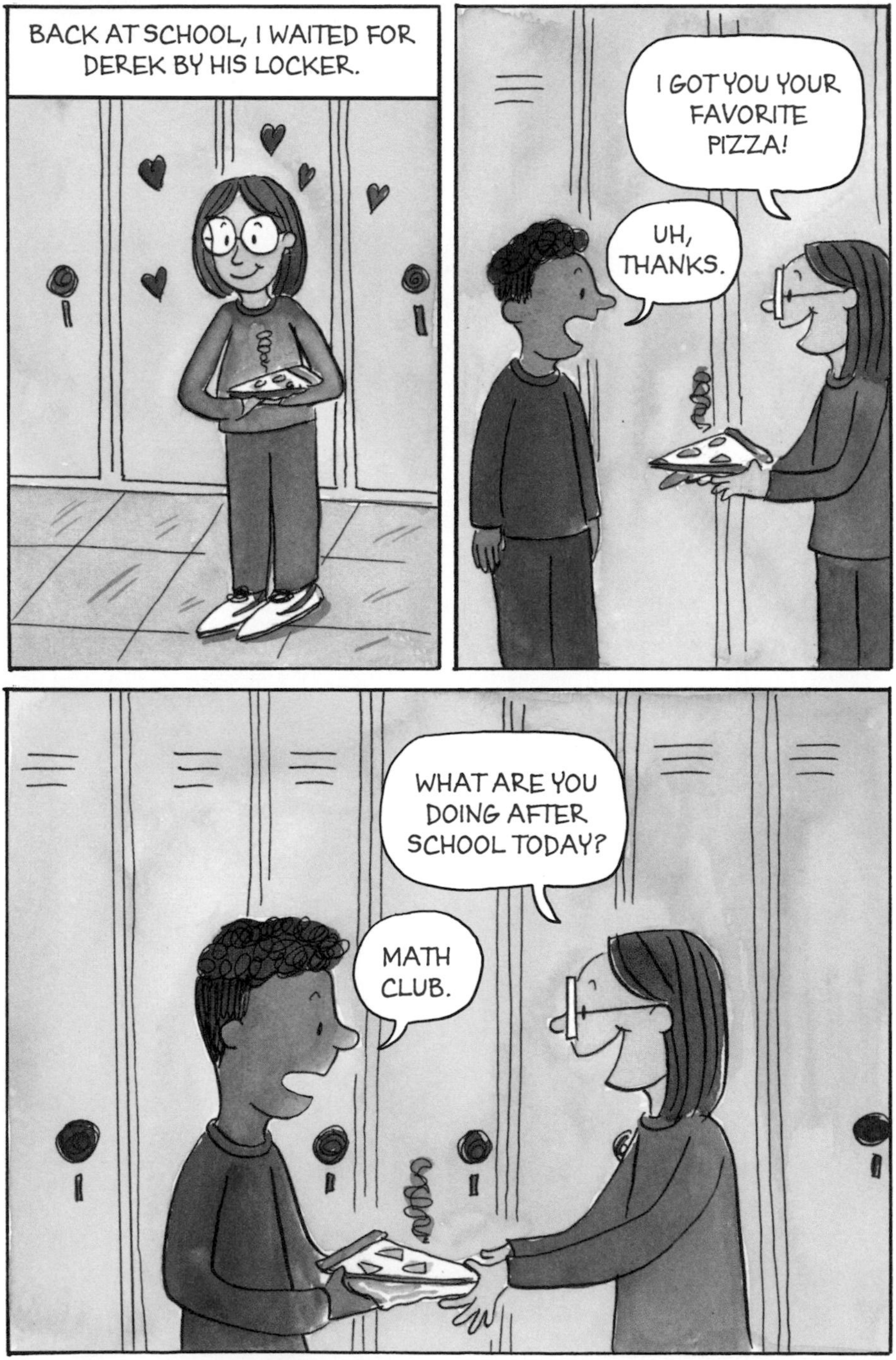
BACK AT SCHOOL, I WAITED FOR DEREK BY HIS LOCKER.
I GOT YOU YOUR FAVORITE PIZZA!
UH, THANKS.
WHAT ARE YOU DOING AFTER SCHOOL TODAY?
MATH CLUB.

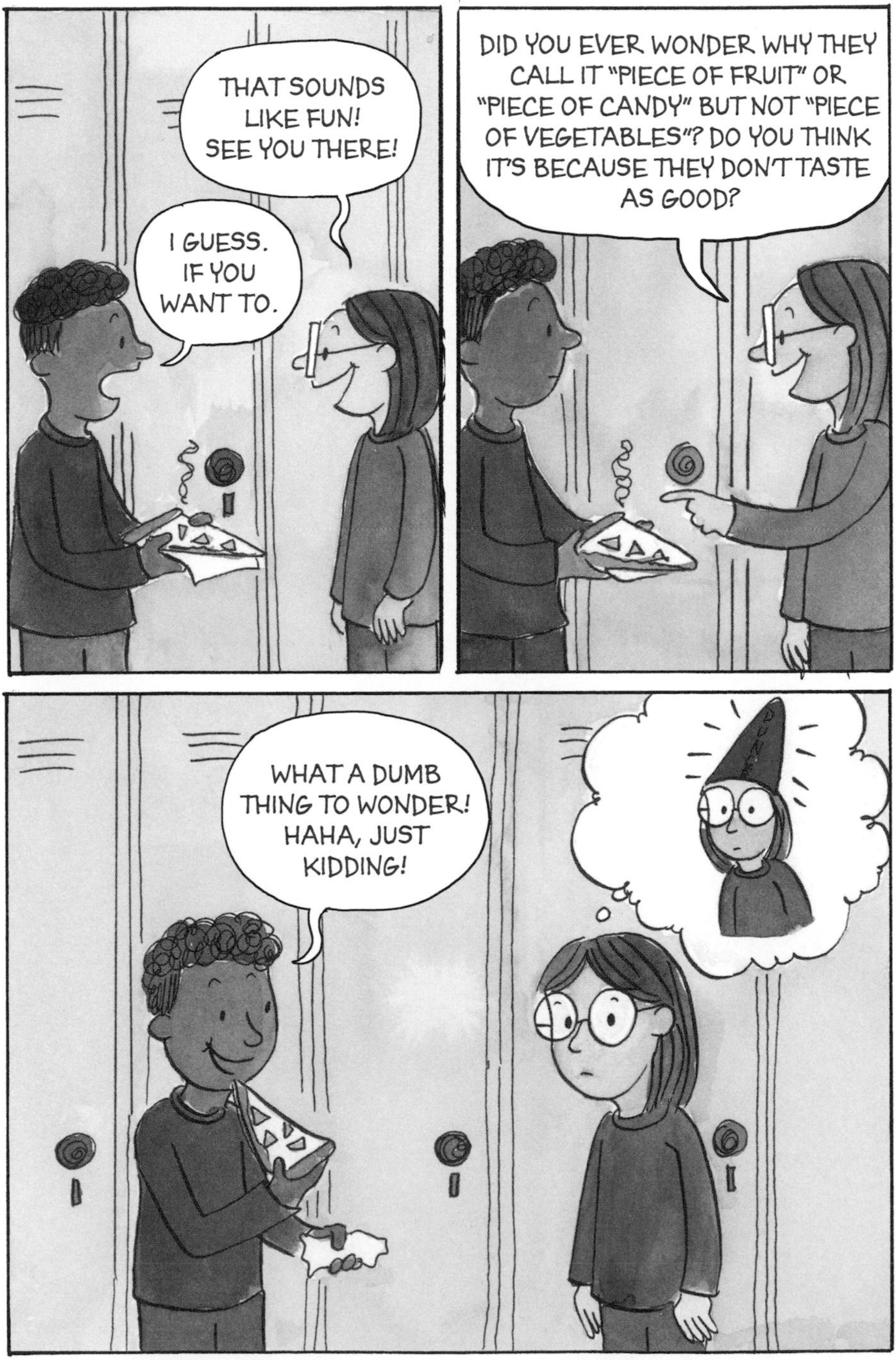
THAT SOUNDS LIKE FUN! SEE YOU THERE!
I GUESS. IF YOU WANT TO.
DID YOU EVER WONDER WHY THEY CALL IT "PIECE OF FRUIT" OR "PIECE OF CANDY" BUT NOT "PIECE OF VEGETABLES"? DO YOU THINK IT'S BECAUSE THEY DON'T TASTE AS GOOD?
WHAT A DUMB THING TO WONDER! HAHA, JUST KIDDING!

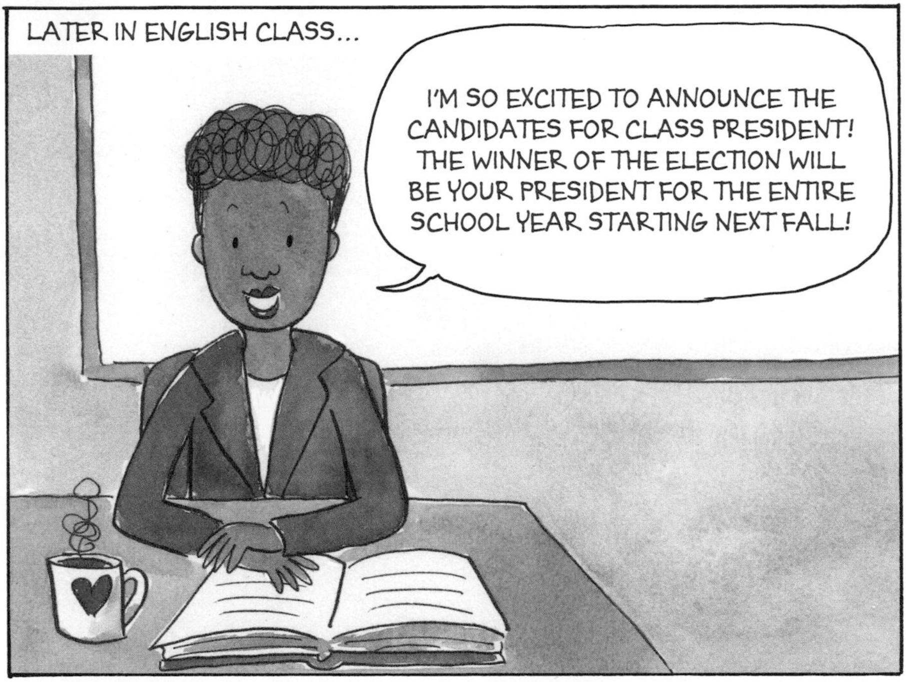
LATER IN ENGLISH CLASS...
I'M SO EXCITED TO ANNOUNCE THE CANDIDATES FOR CLASS PRESIDENT! THE WINNER OF THE ELECTION WILL BE YOUR PRESIDENT FOR THE ENTIRE SCHOOL YEAR STARTING NEXT FALL!

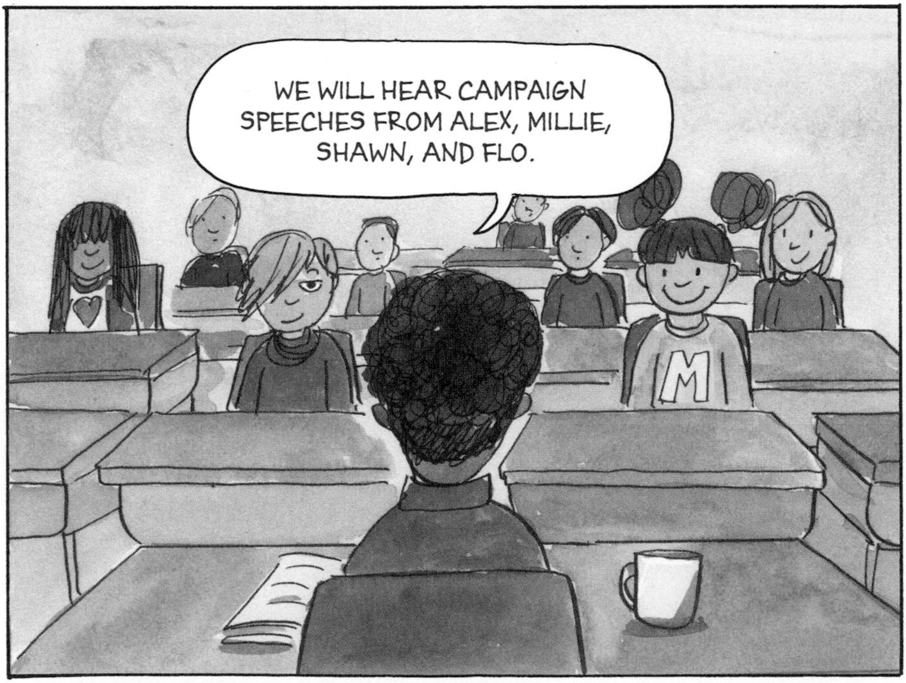
WE WILL HEAR CAMPAIGN SPEECHES FROM ALEX, MILLIE, SHAWN, AND FLO.
M

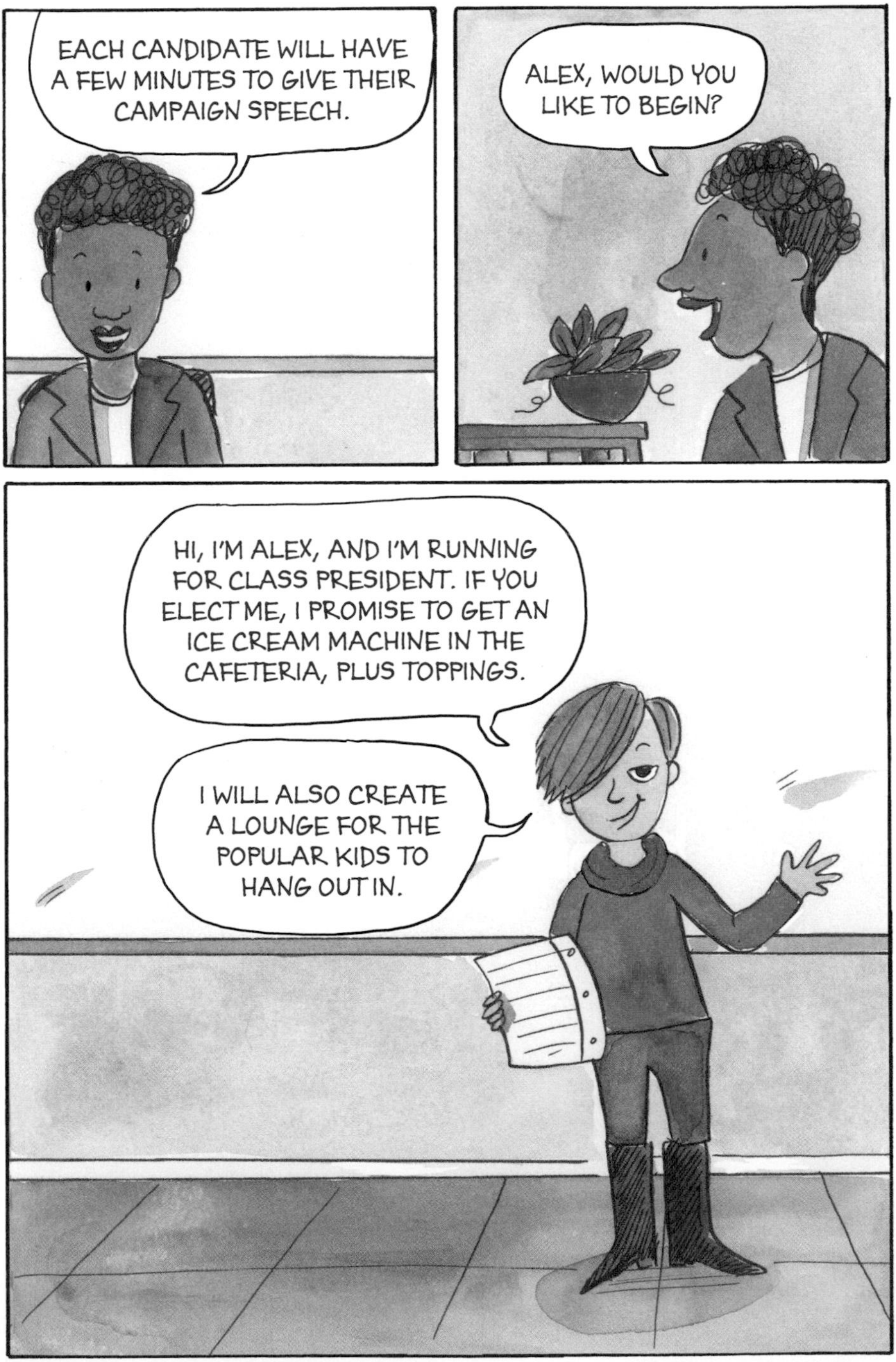
EACH CANDIDATE WILL HAVE A FEW MINUTES TO GIVE THEIR CAMPAIGN SPEECH.
ALEX, WOULD YOU LIKE TO BEGIN?
HI, I'M ALEX, AND I'M RUNNING FOR CLASS PRESIDENT. IF YOU ELECT ME, I PROMISE TO GET AN ICE CREAM MACHINE IN THE CAFETERIA, PLUS TOPPINGS.
I WILL ALSO CREATE A LOUNGE FOR THE POPULAR KIDS TO HANG OUT IN.

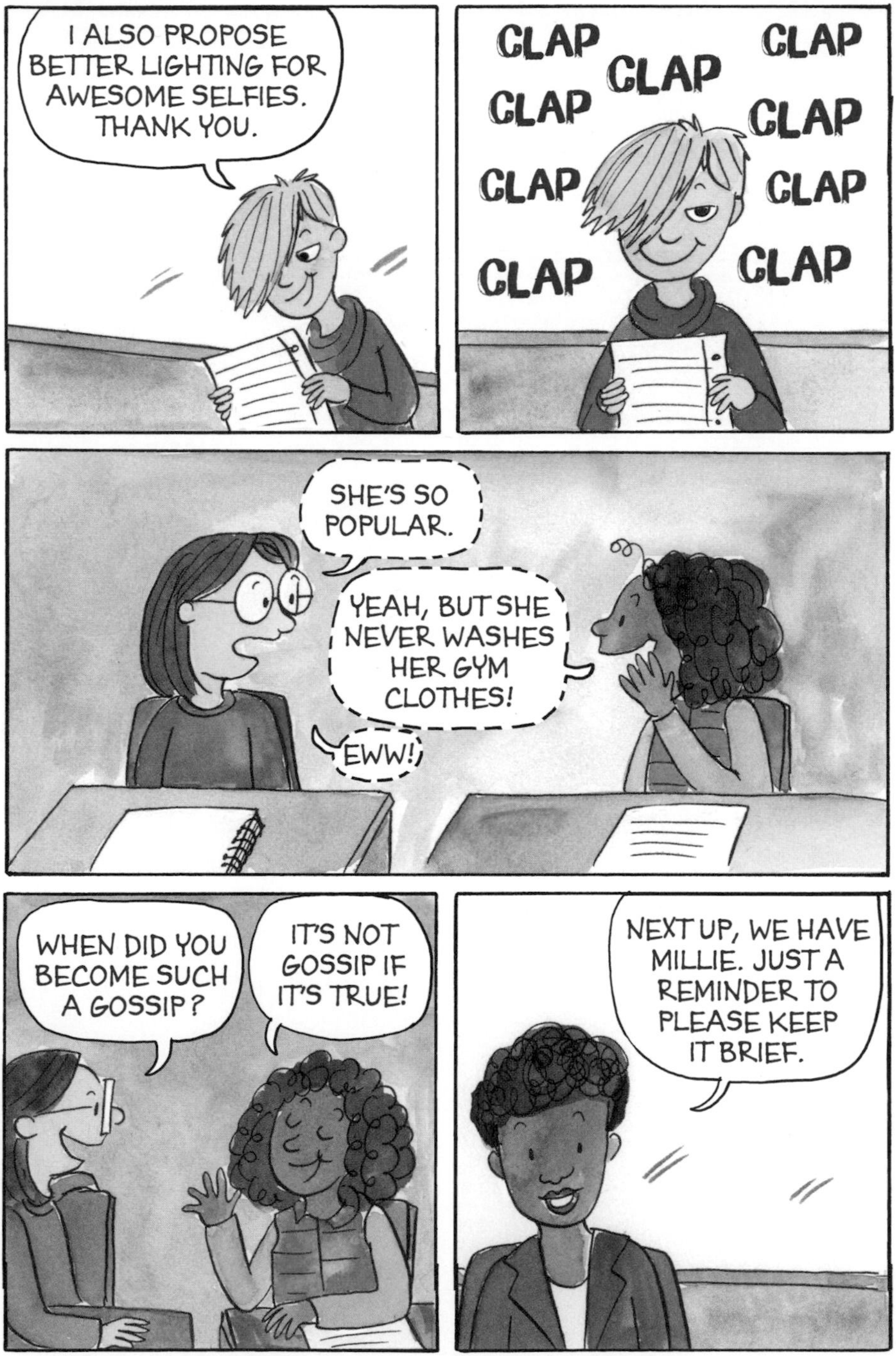
I ALSO PROPOSE BETTER LIGHTING FOR AWESOME SELFIES. THANK YOU.
CLAP CLAP CLAP CLAP CLAP CLAP CLAP CLAP CLAP
SHE'S SO POPULAR.
YEAH, BUT SHE NEVER WASHES HER GYM CLOTHES!
EWW!
WHEN DID YOU BECOME SUCH A GOSSIP?
IT'S NOT GOSSIP IF IT'S TRUE!
NEXT UP, WE HAVE MILLIE. JUST A REMINDER TO PLEASE KEEP IT BRIEF.

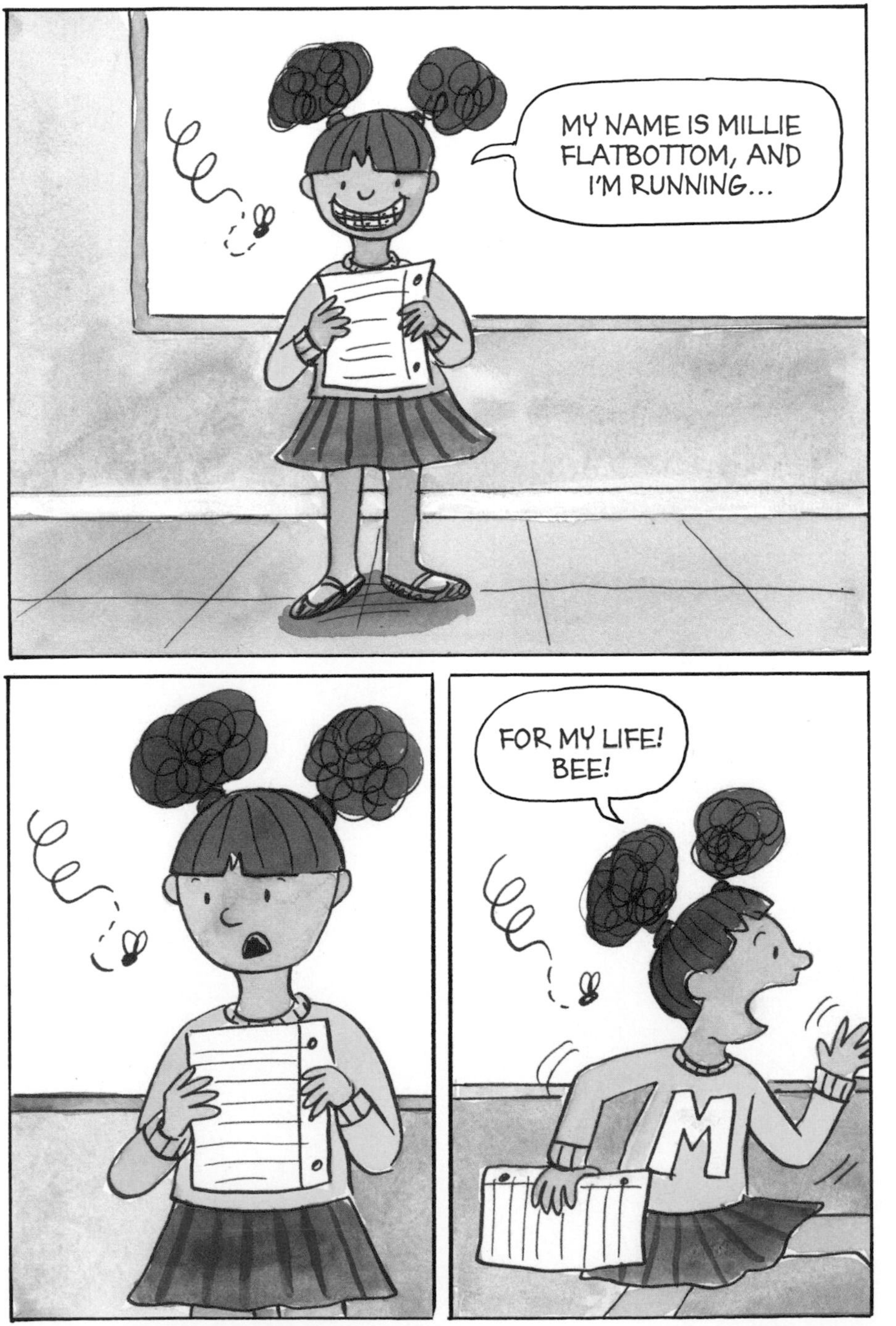
MY NAME IS MILLIE FLATBOTTOM, AND I'M RUNNING...
FOR MY LIFE! BEE!

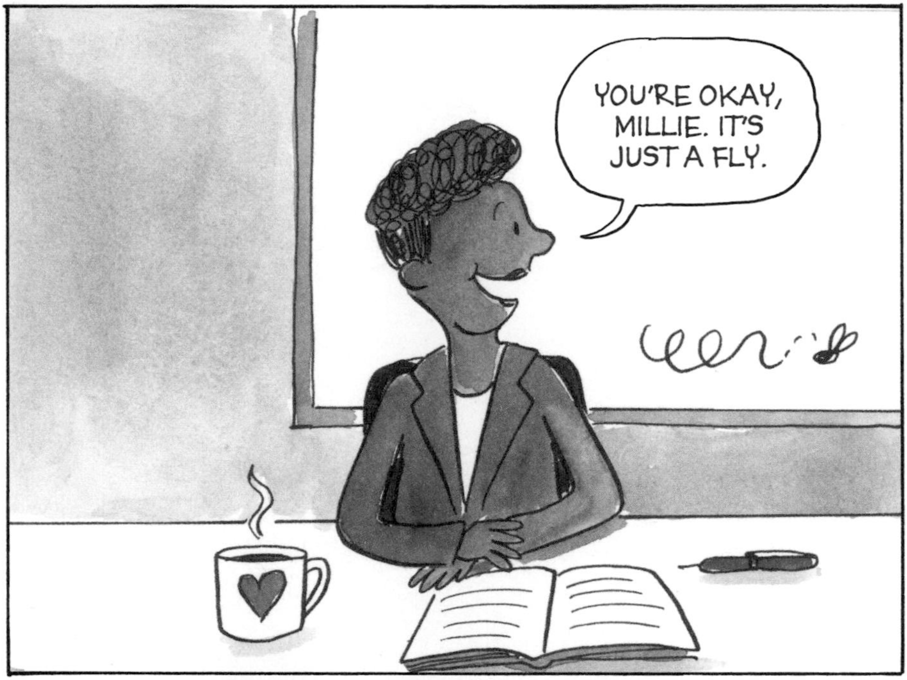
YOU'RE OKAY, MILLIE. IT'S JUST A FLY.

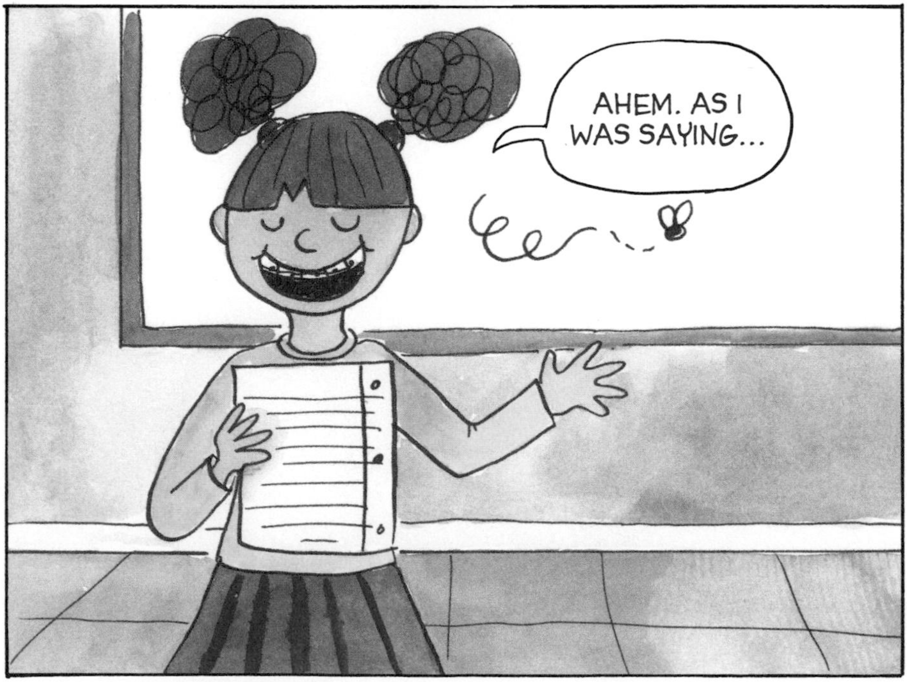
AHEM. AS I WAS SAYING...

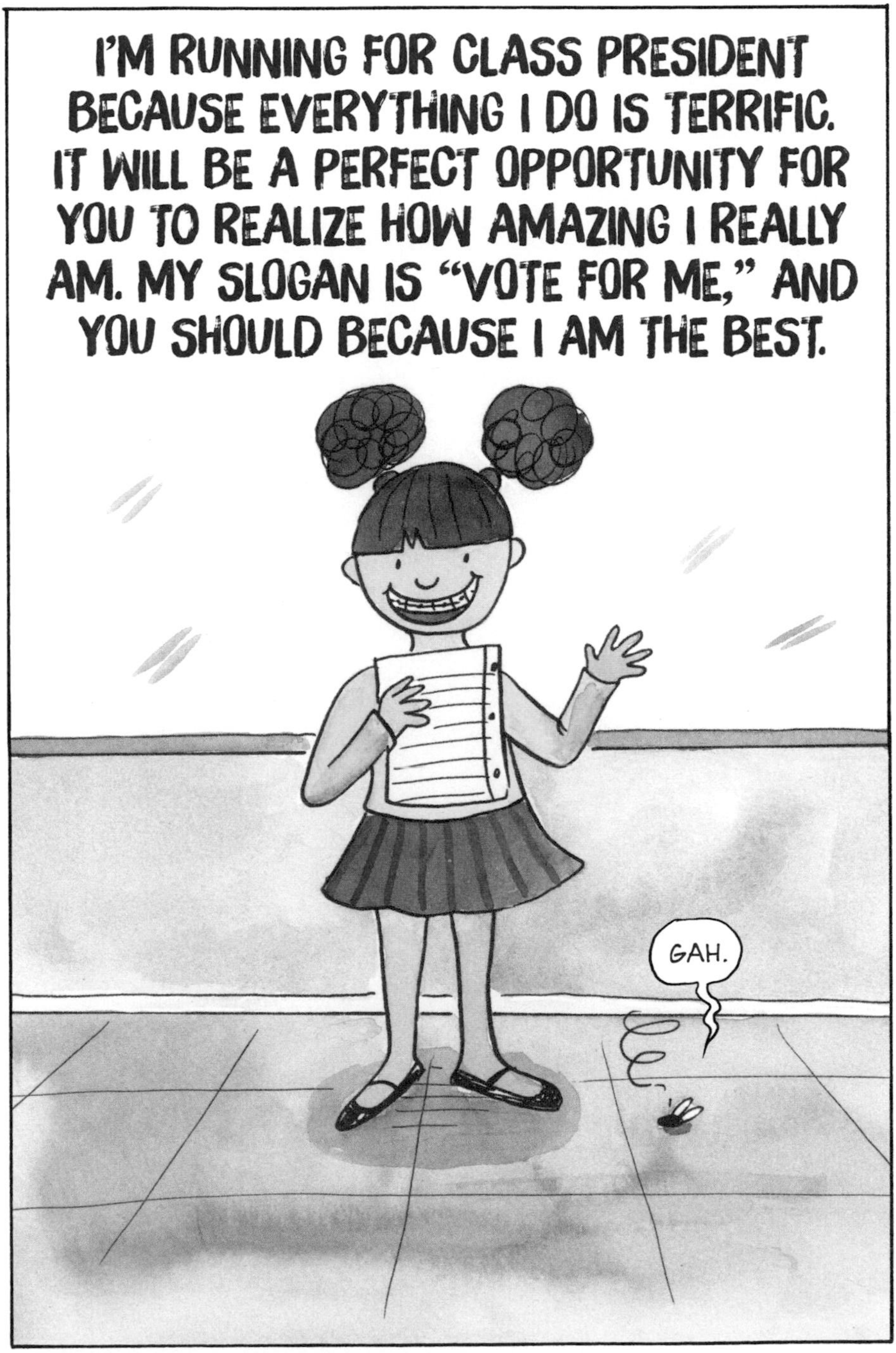
I'M RUNNING FOR CLASS PRESIDENT BECAUSE EVERYTHING I DO IS TERRIFIC. IT WILL BE A PERFECT OPPORTUNITY FOR YOU TO REALIZE HOW AMAZING I REALLY AM. MY SLOGAN IS "VOTE FOR ME," AND YOU SHOULD BECAUSE I AM THE BEST.
GAH.

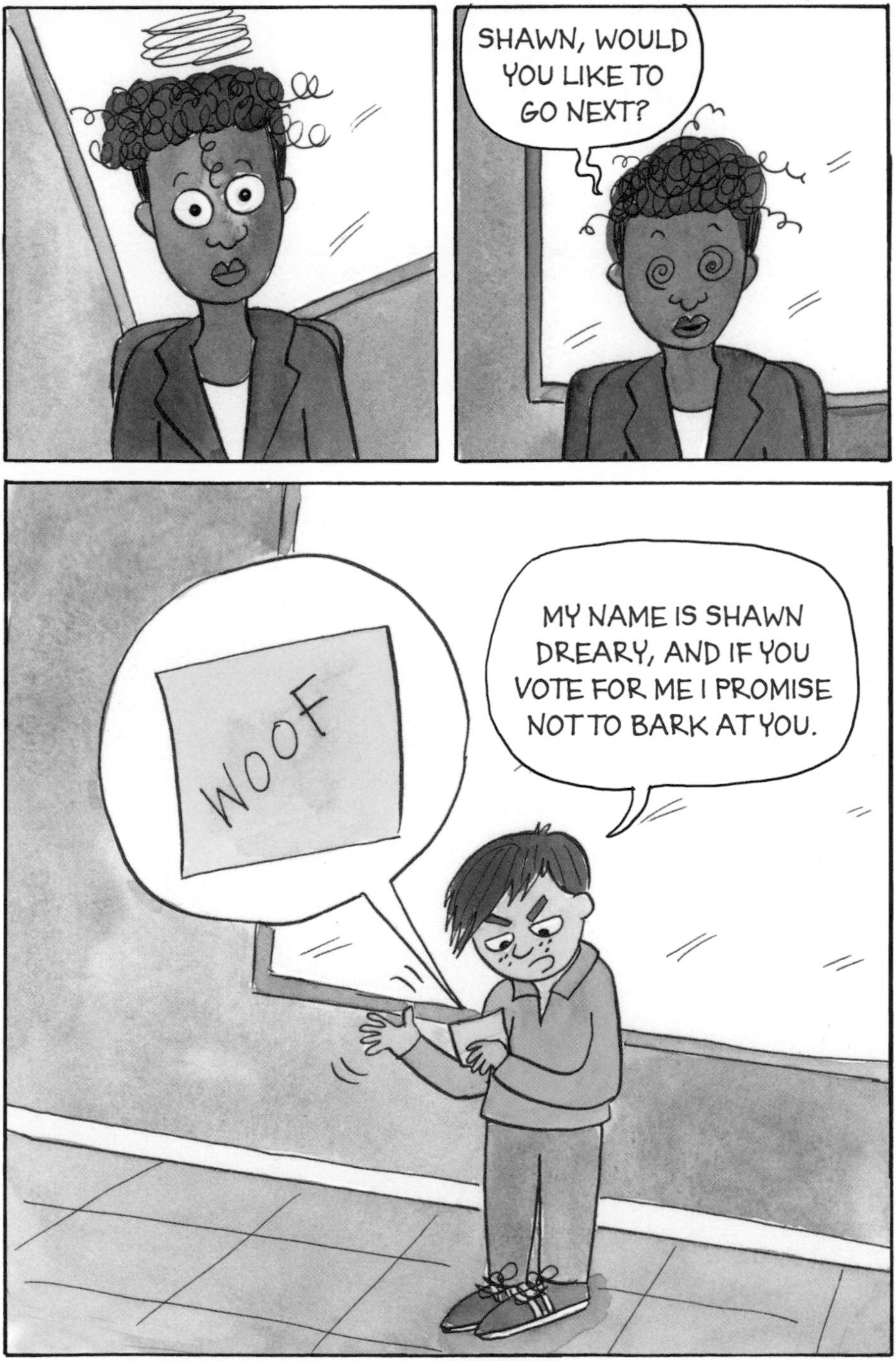
SHAWN, WOULD YOU LIKE TO GO NEXT?
WOOF
MY NAME IS SHAWN DREARY, AND IF YOU VOTE FOR ME I PROMISE NOT TO BARK AT YOU.

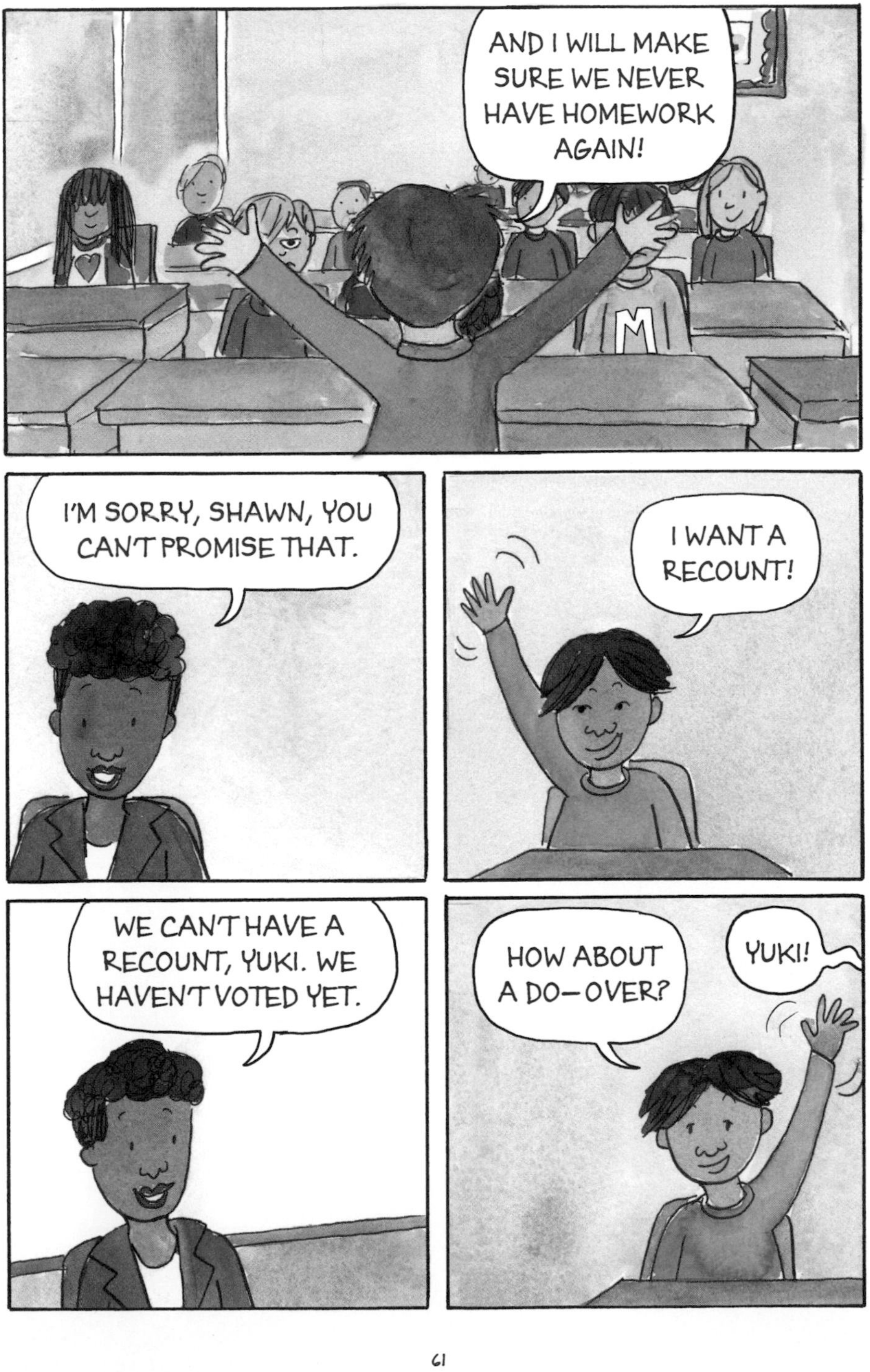
AND I WILL MAKE SURE WE NEVER HAVE HOMEWORK AGAIN!
I'M SORRY, SHAWN, YOU CAN'T PROMISE THAT.
I WANT A RECOUNT!
WE CAN'T HAVE A RECOUNT, YUKI. WE HAVEN'T VOTED YET.
HOW ABOUT A DO-OVER?
YUKI!

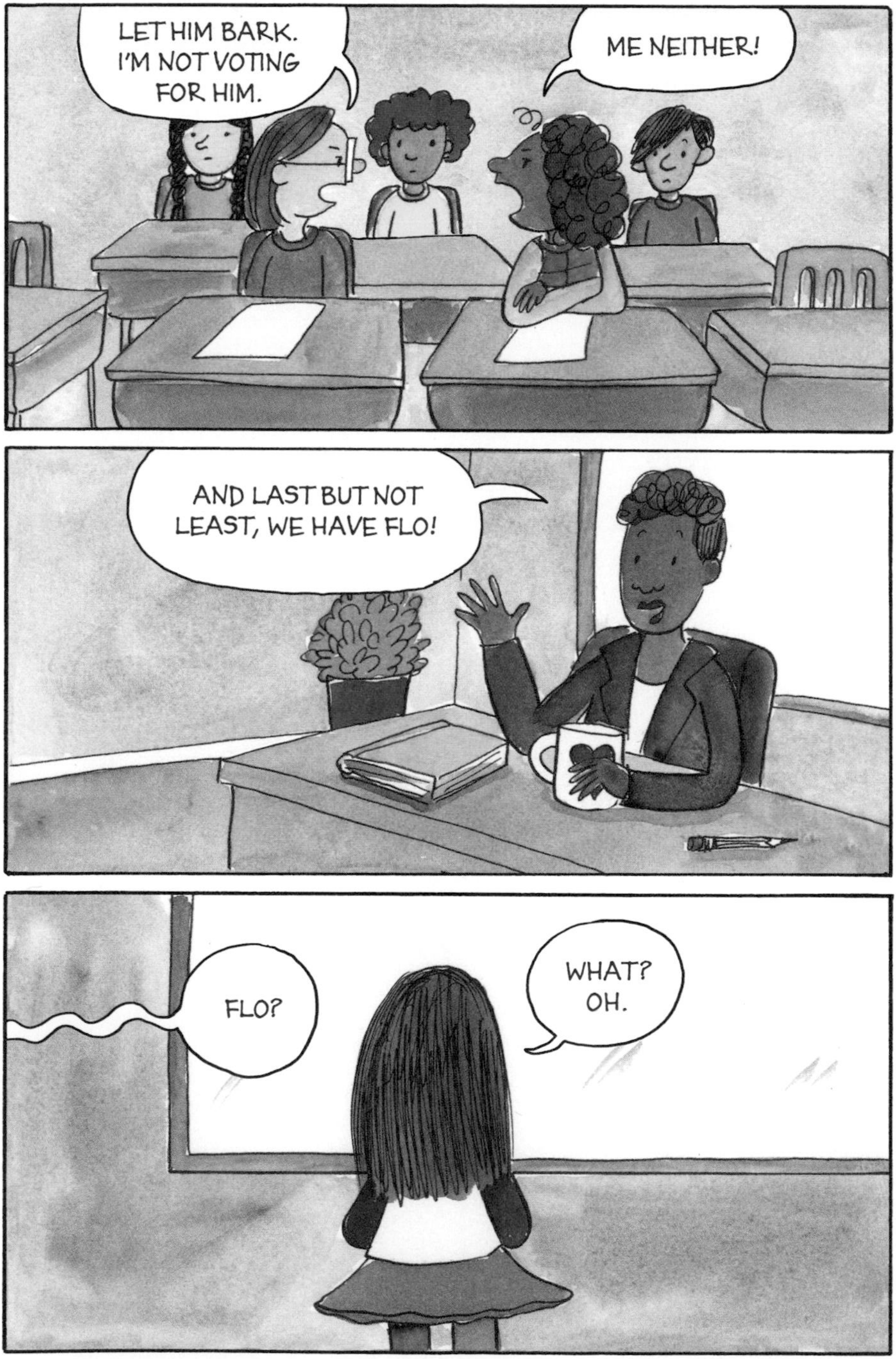
LET HIM BARK. I'M NOT VOTING FOR HIM.
ME NEITHER!
AND LAST BUT NOT LEAST, WE HAVE FLO!
FLO?
WHAT? OH.

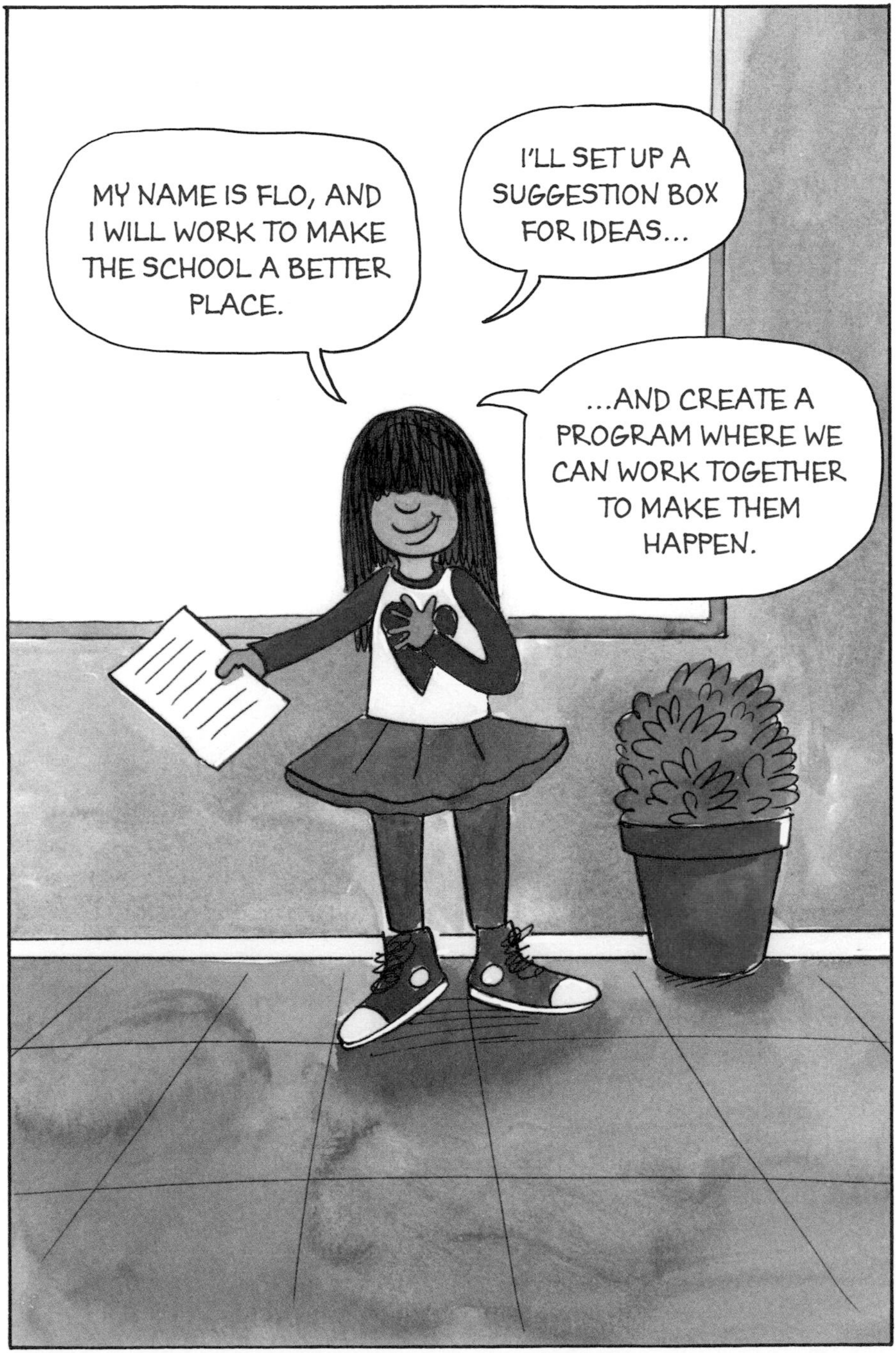
MY NAME IS FLO, AND I WILL WORK TO MAKE THE SCHOOL A BETTER PLACE.
I'LL SET UP A SUGGESTION BOX FOR IDEAS...
...AND CREATE A PROGRAM WHERE WE CAN WORK TOGETHER TO MAKE THEM HAPPEN.

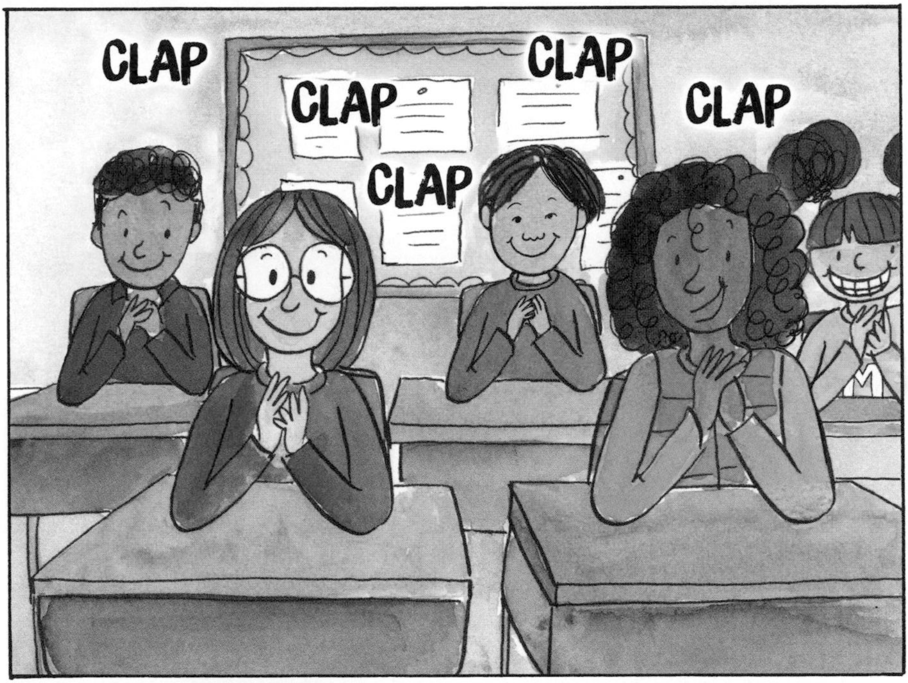
CLAP
CLAP
CLAP
CLAP
CLAP

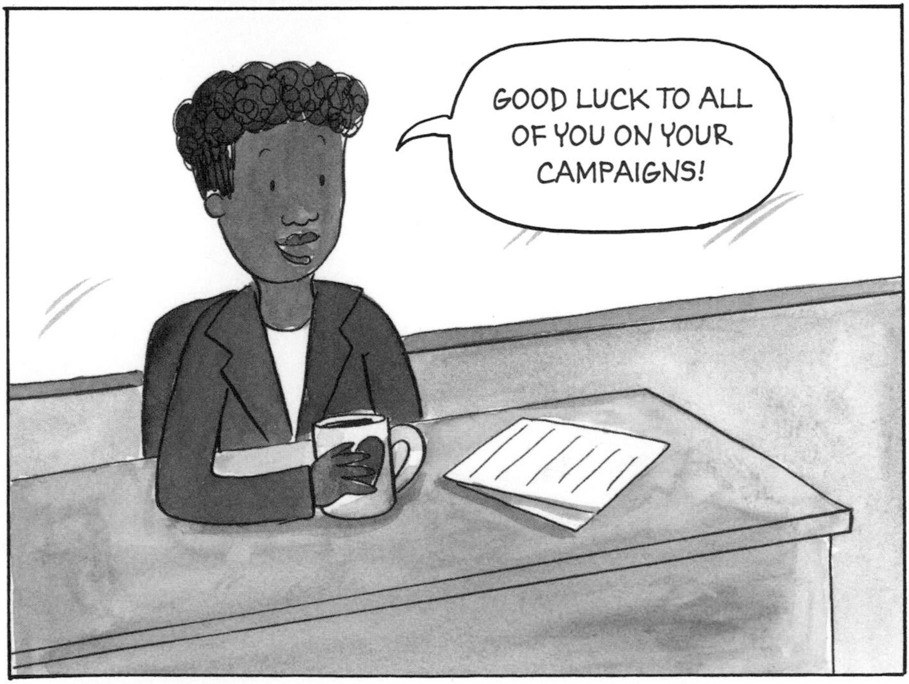
GOOD LUCK TO ALL OF YOU ON YOUR CAMPAIGNS!

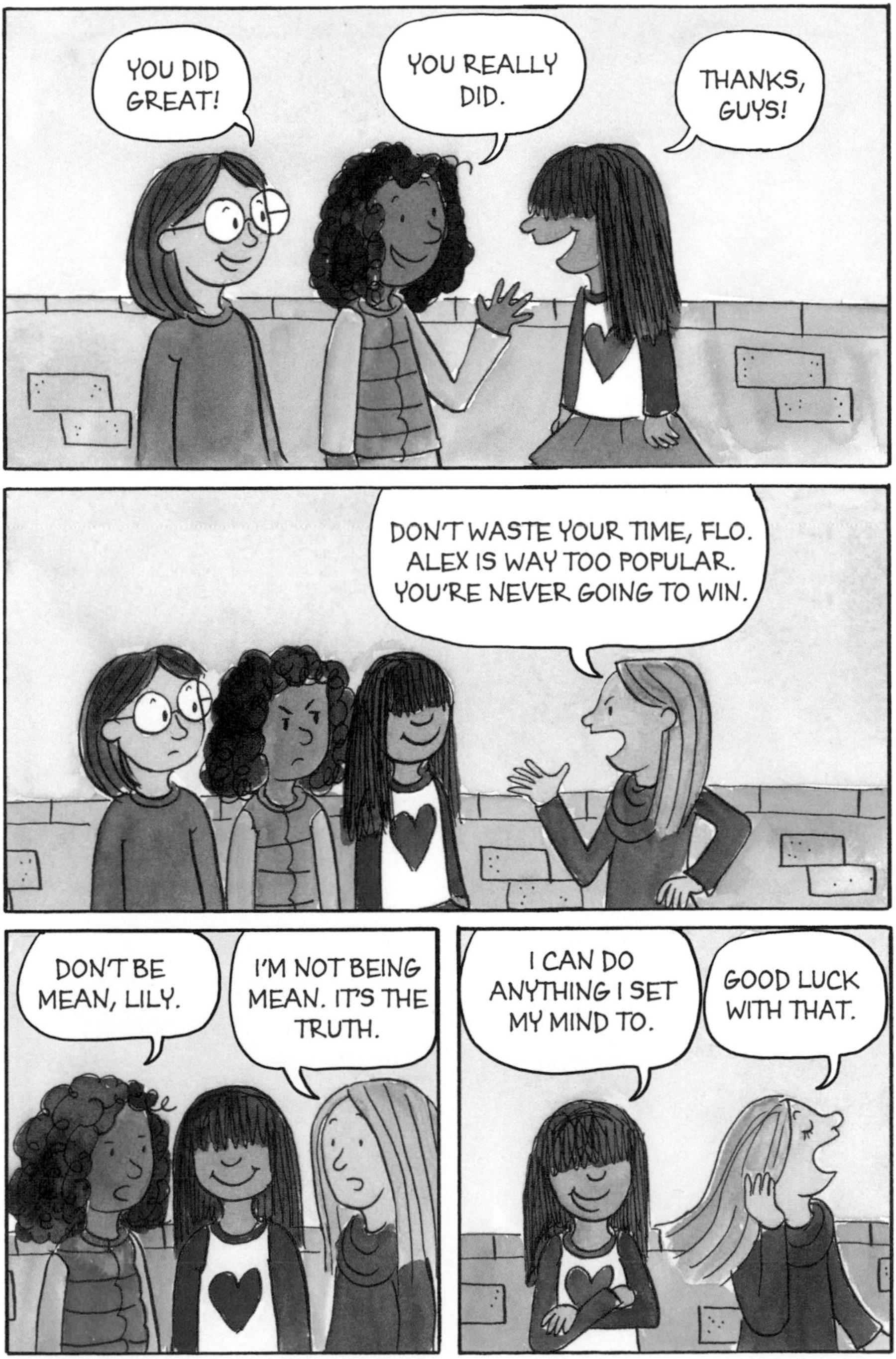
YOU DID GREAT!
YOU REALLY DID.
THANKS, GUYS!
DON'T WASTE YOUR TIME, FLO. ALEX IS WAY TOO POPULAR. YOU'RE NEVER GOING TO WIN.
DON'T BE MEAN, LILY.
I'M NOT BEING MEAN. IT'S THE TRUTH.
I CAN DO ANYTHING I SET MY MIND TO.
GOOD LUCK WITH THAT.

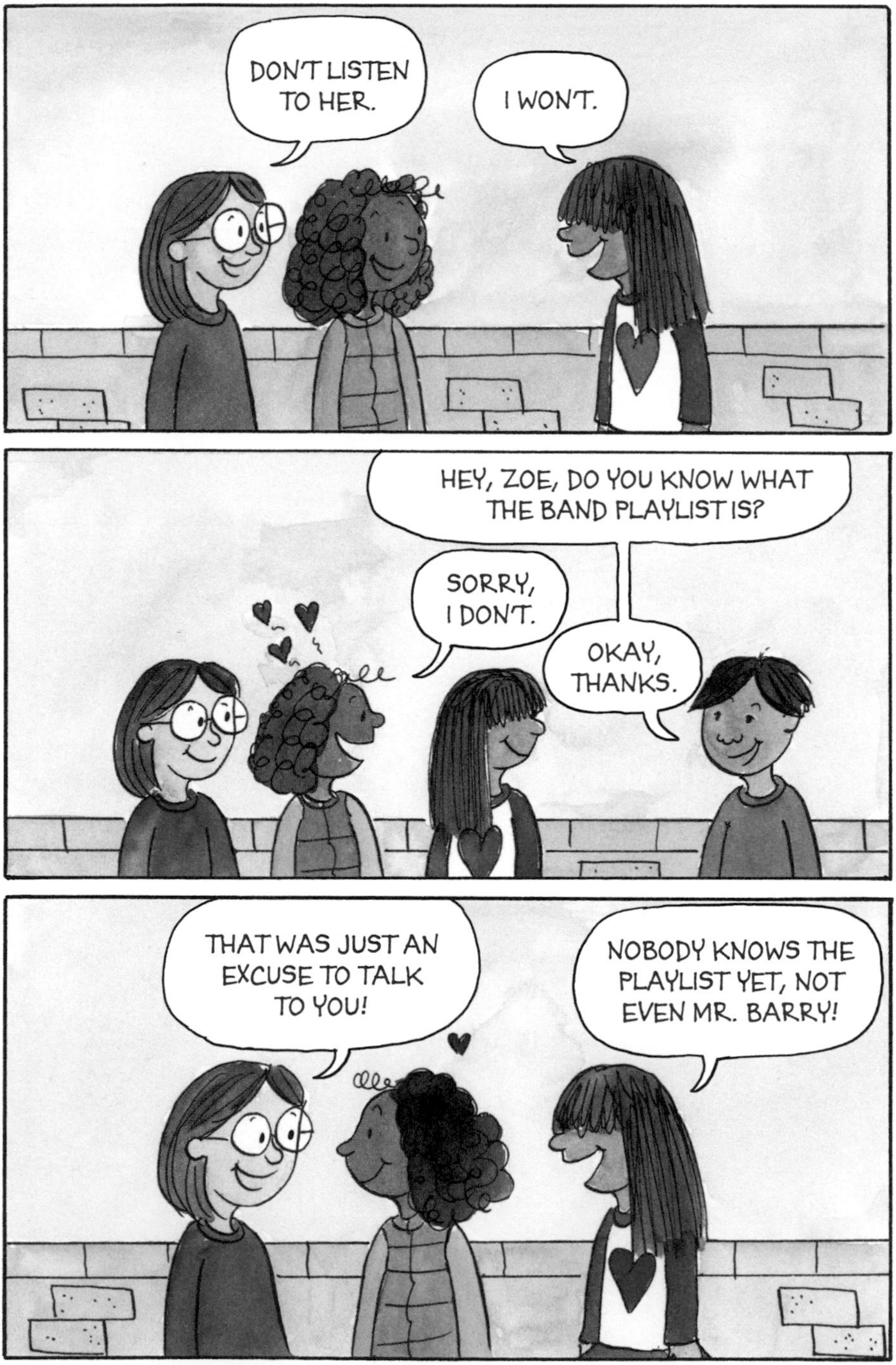
DON'T LISTEN TO HER.
I WON'T.
HEY, ZOE, DO YOU KNOW WHAT THE BAND PLAYLIST IS?
SORRY, I DON'T.
OKAY, THANKS.
THAT WAS JUST AN EXCUSE TO TALK TO YOU!
NOBODY KNOWS THE PLAYLIST YET, NOT EVEN MR. BARRY!

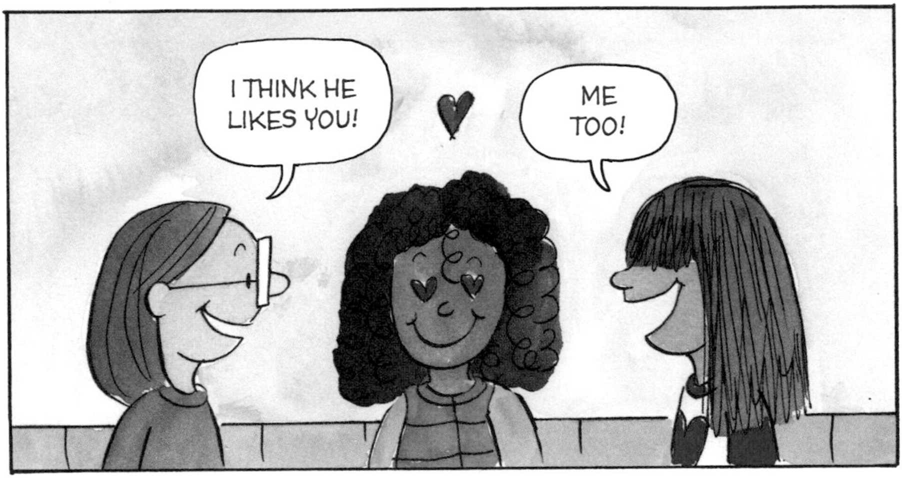
I THINK HE LIKES YOU!
ME TOO!

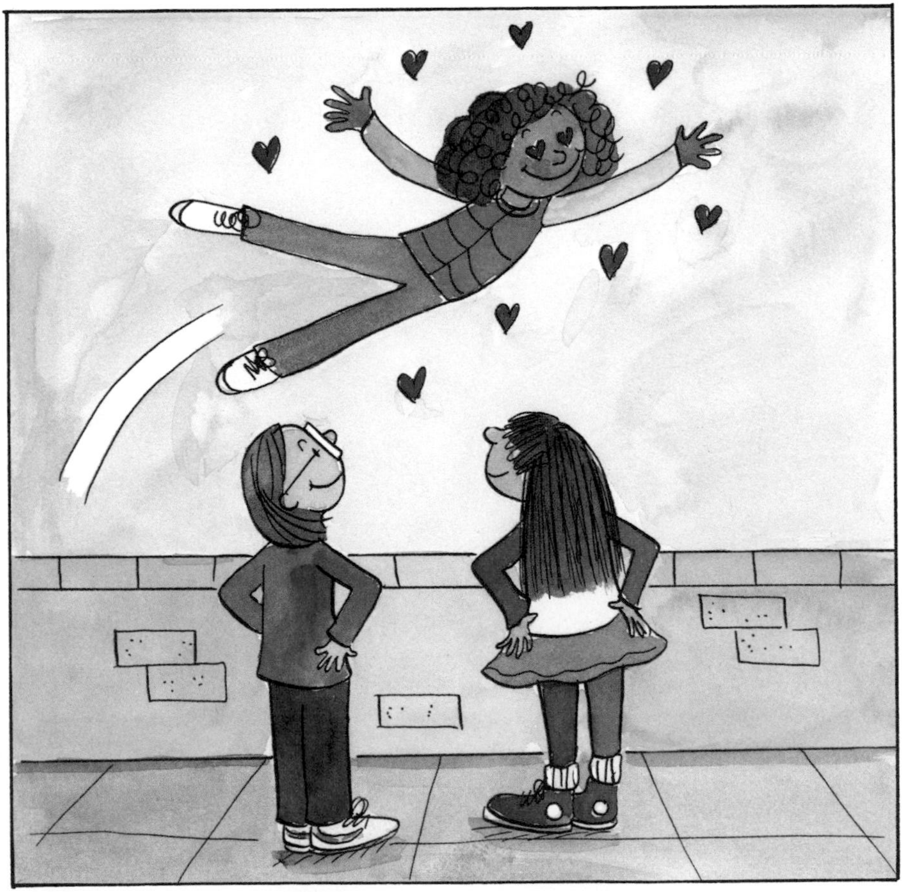

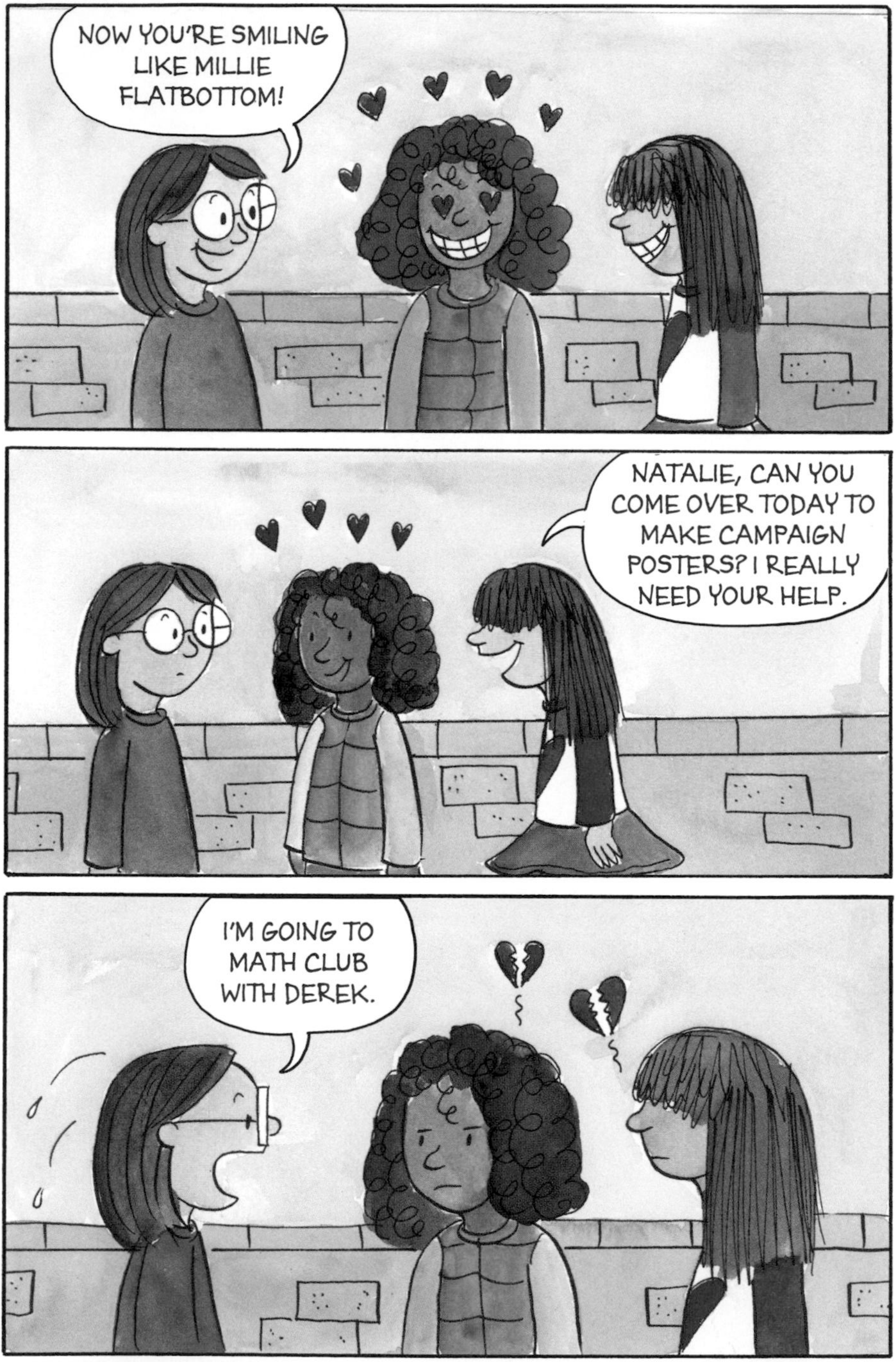
NOW YOU'RE SMILING LIKE MILLIE FLATBOTTOM!
NATALIE, CAN YOU COME OVER TODAY TO MAKE CAMPAIGN POSTERS? I REALLY NEED YOUR HELP.
I'M GOING TO MATH CLUB WITH DEREK.

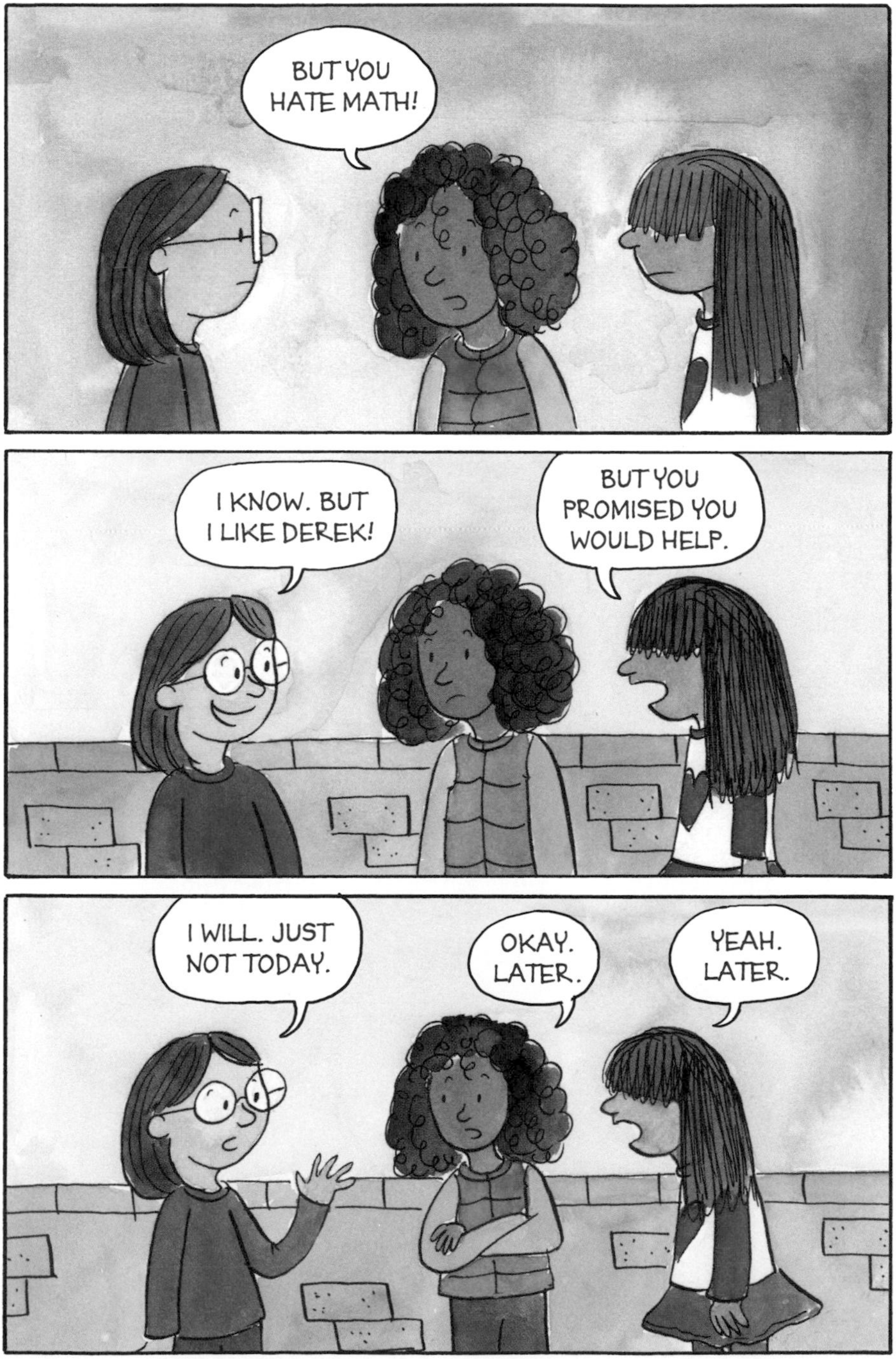
BUT YOU HATE MATH!
I KNOW. BUT I LIKE DEREK!
BUT YOU PROMISED YOU WOULD HELP.
I WILL. JUST NOT TODAY.
OKAY. LATER.
YEAH. LATER.

OOH, I LOVE POTTERY!
POTTERY CLUB TODAY!
TAKE THE WHEEL!
MISSING
"FLIP"
LAST SEEN WITH
"FLOP"

POTTERY CLUB TODAY!
TAKE THE WHEEL!
MISSING
"FLIP"
LAST SEEN WITH
"FLOP"
BUT I REALLY WANT TO SEE DEREK...

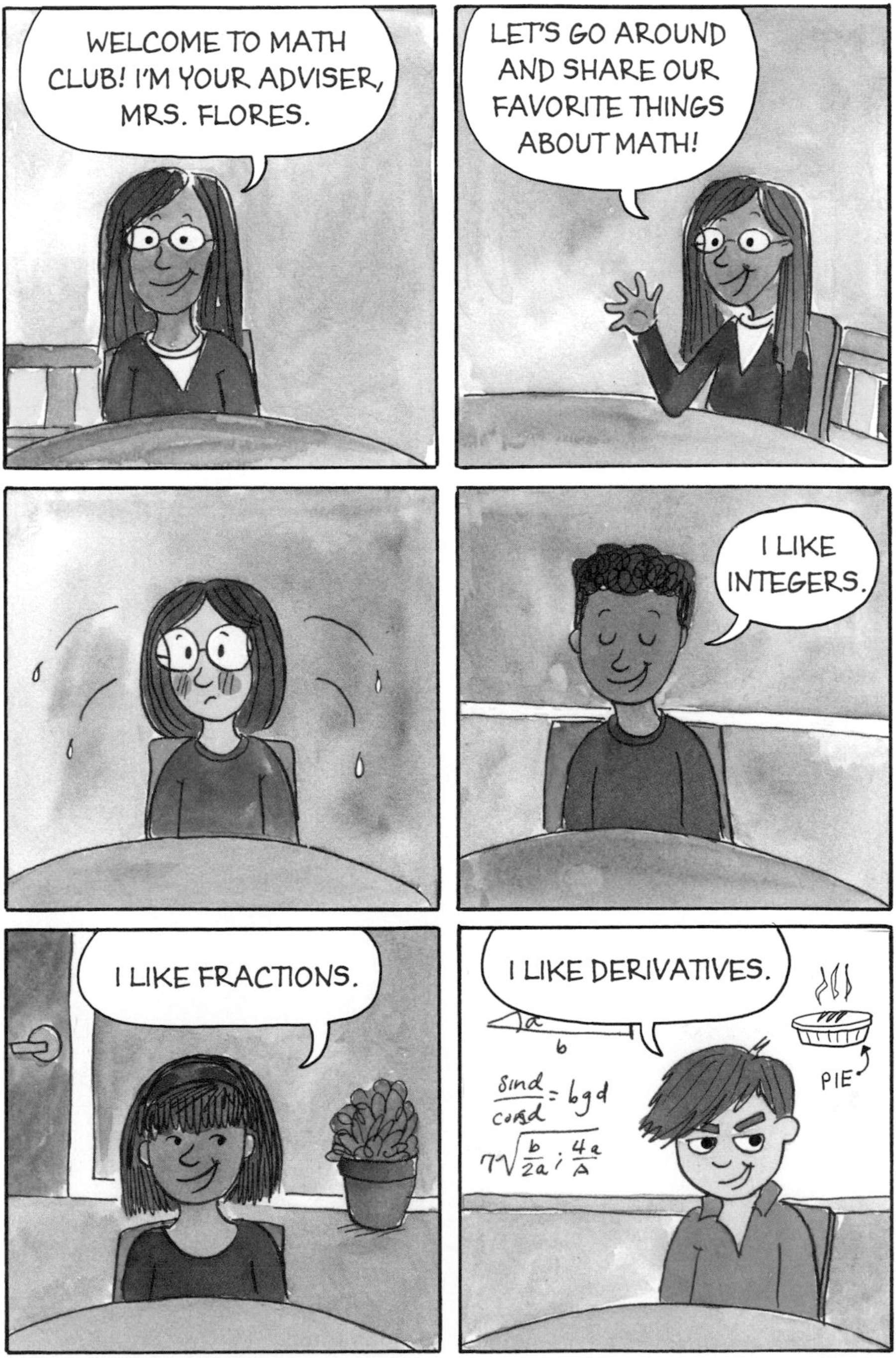
WELCOME TO MATH CLUB! I'M YOUR ADVISER, MRS. FLORES.
LET'S GO AROUND AND SHARE OUR FAVORITE THINGS ABOUT MATH!
I LIKE INTEGERS.
I LIKE FRACTIONS.
I LIKE DERIVATIVES.
PIE

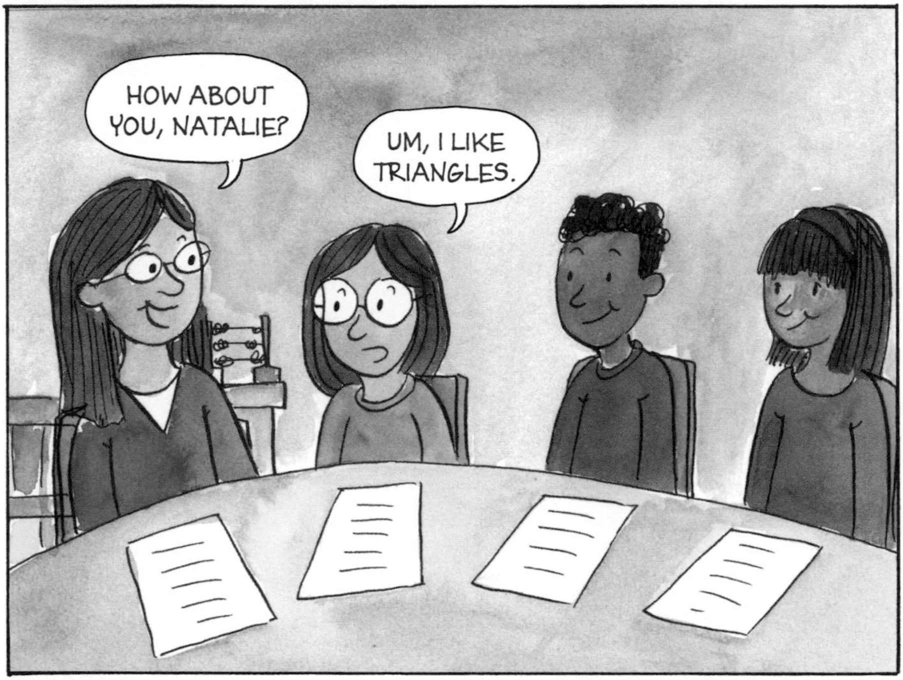
HOW ABOUT YOU, NATALIE?
UM, I LIKE TRIANGLES.

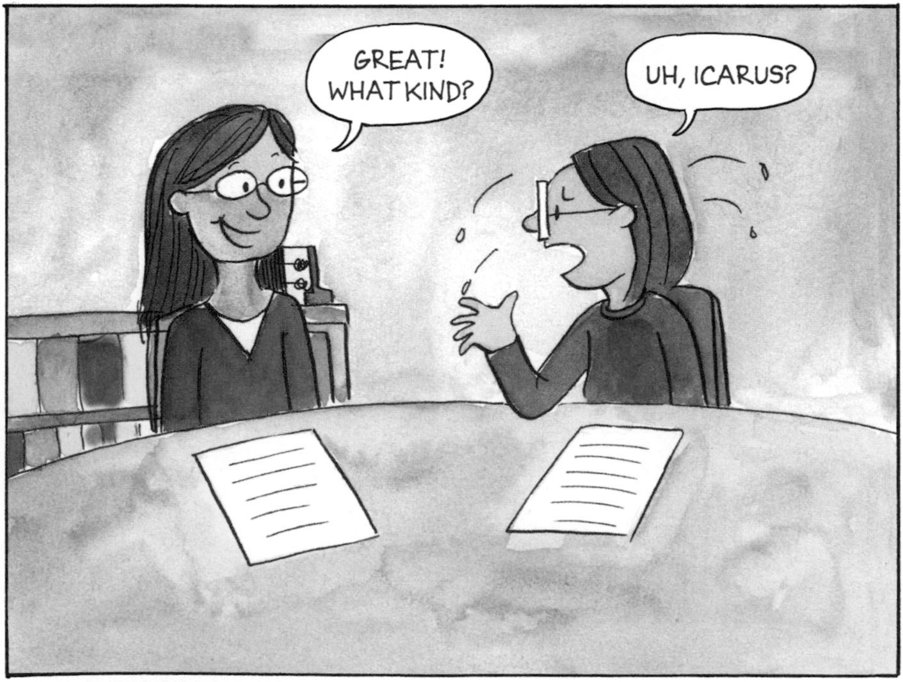
GREAT! WHAT KIND?
UH, ICARUS?

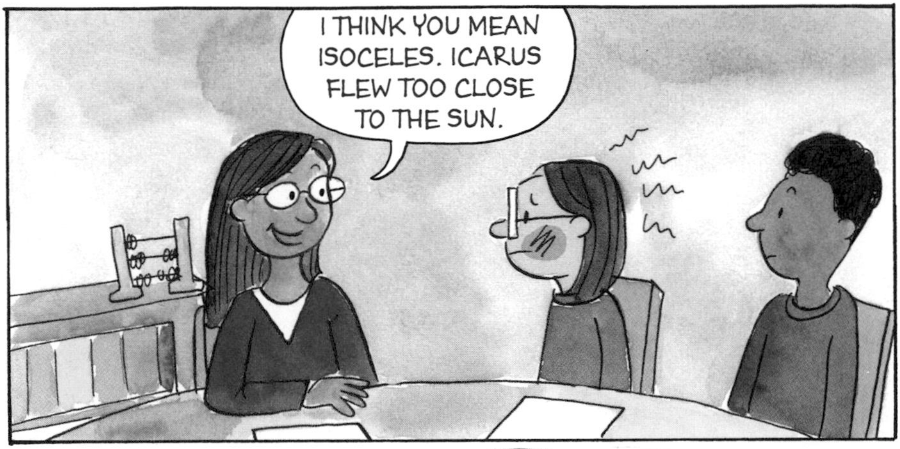
I THINK YOU MEAN ISOCELES. ICARUS FLEW TOO CLOSE TO THE SUN.

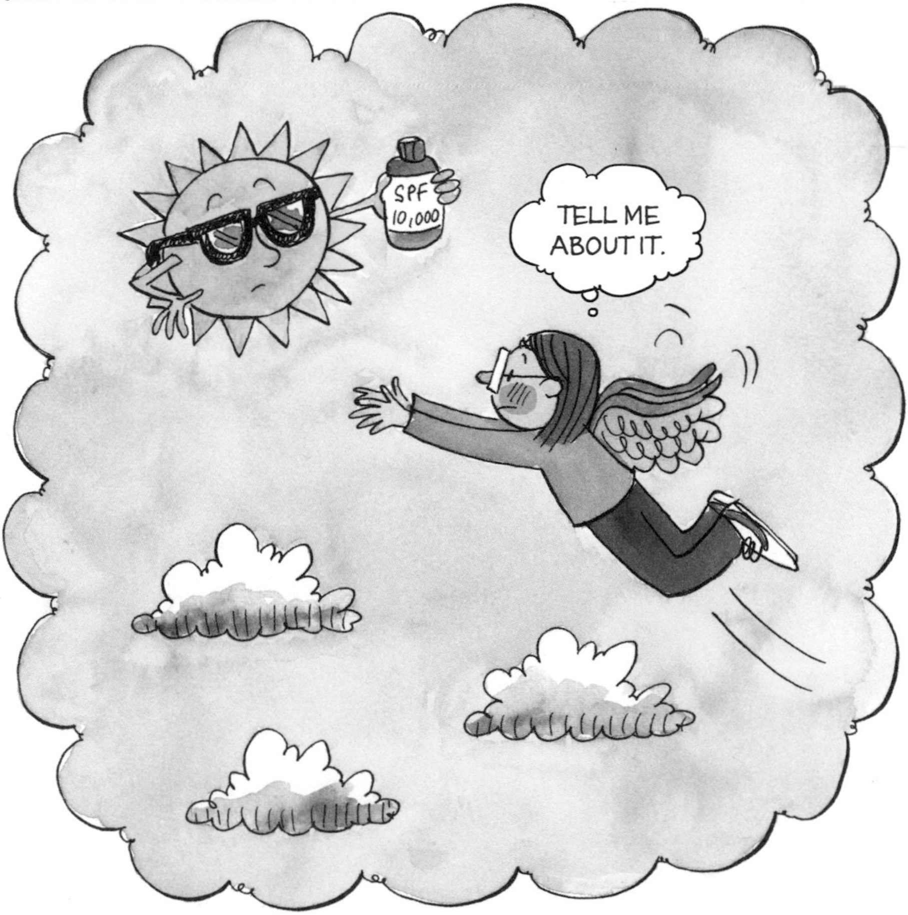
SPF 10,000
TELL ME ABOUT IT.

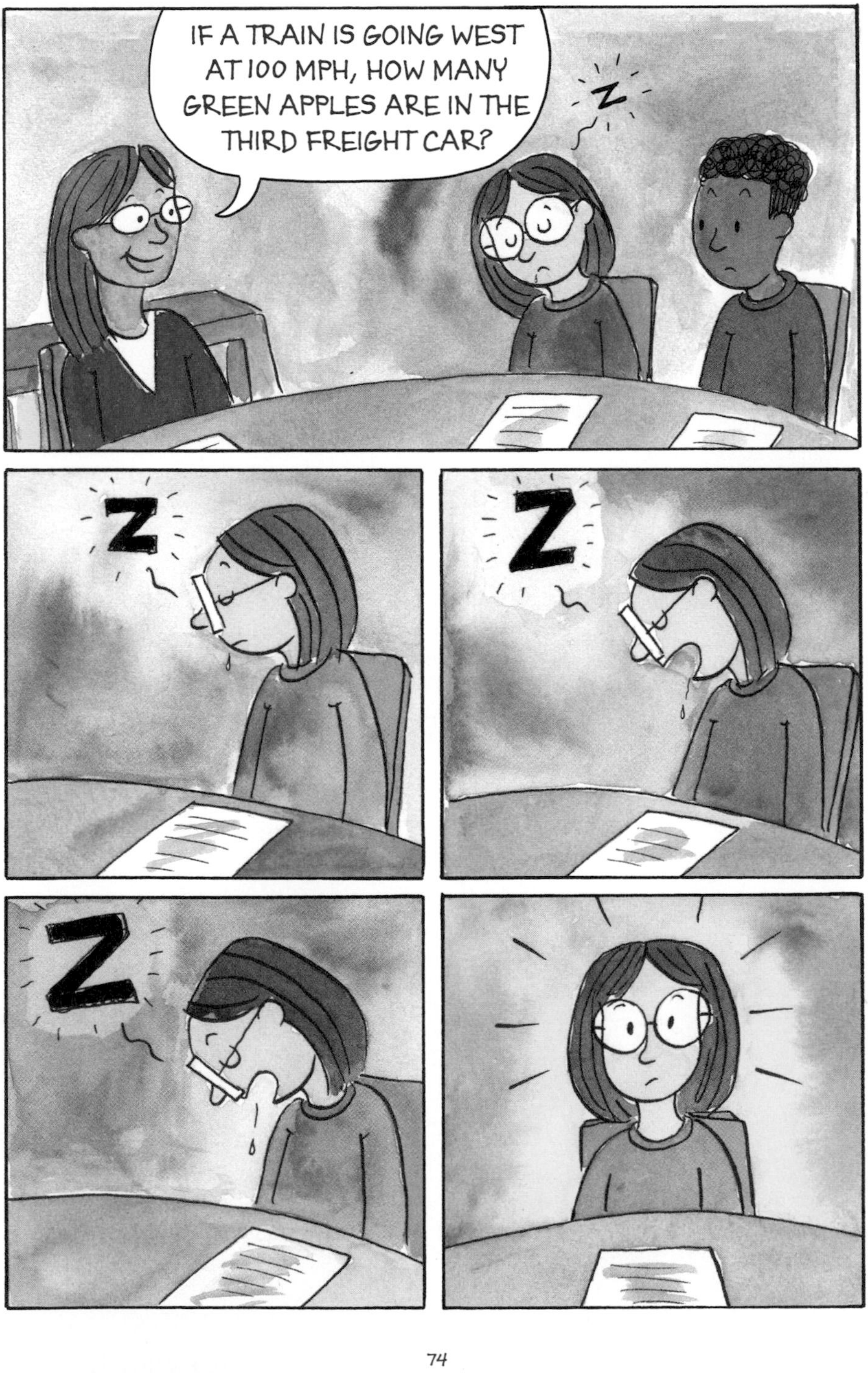
IF A TRAIN IS GOING WEST AT 100 MPH, HOW MANY GREEN APPLES ARE IN THE THIRD FREIGHT CAR?
Z
Z
Z
Z

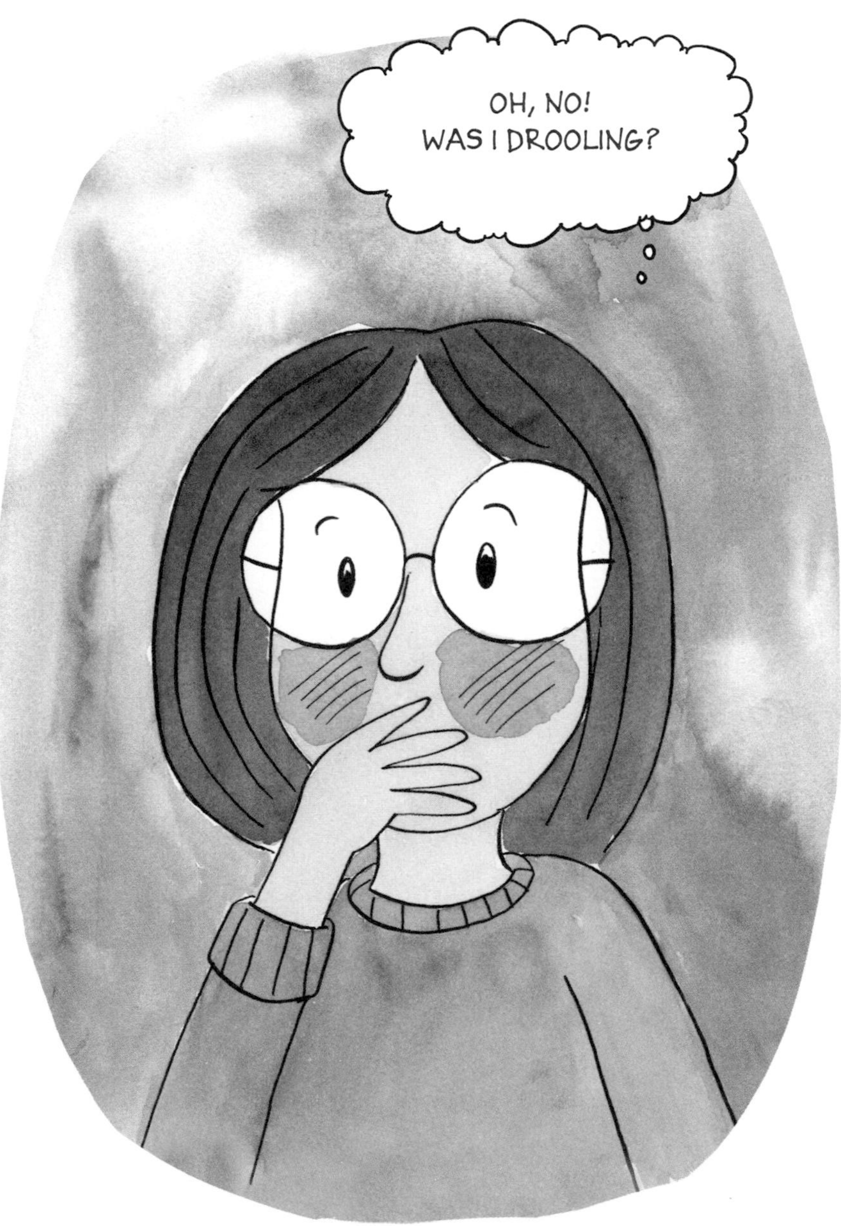
OH, NO!
WAS I DROOLING?

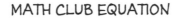

MATH CLUB EQUATION

SPENDING TIME
WITH YOUR
CRUSH

FALLING ASLEEP
IN FRONT OF
YOUR CRUSH

COMPLETE AND TOTAL HUMILIATION

CHAPTER 5
BRACE YOURSELF

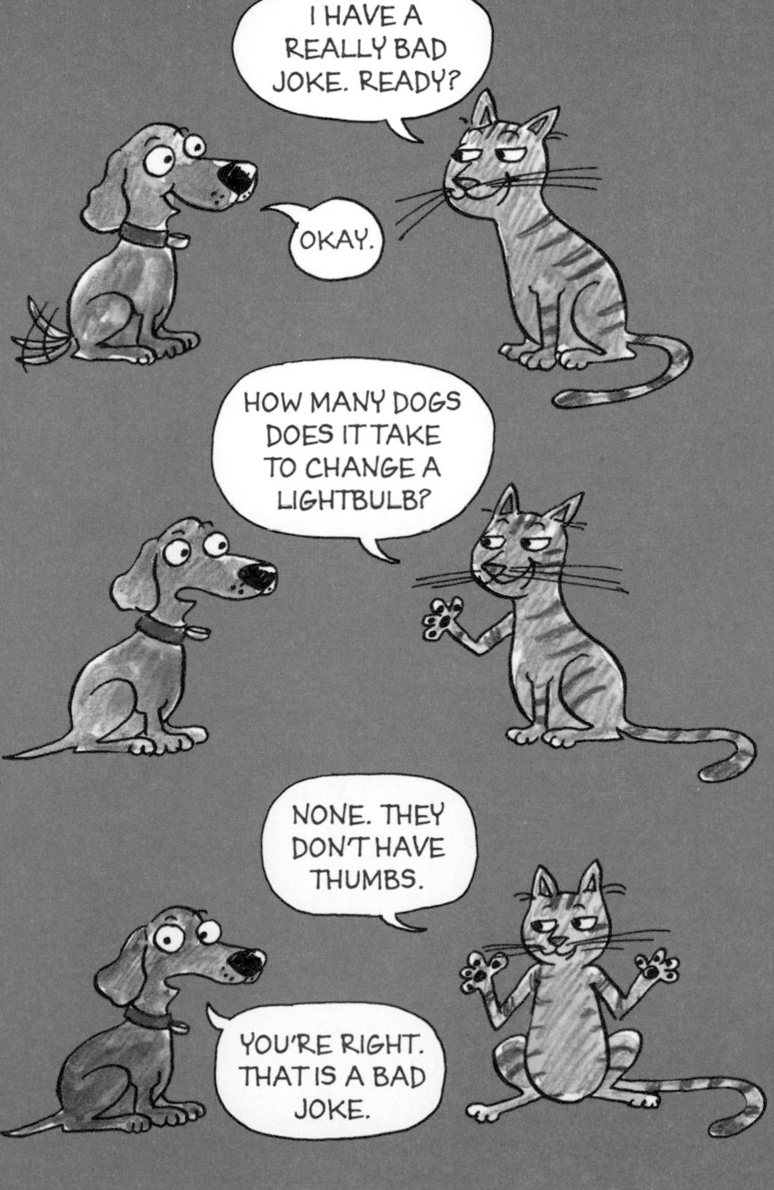
I HAVE A REALLY BAD JOKE. READY?
OKAY.
HOW MANY DOGS DOES IT TAKE TO CHANGE A LIGHTBULB?
NONE. THEY DON'T HAVE THUMBS.
YOU'RE RIGHT. THAT IS A BAD JOKE.

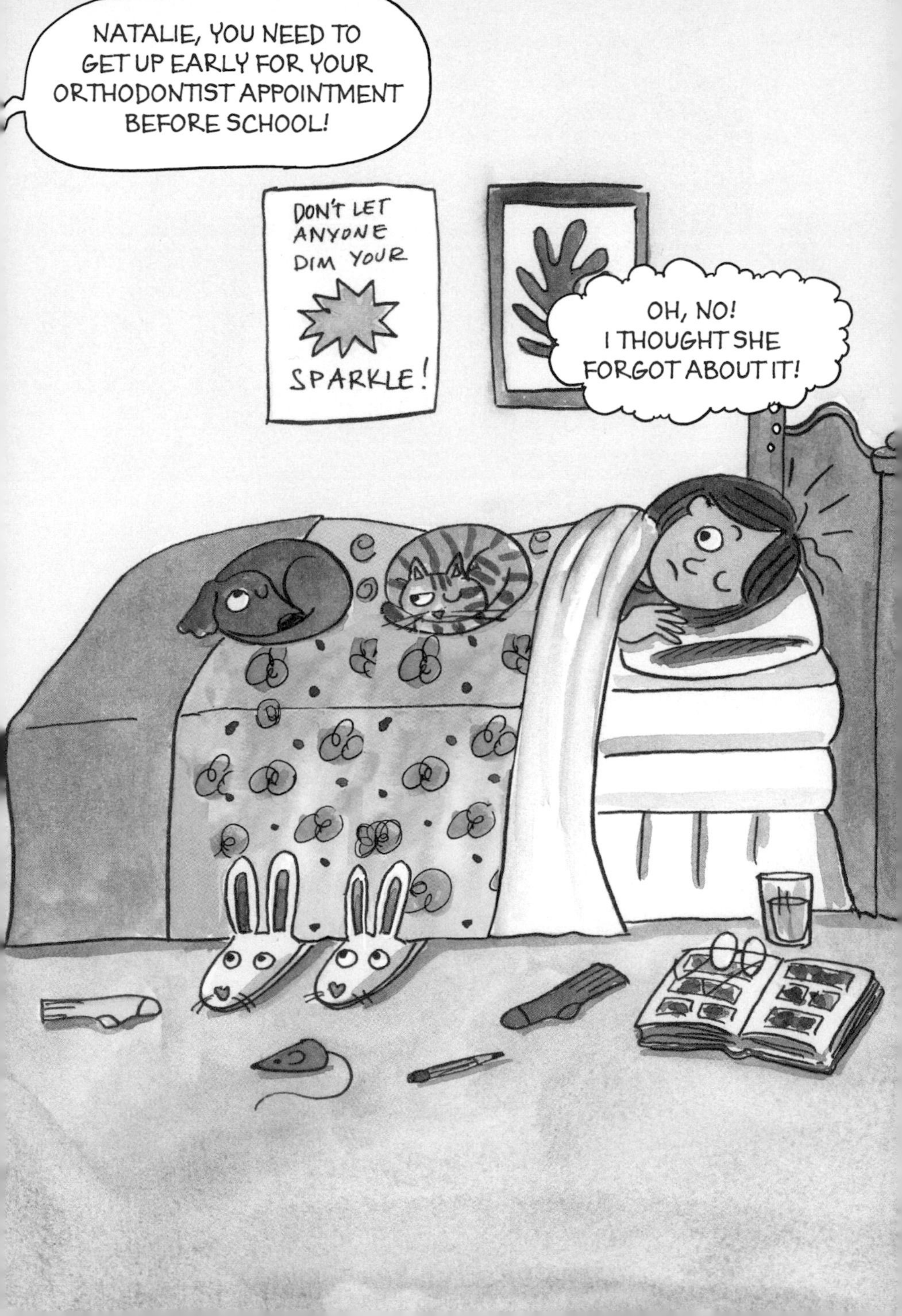
NATALIE, YOU NEED TO GET UP EARLY FOR YOUR ORTHODONTIST APPOINTMENT BEFORE SCHOOL!
DON'T LET ANYONE DIM YOUR SPARKLE!
OH, NO! I THOUGHT SHE FORGOT ABOUT IT!

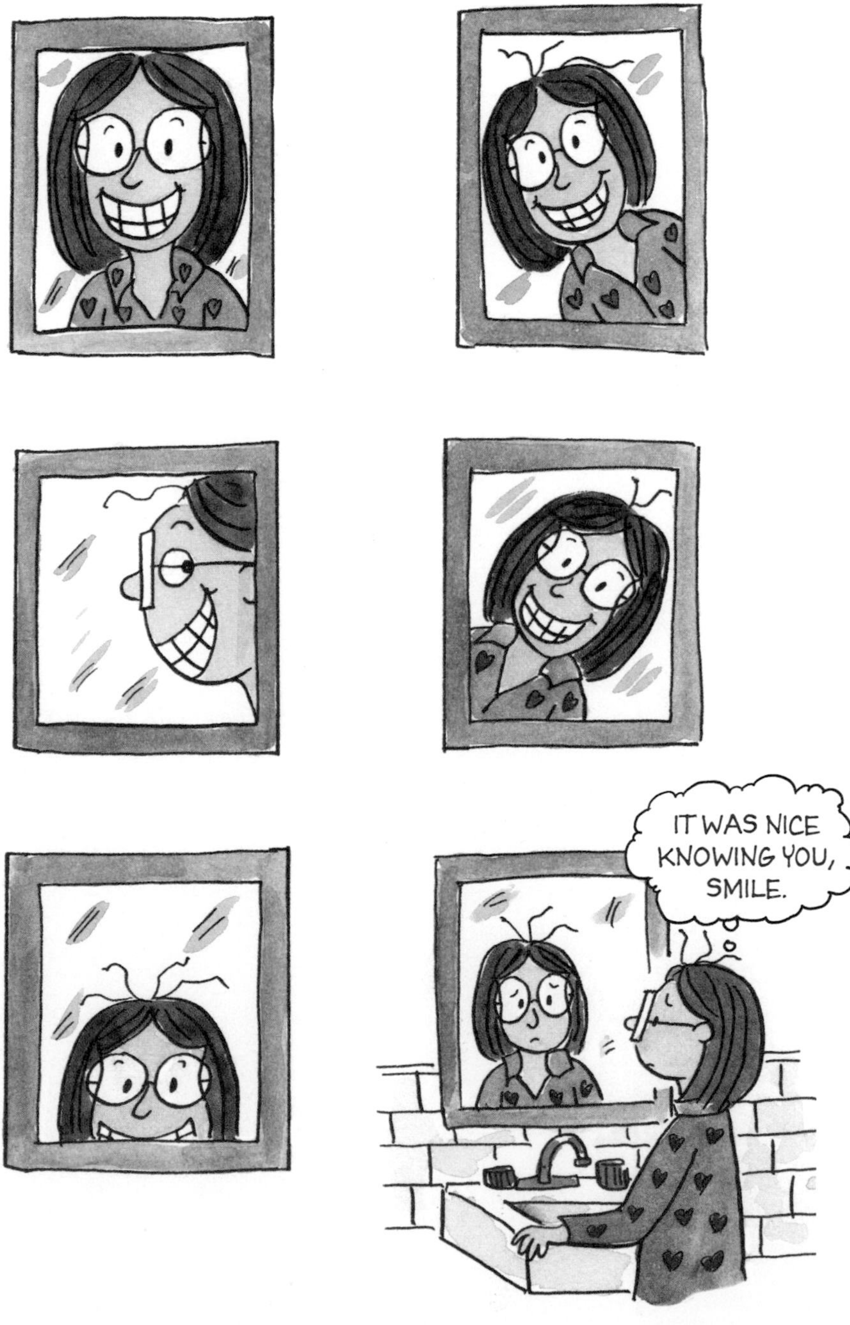
IT WAS NICE
KNOWING YOU,
SMILE.

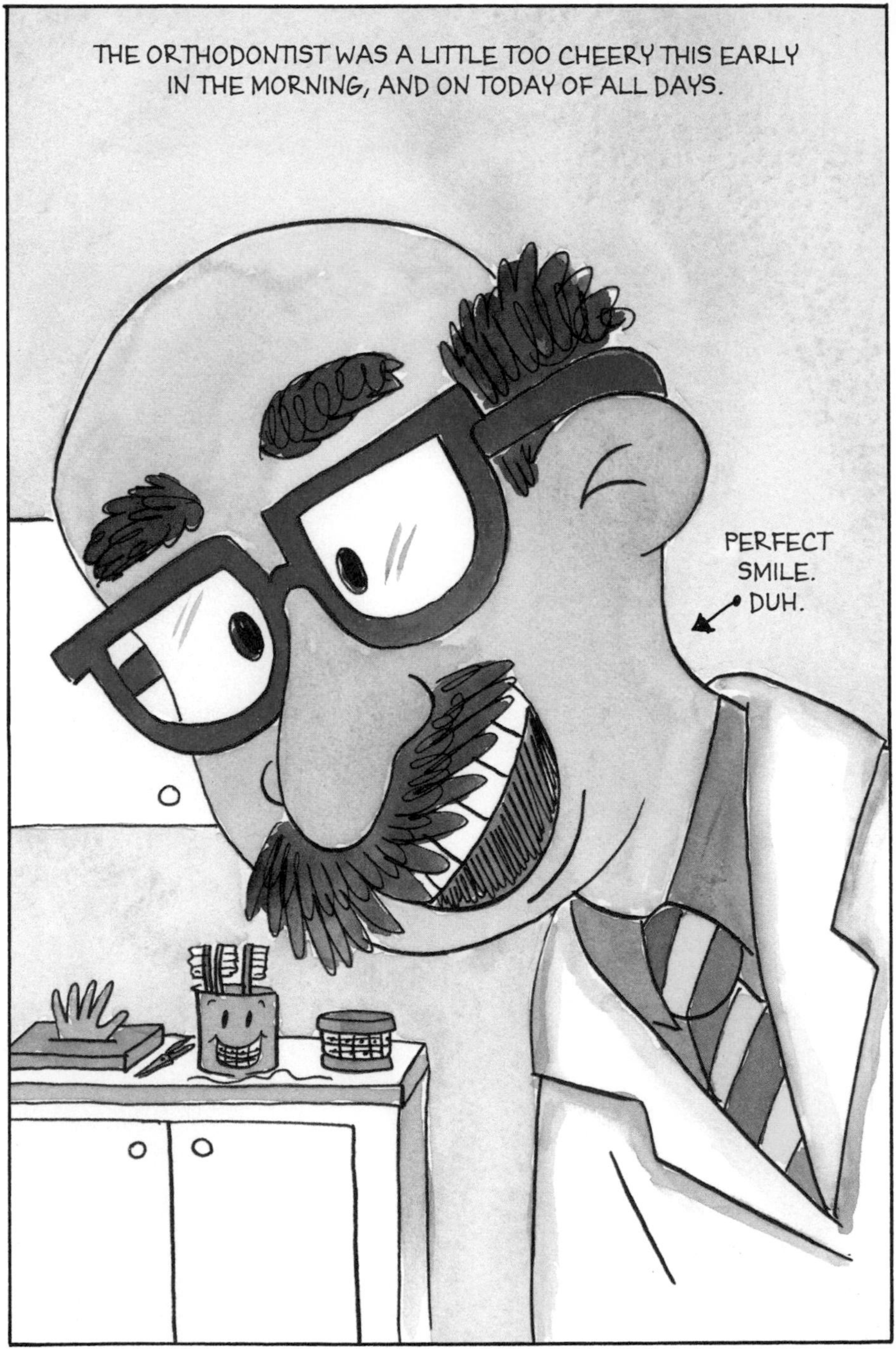
THE ORTHODONTIST WAS A LITTLE TOO CHEERY THIS EARLY IN THE MORNING, AND ON TODAY OF ALL DAYS.
PERFECT SMILE. DUH.

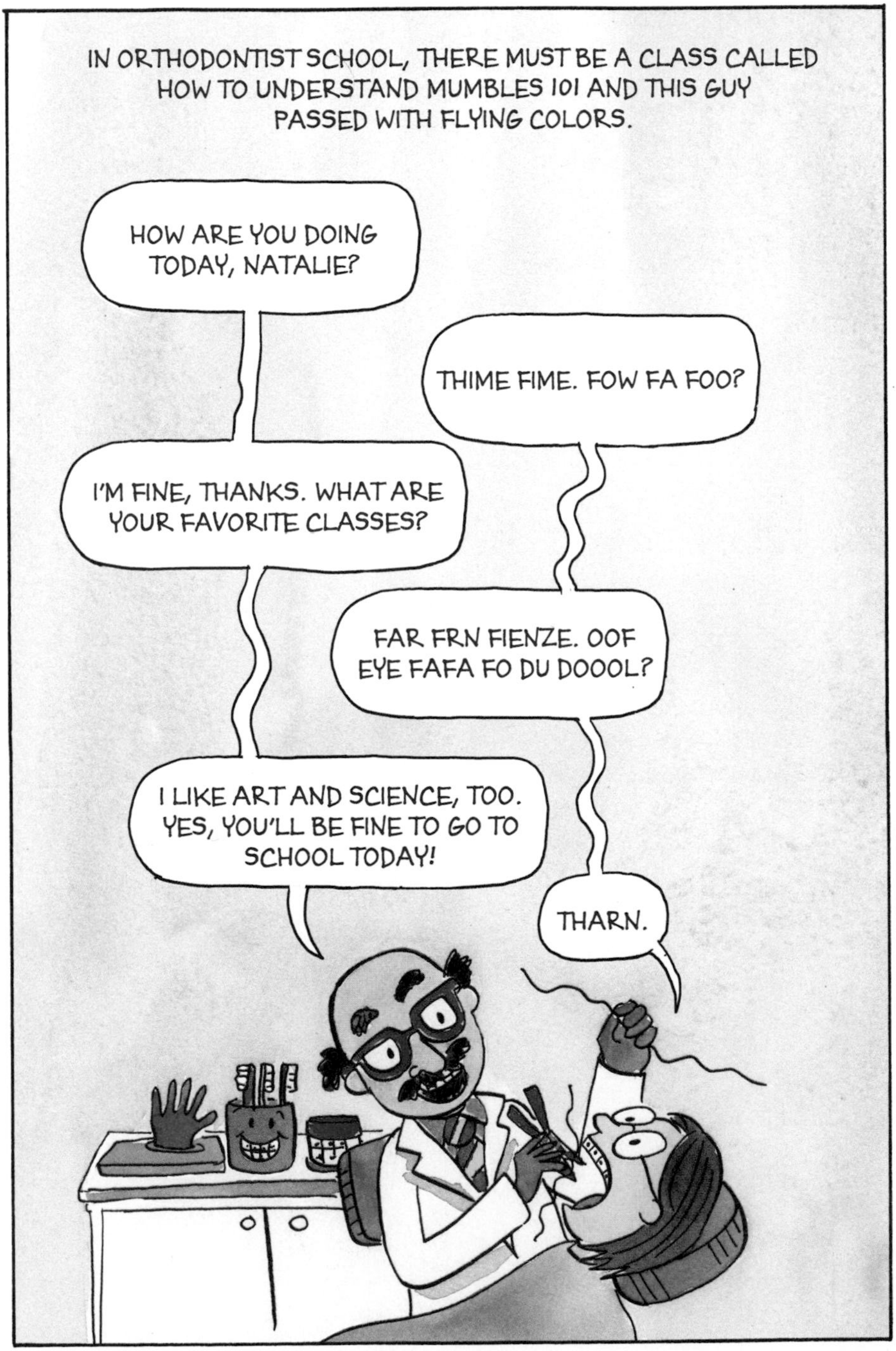
IN ORTHODONTIST SCHOOL, THERE MUST BE A CLASS CALLED HOW TO UNDERSTAND MUMBLES 101 AND THIS GUY PASSED WITH FLYING COLORS.
HOW ARE YOU DOING TODAY, NATALIE?
THIME FIME. FOW FA FOO?
I'M FINE, THANKS. WHAT ARE YOUR FAVORITE CLASSES?
FAR FRN FIENZE. OOF EYE FAFA FO DU DOOOL?
I LIKE ART AND SCIENCE, TOO. YES, YOU'LL BE FINE TO GO TO SCHOOL TODAY!
THARN.

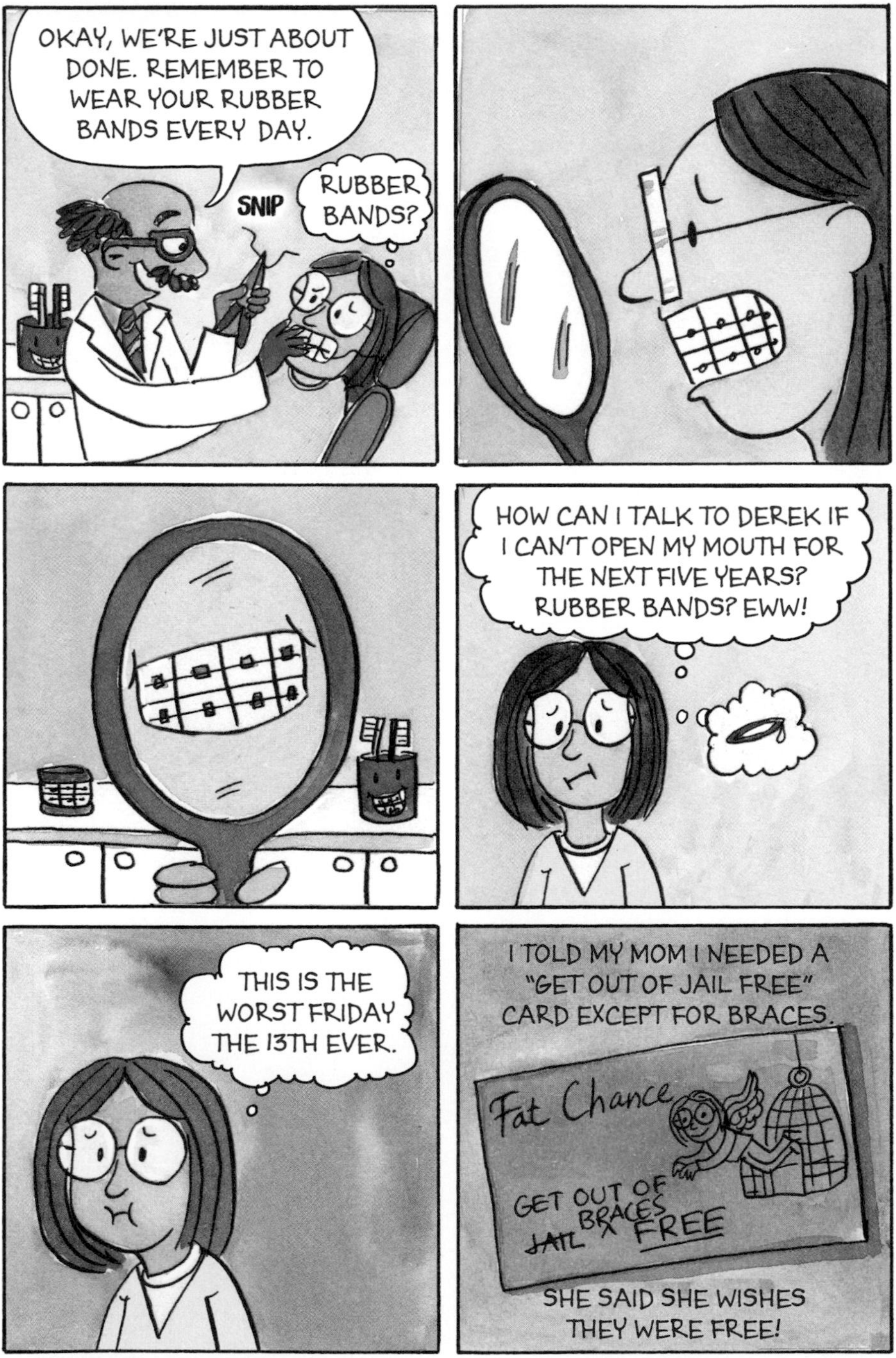
OKAY, WE'RE JUST ABOUT DONE. REMEMBER TO WEAR YOUR RUBBER BANDS EVERY DAY.
SNIP
RUBBER BANDS?
HOW CAN I TALK TO DEREK IF I CAN'T OPEN MY MOUTH FOR THE NEXT FIVE YEARS? RUBBER BANDS? EWW!
THIS IS THE WORST FRIDAY THE 13TH EVER.
I TOLD MY MOM I NEEDED A "GET OUT OF JAIL FREE" CARD EXCEPT FOR BRACES.
Fat Chance
GET OUT OF JAIL BRACES FREE
SHE SAID SHE WISHES THEY WERE FREE!

"BRACES" IS ONE OF THOSE WORDS THAT LOOKS EXACTLY LIKE IT SOUNDS, EXCEPT WHEN YOU'RE WEARING THEM. THEN IT'S MORE LIKE "BRATHES."

HERE ARE SOME OF THE THINGS I'M SUPPOSED TO AVOID WHILE WEARING BRACES:

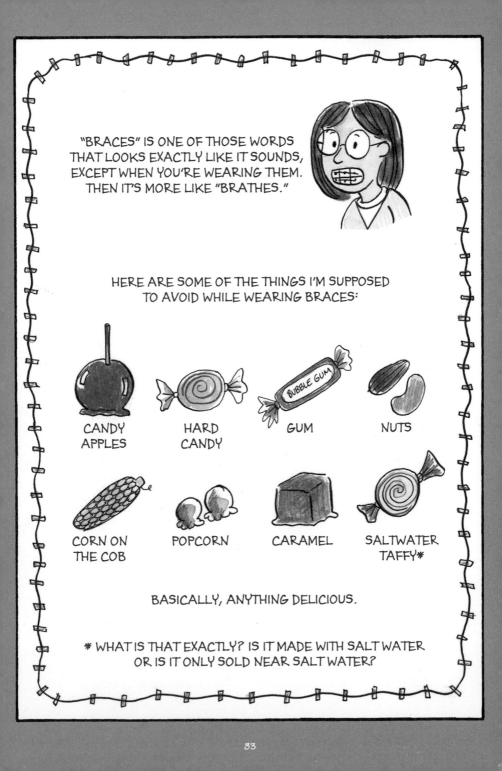

CANDY APPLES

HARD CANDY

GUM

NUTS

CORN ON THE COB

POPCORN

CARAMEL

SALTWATER TAFFY*

BASICALLY, ANYTHING DELICIOUS.

* WHAT IS THAT EXACTLY? IS IT MADE WITH SALT WATER OR IS IT ONLY SOLD NEAR SALT WATER?

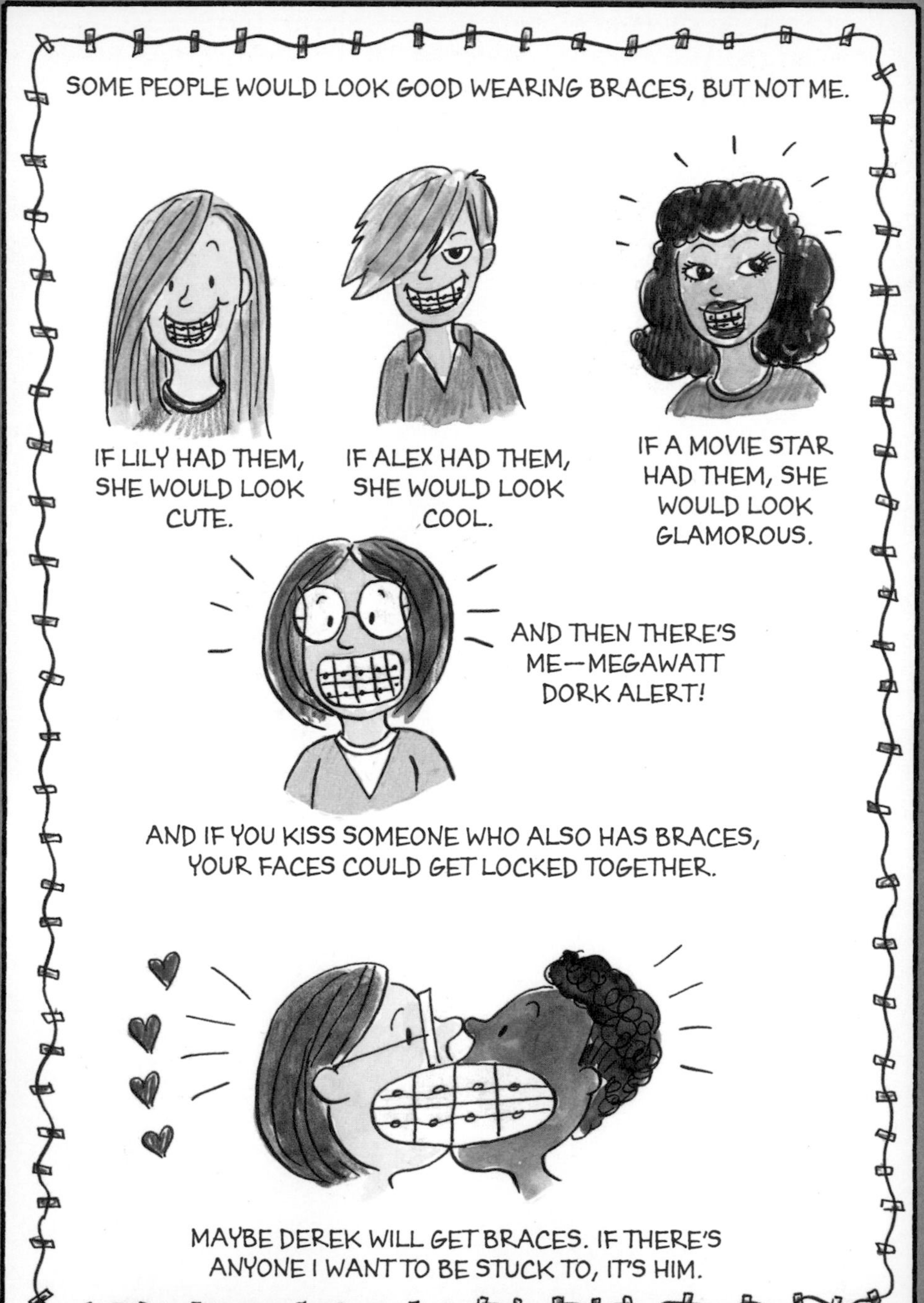
SOME PEOPLE WOULD LOOK GOOD WEARING BRACES, BUT NOT ME.
IF LILY HAD THEM, SHE WOULD LOOK CUTE.
IF ALEX HAD THEM, SHE WOULD LOOK COOL.
IF A MOVIE STAR HAD THEM, SHE WOULD LOOK GLAMOROUS.
AND THEN THERE'S ME—MEGAWATT DORK ALERT!
AND IF YOU KISS SOMEONE WHO ALSO HAS BRACES, YOUR FACES COULD GET LOCKED TOGETHER.
MAYBE DEREK WILL GET BRACES. IF THERE'S ANYONE I WANT TO BE STUCK TO, IT'S HIM.

I CAN'T BELIEVE I HAVE TO GO TO SCHOOL AFTER GETTING BRACES. I GUESS I CAN JUST TALK OUT OF THE SIDE OF MY MOUTH OR MAYBE THROUGH A VENTRILOQUIST PUPPET, BUT THAT MIGHT BE WEIRD.

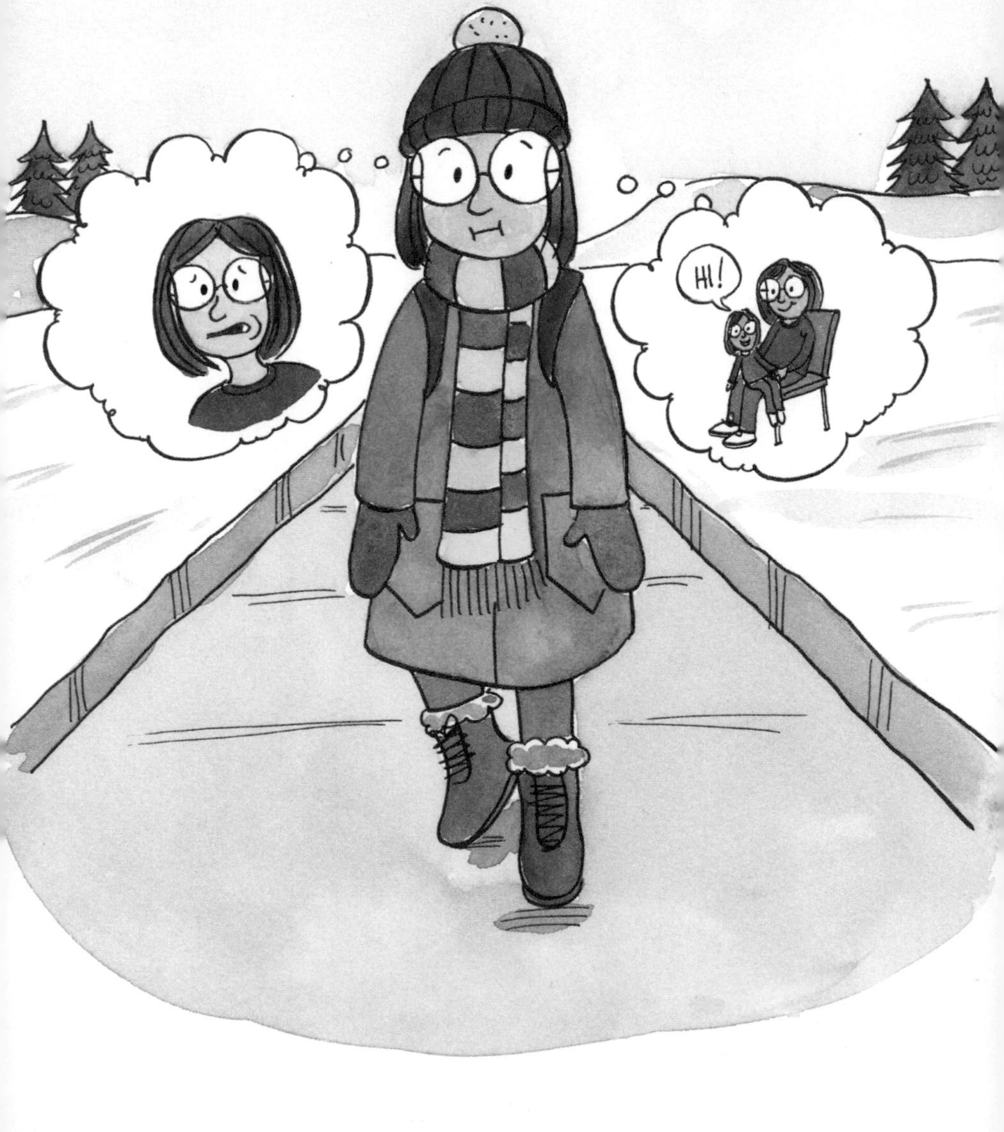
HI!

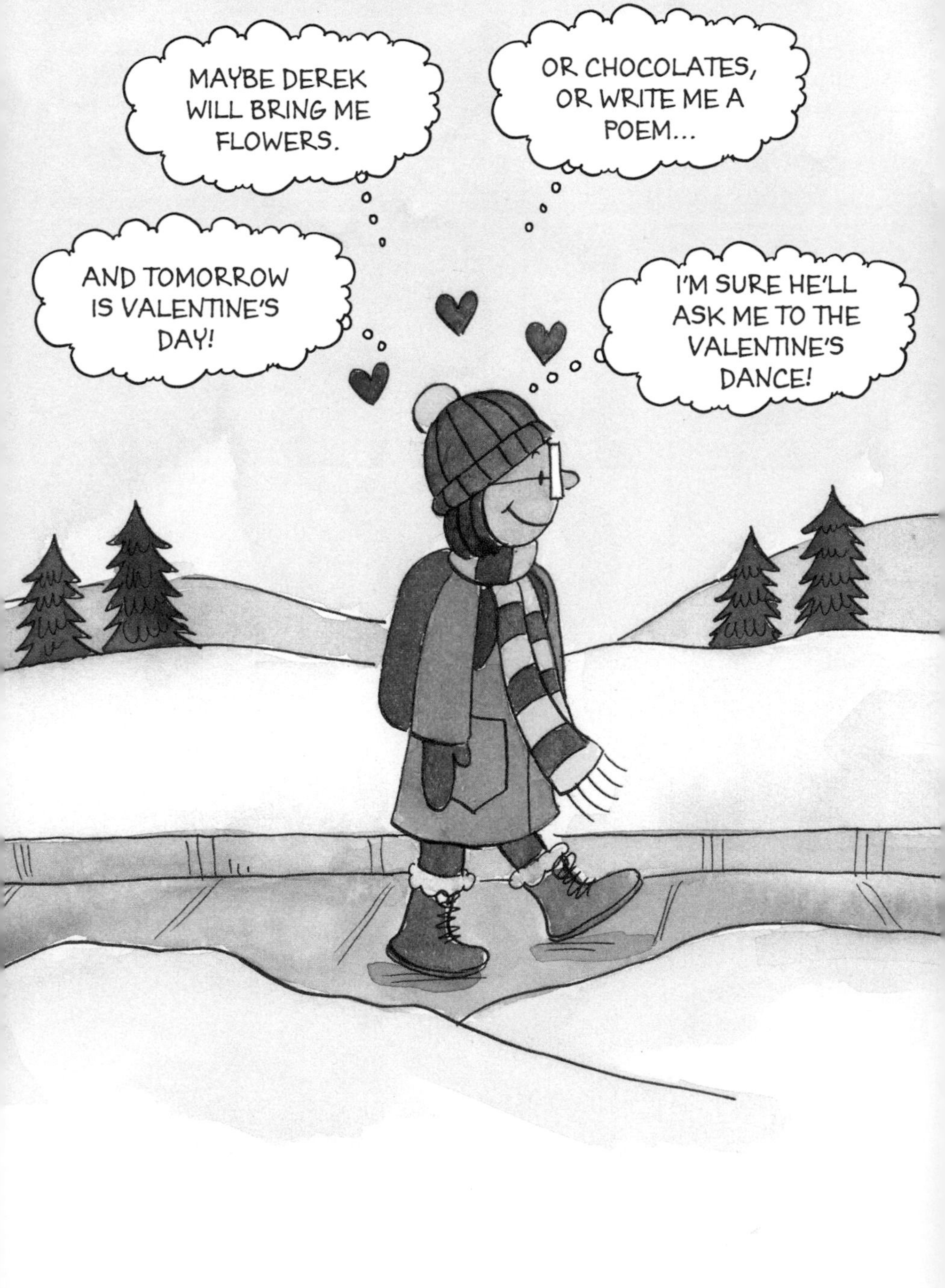
MAYBE DEREK WILL BRING ME FLOWERS.
OR CHOCOLATES, OR WRITE ME A POEM...
AND TOMORROW IS VALENTINE'S DAY!
I'M SURE HE'LL ASK ME TO THE VALENTINE'S DANCE!

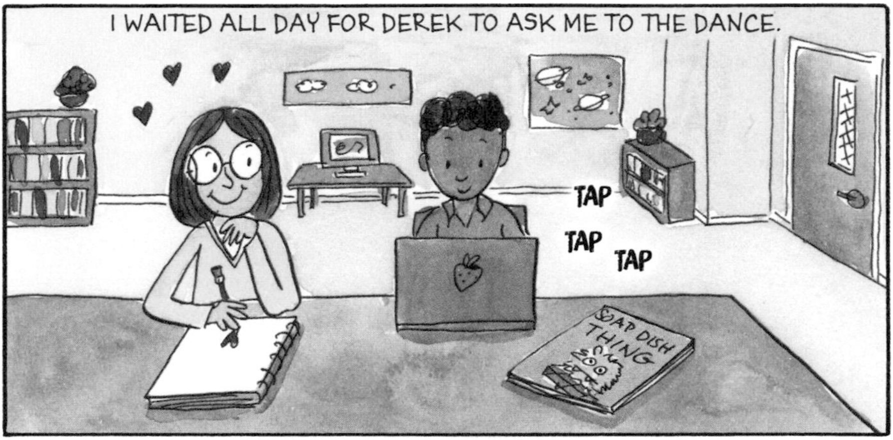
I WAITED ALL DAY FOR DEREK TO ASK ME TO THE DANCE.
TAP
TAP
TAP
SOAP DISH THING

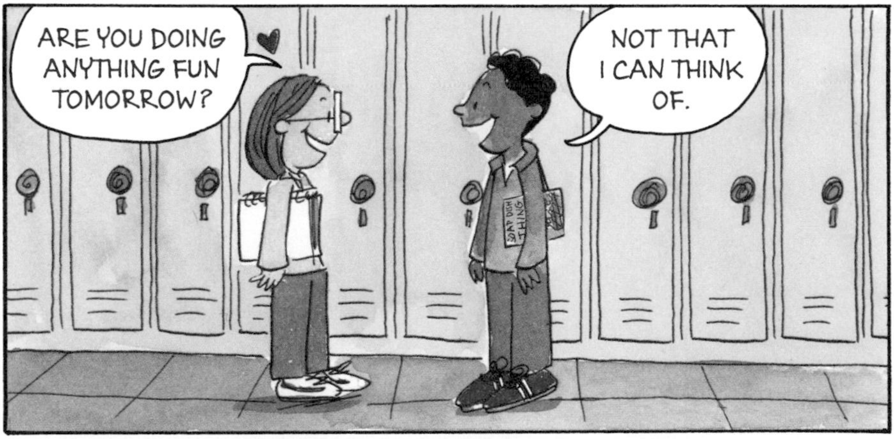
ARE YOU DOING ANYTHING FUN TOMORROW?
NOT THAT I CAN THINK OF.
SOAP DISH THING

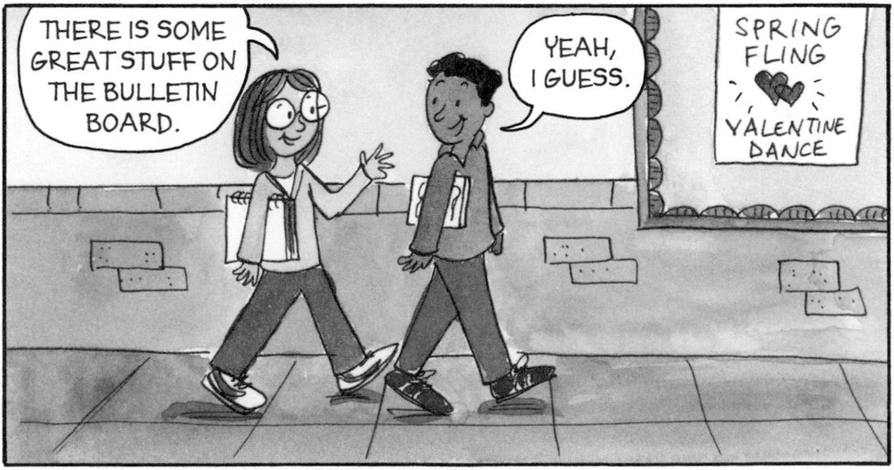
THERE IS SOME GREAT STUFF ON THE BULLETIN BOARD.
YEAH, I GUESS.
SPRING FLING
VALENTINE DANCE

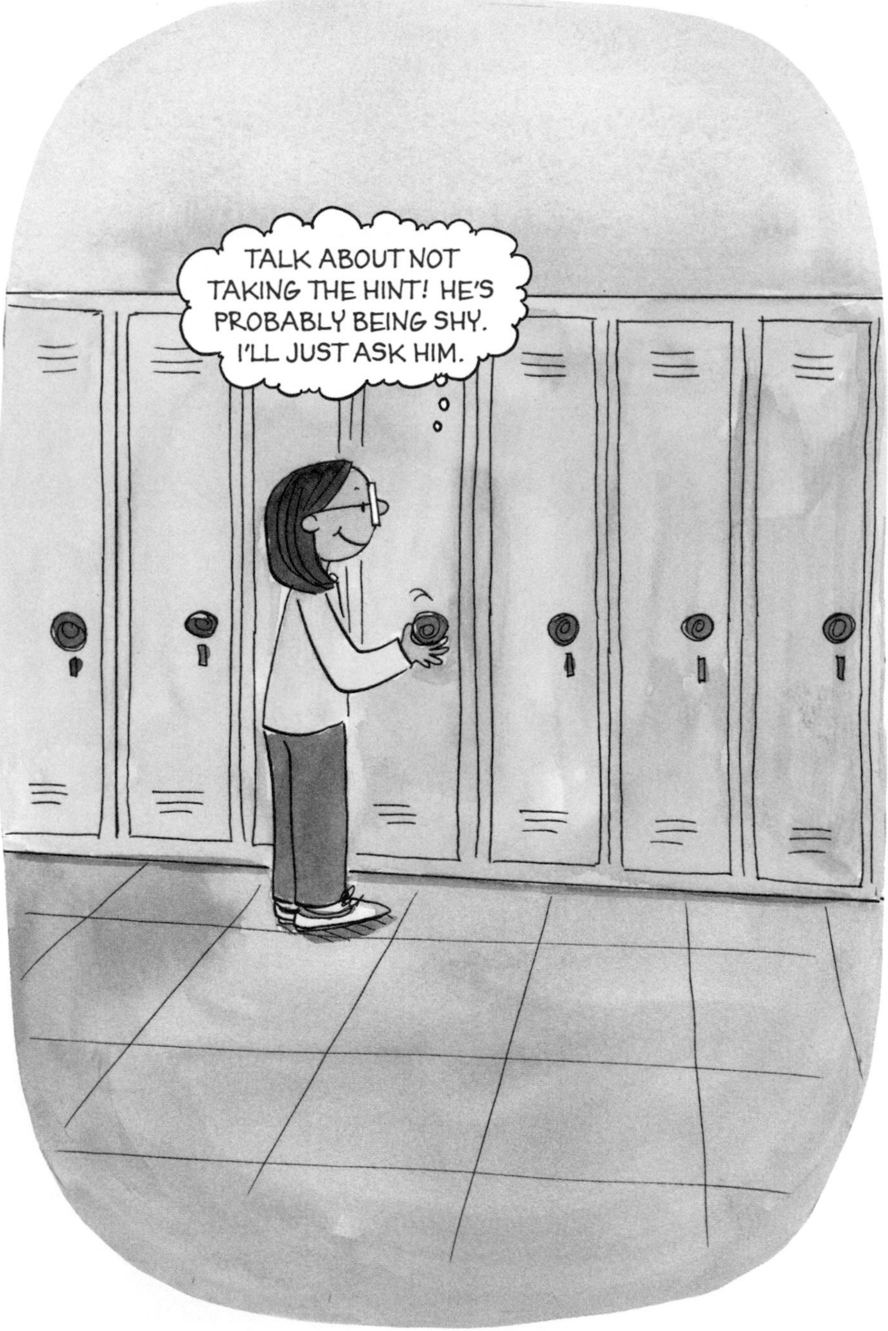
TALK ABOUT NOT TAKING THE HINT! HE'S PROBABLY BEING SHY. I'LL JUST ASK HIM.

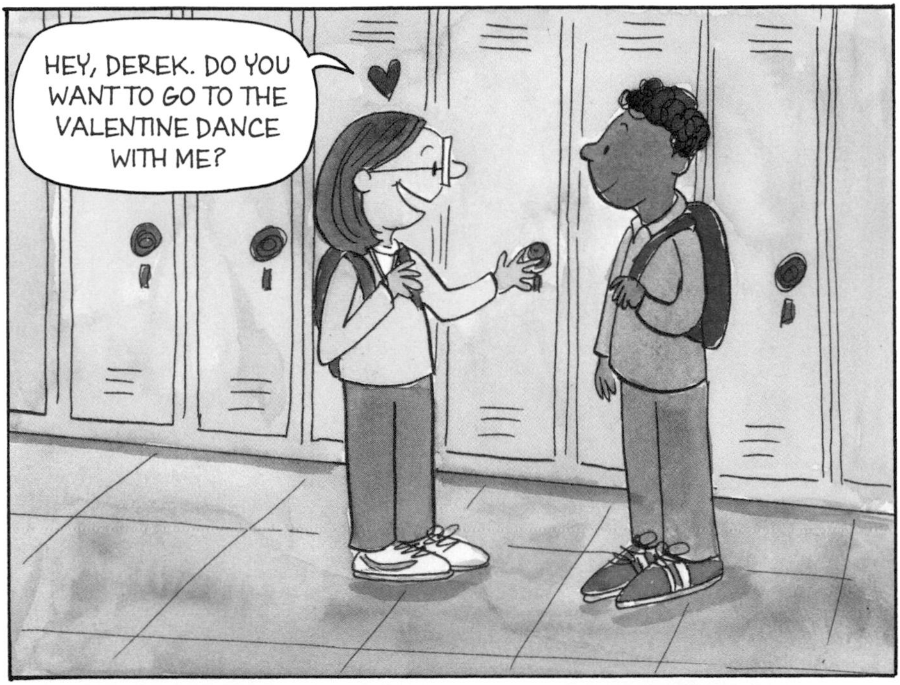
HEY, DEREK. DO YOU WANT TO GO TO THE VALENTINE DANCE WITH ME?

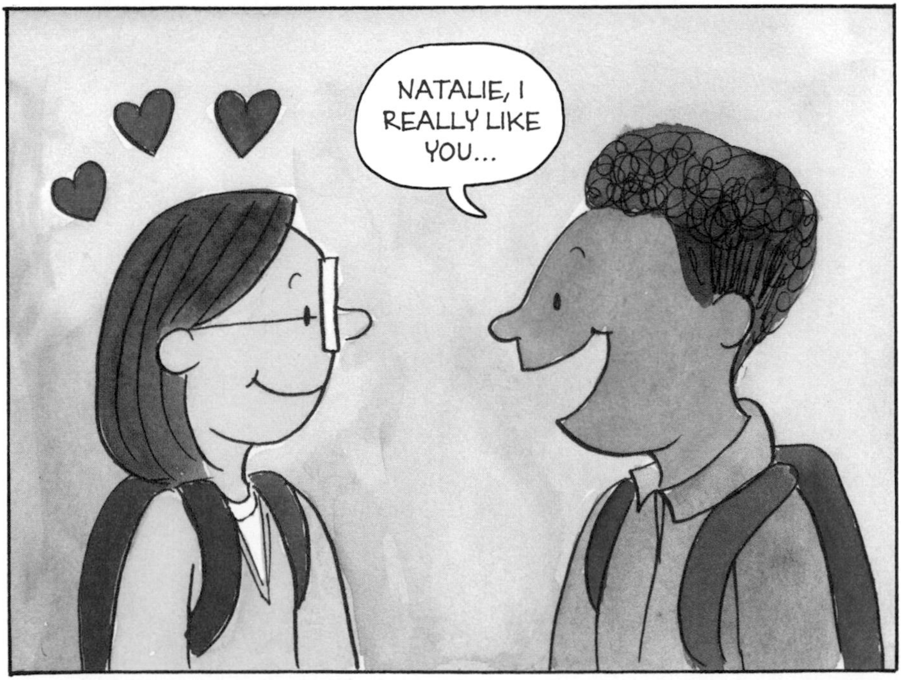
NATALIE, I REALLY LIKE YOU...

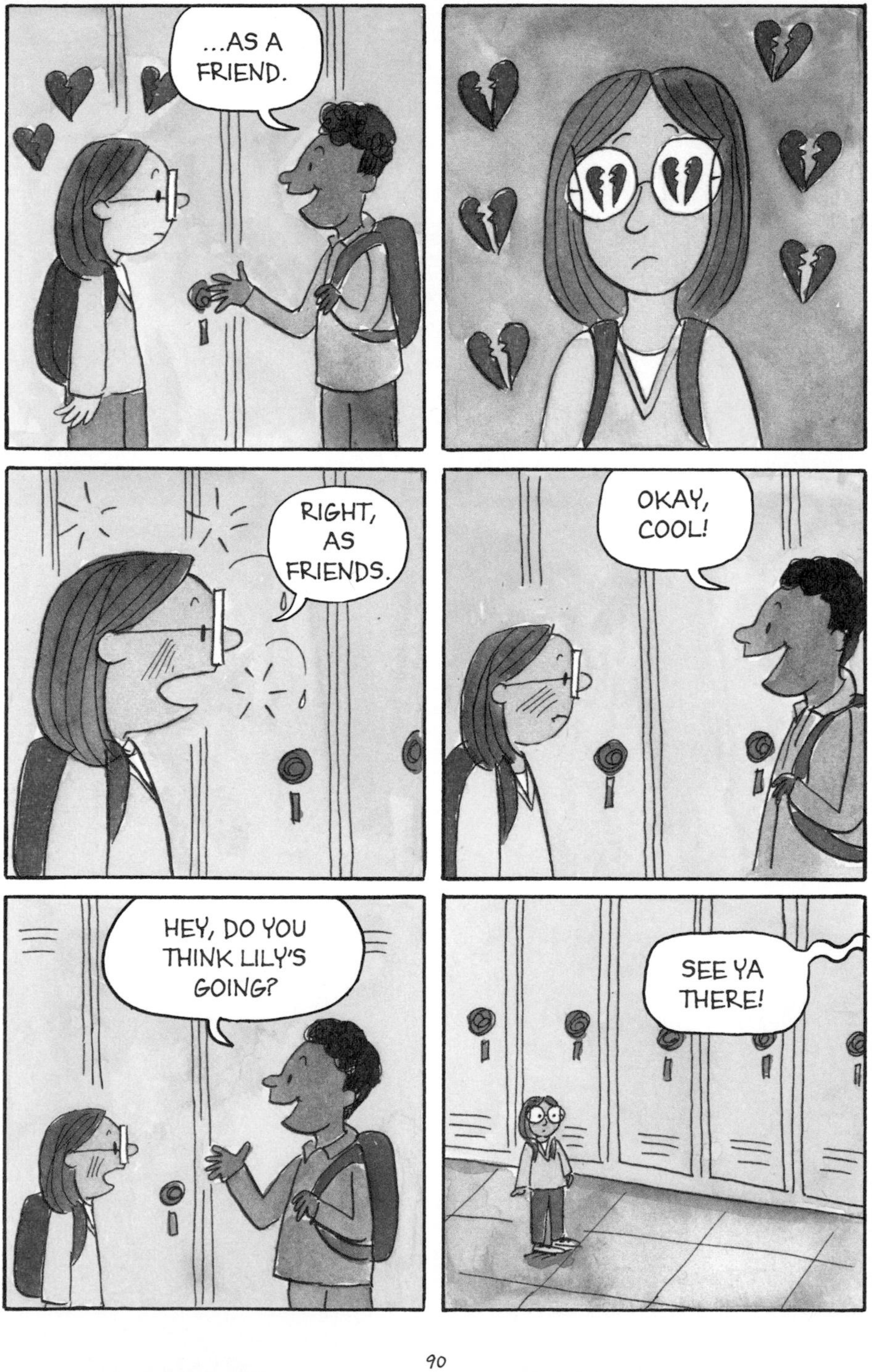
...AS A FRIEND.
RIGHT, AS FRIENDS.
OKAY, COOL!
HEY, DO YOU THINK LILY'S GOING?
SEE YA THERE!

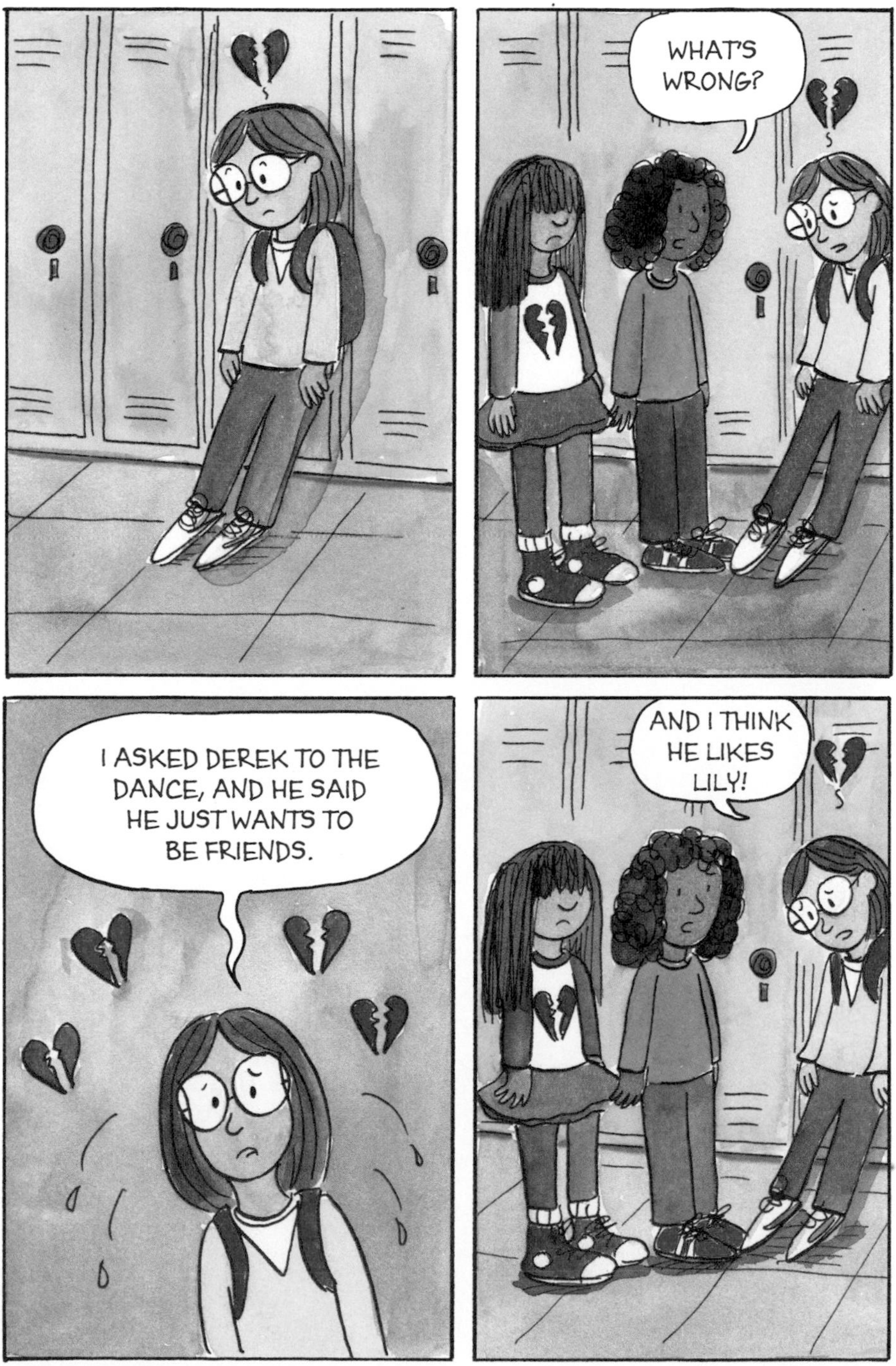
WHAT'S WRONG?
I ASKED DEREK TO THE DANCE, AND HE SAID HE JUST WANTS TO BE FRIENDS.
AND I THINK HE LIKES LILY!

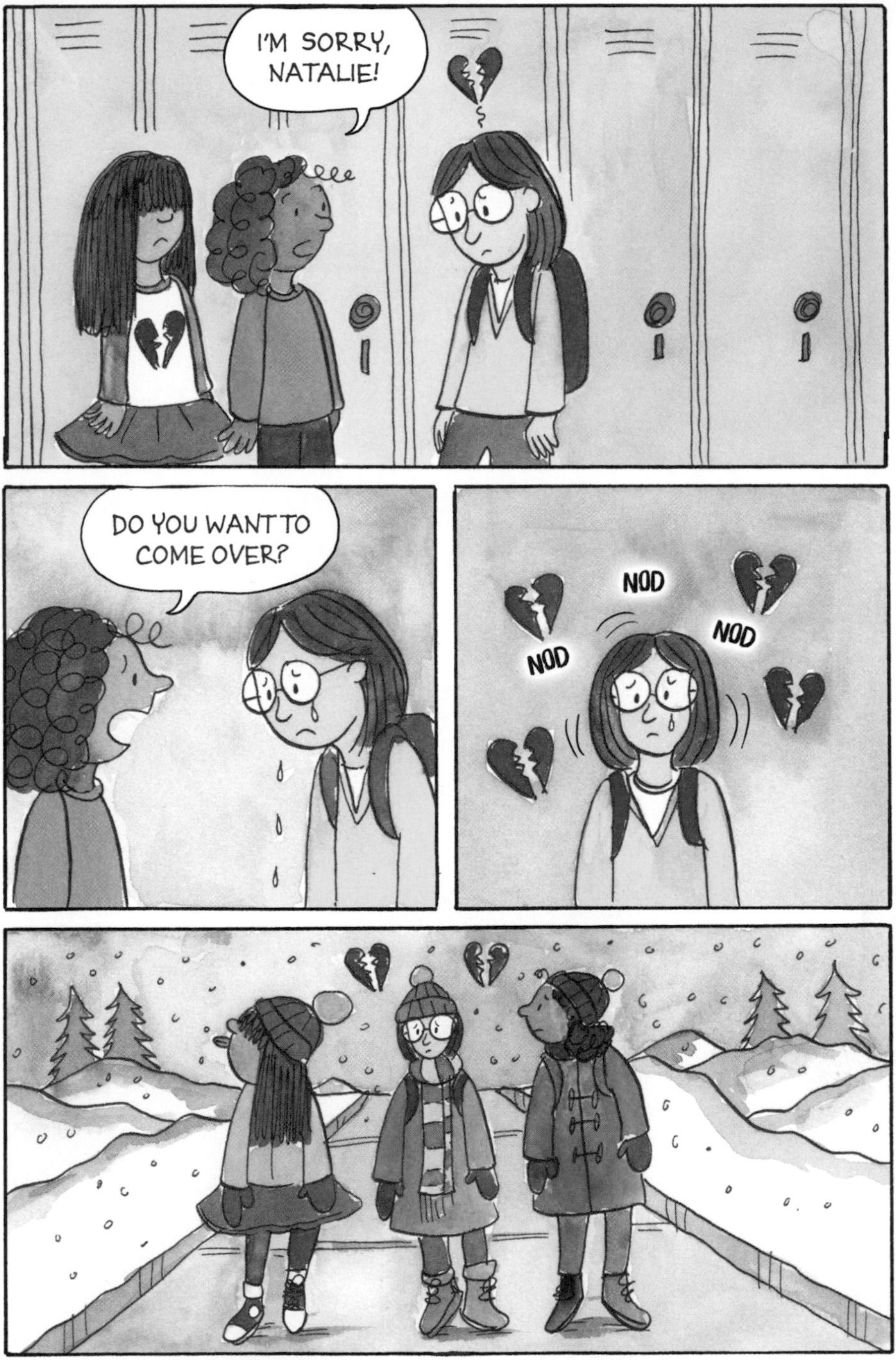
I'M SORRY, NATALIE!
DO YOU WANT TO COME OVER?
NOD
NOD
NOD

CHAPTER 6
THE DAY BEFORE VALENTINE'S DAY

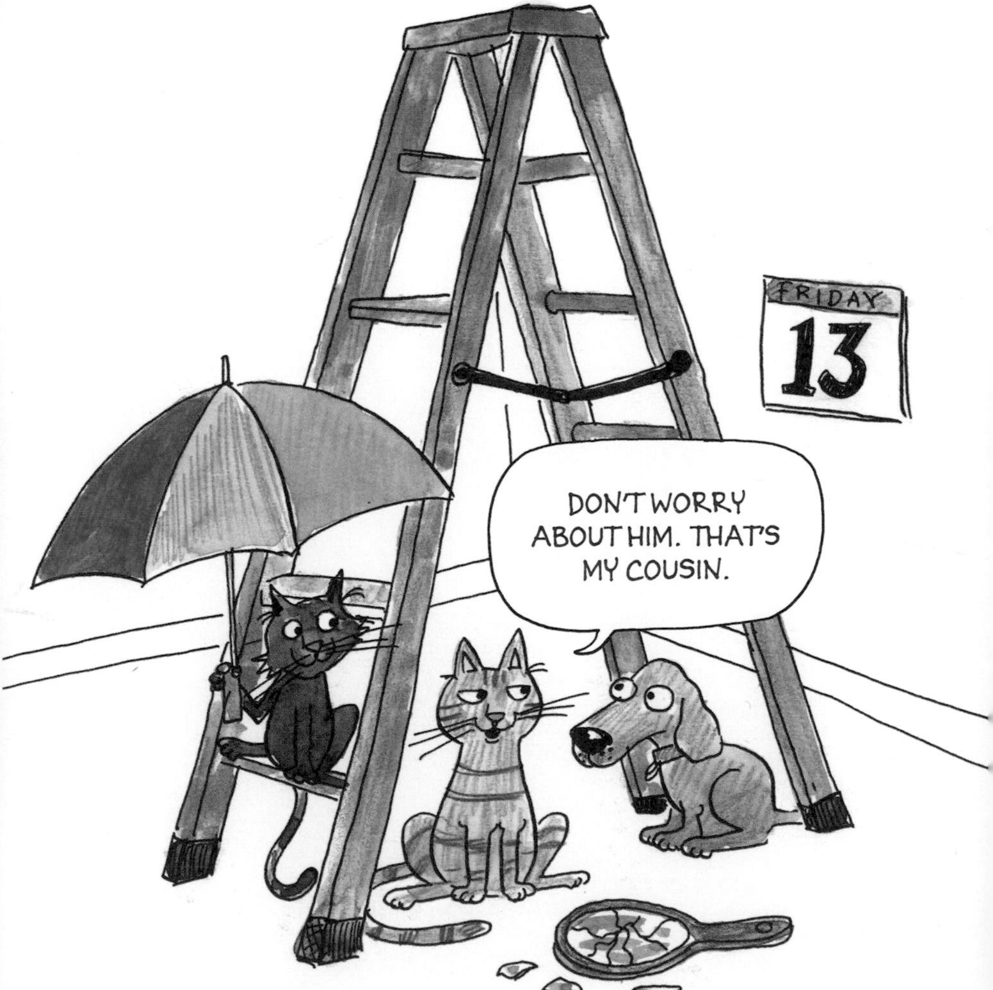
FRIDAY
13
DON'T WORRY ABOUT HIM. THAT'S MY COUSIN.

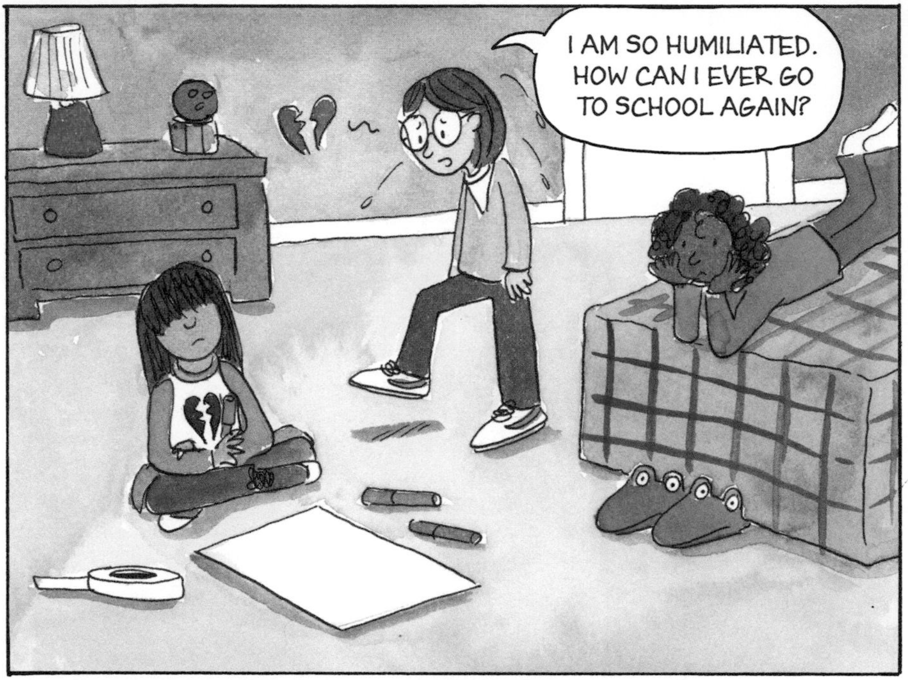
I AM SO HUMILIATED. HOW CAN I EVER GO TO SCHOOL AGAIN?

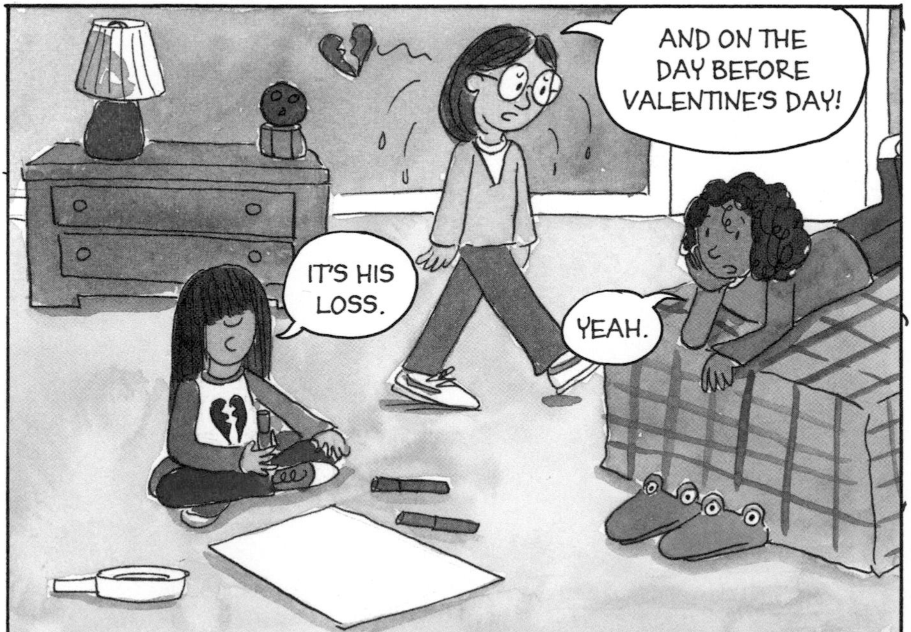
AND ON THE DAY BEFORE VALENTINE'S DAY!
IT'S HIS LOSS.
YEAH.

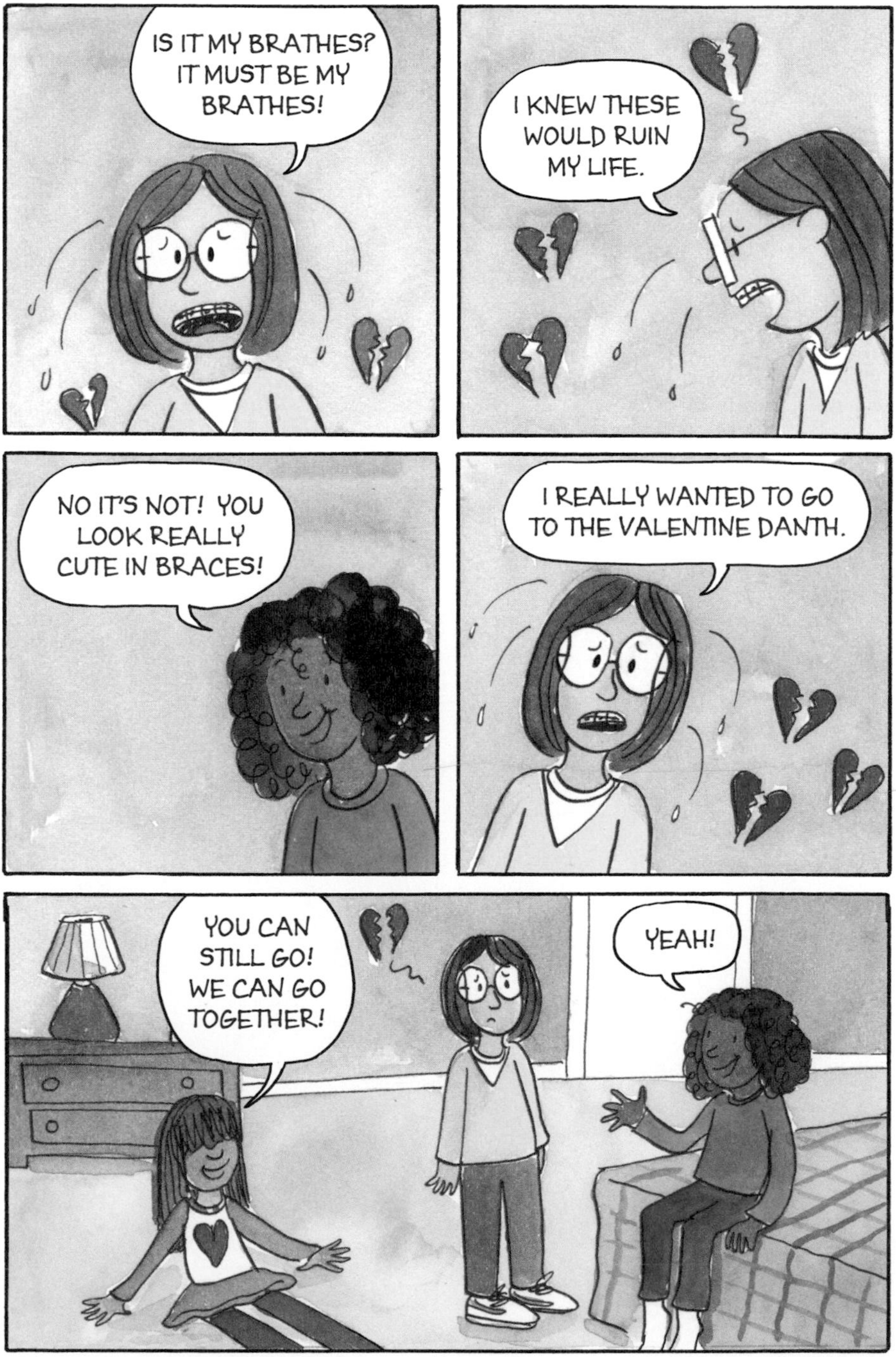
IS IT MY BRATHES? IT MUST BE MY BRATHES!
I KNEW THESE WOULD RUIN MY LIFE.
NO IT'S NOT! YOU LOOK REALLY CUTE IN BRACES!
I REALLY WANTED TO GO TO THE VALENTINE DANTH.
YOU CAN STILL GO! WE CAN GO TOGETHER!
YEAH!

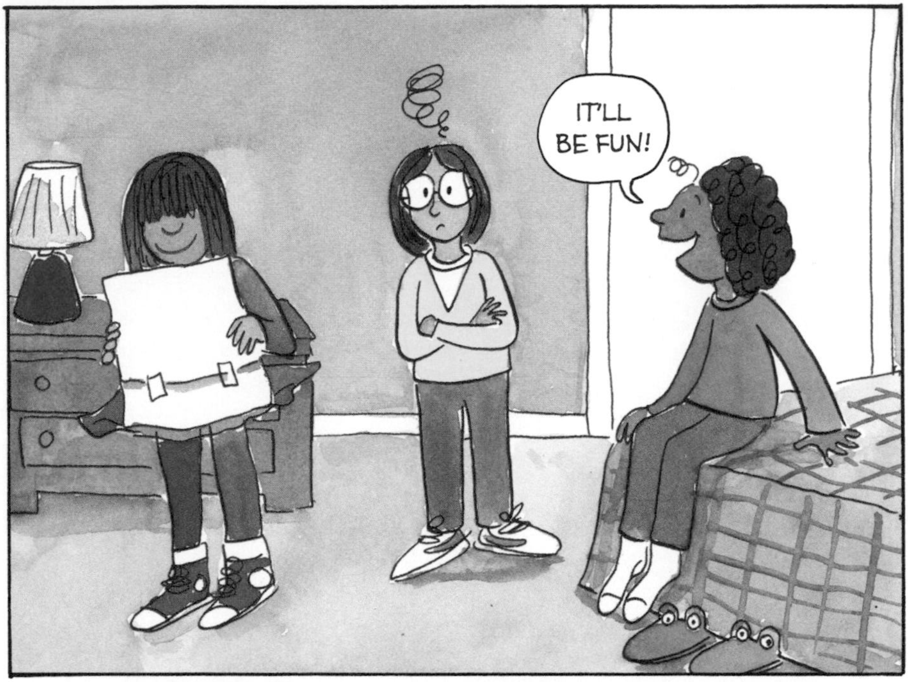
IT'LL BE FUN!

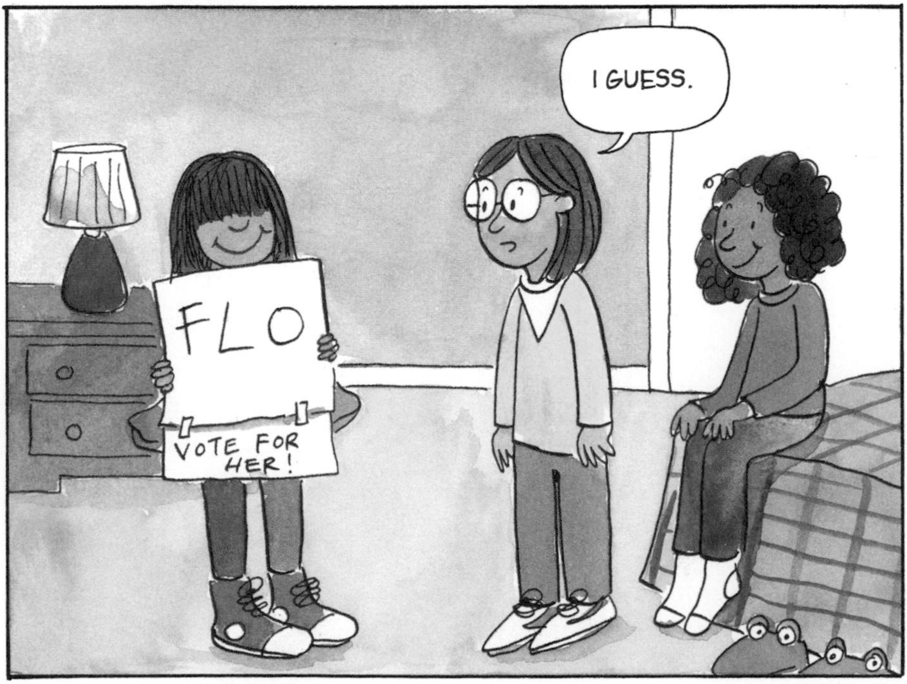
I GUESS.
FLO
VOTE FOR HER!

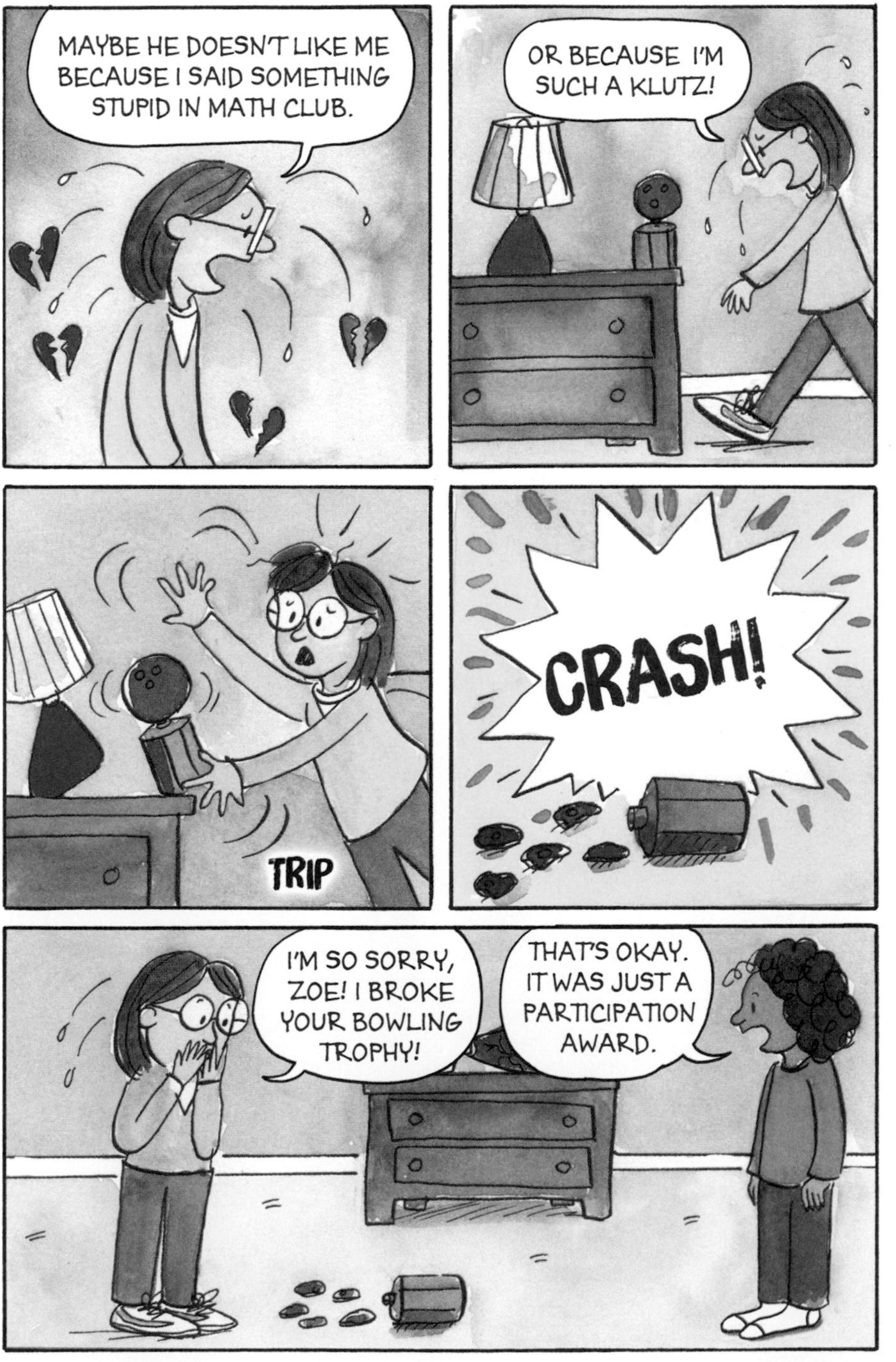
MAYBE HE DOESN'T LIKE ME BECAUSE I SAID SOMETHING STUPID IN MATH CLUB.
OR BECAUSE I'M SUCH A KLUTZ!
TRIP
CRASH!
I'M SO SORRY, ZOE! I BROKE YOUR BOWLING TROPHY!
THAT'S OKAY. IT WAS JUST A PARTICIPATION AWARD.

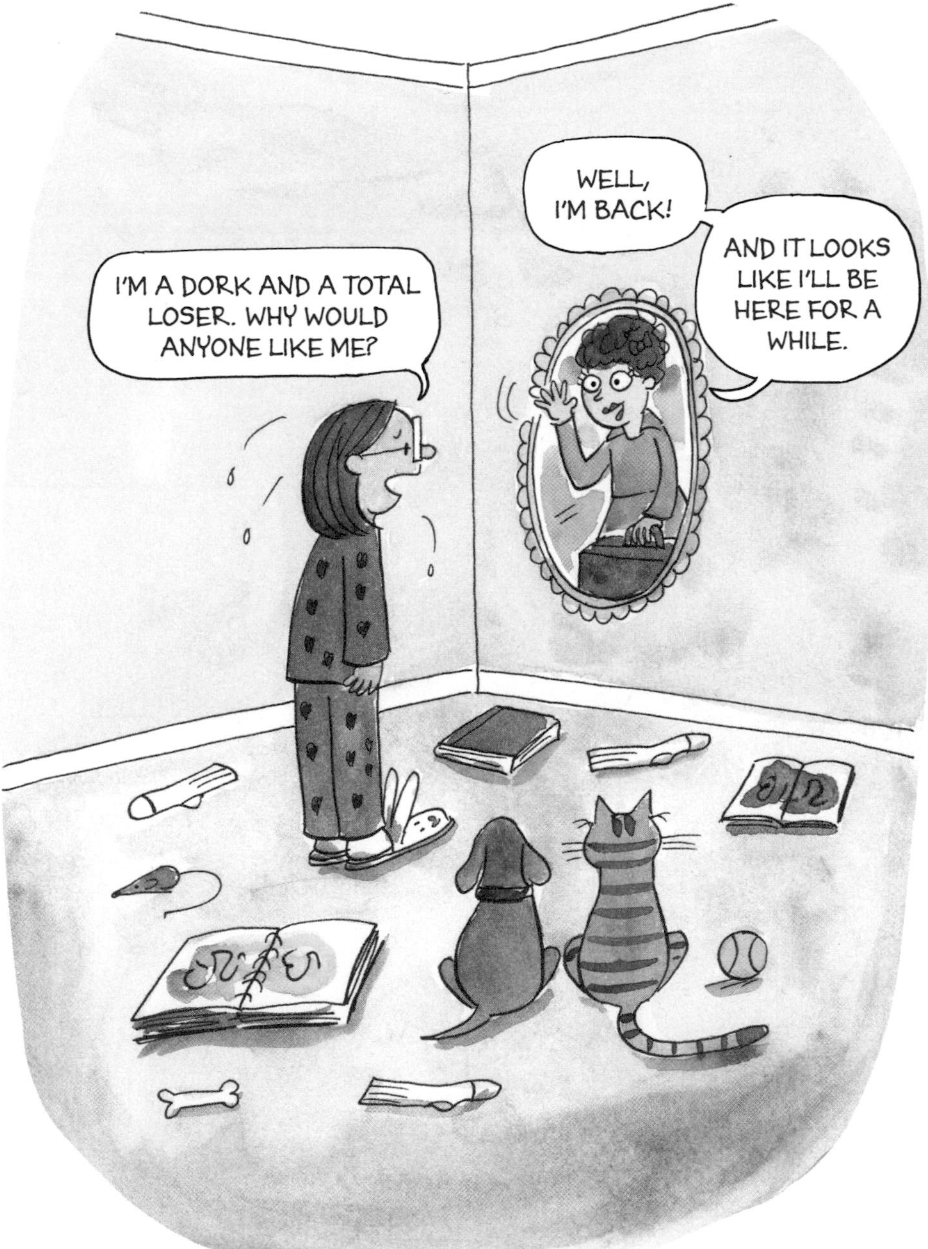
I'M A DORK AND A TOTAL LOSER. WHY WOULD ANYONE LIKE ME?
WELL, I'M BACK!
AND IT LOOKS LIKE I'LL BE HERE FOR A WHILE.

CHAPTER 7
STUCK ON YOU

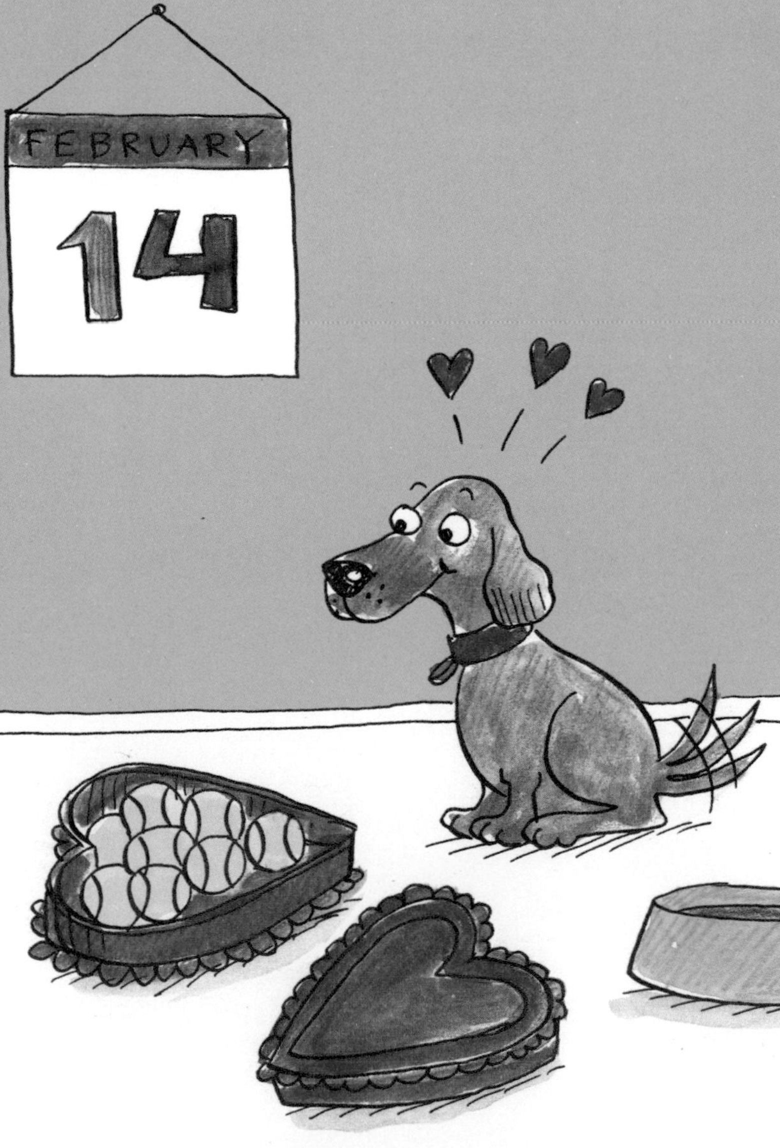
FEBRUARY
14

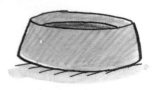

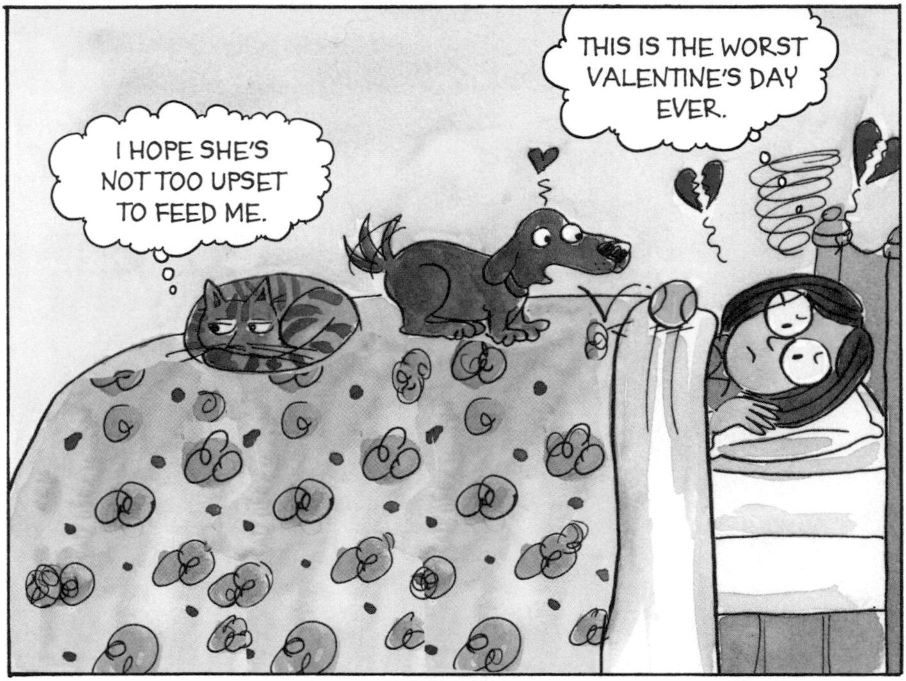
I HOPE SHE'S NOT TOO UPSET TO FEED ME.
THIS IS THE WORST VALENTINE'S DAY EVER.

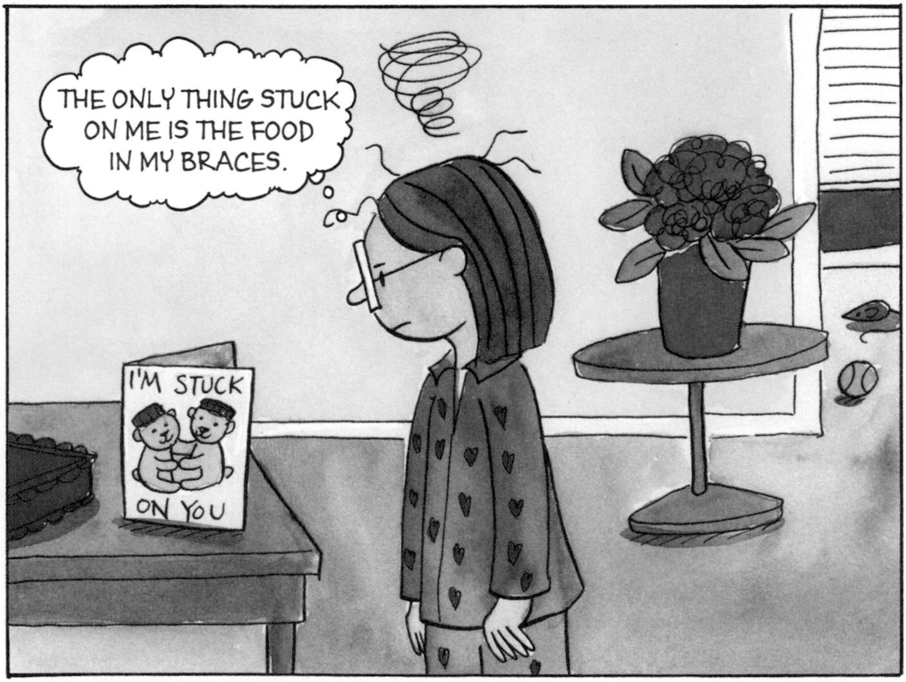
THE ONLY THING STUCK ON ME IS THE FOOD IN MY BRACES.
I'M STUCK ON YOU

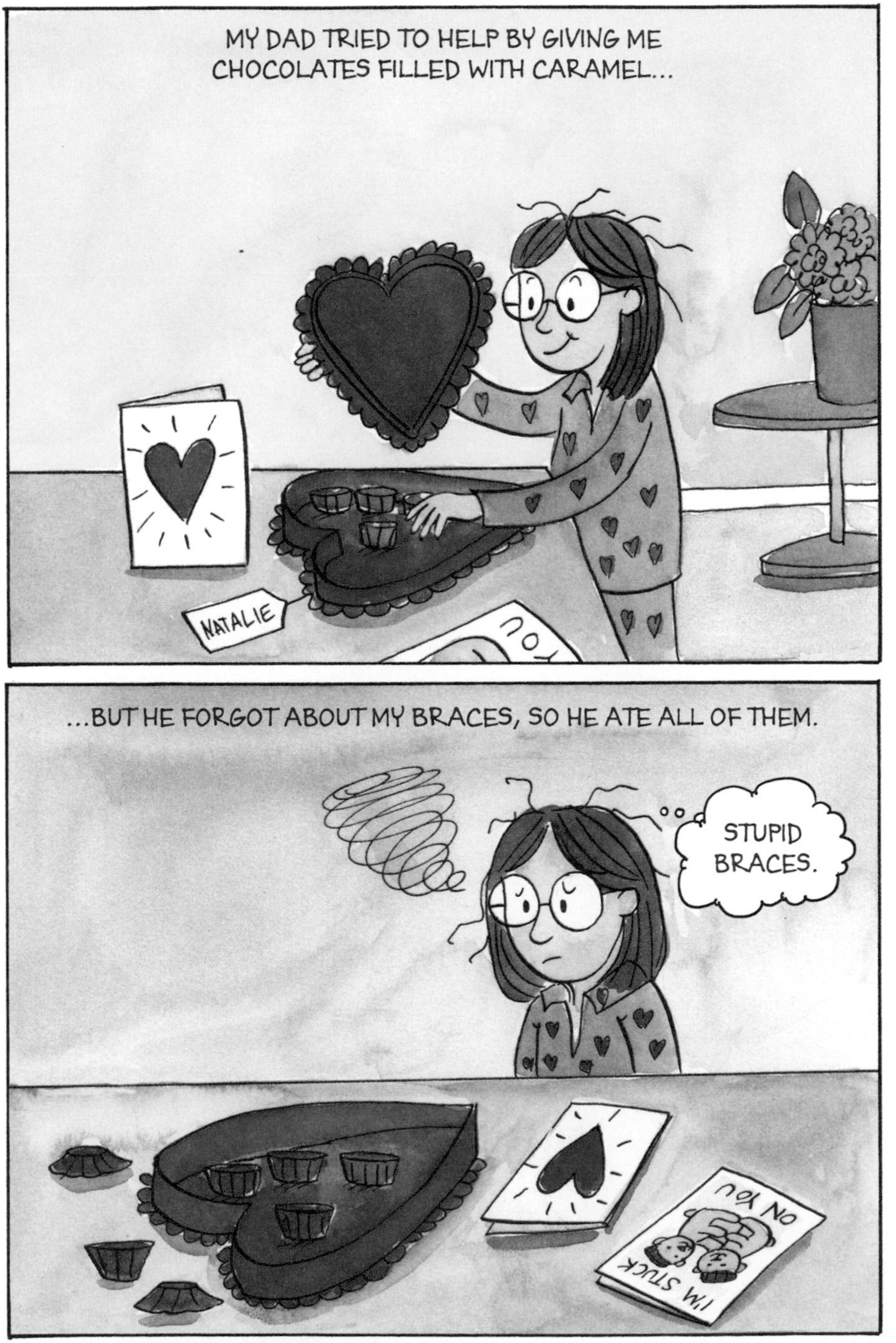
MY DAD TRIED TO HELP BY GIVING ME CHOCOLATES FILLED WITH CARAMEL...
NATALIE
...BUT HE FORGOT ABOUT MY BRACES, SO HE ATE ALL OF THEM.
STUPID BRACES.
I'M STUCK ON YOU

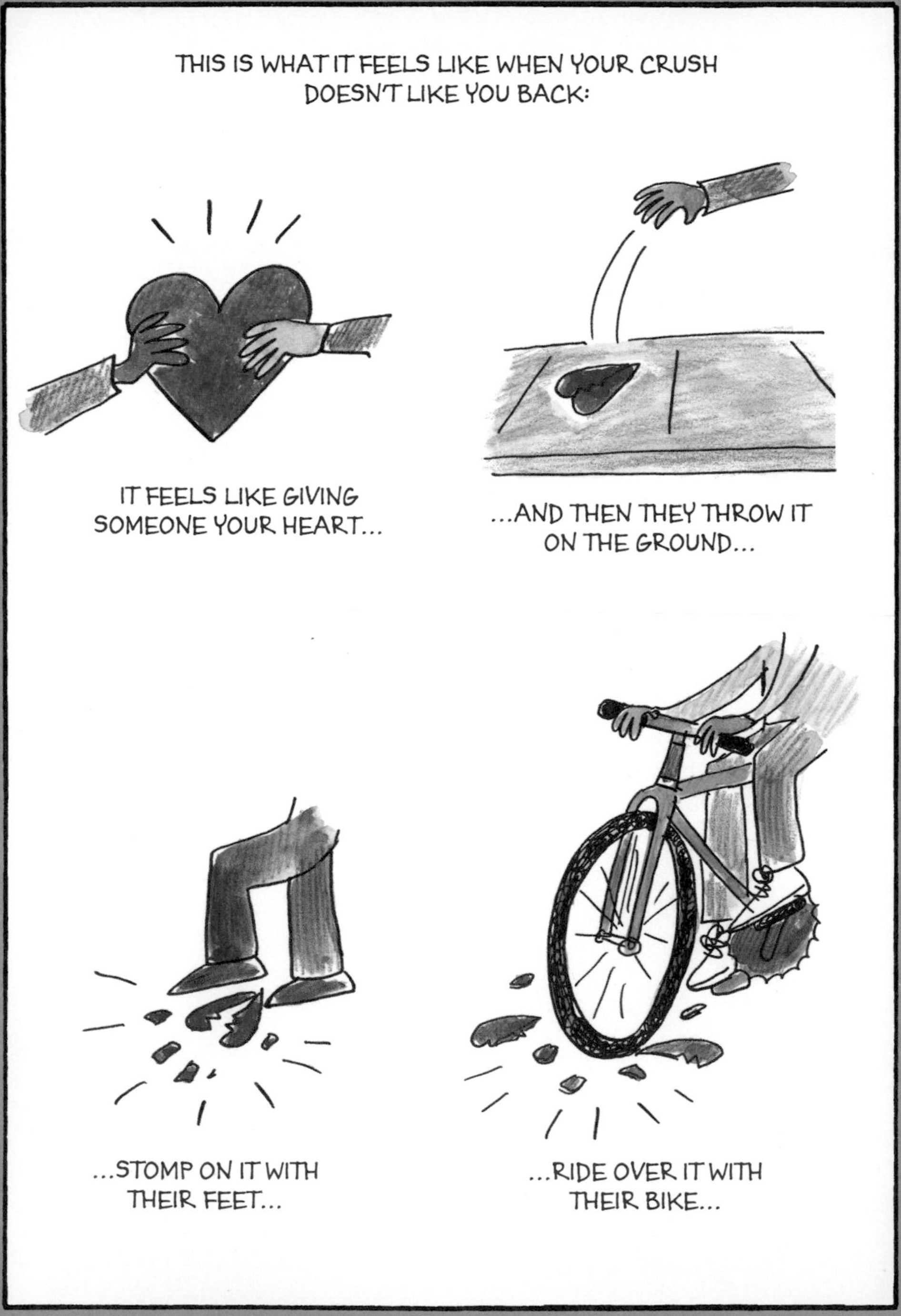
THIS IS WHAT IT FEELS LIKE WHEN YOUR CRUSH DOESN'T LIKE YOU BACK:
IT FEELS LIKE GIVING SOMEONE YOUR HEART...
...AND THEN THEY THROW IT ON THE GROUND...
...STOMP ON IT WITH THEIR FEET...
...RIDE OVER IT WITH THEIR BIKE...

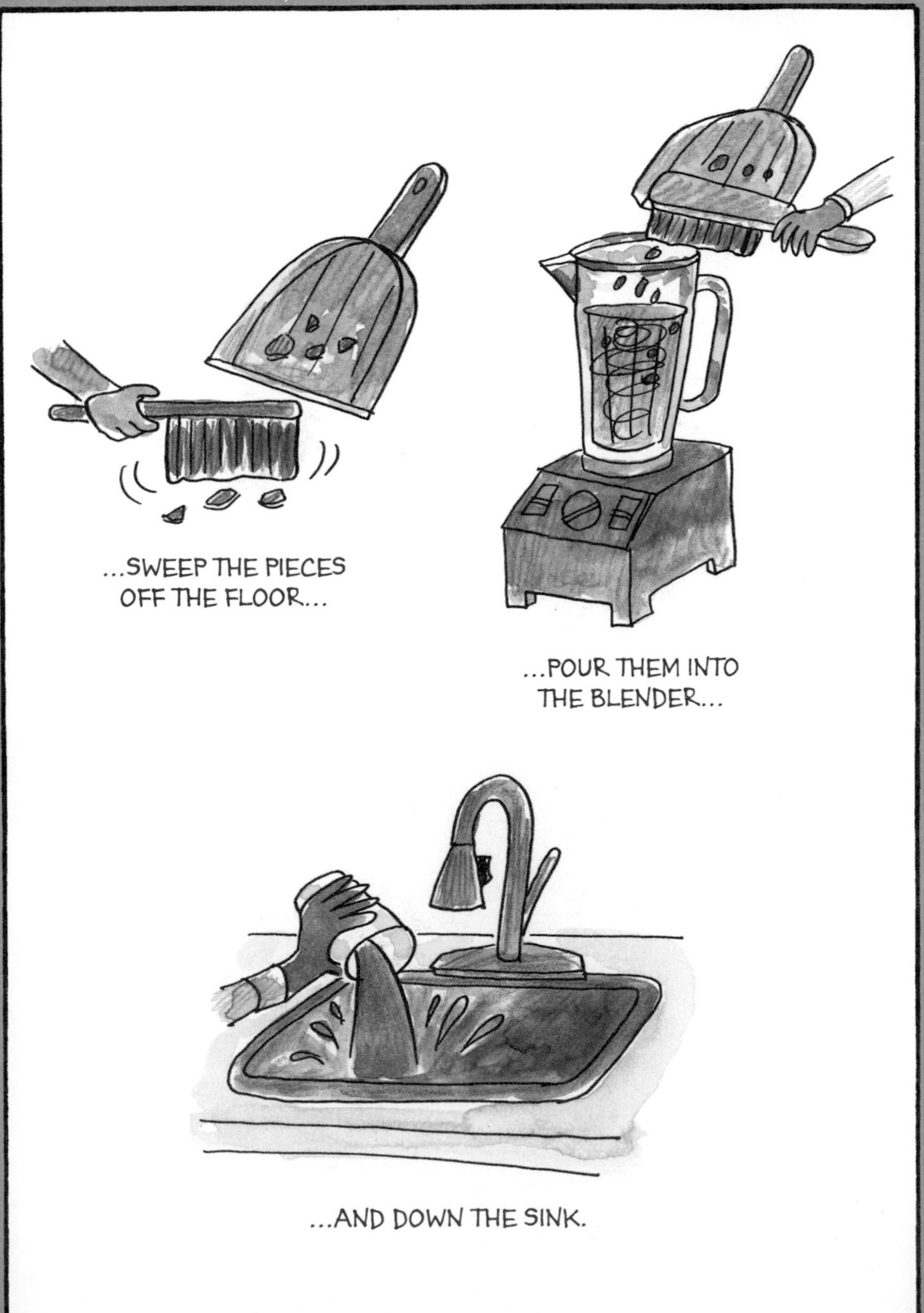
...SWEEP THE PIECES OFF THE FLOOR...
...POUR THEM INTO THE BLENDER...
...AND DOWN THE SINK.

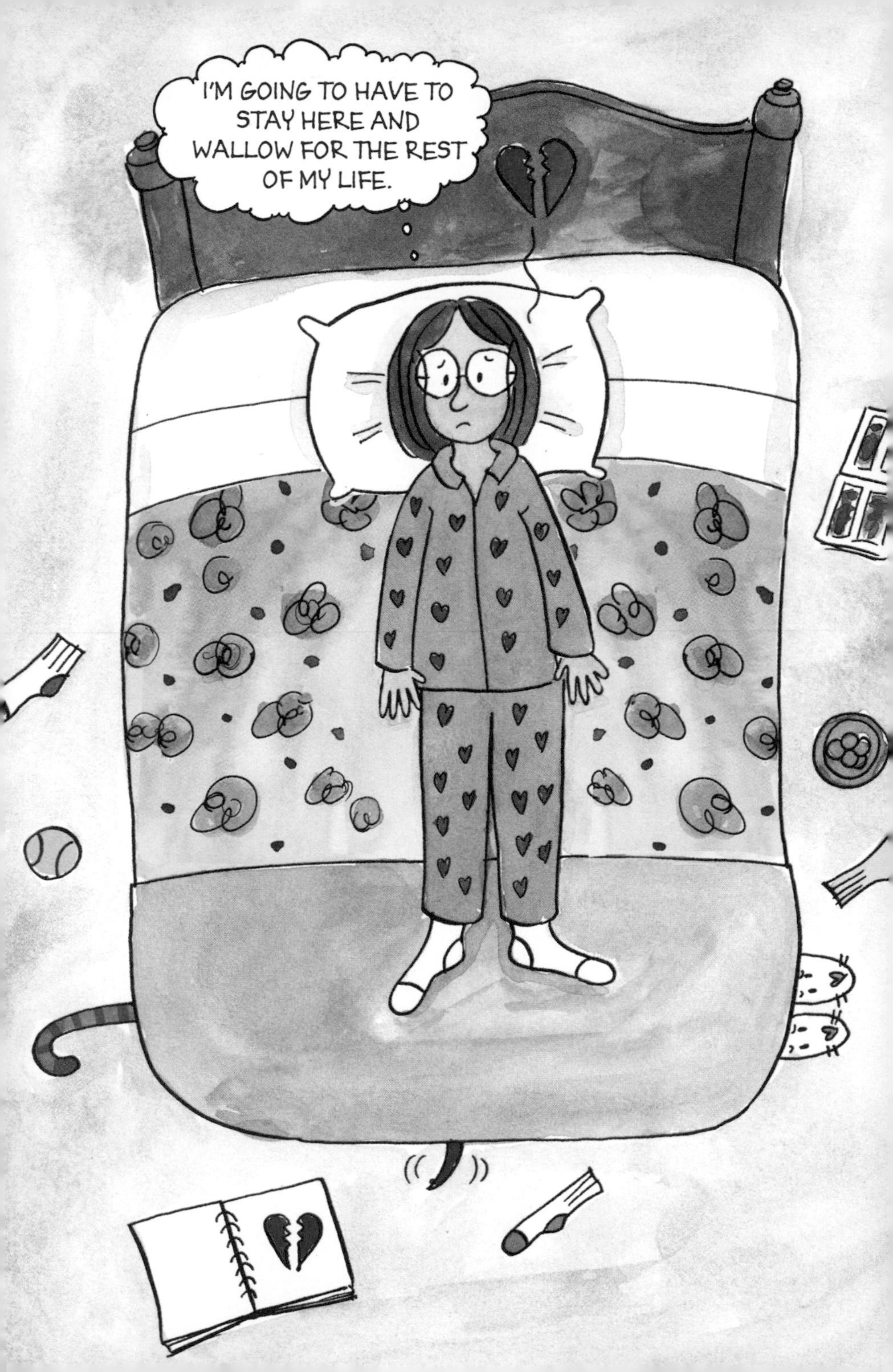
I'M GOING TO HAVE TO STAY HERE AND WALLOW FOR THE REST OF MY LIFE.

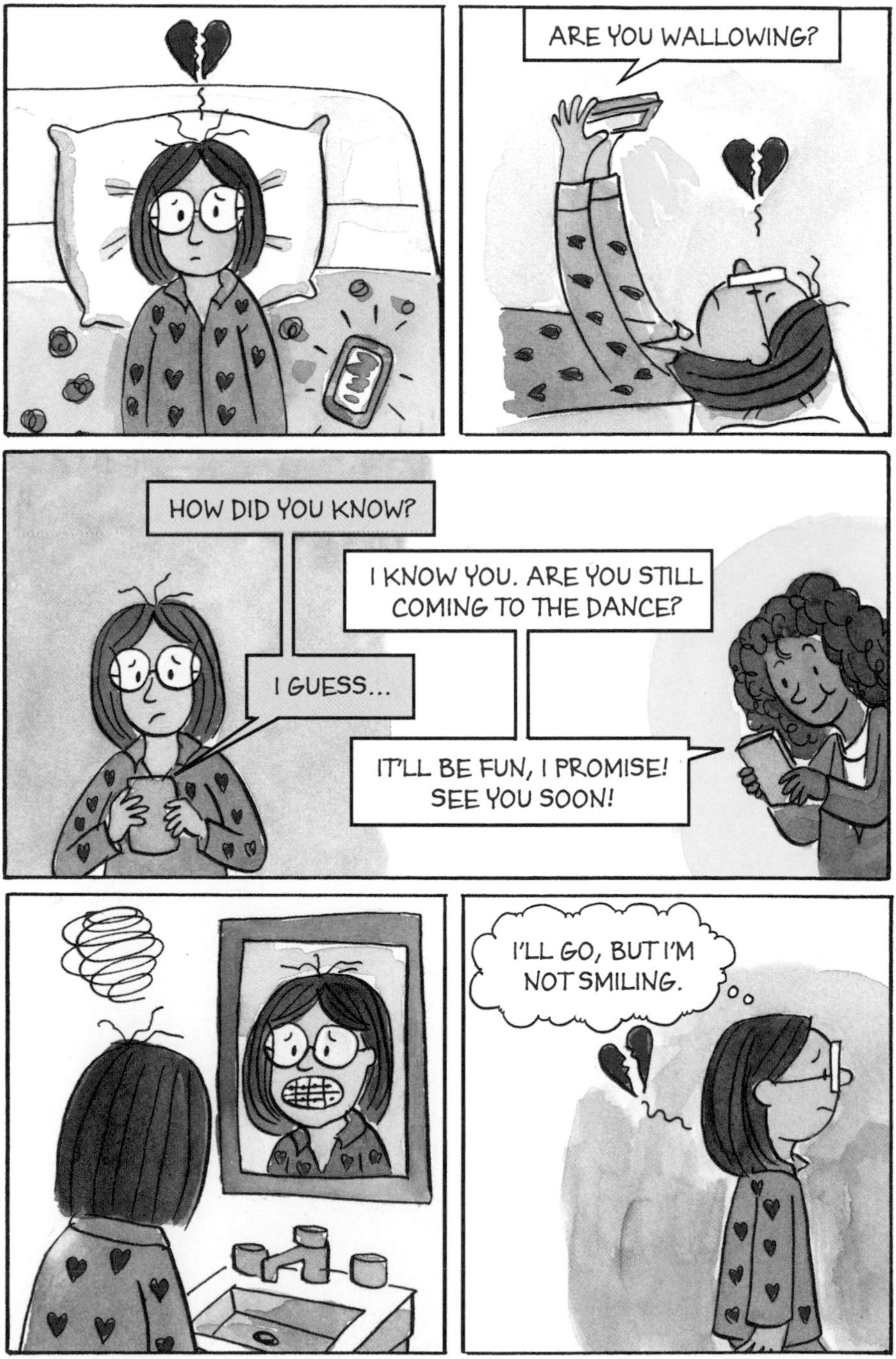
ARE YOU WALLOWING?
HOW DID YOU KNOW?
I KNOW YOU. ARE YOU STILL COMING TO THE DANCE?
I GUESS...
IT'LL BE FUN, I PROMISE! SEE YOU SOON!
I'LL GO, BUT I'M NOT SMILING.

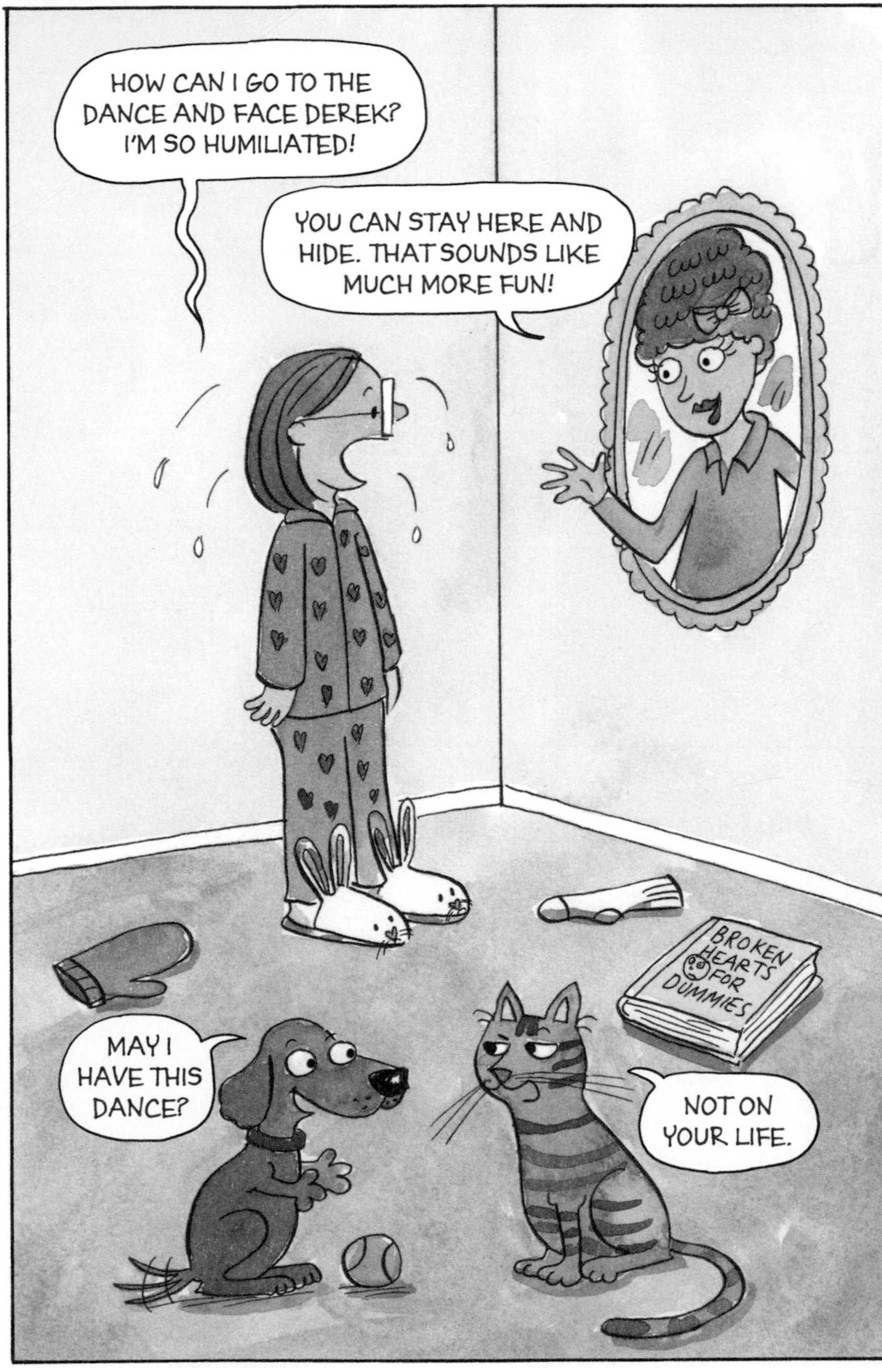
HOW CAN I GO TO THE DANCE AND FACE DEREK? I'M SO HUMILIATED!
YOU CAN STAY HERE AND HIDE. THAT SOUNDS LIKE MUCH MORE FUN!
BROKEN HEARTS FOR DUMMIES
MAY I HAVE THIS DANCE?
NOT ON YOUR LIFE.

CHAPTER 8
THE DANCE

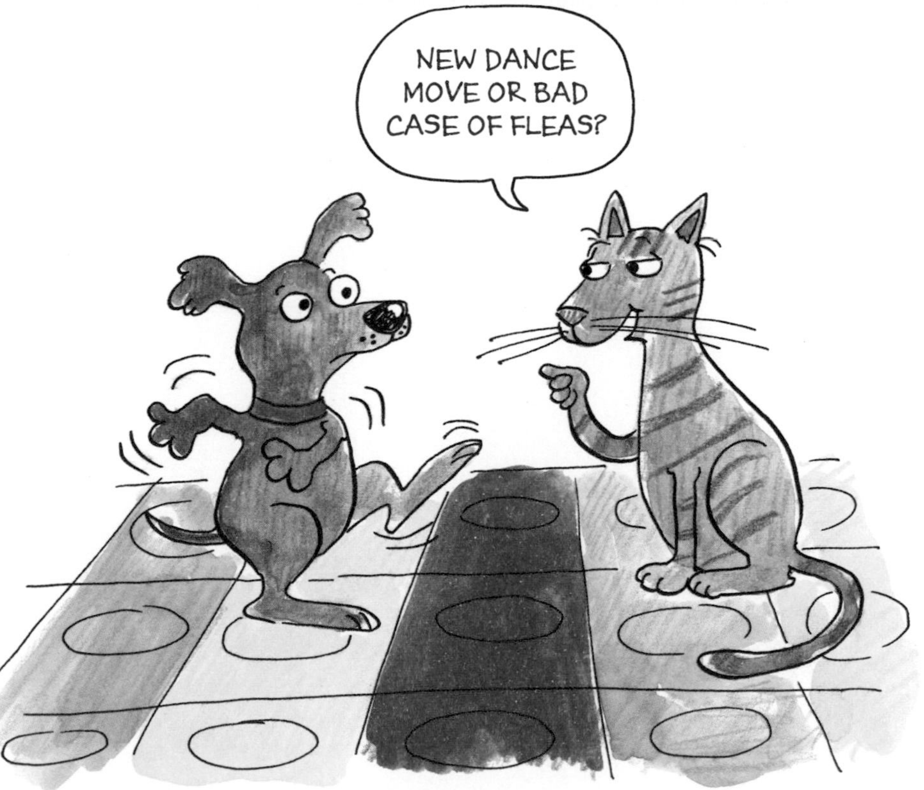
NEW DANCE
MOVE OR BAD
CASE OF FLEAS?

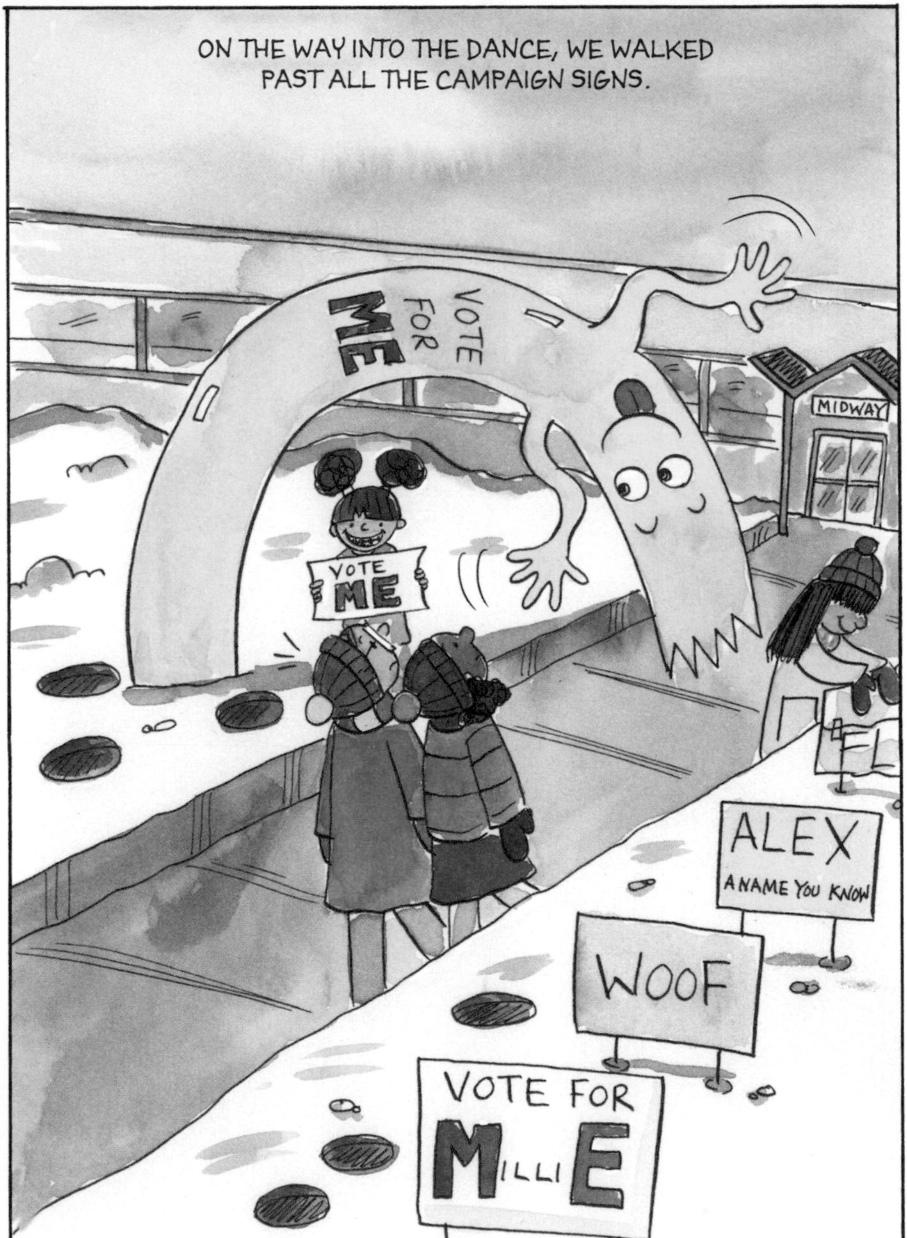
ON THE WAY INTO THE DANCE, WE WALKED PAST ALL THE CAMPAIGN SIGNS.
VOTE FOR ME
MIDWAY
VOTE ME
ALEX
A NAME YOU KNOW
WOOF
VOTE FOR
MILLIE

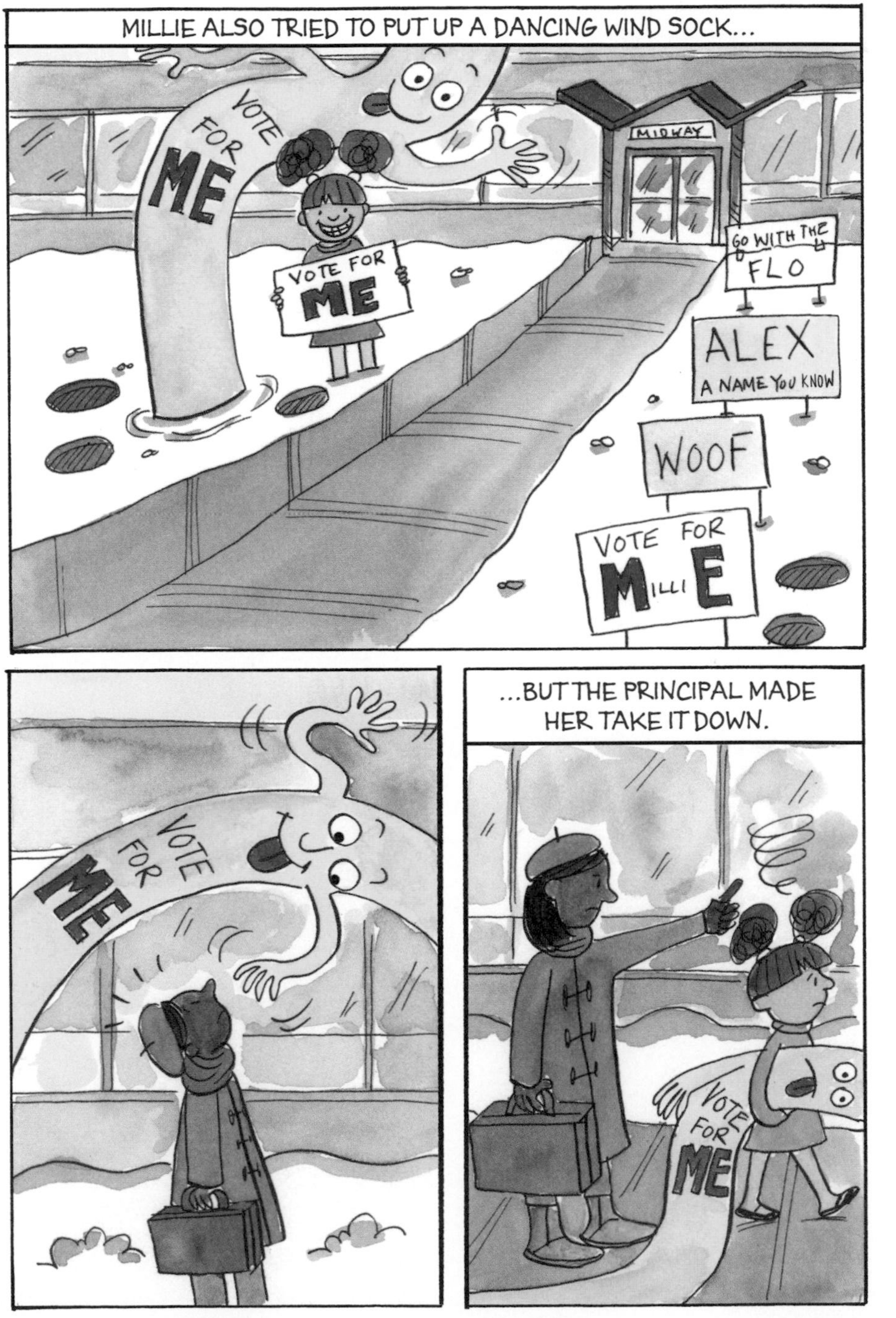
MILLIE ALSO TRIED TO PUT UP A DANCING WIND SOCK...
VOTE FOR ME
VOTE FOR ME
MIDWAY
GO WITH THE FLO
ALEX
A NAME YOU KNOW
WOOF
VOTE FOR MILLIE
VOTE FOR ME
...BUT THE PRINCIPAL MADE HER TAKE IT DOWN.
VOTE FOR ME

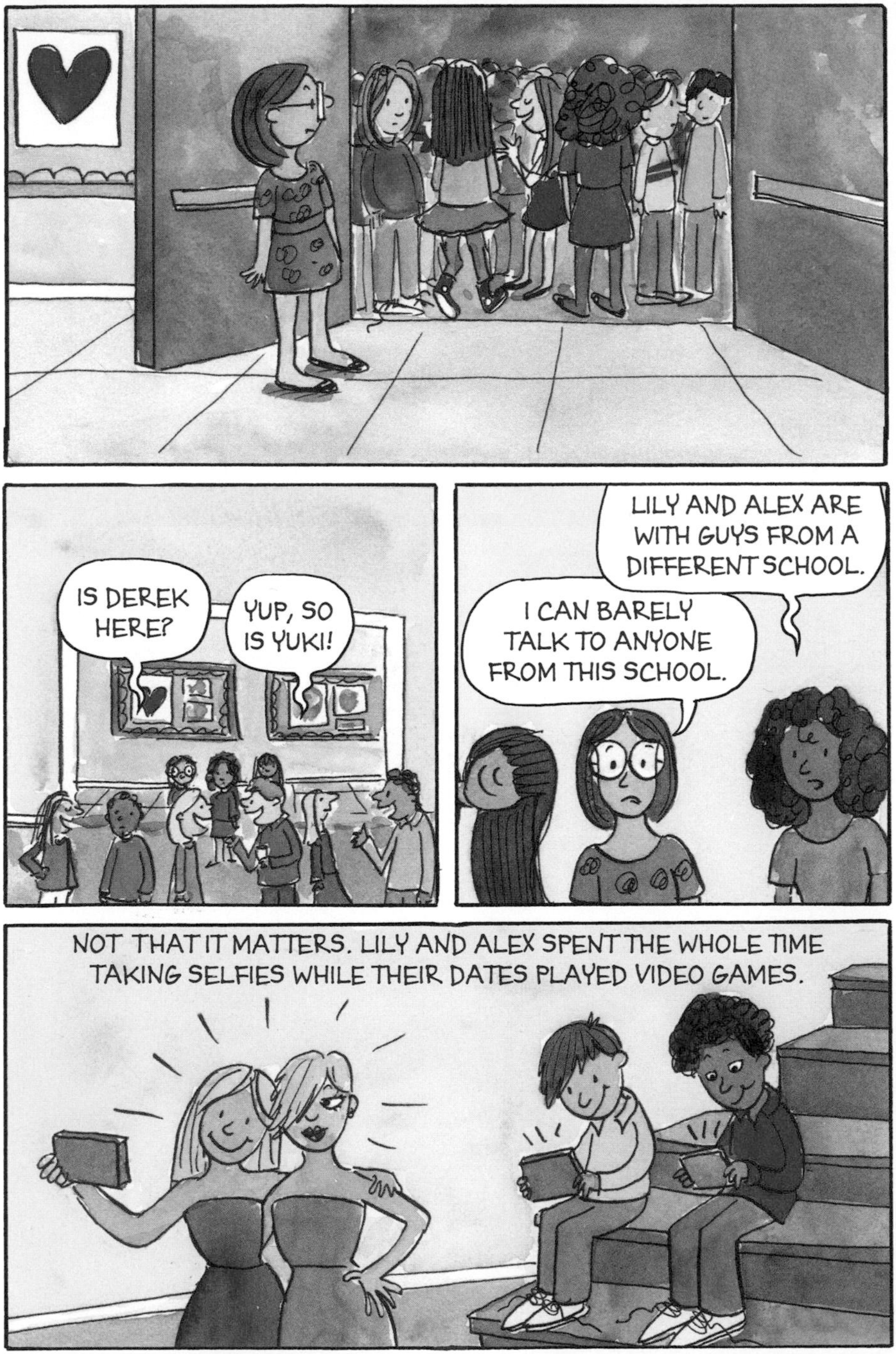
IS DEREK HERE?
YUP, SO IS YUKI!
LILY AND ALEX ARE WITH GUYS FROM A DIFFERENT SCHOOL.
I CAN BARELY TALK TO ANYONE FROM THIS SCHOOL.
NOT THAT IT MATTERS. LILY AND ALEX SPENT THE WHOLE TIME TAKING SELFIES WHILE THEIR DATES PLAYED VIDEO GAMES.

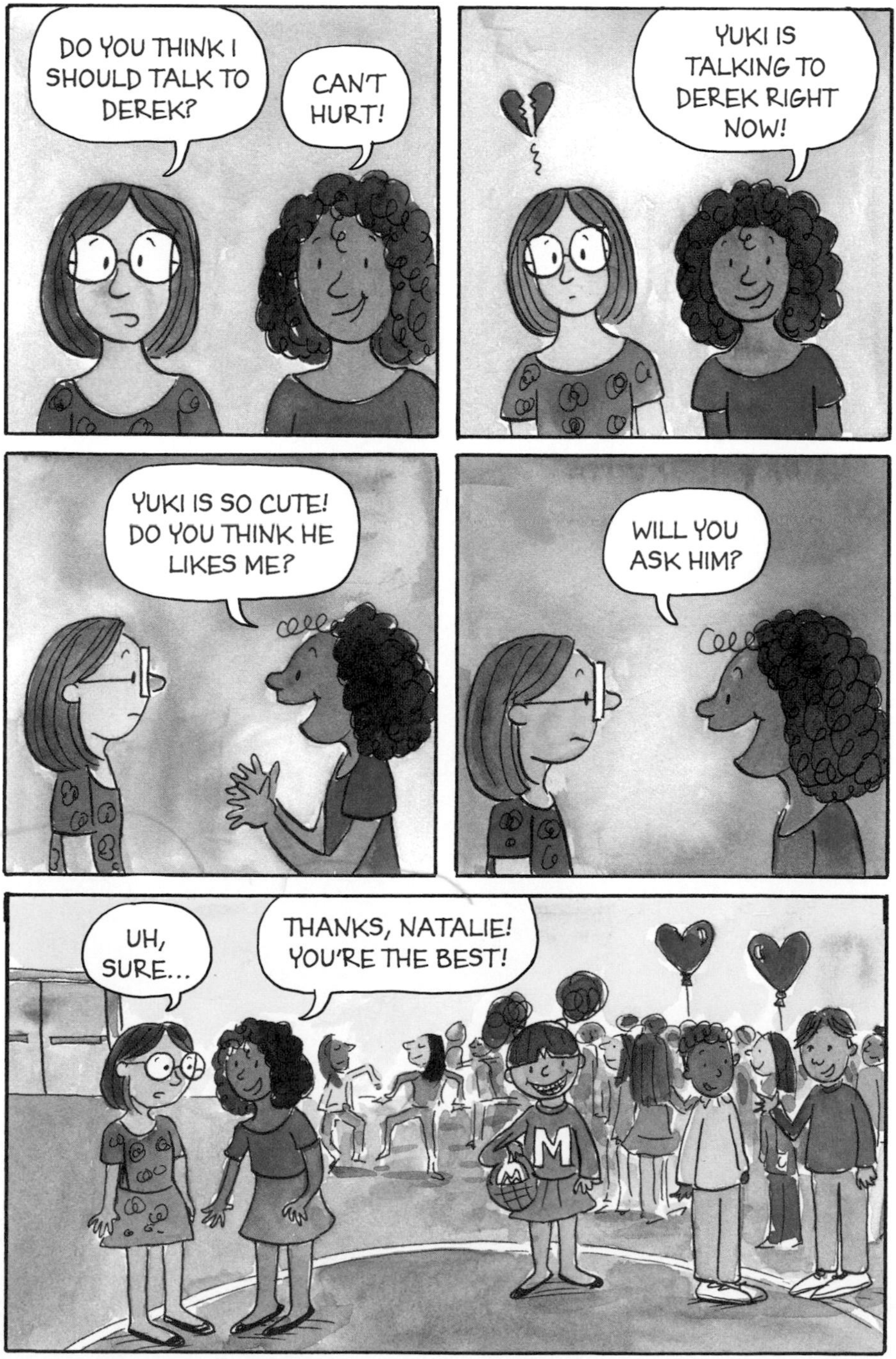
DO YOU THINK I SHOULD TALK TO DEREK?
CAN'T HURT!
YUKI IS TALKING TO DEREK RIGHT NOW!
YUKI IS SO CUTE! DO YOU THINK HE LIKES ME?
WILL YOU ASK HIM?
UH, SURE...
THANKS, NATALIE! YOU'RE THE BEST!
M

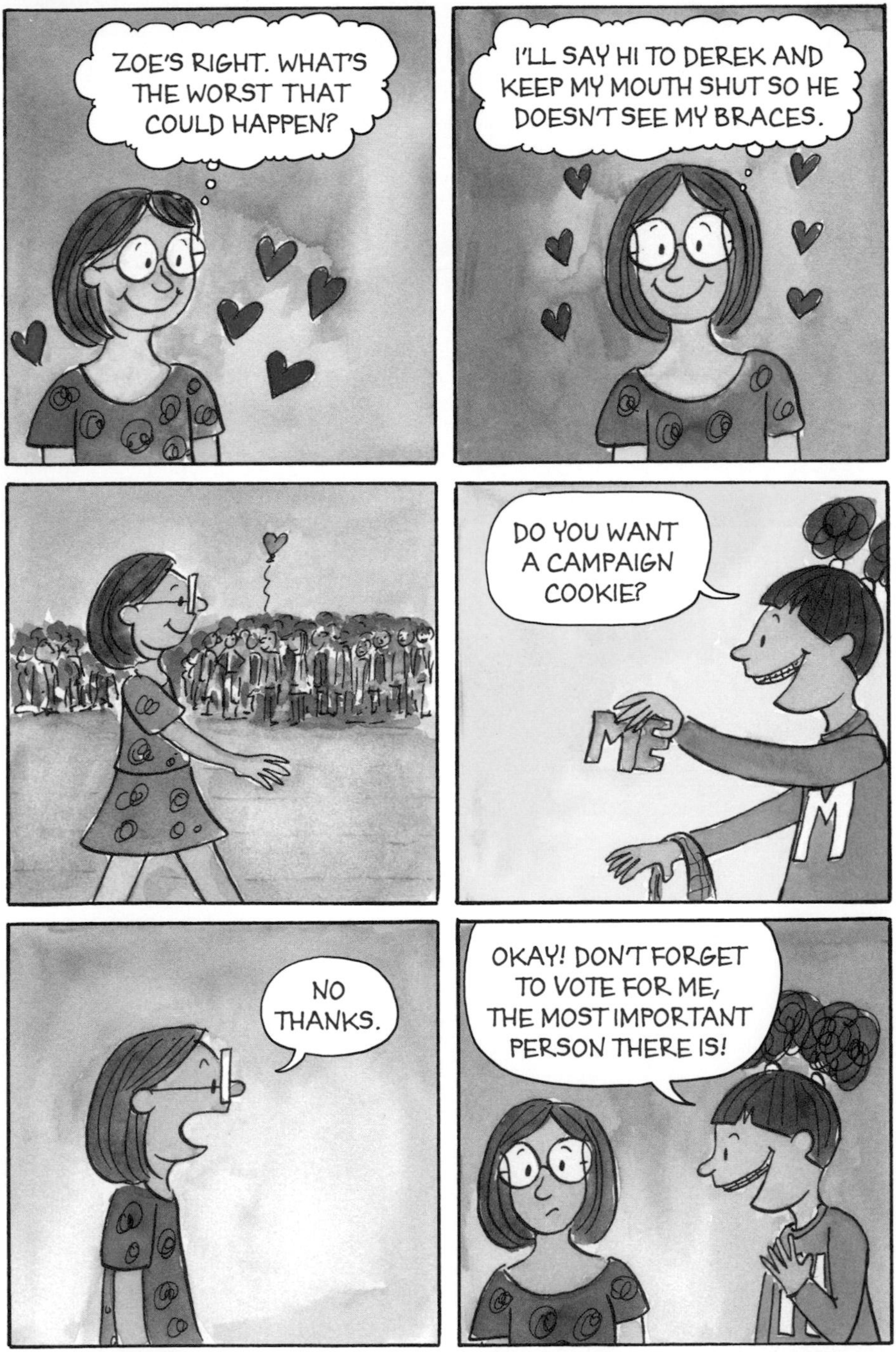
ZOE'S RIGHT. WHAT'S THE WORST THAT COULD HAPPEN?
I'LL SAY HI TO DEREK AND KEEP MY MOUTH SHUT SO HE DOESN'T SEE MY BRACES.
DO YOU WANT A CAMPAIGN COOKIE?
ME
M
NO THANKS.
OKAY! DON'T FORGET TO VOTE FOR ME, THE MOST IMPORTANT PERSON THERE IS!

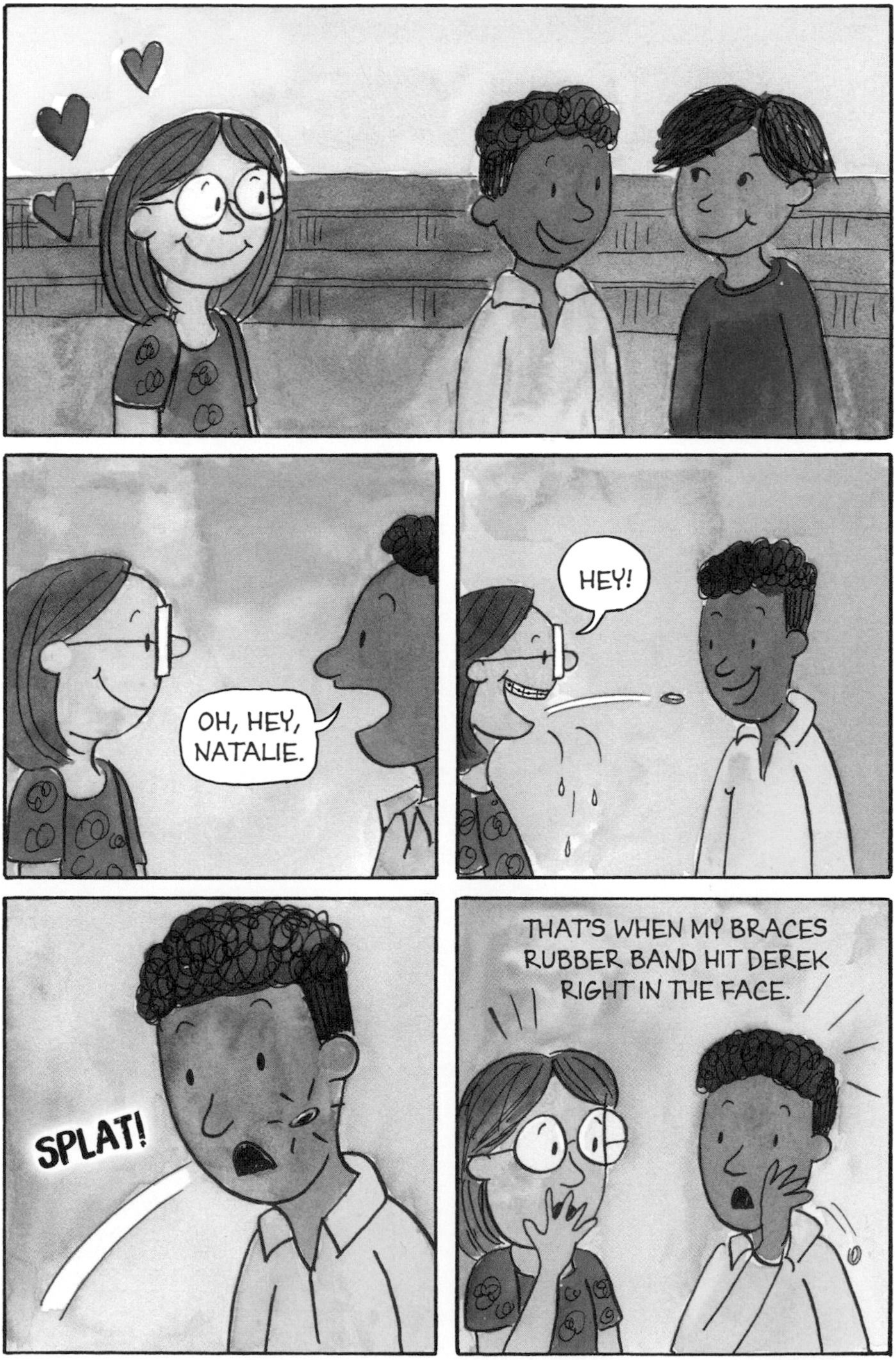
OH, HEY, NATALIE.
HEY!
SPLAT!
THAT'S WHEN MY BRACES RUBBER BAND HIT DEREK RIGHT IN THE FACE.

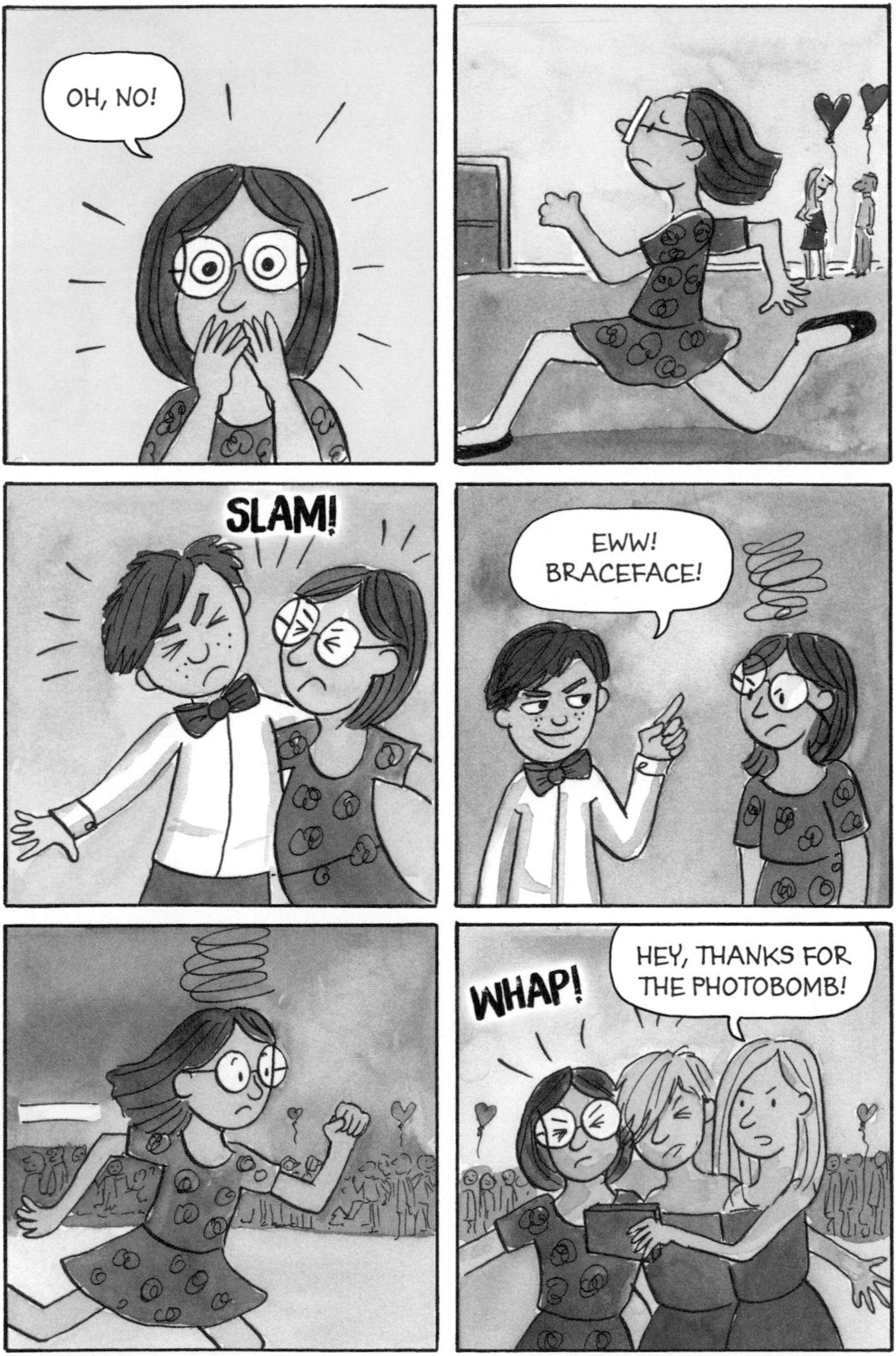
OH, NO!
SLAM!
EWW! BRACEFACE!
WHAP!
HEY, THANKS FOR THE PHOTOBOMB!

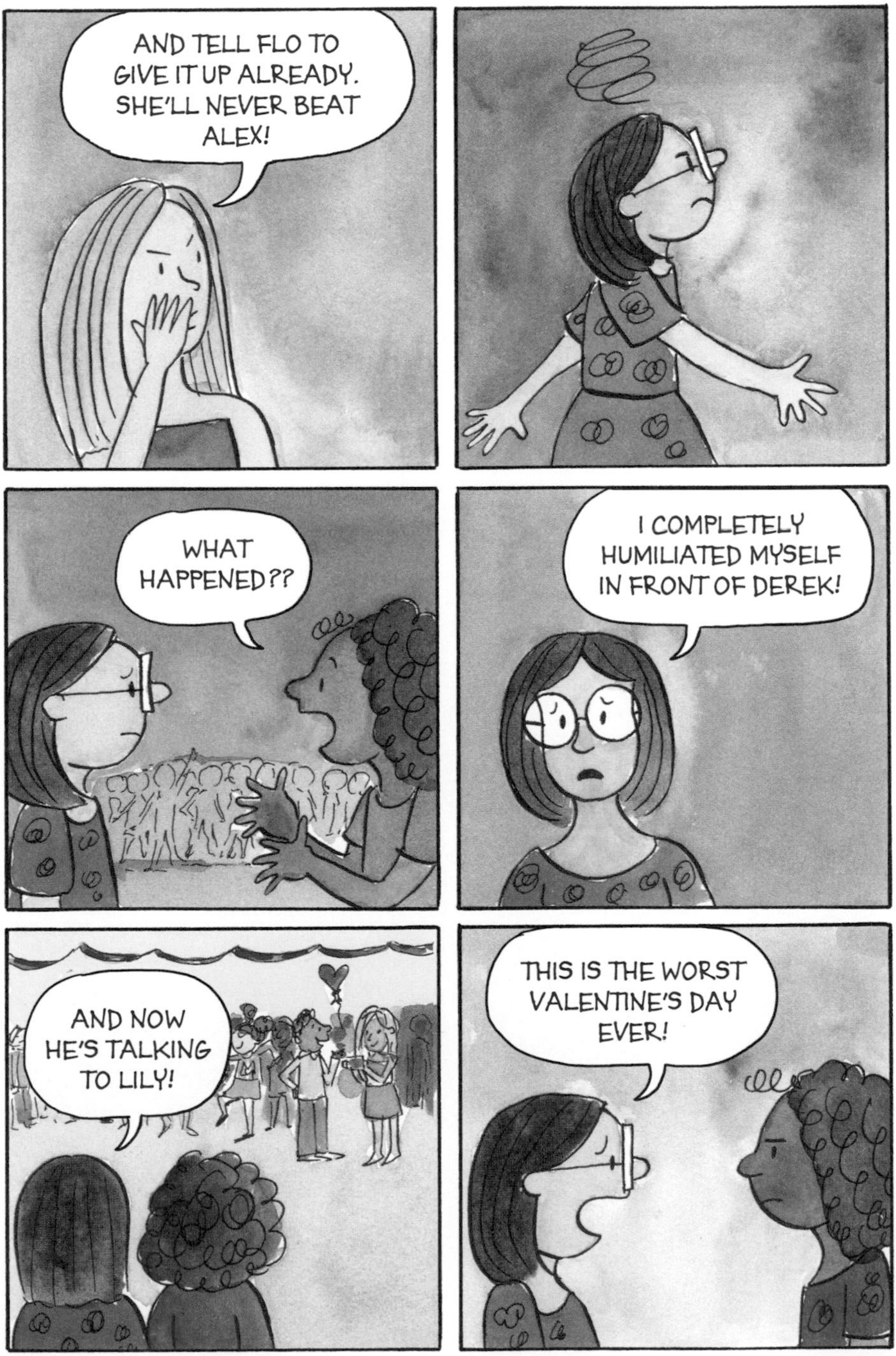
AND TELL FLO TO GIVE IT UP ALREADY. SHE'LL NEVER BEAT ALEX!
WHAT HAPPENED??
I COMPLETELY HUMILIATED MYSELF IN FRONT OF DEREK!
AND NOW HE'S TALKING TO LILY!
THIS IS THE WORST VALENTINE'S DAY EVER!

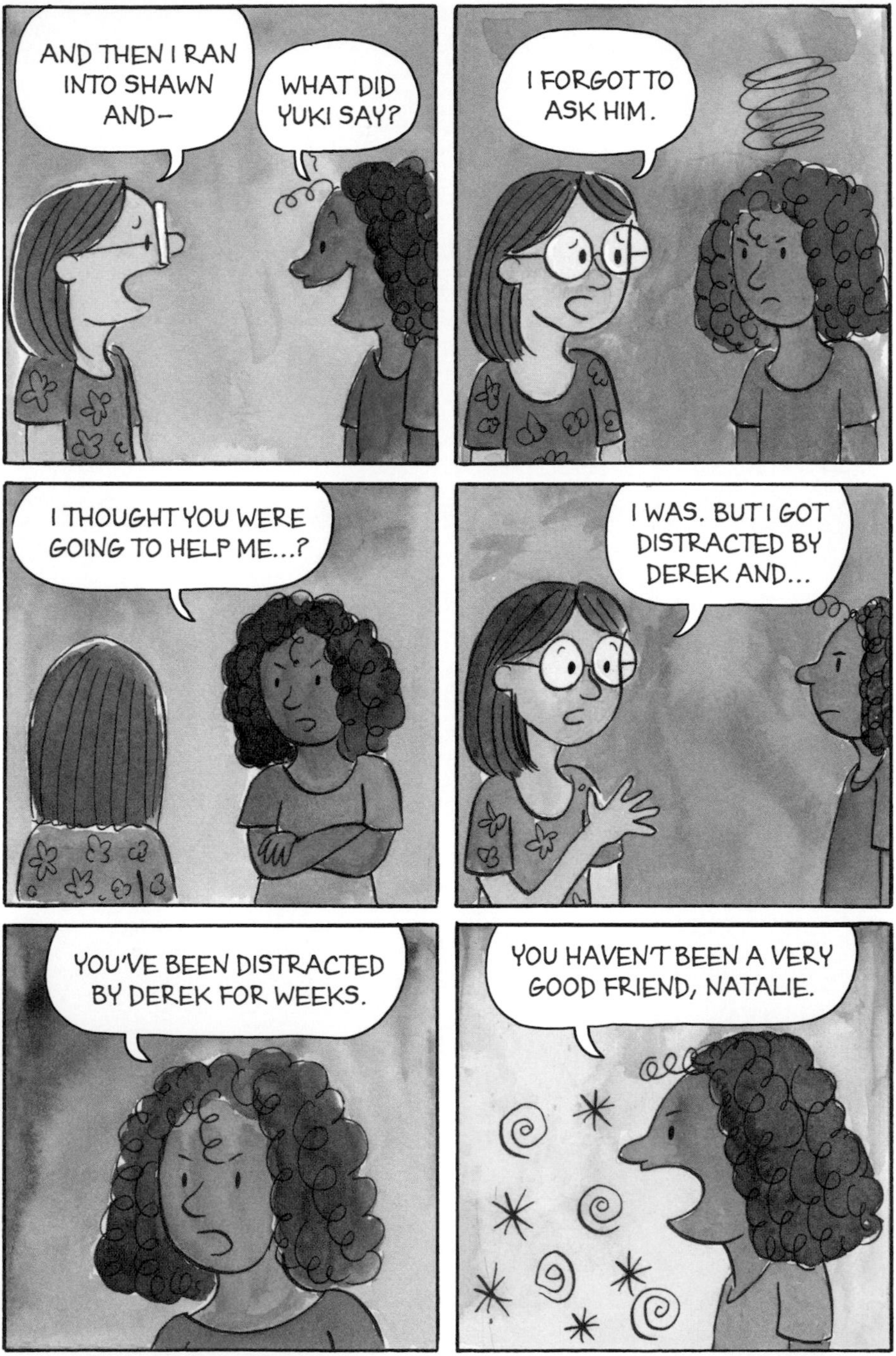
AND THEN I RAN INTO SHAWN AND–
WHAT DID YUKI SAY?
I FORGOT TO ASK HIM.
I THOUGHT YOU WERE GOING TO HELP ME...?
I WAS. BUT I GOT DISTRACTED BY DEREK AND...
YOU'VE BEEN DISTRACTED BY DEREK FOR WEEKS.
YOU HAVEN'T BEEN A VERY GOOD FRIEND, NATALIE.

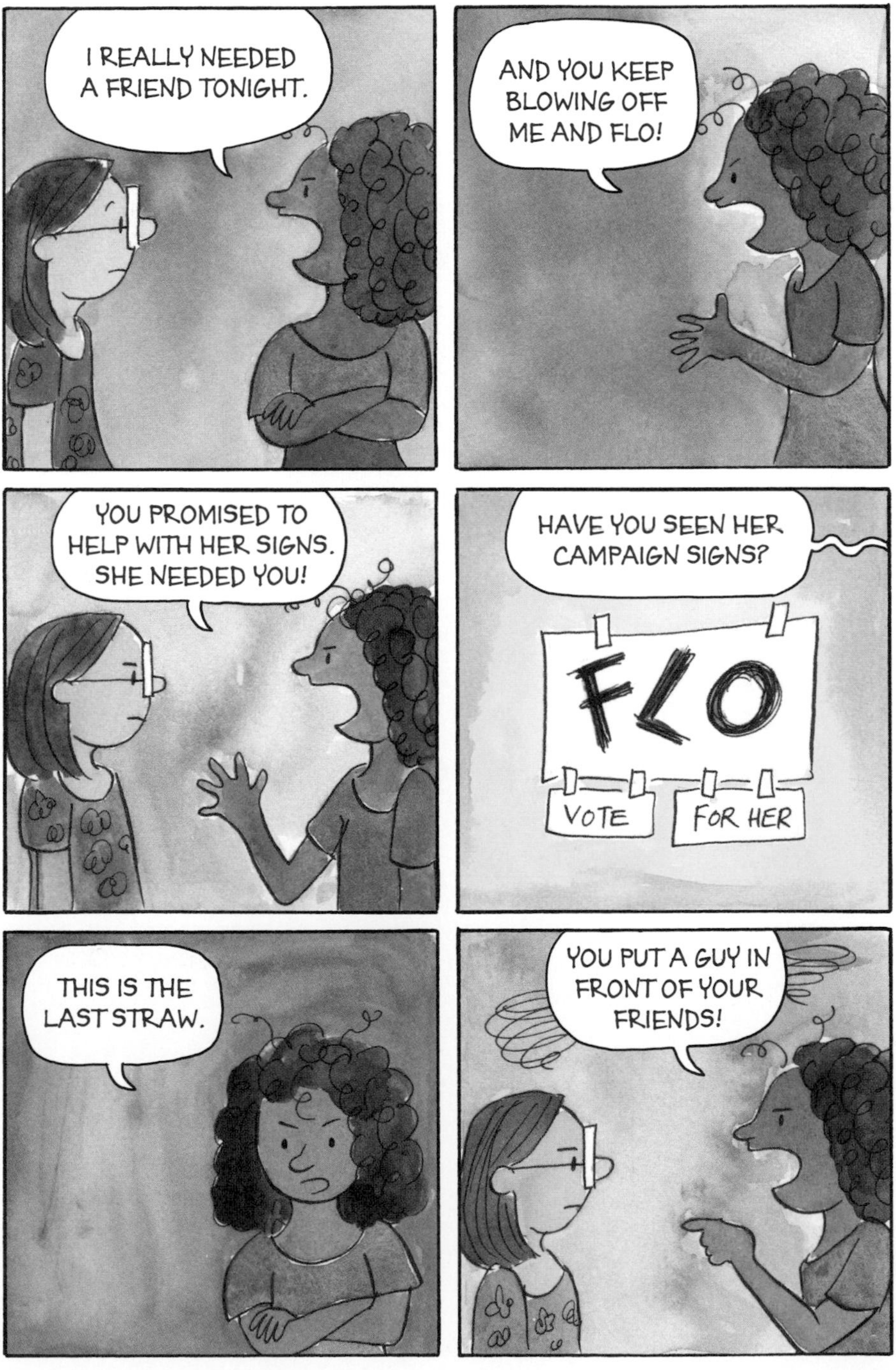
I REALLY NEEDED A FRIEND TONIGHT.
AND YOU KEEP BLOWING OFF ME AND FLO!
YOU PROMISED TO HELP WITH HER SIGNS. SHE NEEDED YOU!
HAVE YOU SEEN HER CAMPAIGN SIGNS?
FLO
VOTE
FOR HER
THIS IS THE LAST STRAW.
YOU PUT A GUY IN FRONT OF YOUR FRIENDS!

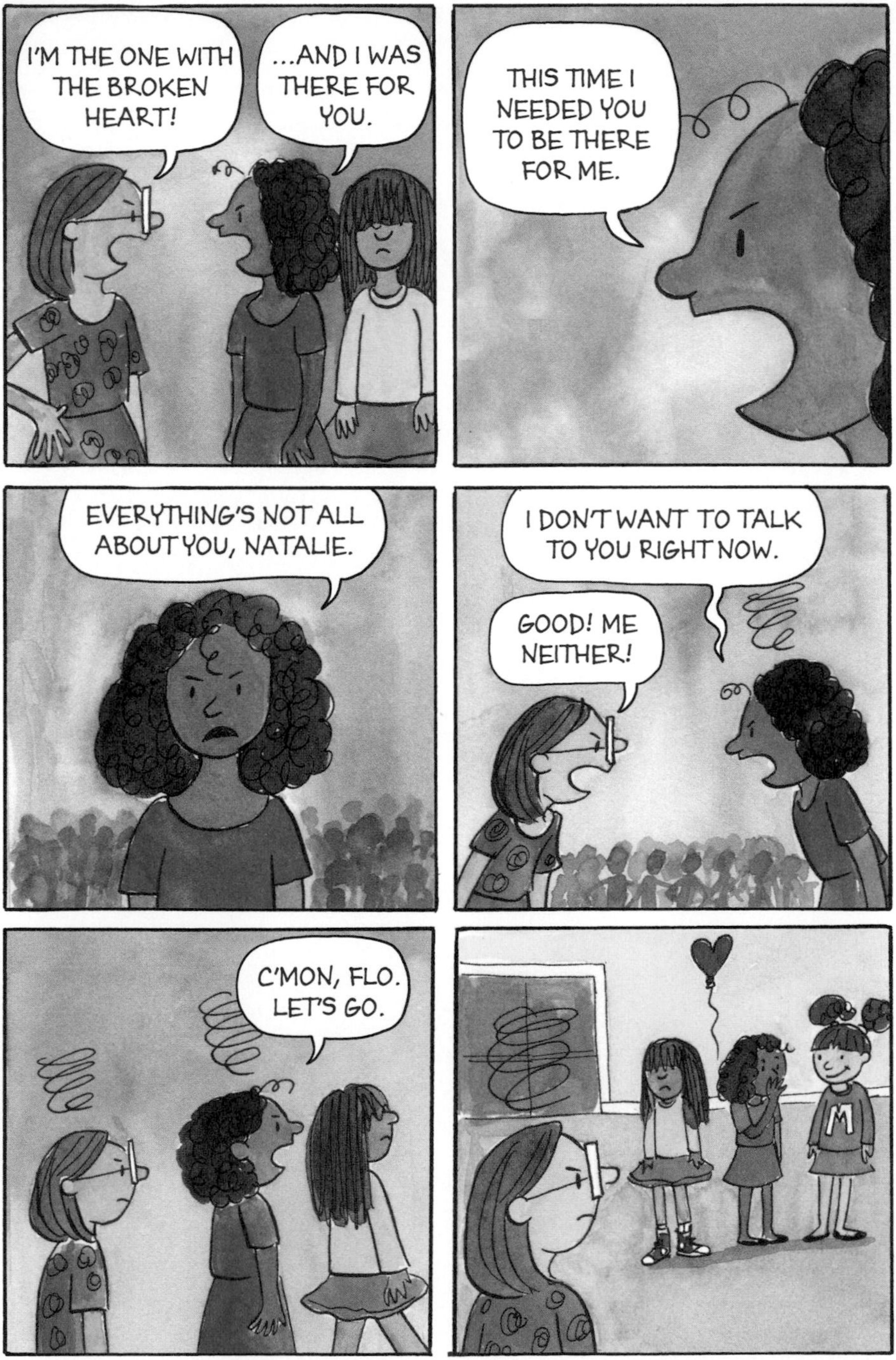
I'M THE ONE WITH THE BROKEN HEART!
...AND I WAS THERE FOR YOU.
THIS TIME I NEEDED YOU TO BE THERE FOR ME.
EVERYTHING'S NOT ALL ABOUT YOU, NATALIE.
I DON'T WANT TO TALK TO YOU RIGHT NOW.
GOOD! ME NEITHER!
C'MON, FLO. LET'S GO.
M

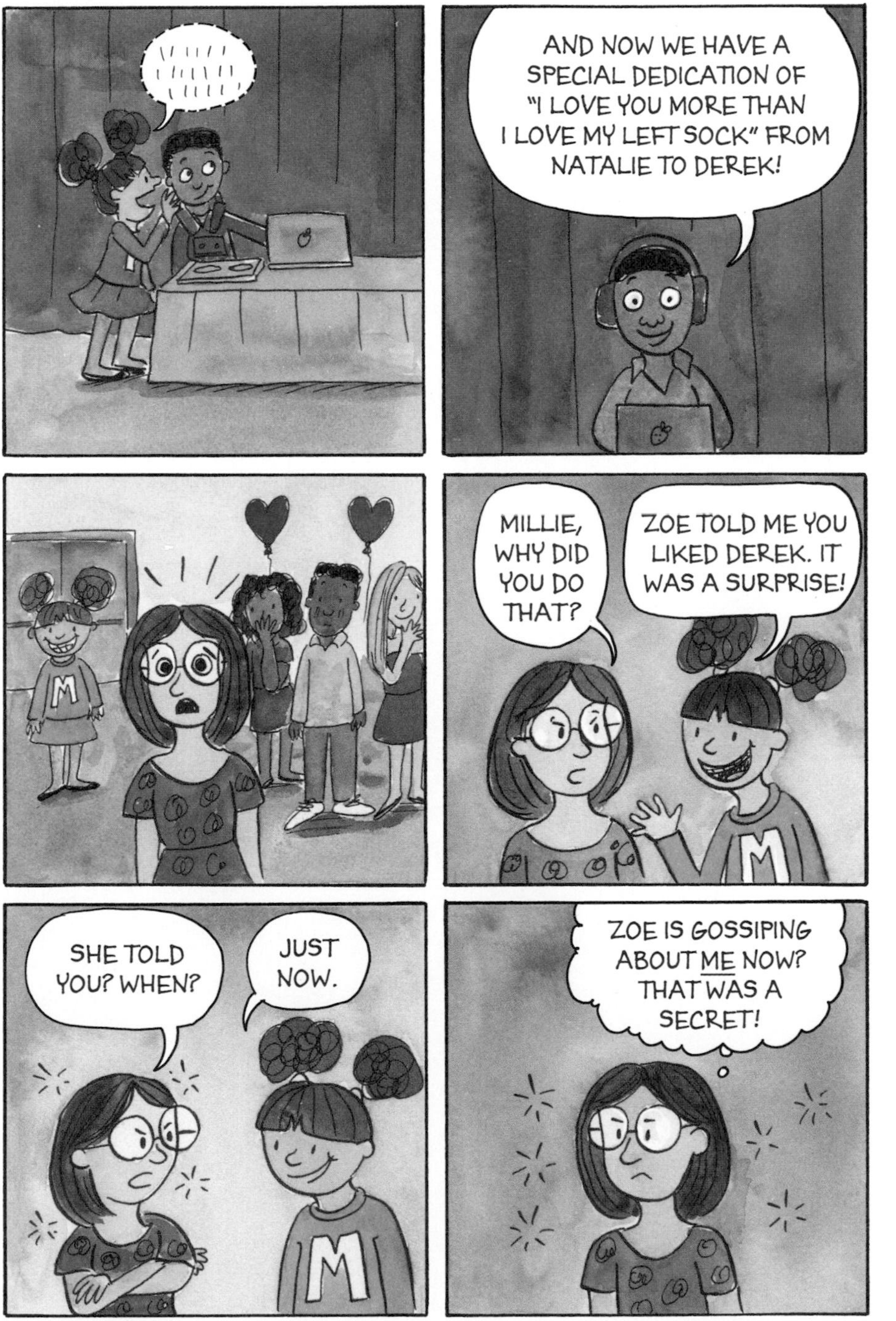
AND NOW WE HAVE A SPECIAL DEDICATION OF "I LOVE YOU MORE THAN I LOVE MY LEFT SOCK" FROM NATALIE TO DEREK!
MILLIE, WHY DID YOU DO THAT?
ZOE TOLD ME YOU LIKED DEREK. IT WAS A SURPRISE!
SHE TOLD YOU? WHEN?
JUST NOW.
ZOE IS GOSSIPING ABOUT ME NOW? THAT WAS A SECRET!
M

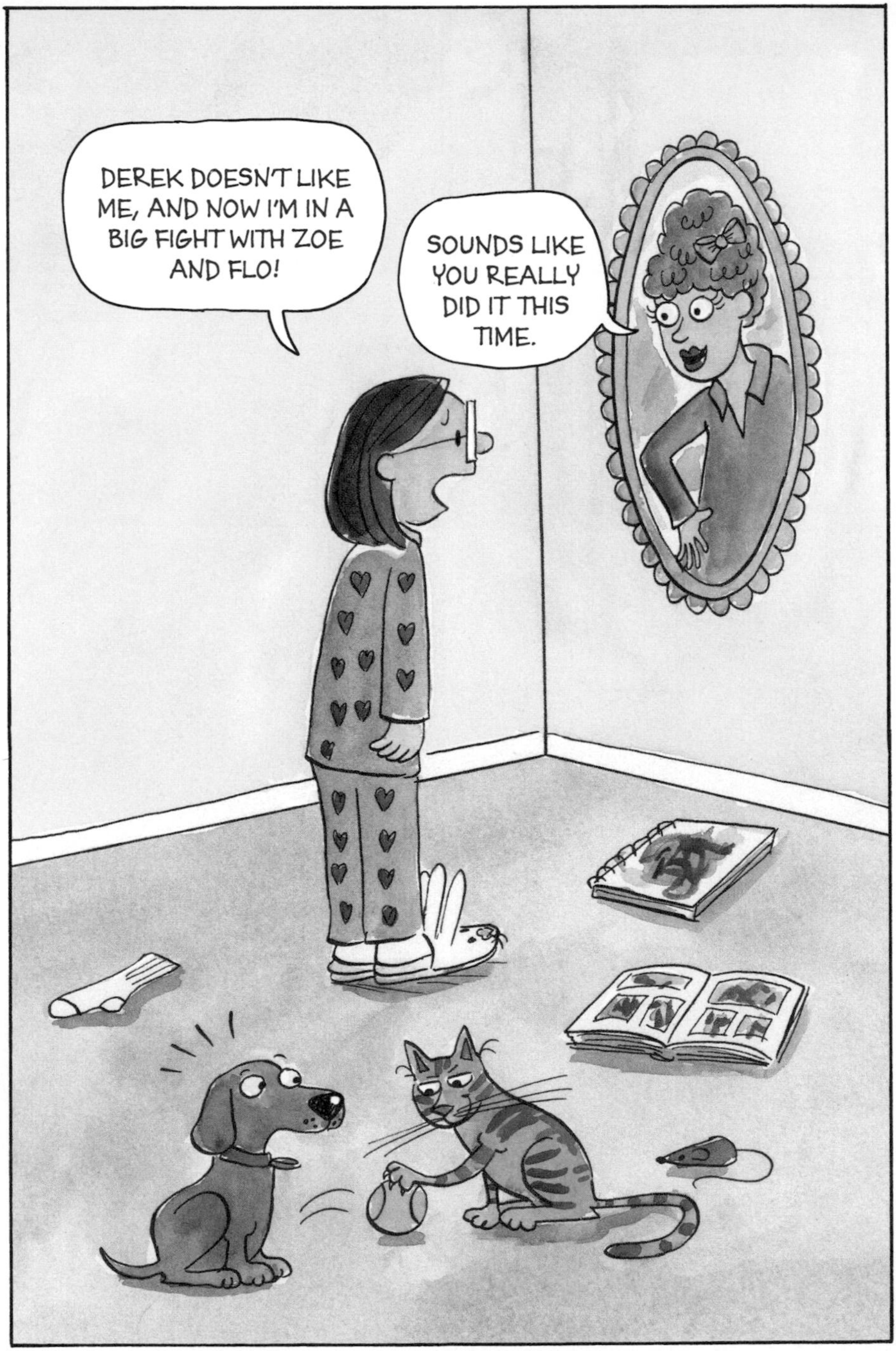
DEREK DOESN'T LIKE ME, AND NOW I'M IN A BIG FIGHT WITH ZOE AND FLO!
SOUNDS LIKE YOU REALLY DID IT THIS TIME.

CHAPTER 9
SOUR GRAPES
(AND EVERYTHING ELSE)

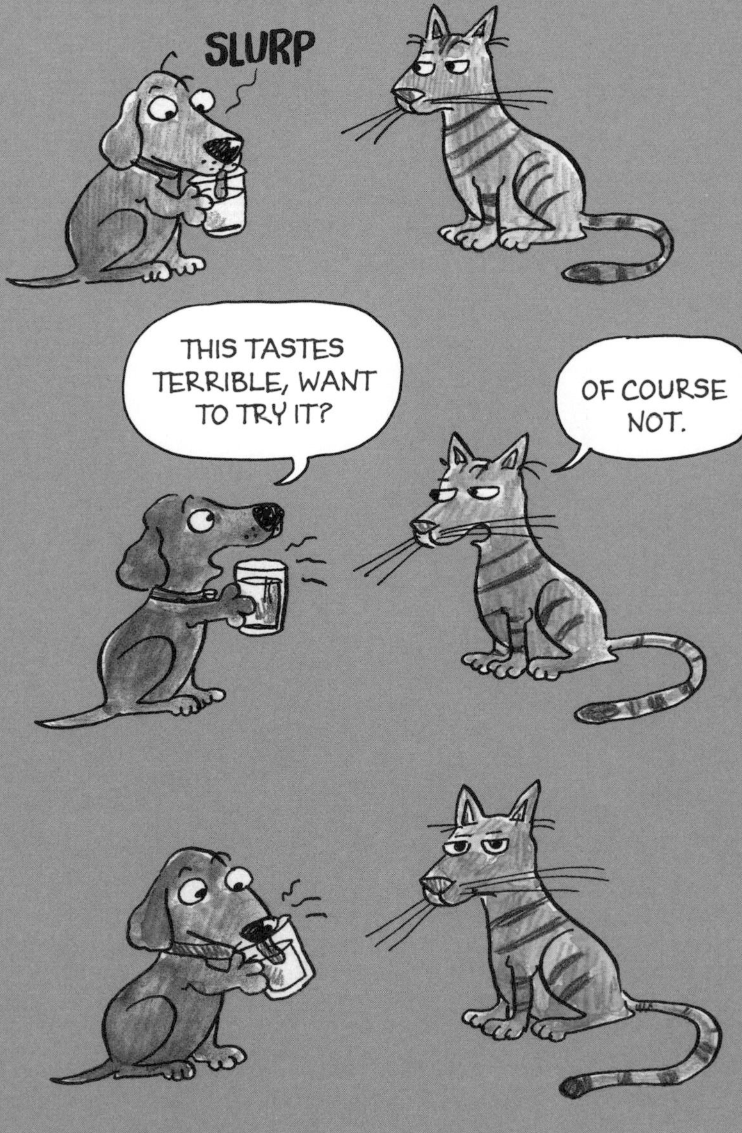

SLURP
THIS TASTES TERRIBLE, WANT TO TRY IT?
OF COURSE NOT.

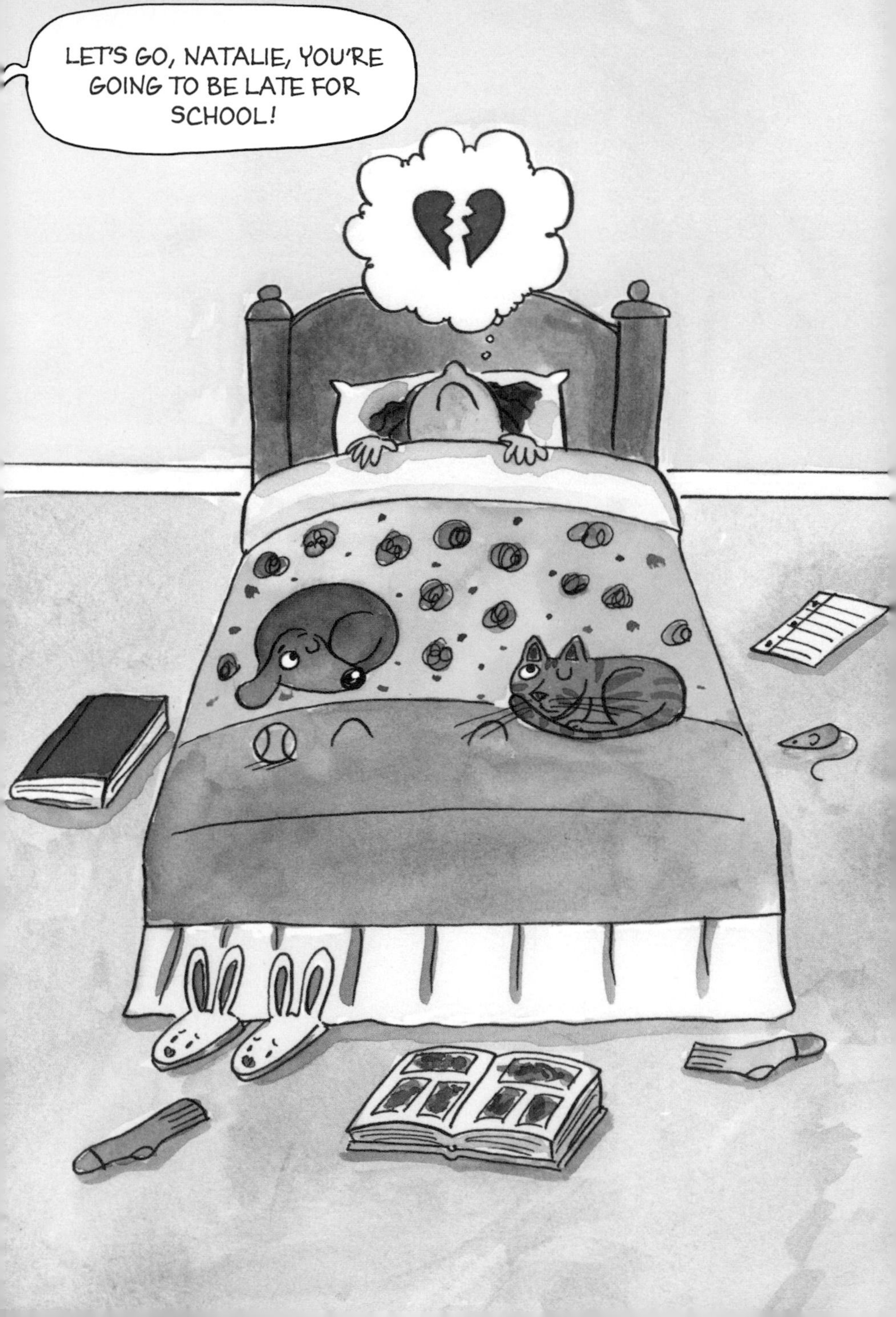
LET'S GO, NATALIE, YOU'RE GOING TO BE LATE FOR SCHOOL!

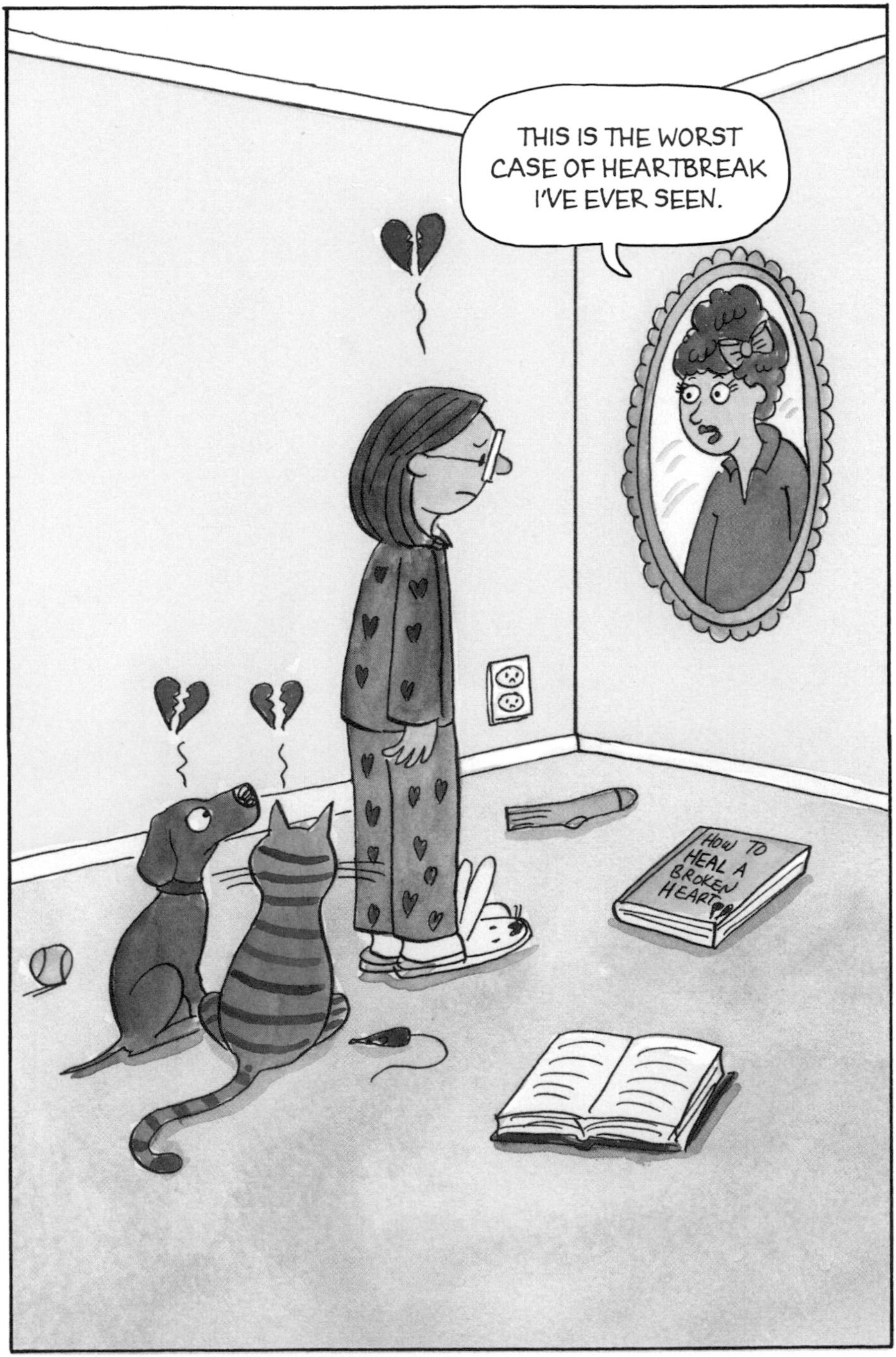
THIS IS THE WORST CASE OF HEARTBREAK I'VE EVER SEEN.
HOW TO HEAL A BROKEN HEART

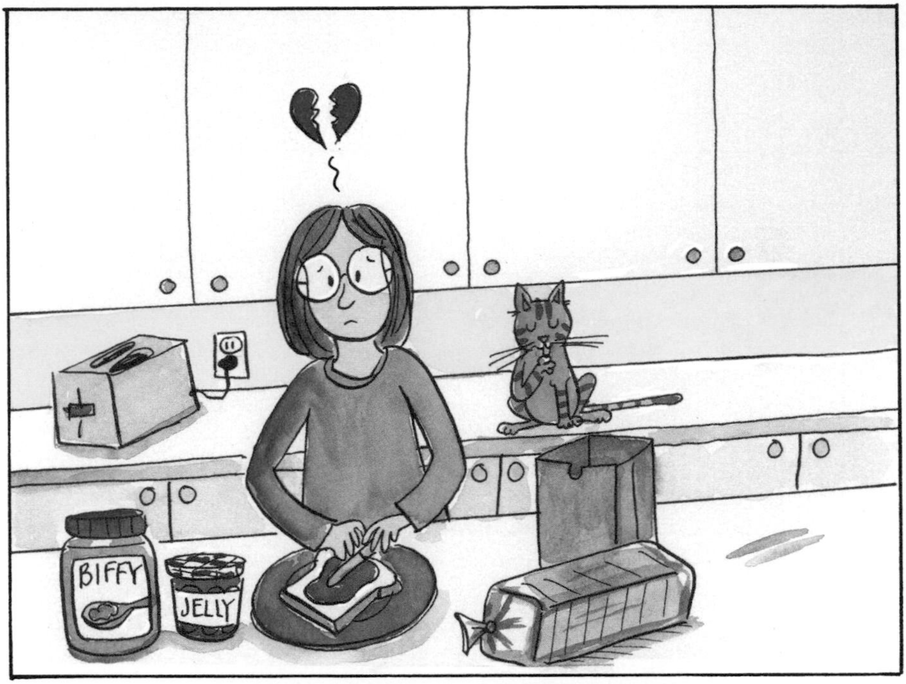
BIFFY
JELLY

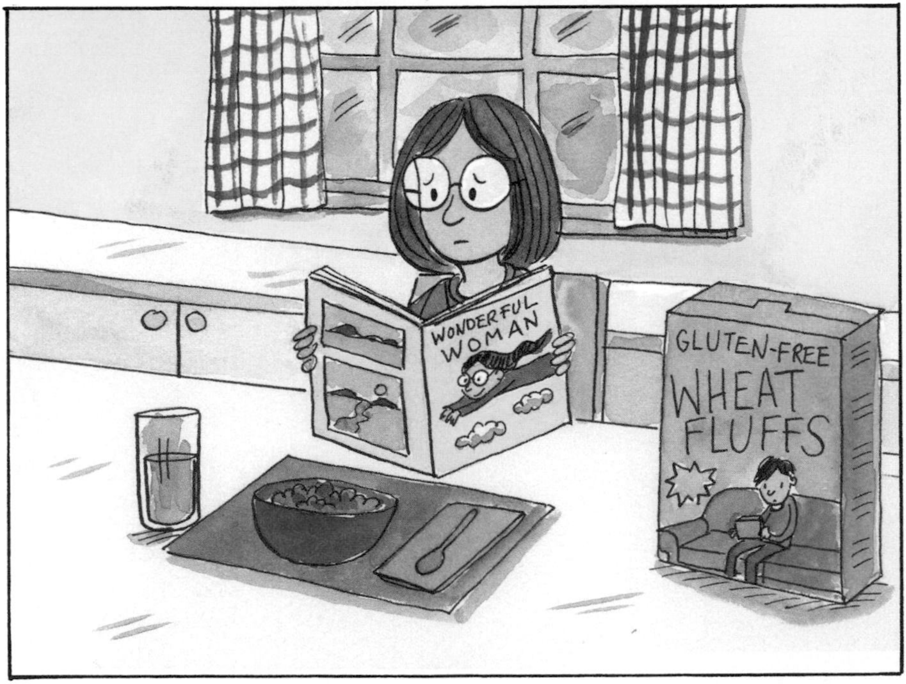
WONDERFUL WOMAN
GLUTEN-FREE
WHEAT FLUFFS

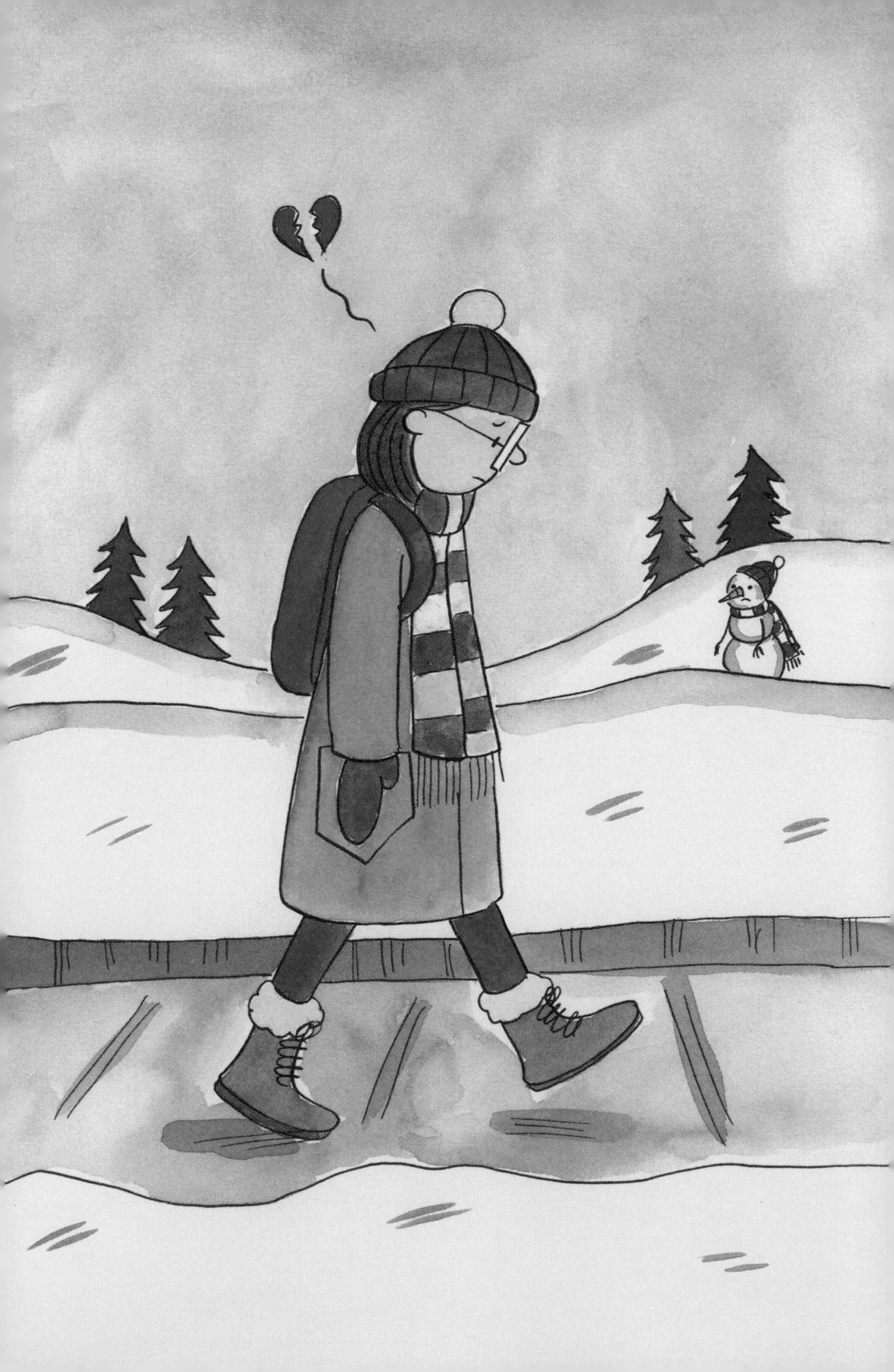

DEREK DIDN'T REALLY WANT TO TALK TO ME AFTER THE SONG DEDICATION INCIDENT.

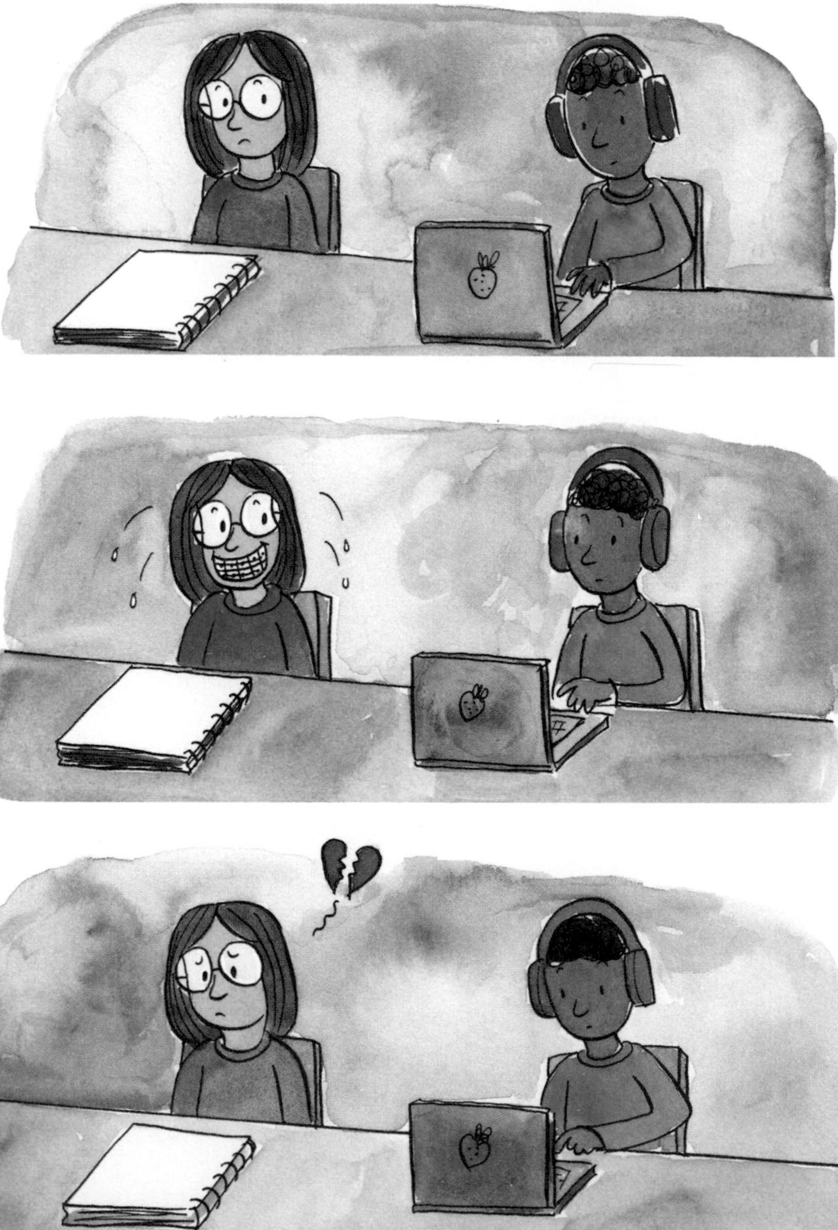

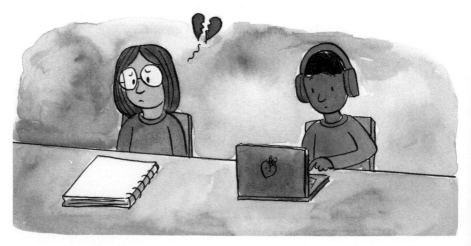

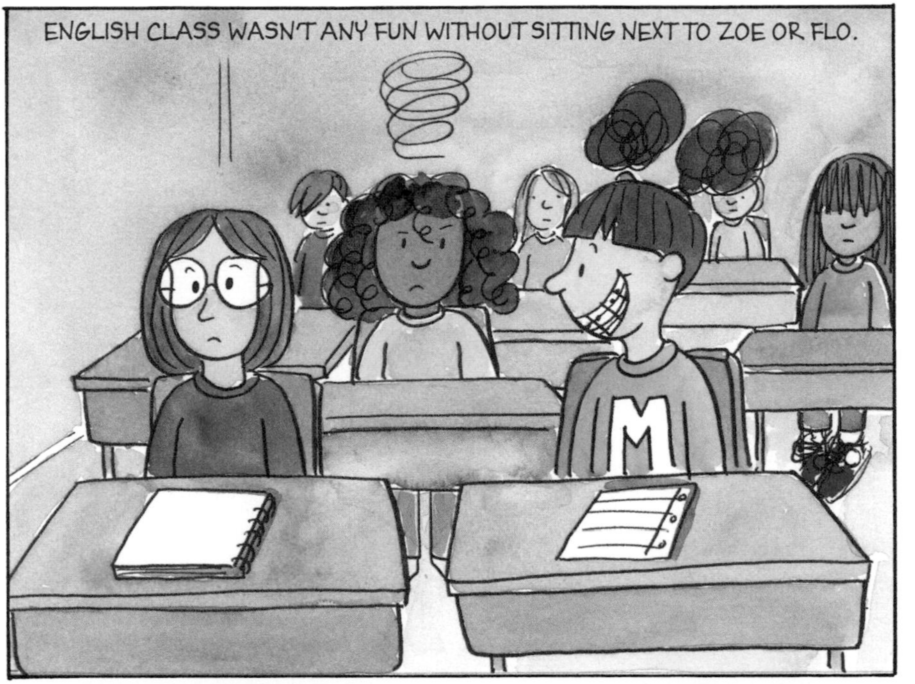
ENGLISH CLASS WASN'T ANY FUN WITHOUT SITTING NEXT TO ZOE OR FLO.

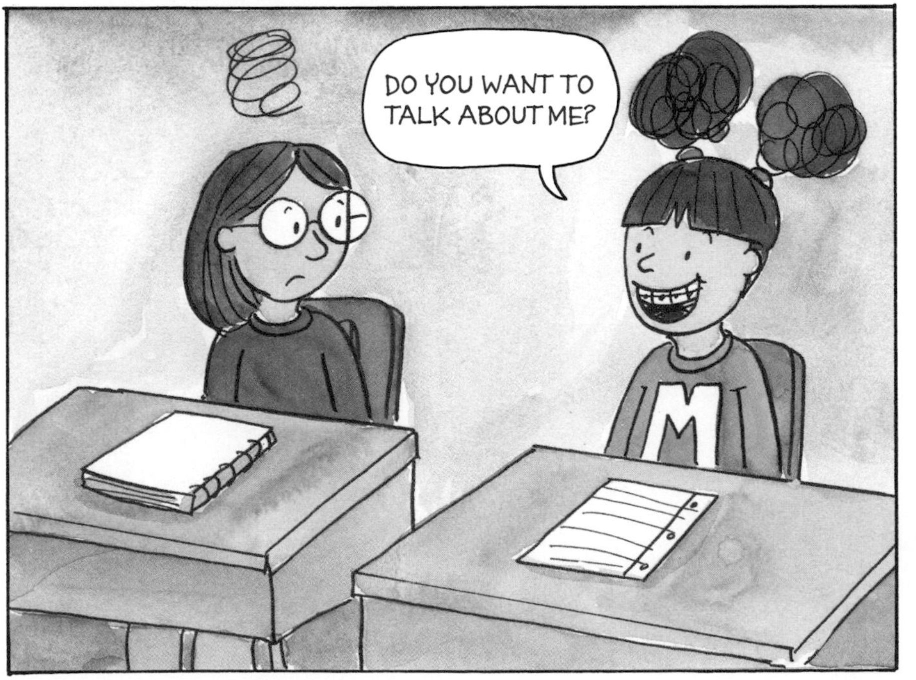
DO YOU WANT TO TALK ABOUT ME?

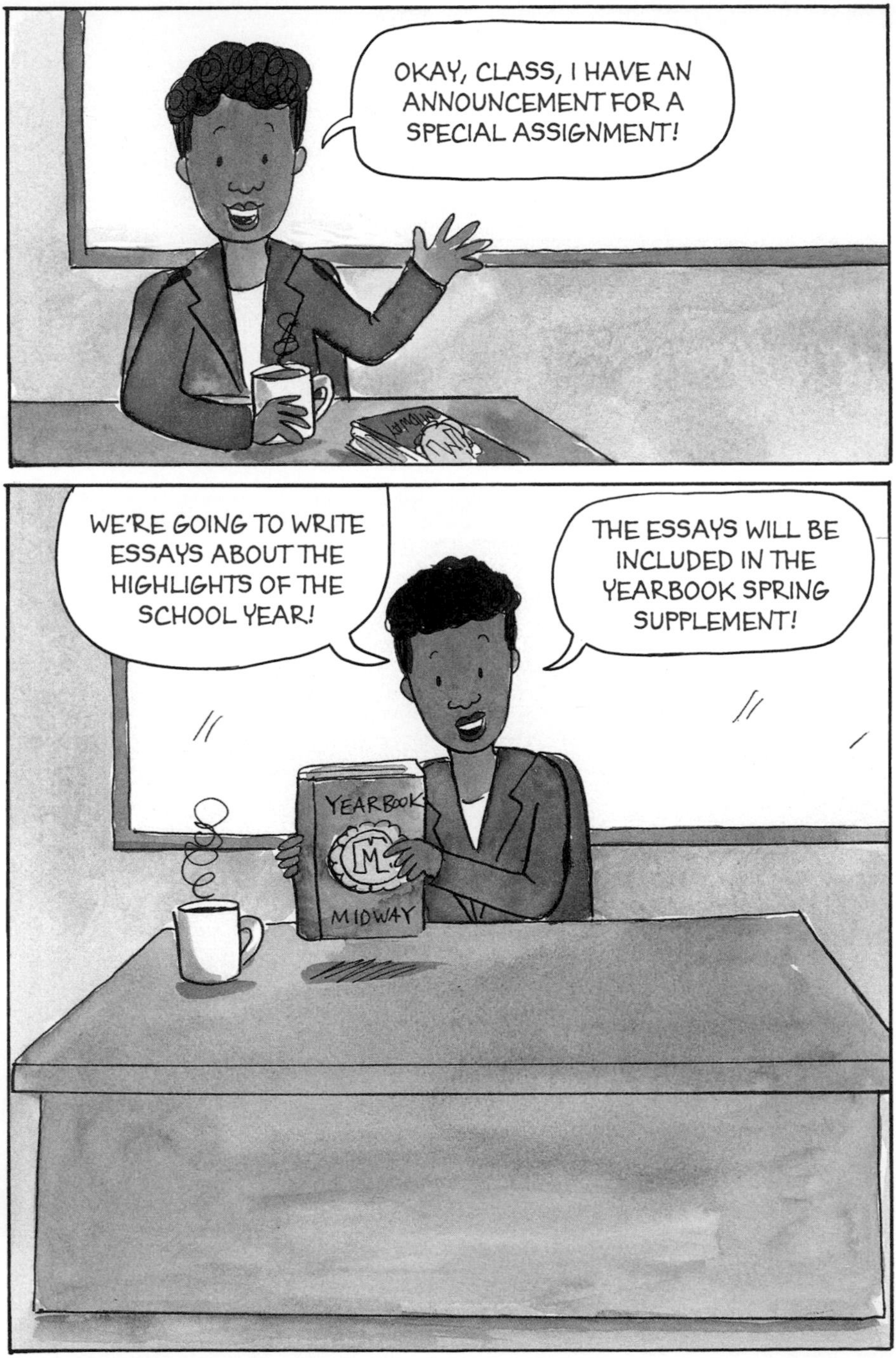
OKAY, CLASS, I HAVE AN ANNOUNCEMENT FOR A SPECIAL ASSIGNMENT!
WE'RE GOING TO WRITE ESSAYS ABOUT THE HIGHLIGHTS OF THE SCHOOL YEAR!
THE ESSAYS WILL BE INCLUDED IN THE YEARBOOK SPRING SUPPLEMENT!
YEARBOOK
M
MIDWAY

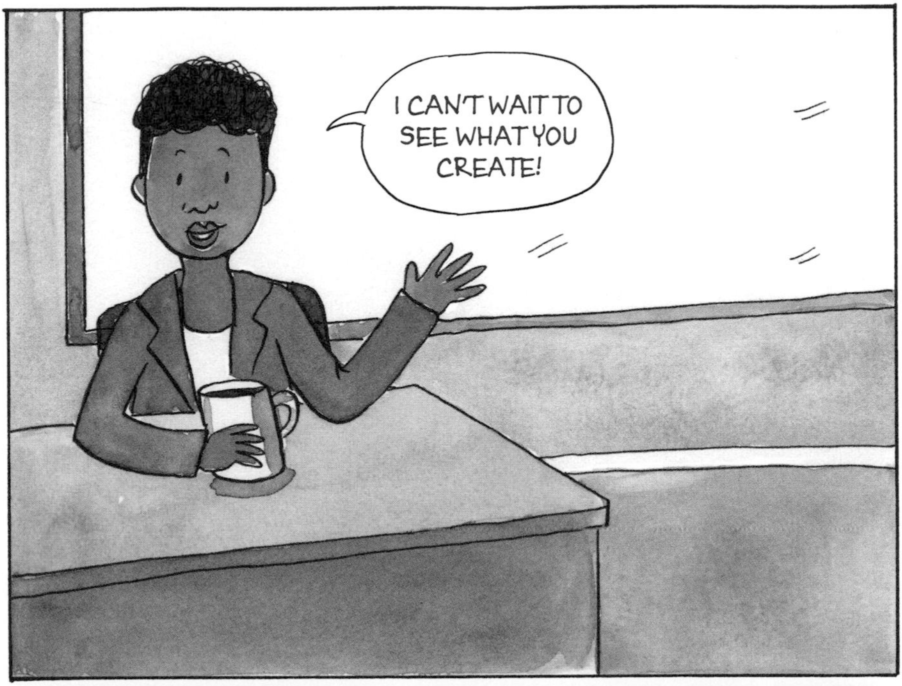
I CAN'T WAIT TO SEE WHAT YOU CREATE!

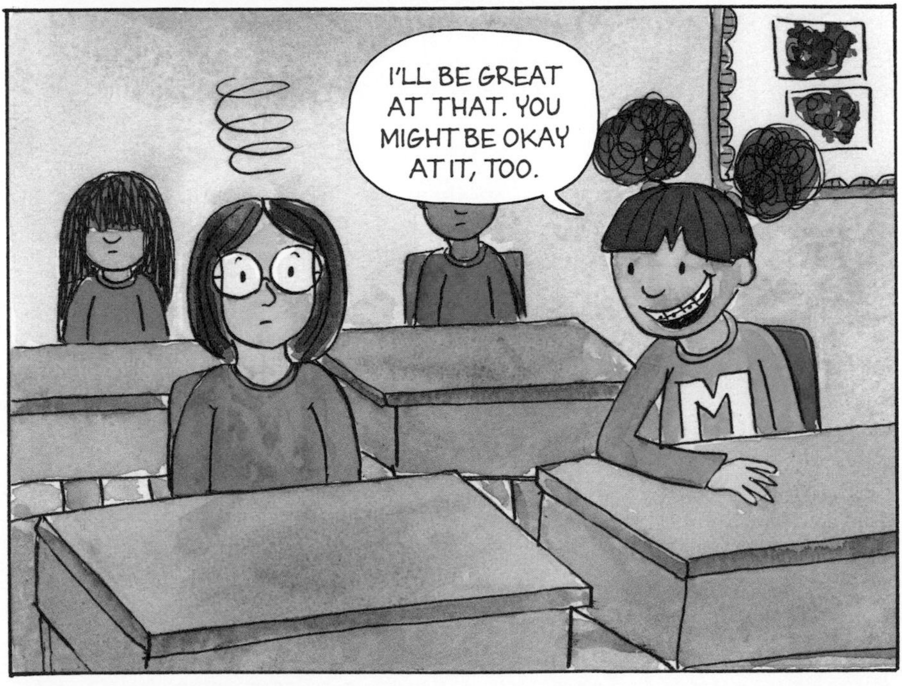
I'LL BE GREAT AT THAT. YOU MIGHT BE OKAY AT IT, TOO.

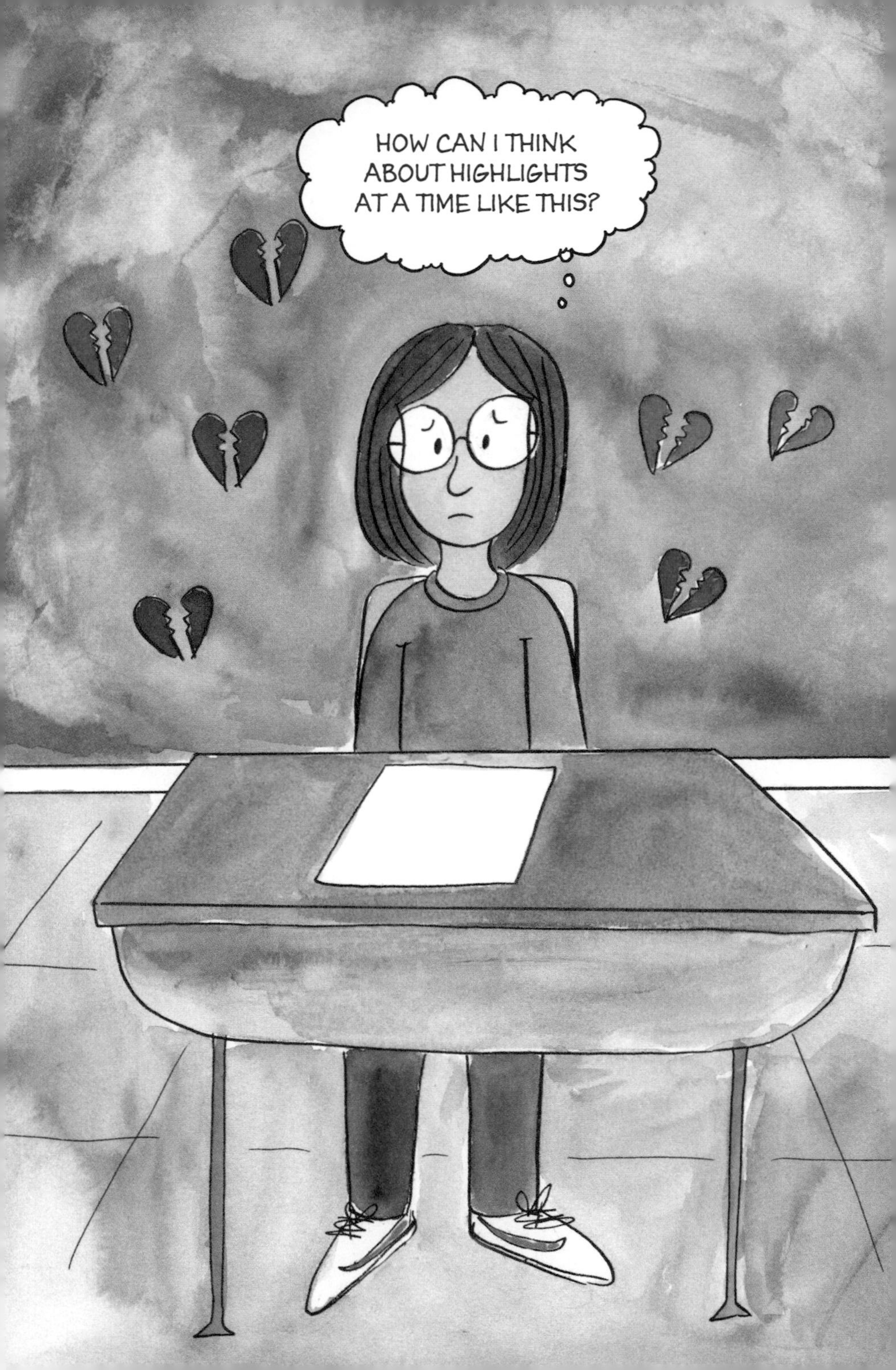
HOW CAN I THINK ABOUT HIGHLIGHTS AT A TIME LIKE THIS?

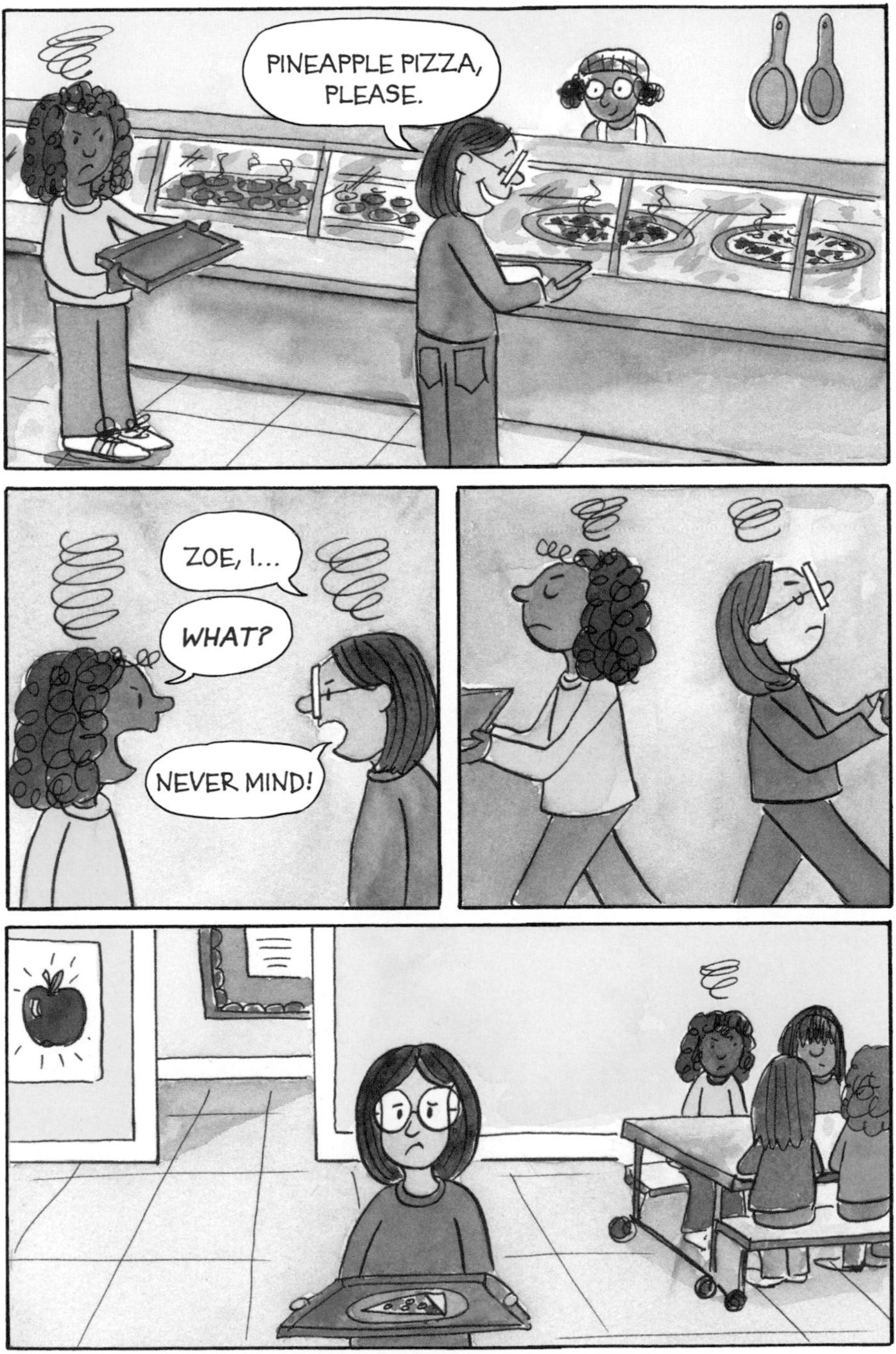
PINEAPPLE PIZZA, PLEASE.
ZOE, I...
WHAT?
NEVER MIND!

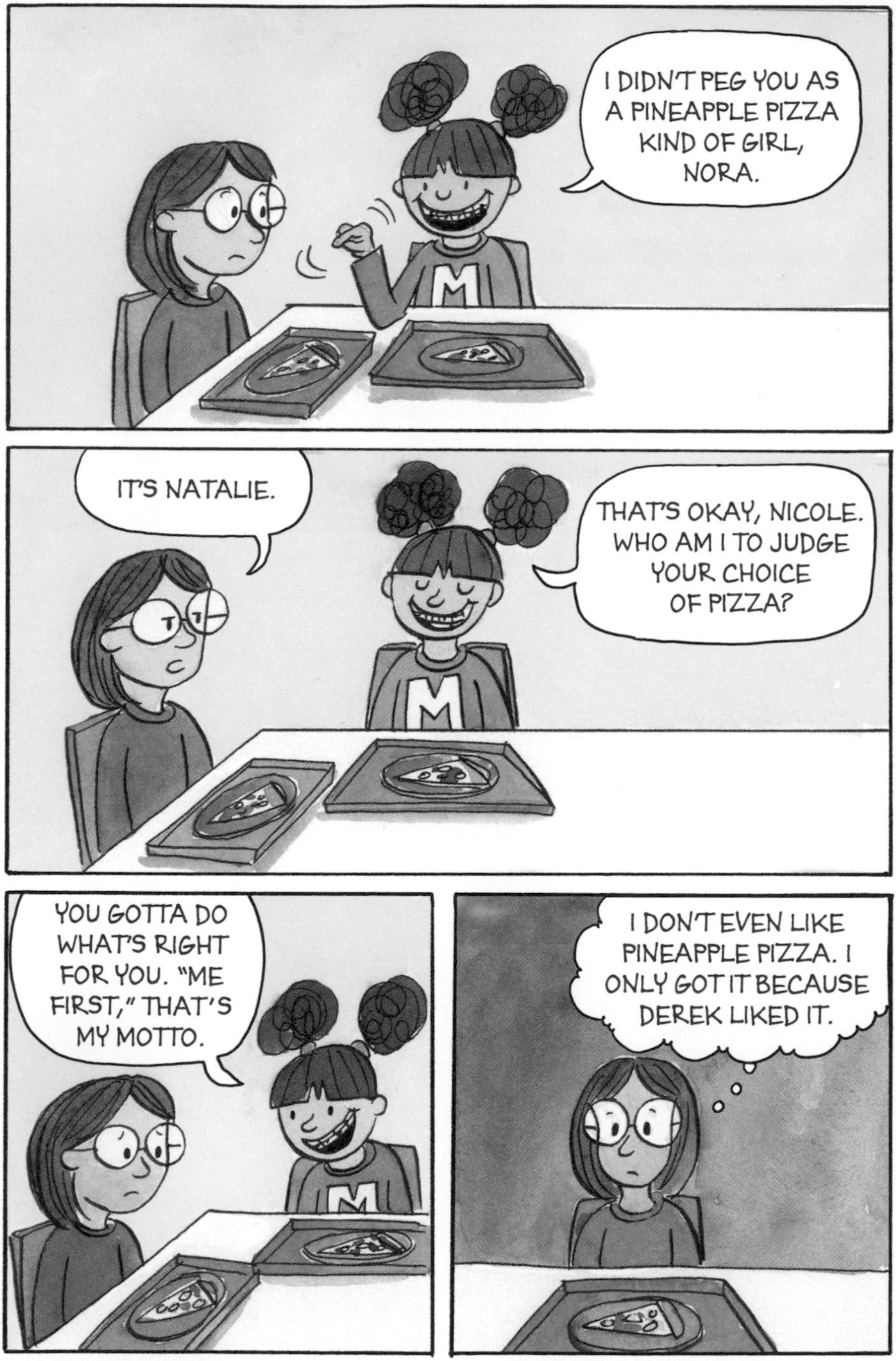
I DIDN'T PEG YOU AS A PINEAPPLE PIZZA KIND OF GIRL, NORA.
IT'S NATALIE.
THAT'S OKAY, NICOLE. WHO AM I TO JUDGE YOUR CHOICE OF PIZZA?
YOU GOTTA DO WHAT'S RIGHT FOR YOU. "ME FIRST," THAT'S MY MOTTO.
I DON'T EVEN LIKE PINEAPPLE PIZZA. I ONLY GOT IT BECAUSE DEREK LIKED IT.

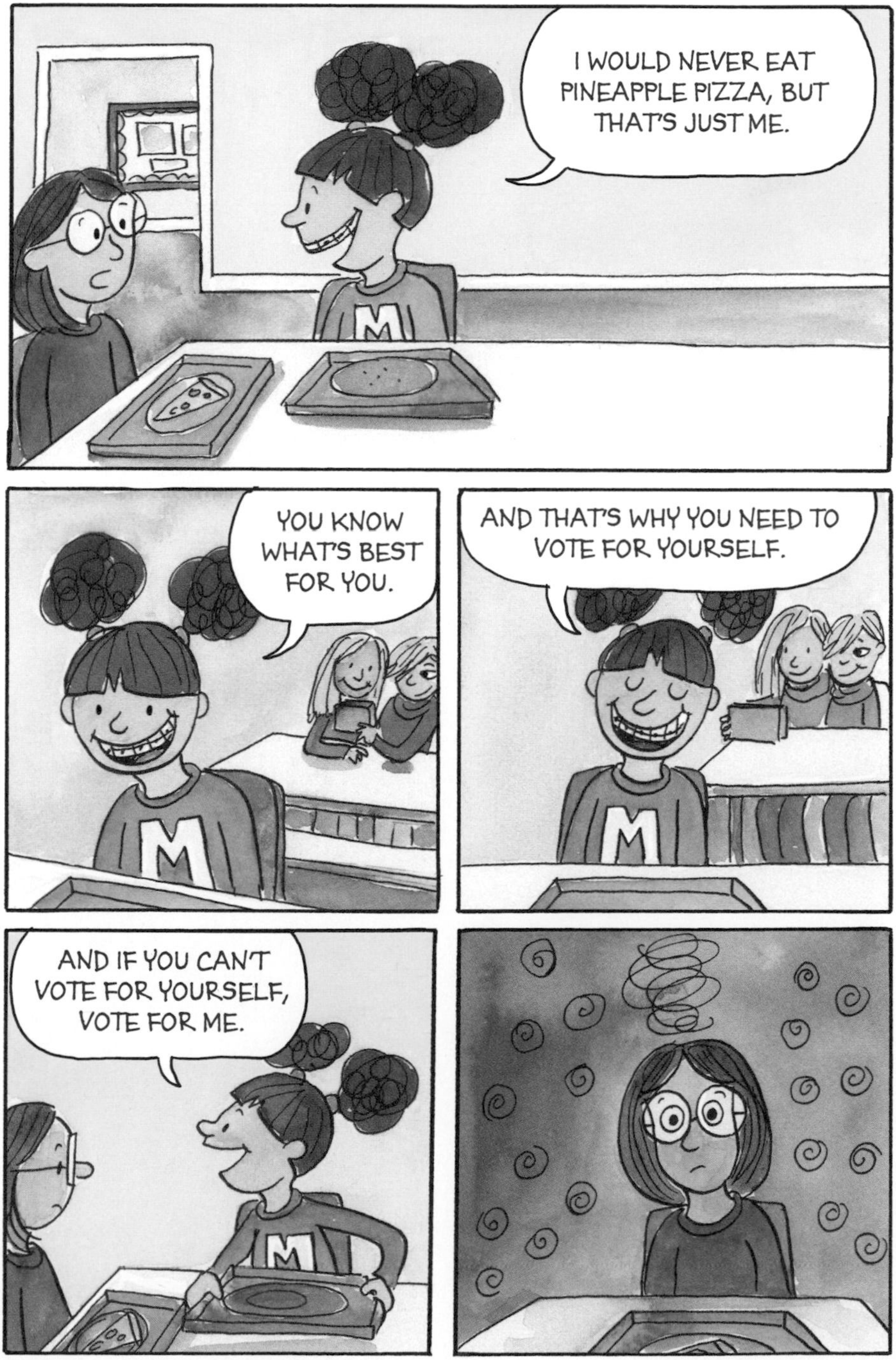
I WOULD NEVER EAT PINEAPPLE PIZZA, BUT THAT'S JUST ME.
YOU KNOW WHAT'S BEST FOR YOU.
AND THAT'S WHY YOU NEED TO VOTE FOR YOURSELF.
AND IF YOU CAN'T VOTE FOR YOURSELF, VOTE FOR ME.

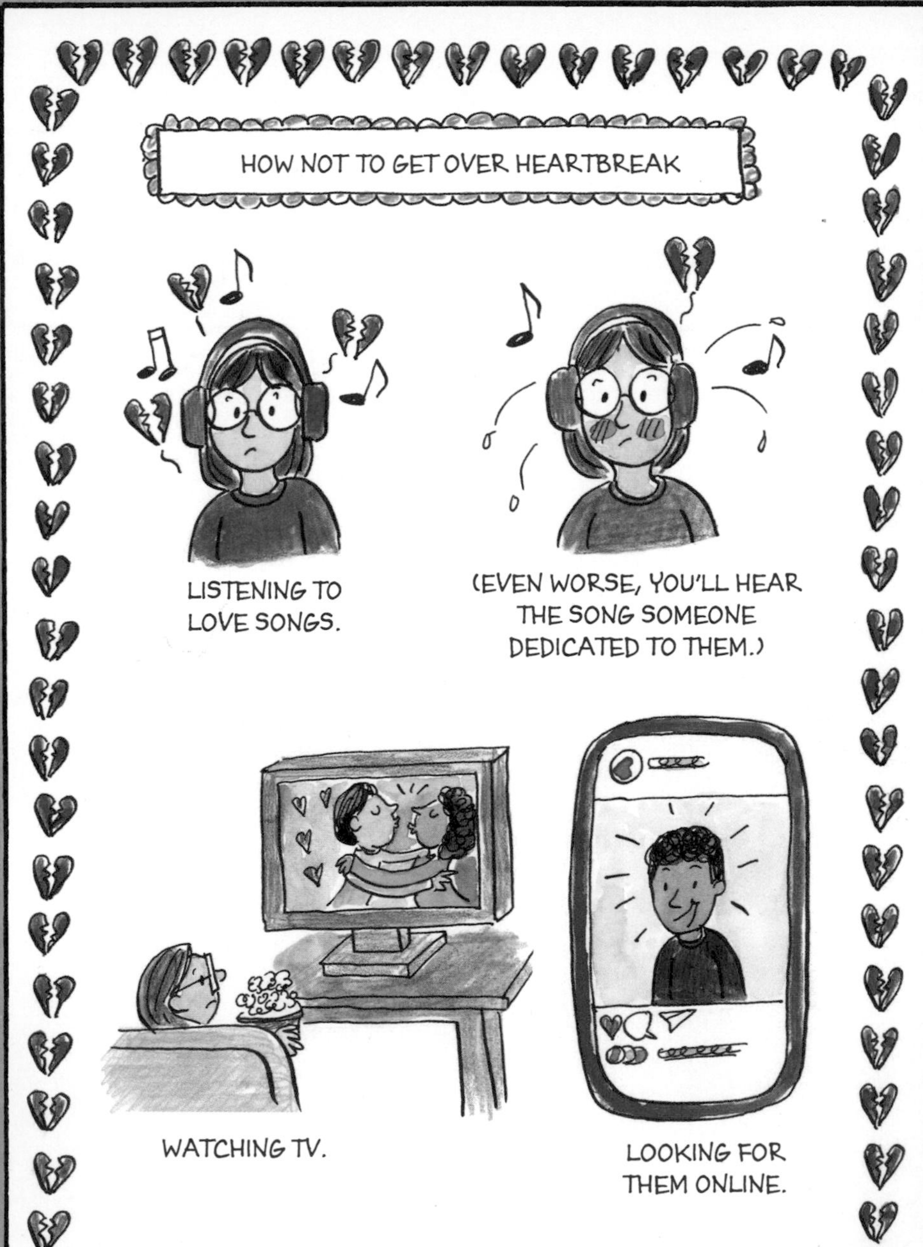
HOW NOT TO GET OVER HEARTBREAK
LISTENING TO LOVE SONGS.
(EVEN WORSE, YOU'LL HEAR THE SONG SOMEONE DEDICATED TO THEM.)
WATCHING TV.
LOOKING FOR THEM ONLINE.

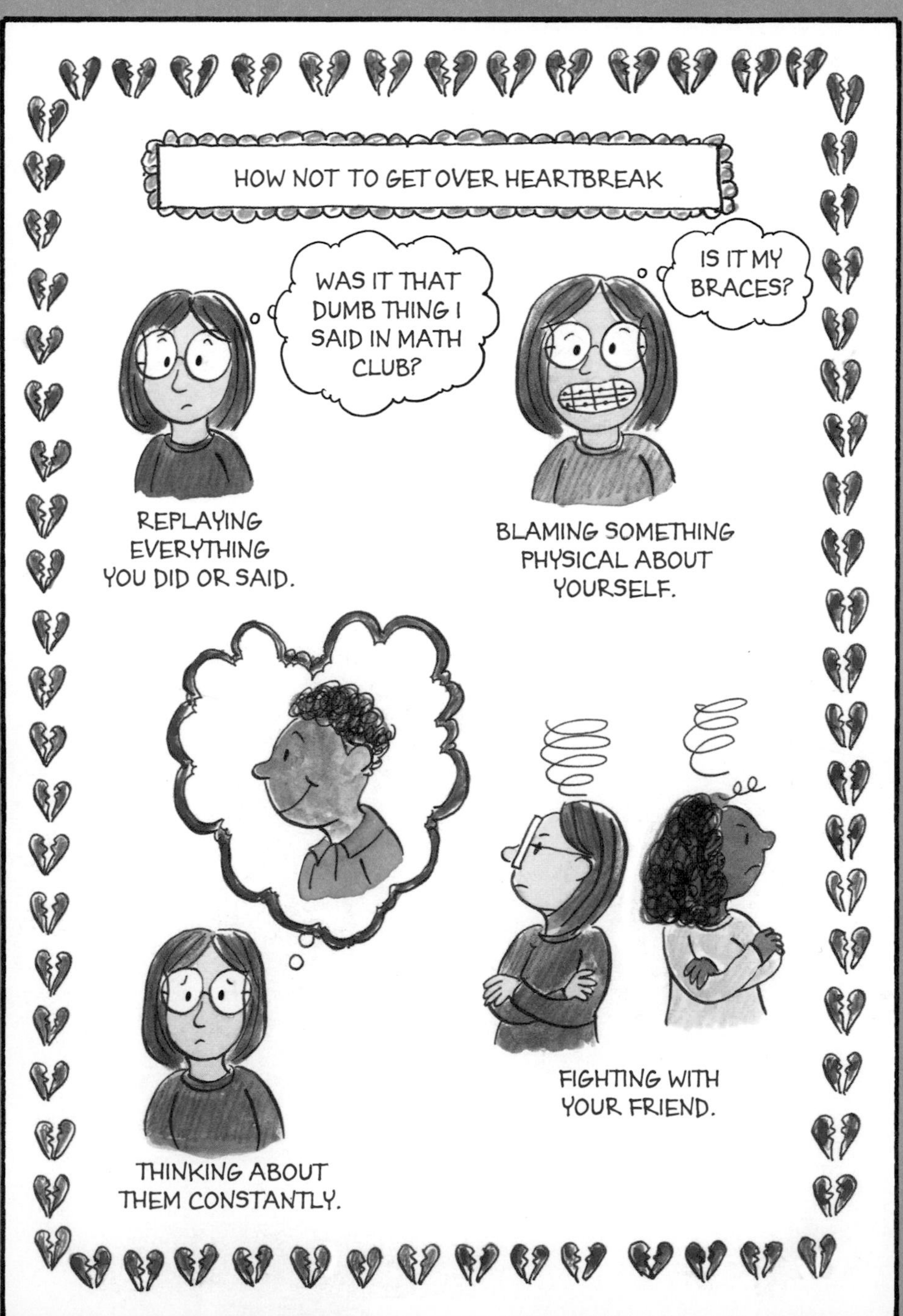
HOW NOT TO GET OVER HEARTBREAK
WAS IT THAT DUMB THING I SAID IN MATH CLUB?
REPLAYING EVERYTHING YOU DID OR SAID.
IS IT MY BRACES?
BLAMING SOMETHING PHYSICAL ABOUT YOURSELF.
THINKING ABOUT THEM CONSTANTLY.
FIGHTING WITH YOUR FRIEND.

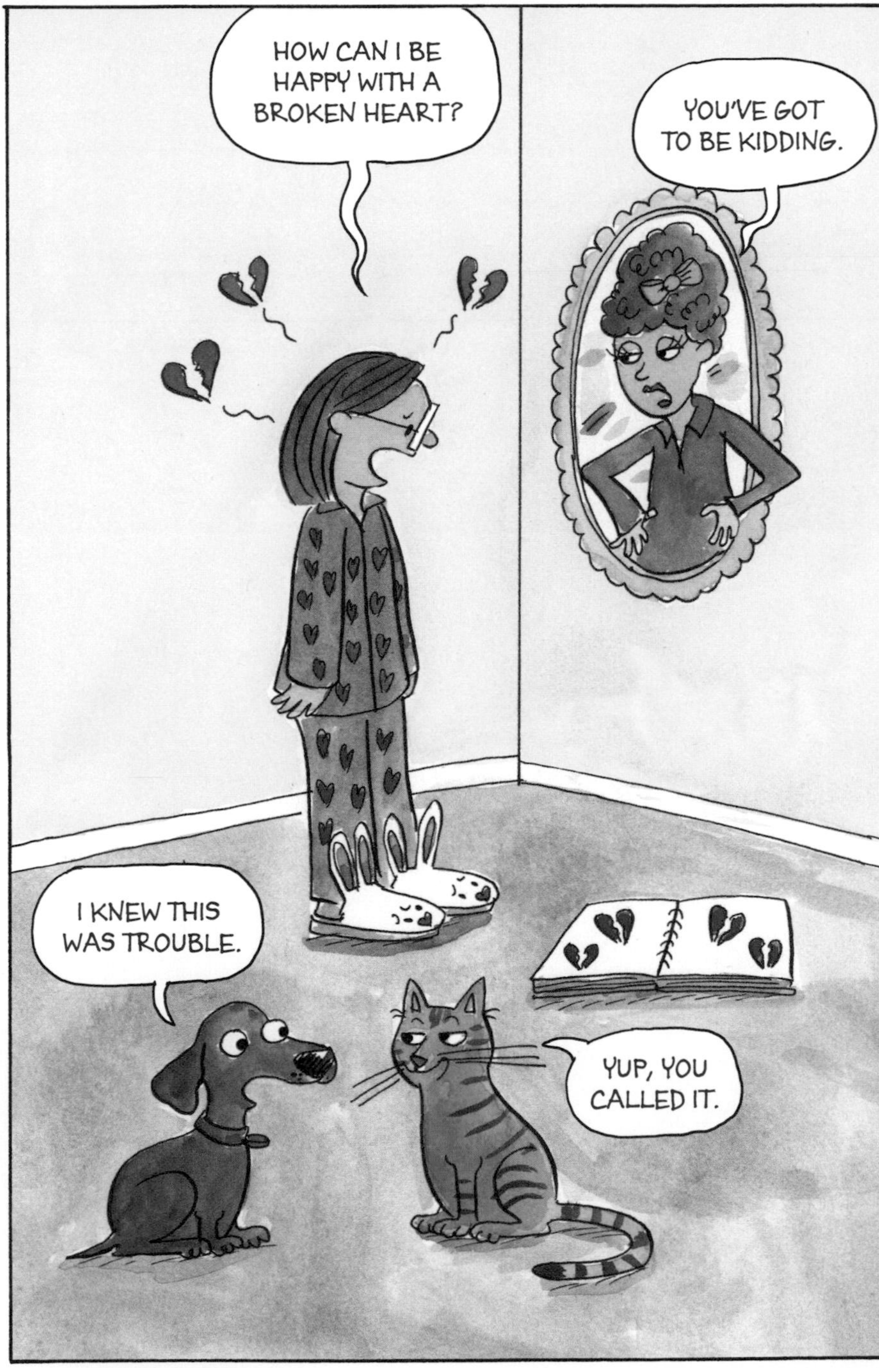
HOW CAN I BE HAPPY WITH A BROKEN HEART?
YOU'VE GOT TO BE KIDDING.
I KNEW THIS WAS TROUBLE.
YUP, YOU CALLED IT.

CHAPTER 10
PRACTICE

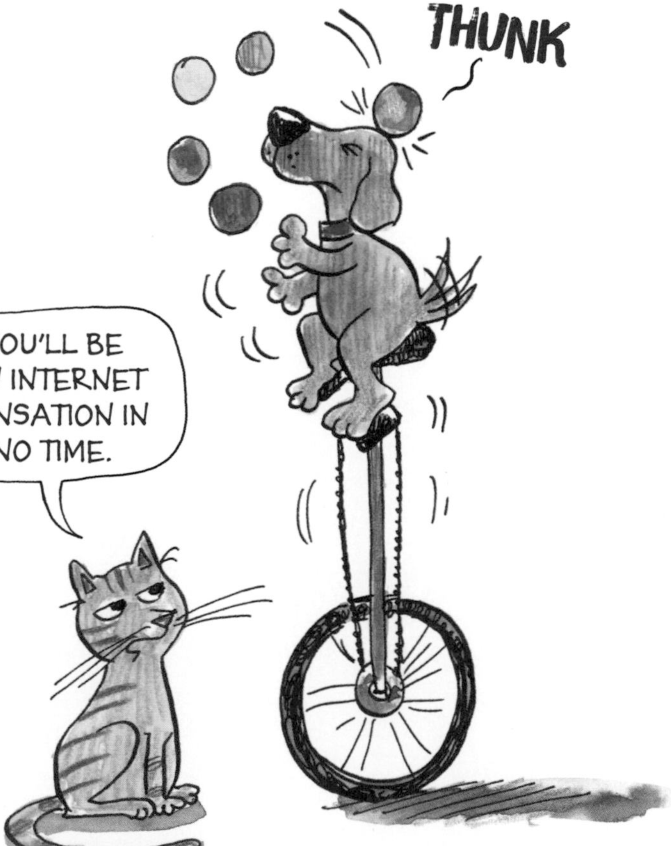
THUNK
YOU'LL BE AN INTERNET SENSATION IN NO TIME.

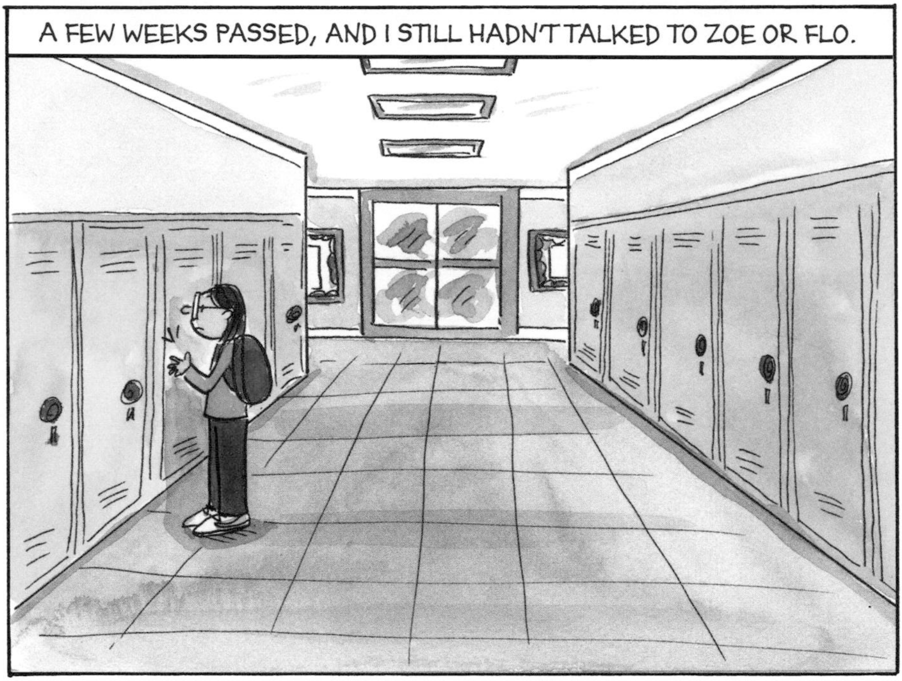
A FEW WEEKS PASSED, AND I STILL HADN'T TALKED TO ZOE OR FLO.

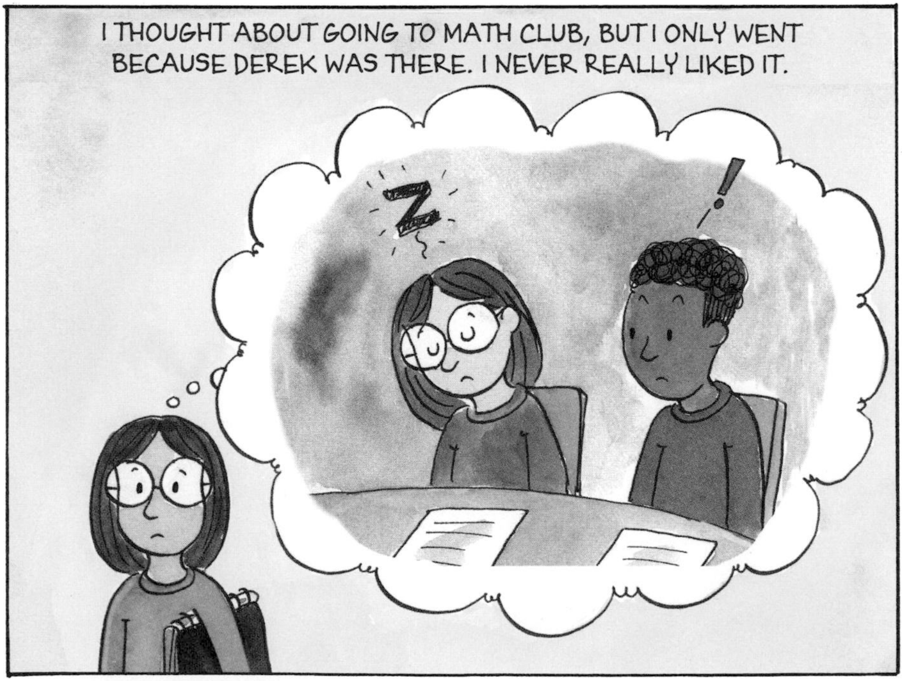
I THOUGHT ABOUT GOING TO MATH CLUB, BUT I ONLY WENT BECAUSE DEREK WAS THERE. I NEVER REALLY LIKED IT.
Z
!

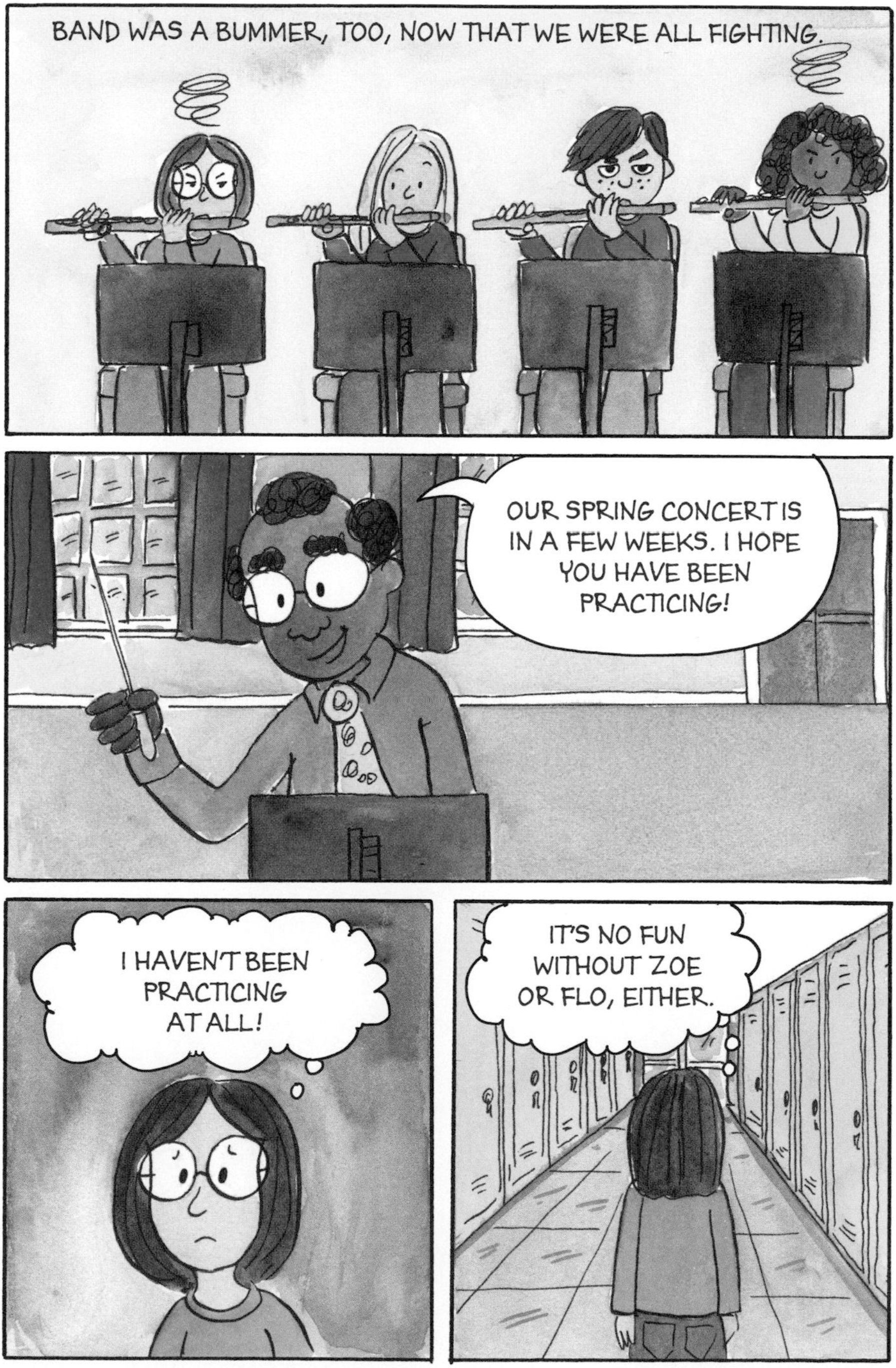
BAND WAS A BUMMER, TOO, NOW THAT WE WERE ALL FIGHTING.
OUR SPRING CONCERT IS IN A FEW WEEKS. I HOPE YOU HAVE BEEN PRACTICING!
I HAVEN'T BEEN PRACTICING AT ALL!
IT'S NO FUN WITHOUT ZOE OR FLO, EITHER.

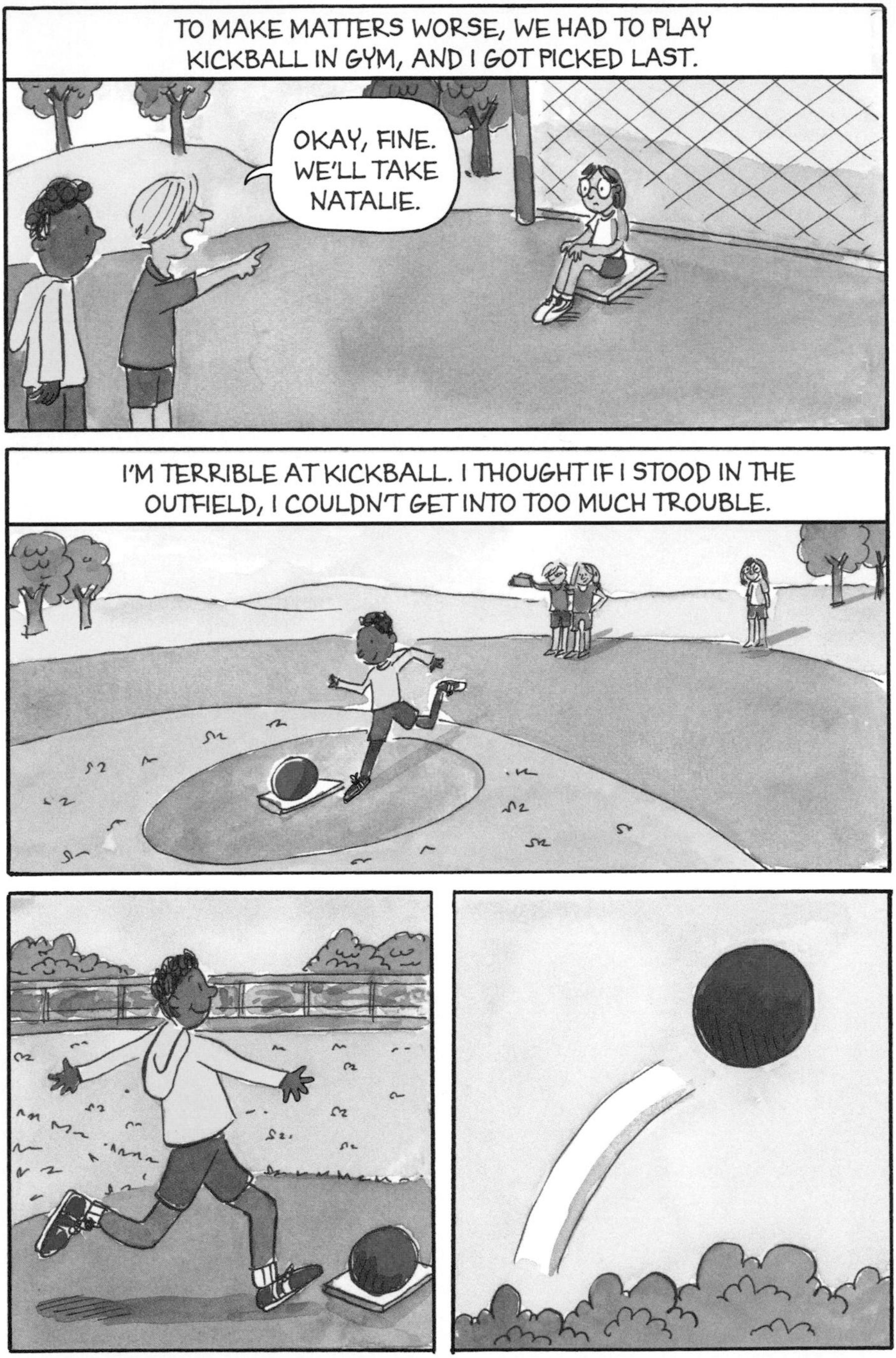
TO MAKE MATTERS WORSE, WE HAD TO PLAY KICKBALL IN GYM, AND I GOT PICKED LAST.
OKAY, FINE. WE'LL TAKE NATALIE.
I'M TERRIBLE AT KICKBALL. I THOUGHT IF I STOOD IN THE OUTFIELD, I COULDN'T GET INTO TOO MUCH TROUBLE.

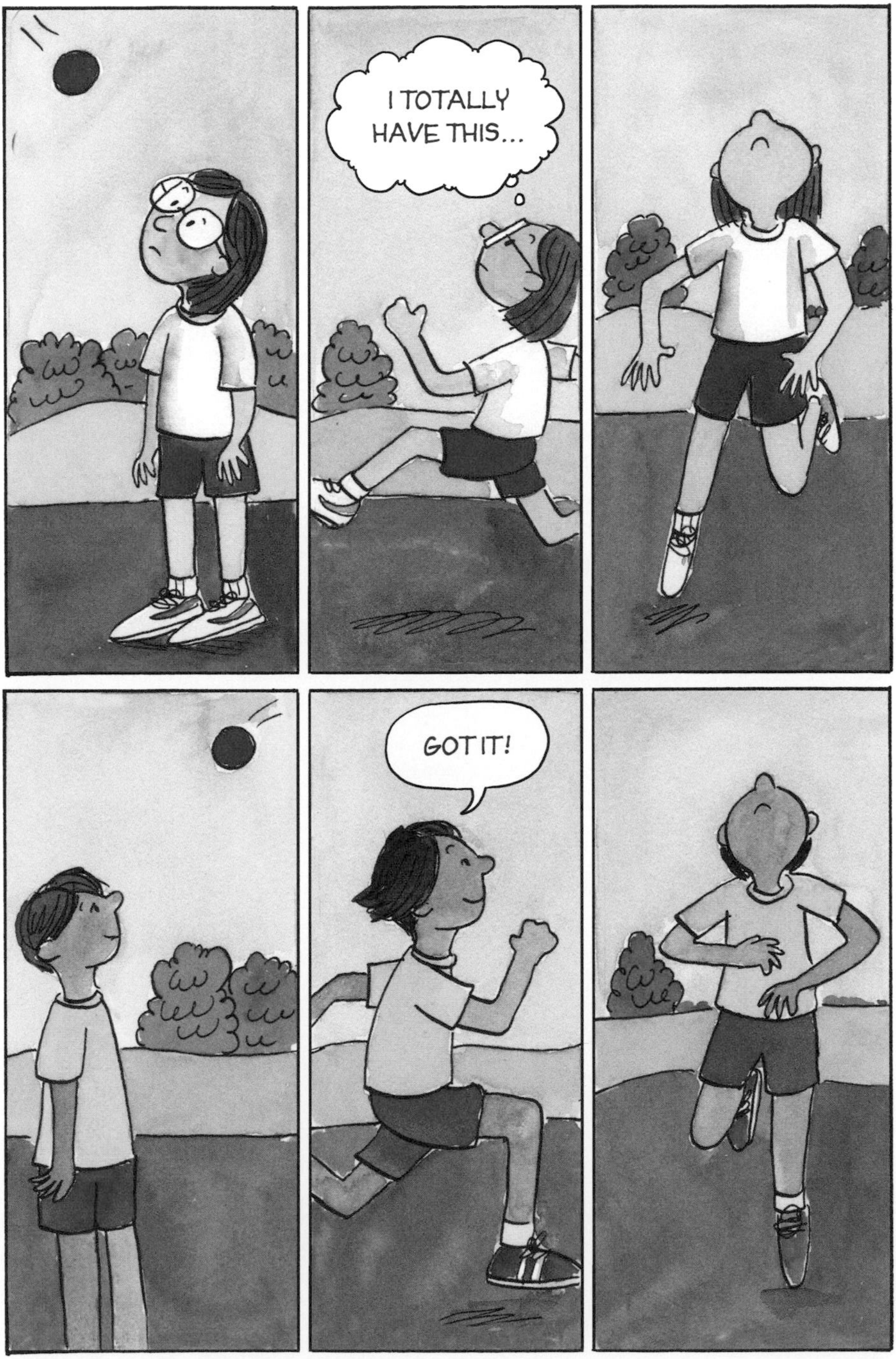
I TOTALLY HAVE THIS...
GOT IT!

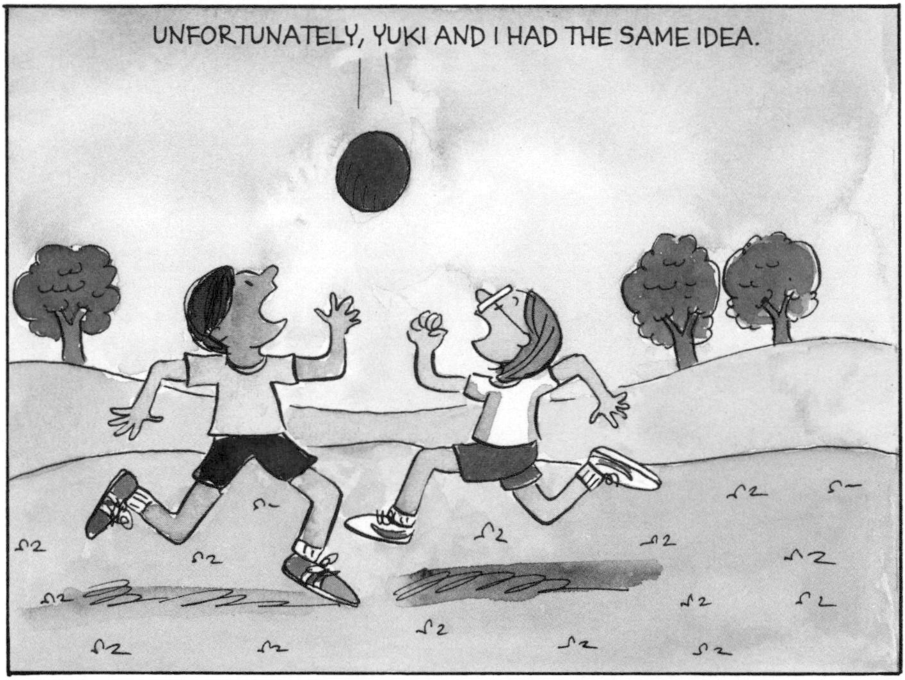
UNFORTUNATELY, YUKI AND I HAD THE SAME IDEA.

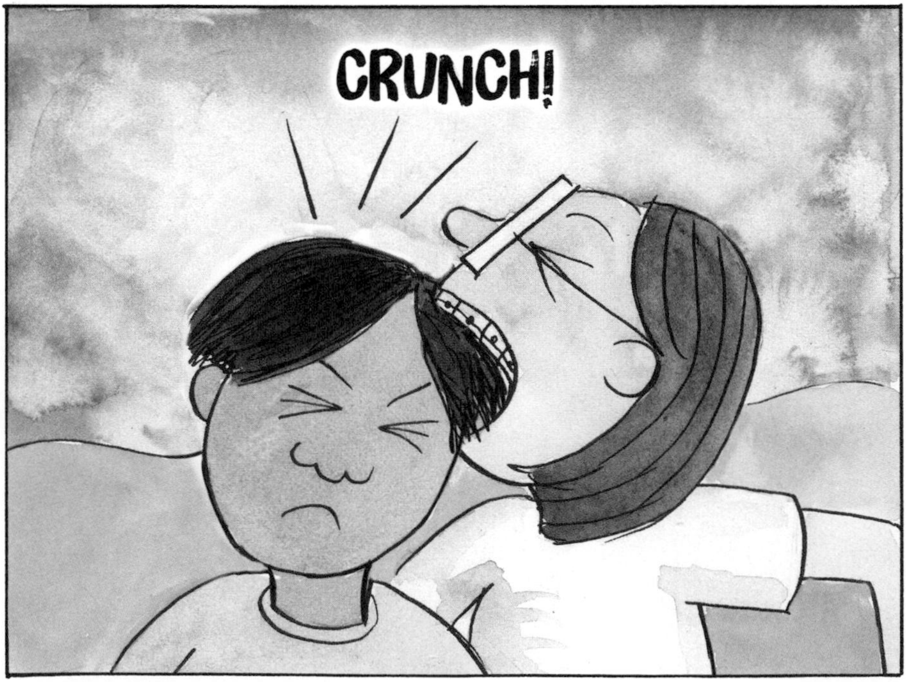
CRUNCH!

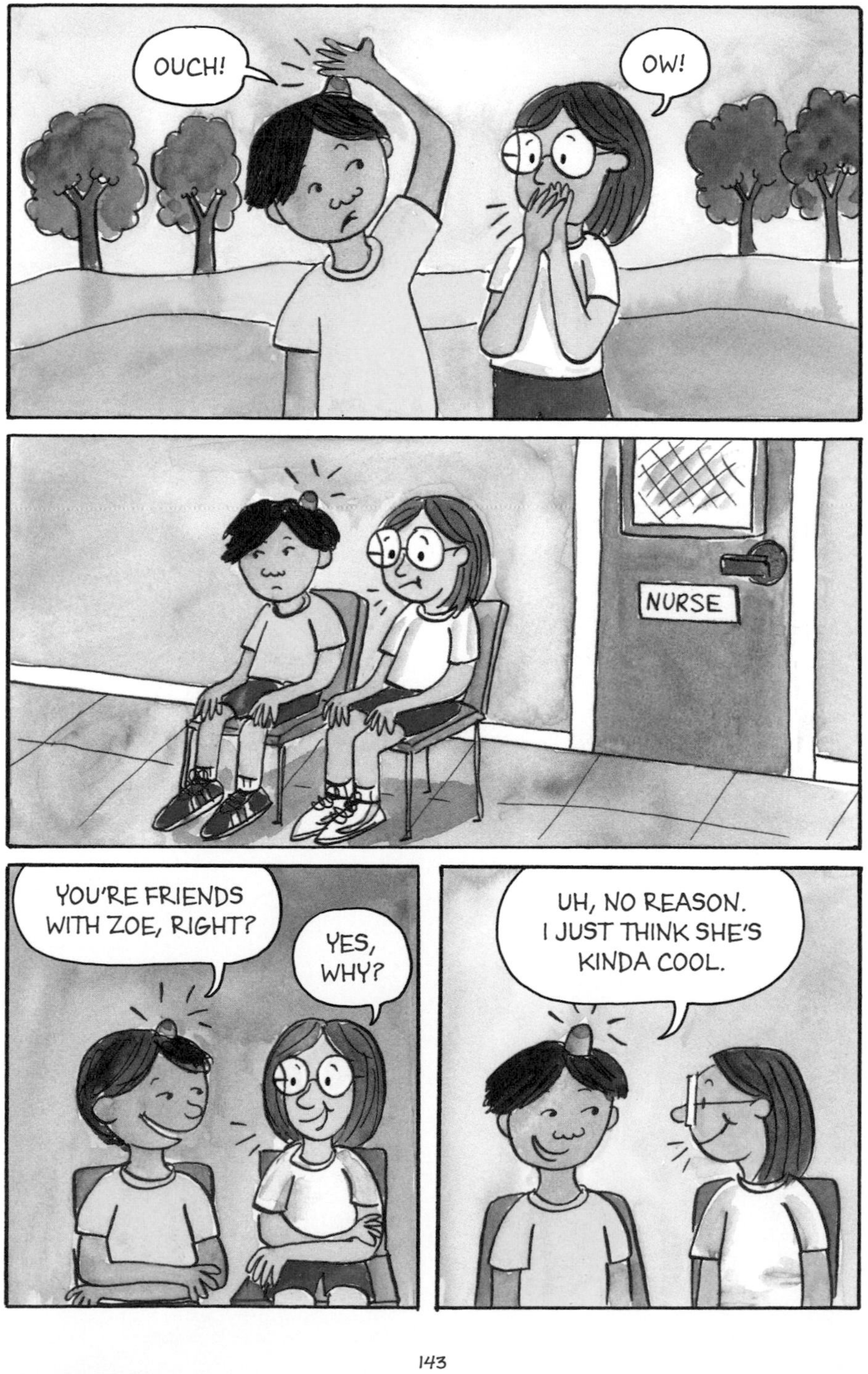
OUCH!
OW!
NURSE
YOU'RE FRIENDS WITH ZOE, RIGHT?
YES, WHY?
UH, NO REASON. I JUST THINK SHE'S KINDA COOL.

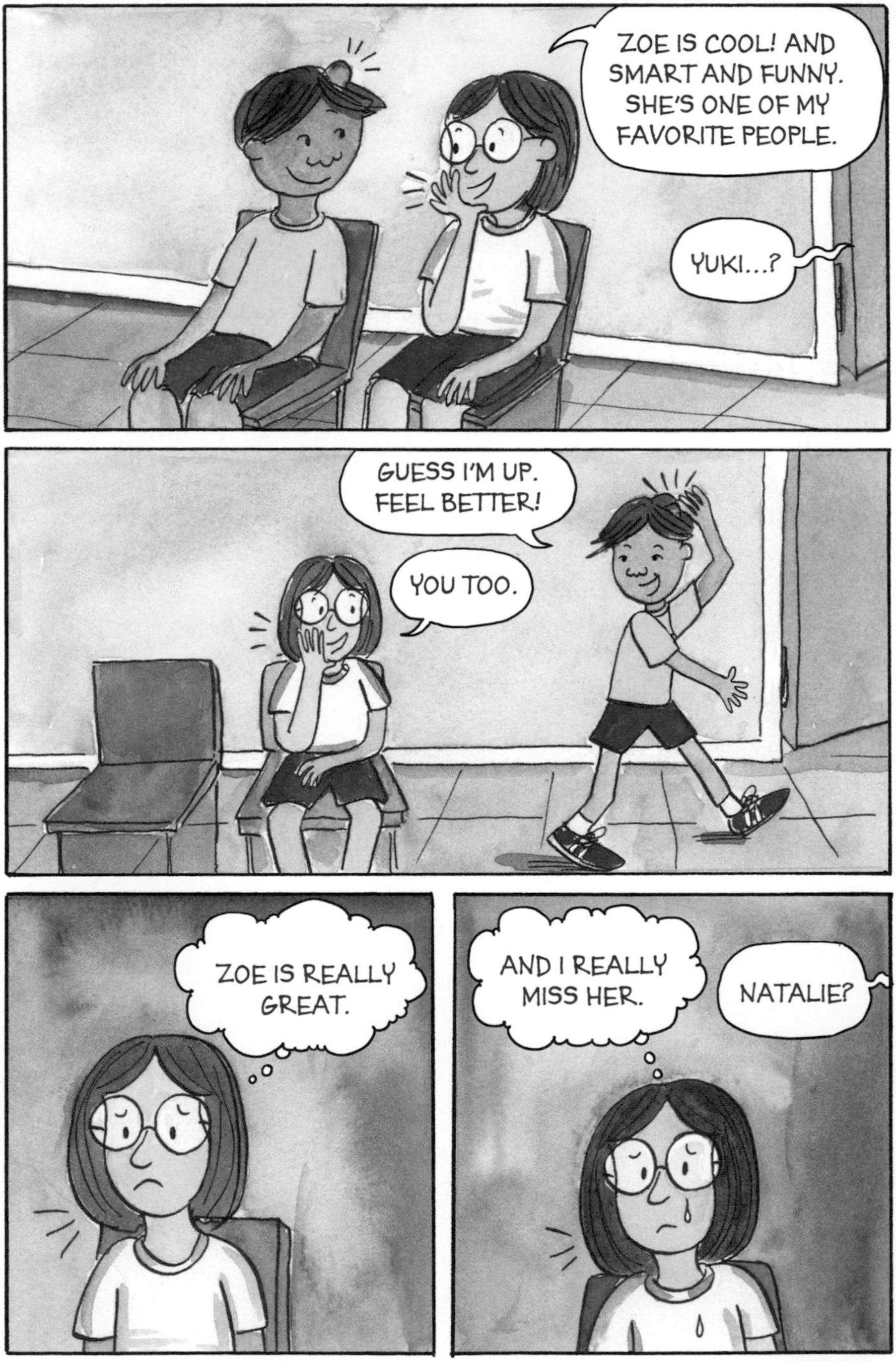
ZOE IS COOL! AND SMART AND FUNNY. SHE'S ONE OF MY FAVORITE PEOPLE.
YUKI...?
GUESS I'M UP. FEEL BETTER!
YOU TOO.
ZOE IS REALLY GREAT.
AND I REALLY MISS HER.
NATALIE?

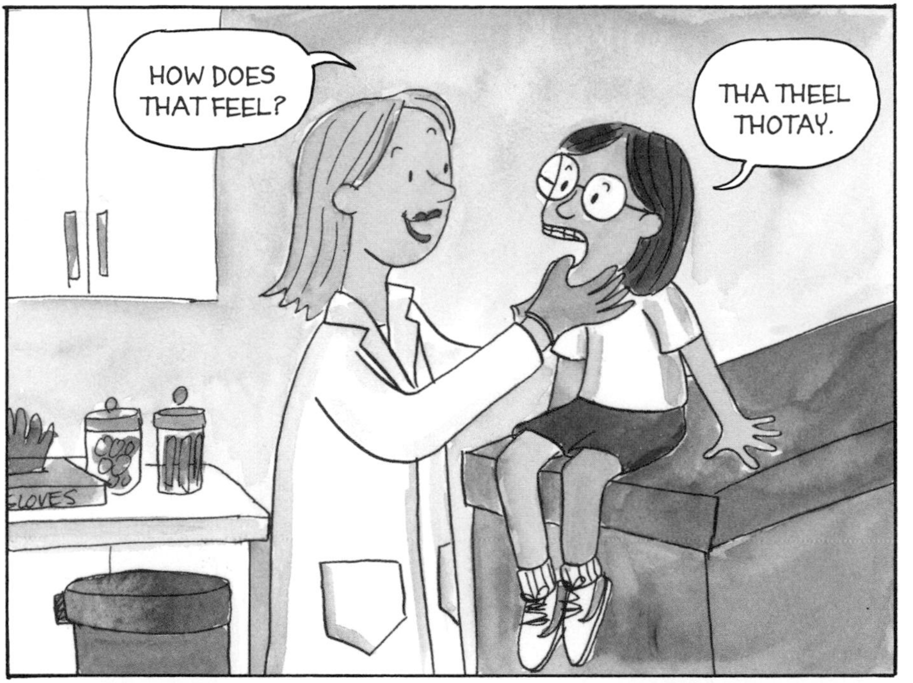
HOW DOES THAT FEEL?
THA THEEL THOTAY.
GLOVES

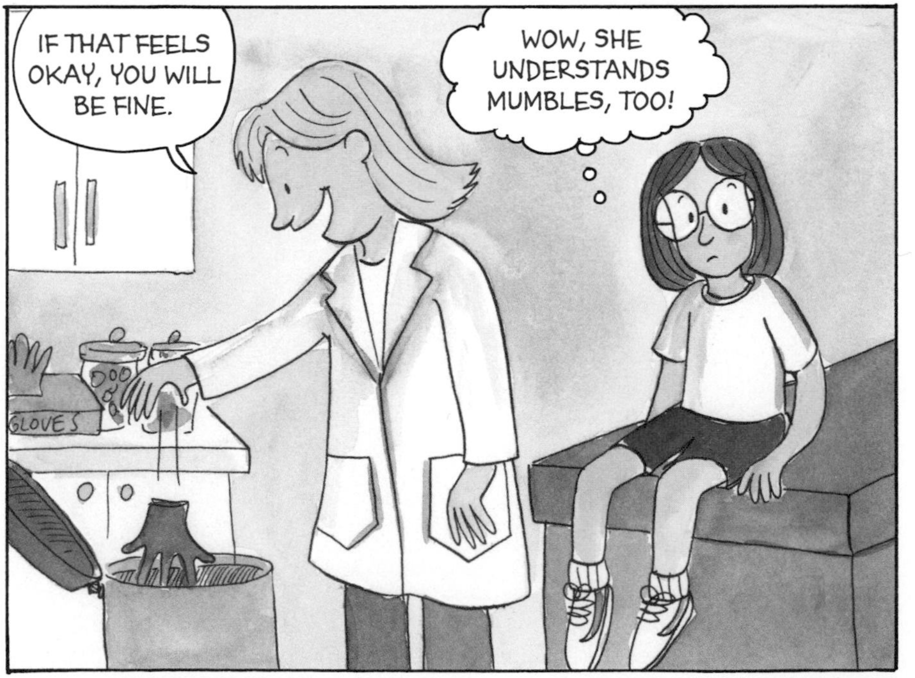
IF THAT FEELS OKAY, YOU WILL BE FINE.
WOW, SHE UNDERSTANDS MUMBLES, TOO!
GLOVES

THERE AREN'T ENOUGH BANDAGES IN THE WORLD TO FIX MY BROKEN HEART.

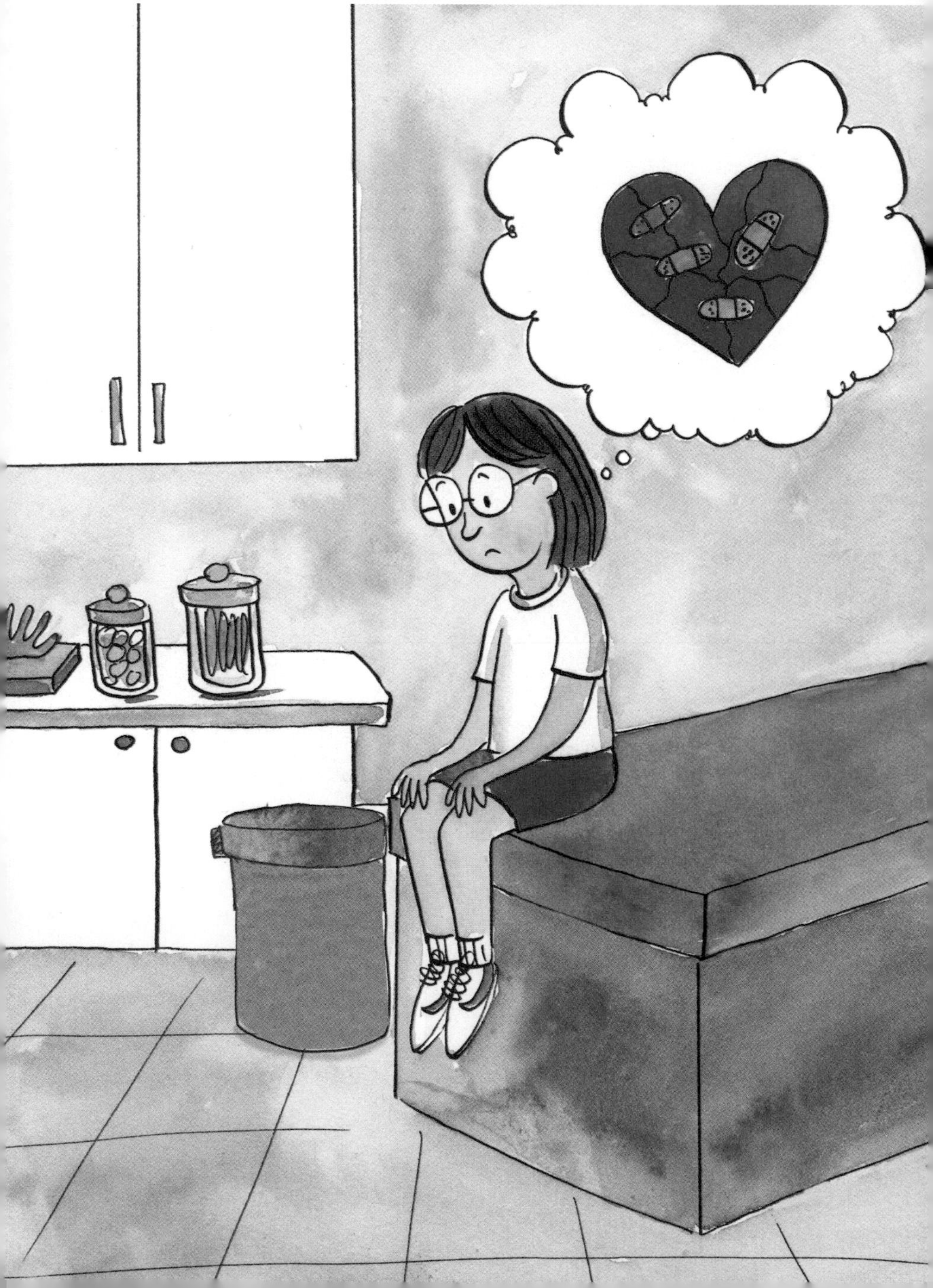

CHAPTER 11
PROMISES

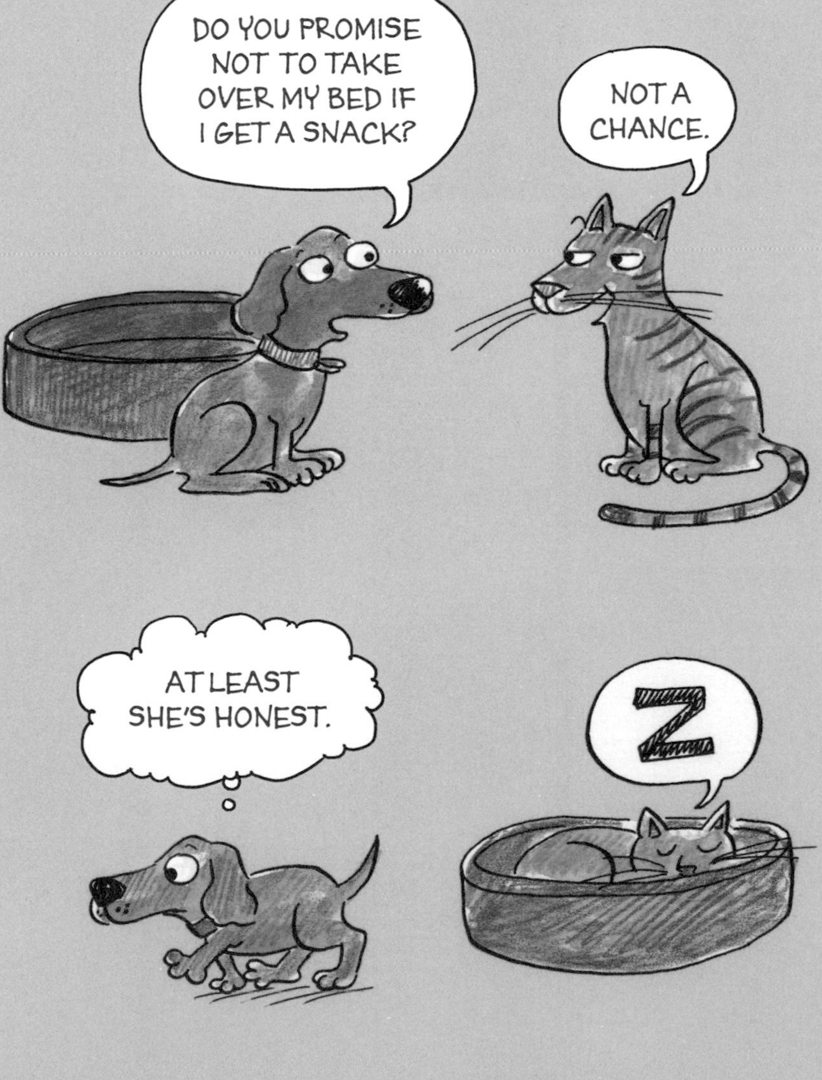
DO YOU PROMISE NOT TO TAKE OVER MY BED IF I GET A SNACK?
NOT A CHANCE.
AT LEAST SHE'S HONEST.
Z

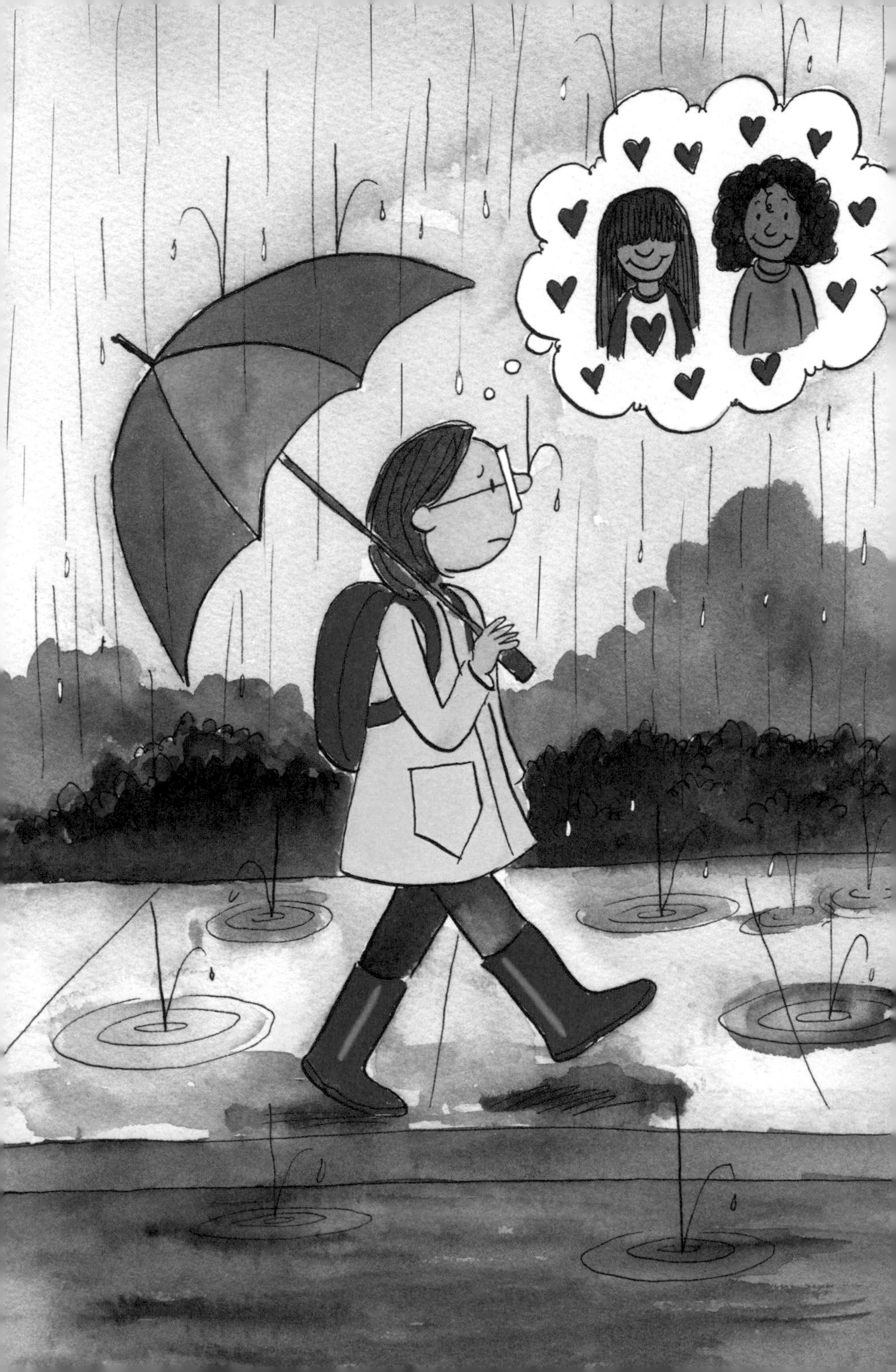

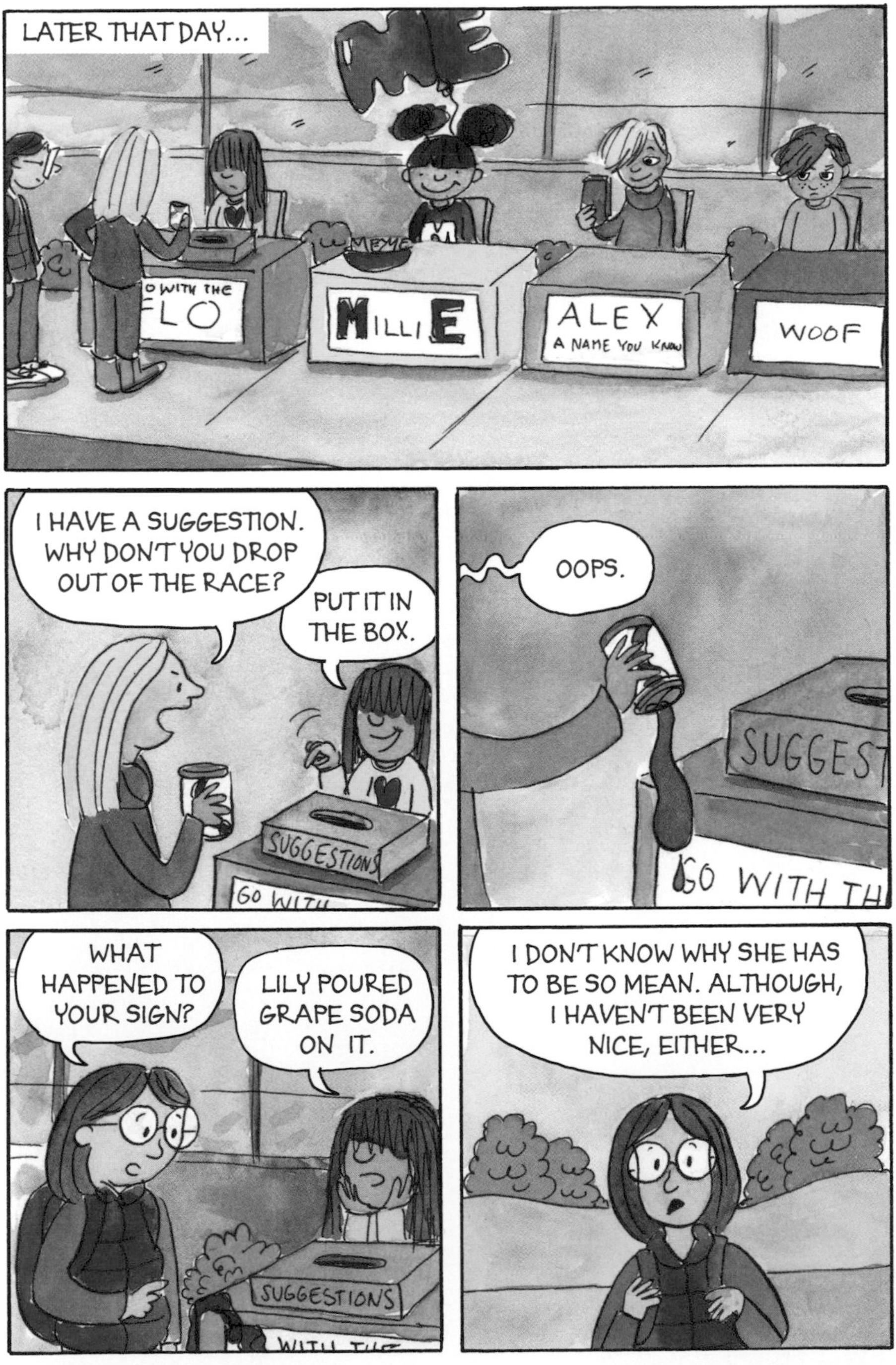
LATER THAT DAY...
ME
MEME
O WITH THE FLO
MILLIE
ALEX A NAME YOU KNOW
WOOF
I HAVE A SUGGESTION. WHY DON'T YOU DROP OUT OF THE RACE?
PUT IT IN THE BOX.
SUGGESTIONS
GO WITH
OOPS.
SUGGEST
GO WITH TH
WHAT HAPPENED TO YOUR SIGN?
LILY POURED GRAPE SODA ON IT.
SUGGESTIONS
I DON'T KNOW WHY SHE HAS TO BE SO MEAN. ALTHOUGH, I HAVEN'T BEEN VERY NICE, EITHER...

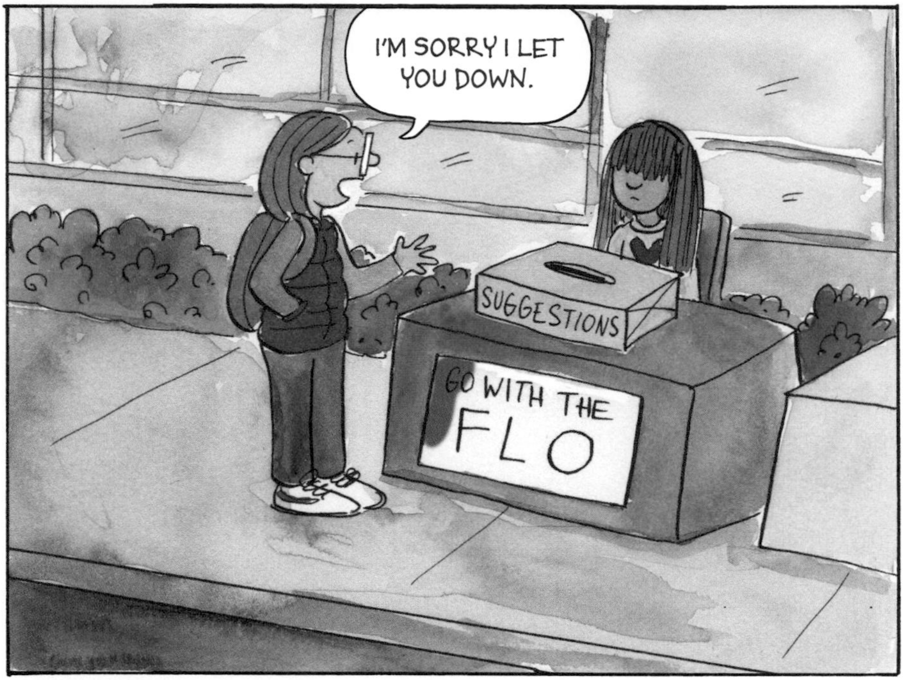
I'M SORRY I LET YOU DOWN.
SUGGESTIONS
GO WITH THE FLO

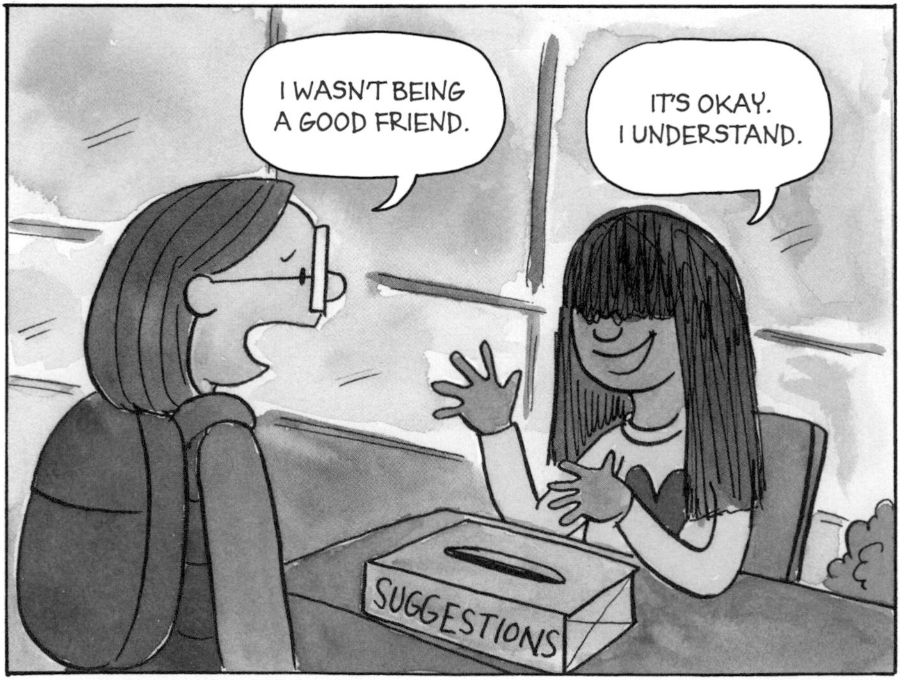
I WASN'T BEING A GOOD FRIEND.
IT'S OKAY. I UNDERSTAND.
SUGGESTIONS

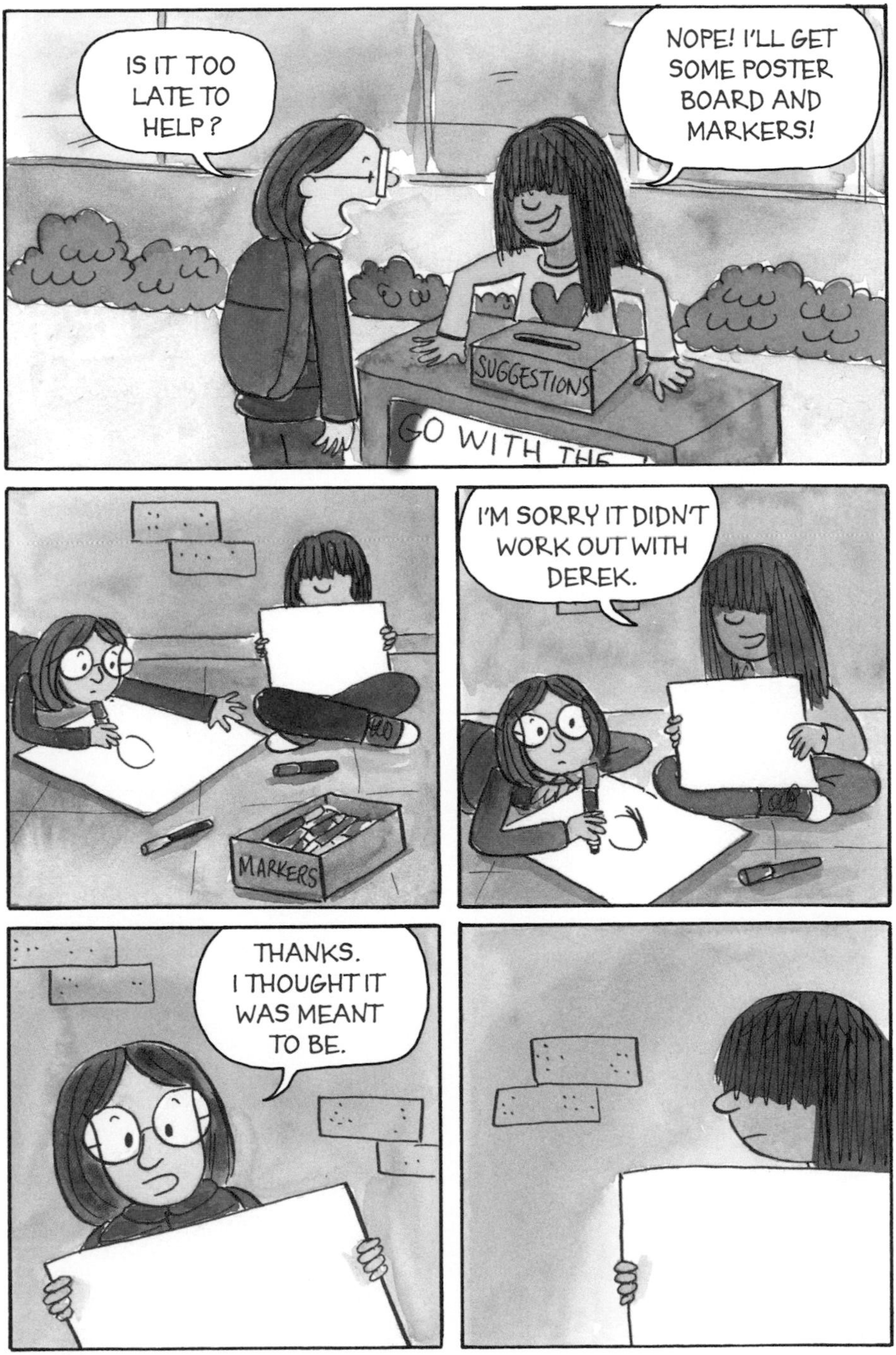
IS IT TOO LATE TO HELP?
NOPE! I'LL GET SOME POSTER BOARD AND MARKERS!
SUGGESTIONS
GO WITH THE
MARKERS
I'M SORRY IT DIDN'T WORK OUT WITH DEREK.
THANKS. I THOUGHT IT WAS MEANT TO BE.

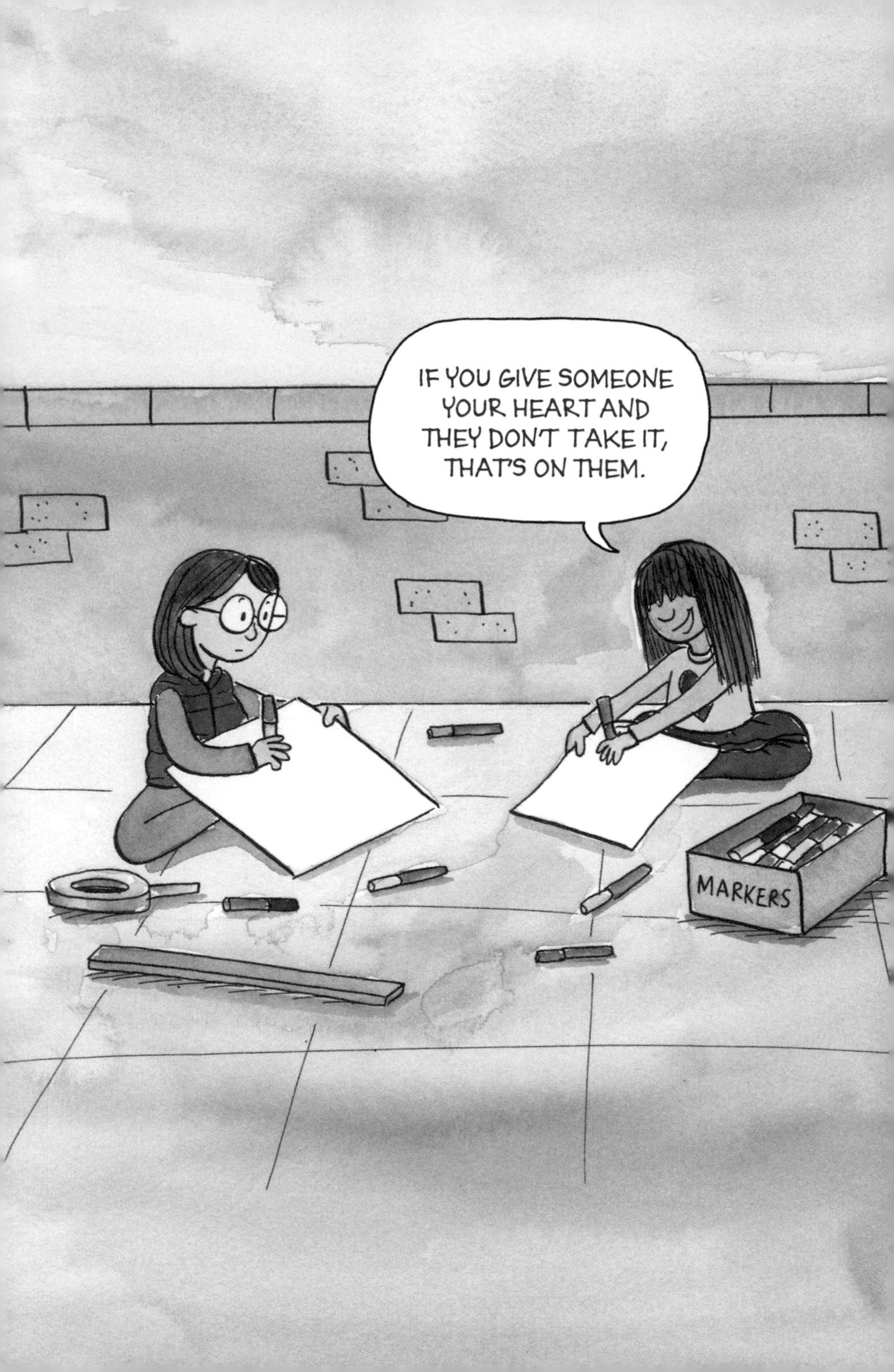
IF YOU GIVE SOMEONE YOUR HEART AND THEY DON'T TAKE IT, THAT'S ON THEM.
MARKERS

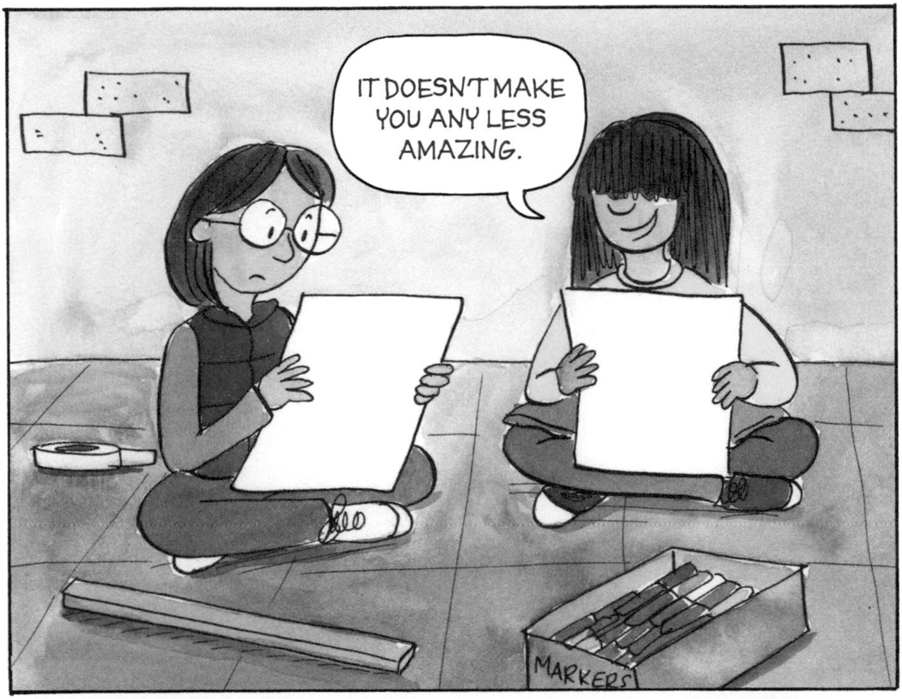
IT DOESN'T MAKE YOU ANY LESS AMAZING.
MARKERS

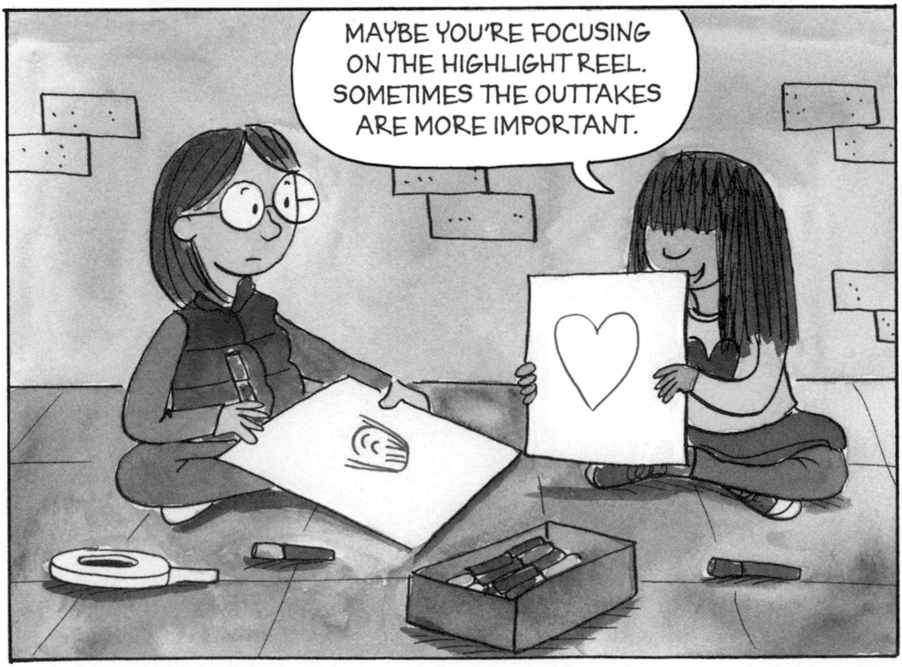
MAYBE YOU'RE FOCUSING ON THE HIGHLIGHT REEL. SOMETIMES THE OUTTAKES ARE MORE IMPORTANT.

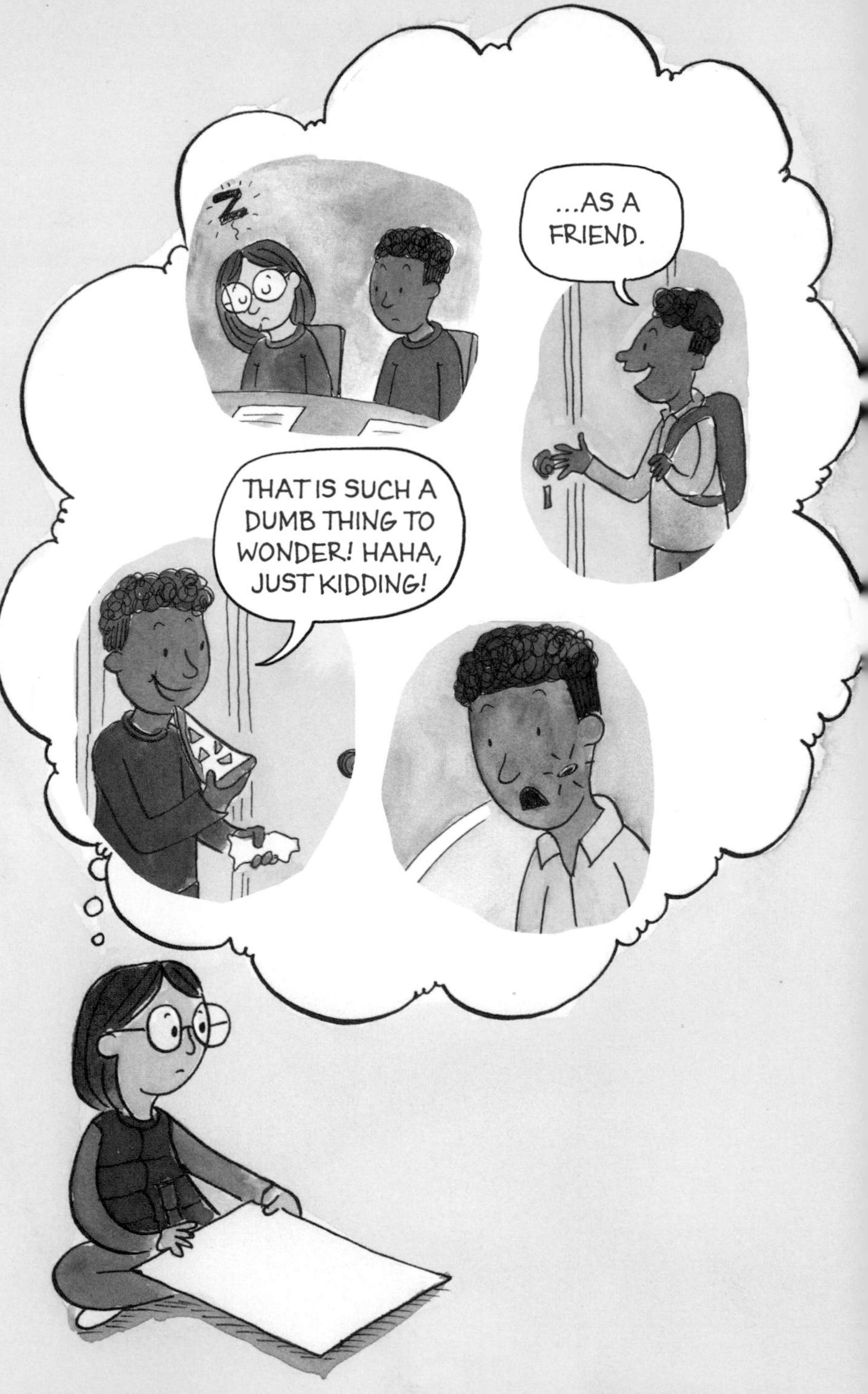

Z
...AS A FRIEND.
THAT IS SUCH A DUMB THING TO WONDER! HAHA, JUST KIDDING!

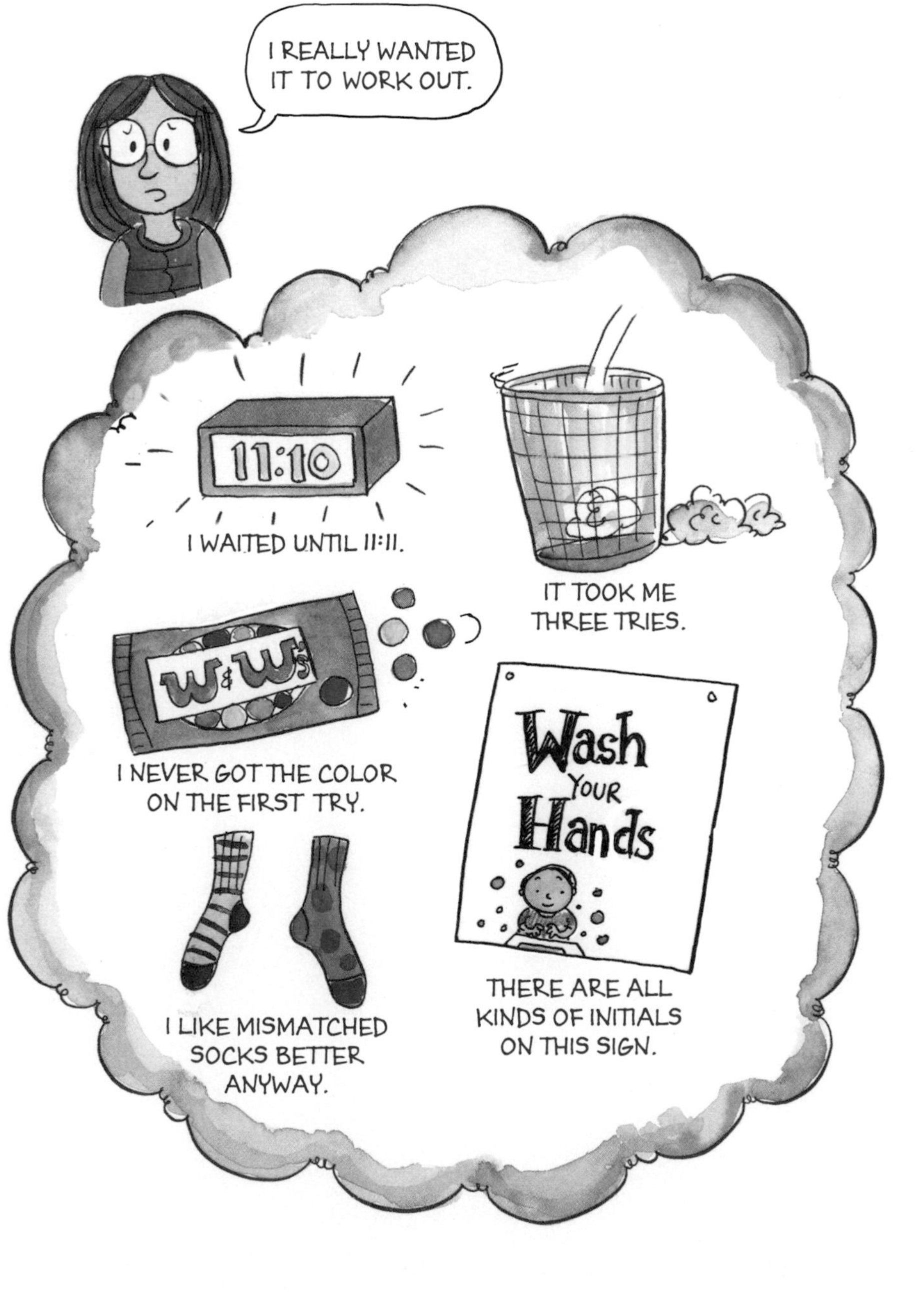
I REALLY WANTED IT TO WORK OUT.
11:10
I WAITED UNTIL 11:11.
IT TOOK ME THREE TRIES.
W&W's
I NEVER GOT THE COLOR ON THE FIRST TRY.
Wash Your Hands
I LIKE MISMATCHED SOCKS BETTER ANYWAY.
THERE ARE ALL KINDS OF INITIALS ON THIS SIGN.

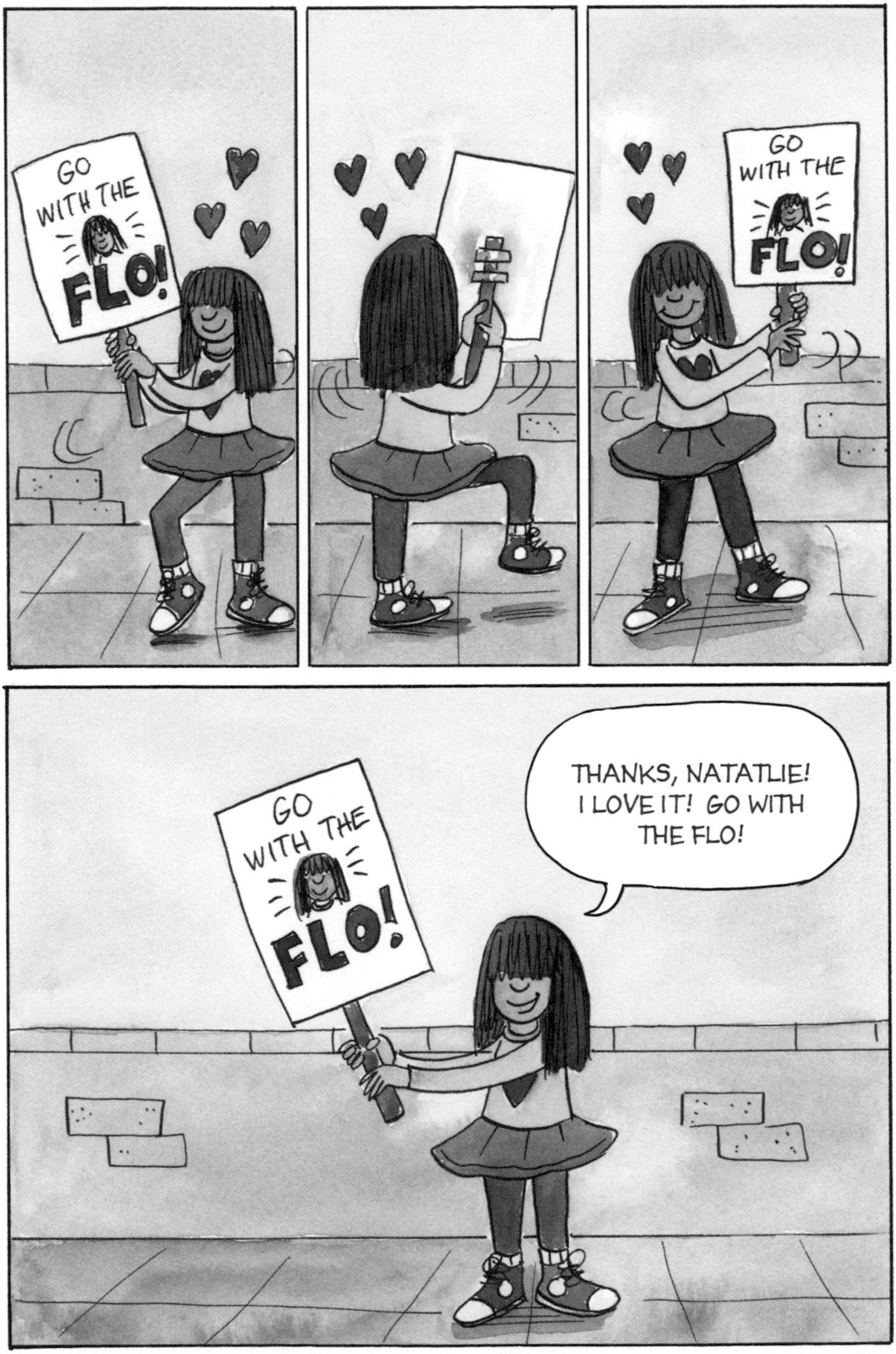
GO WITH THE FLO!
GO WITH THE FLO!
GO WITH THE FLO!
THANKS, NATATLIE! I LOVE IT! GO WITH THE FLO!

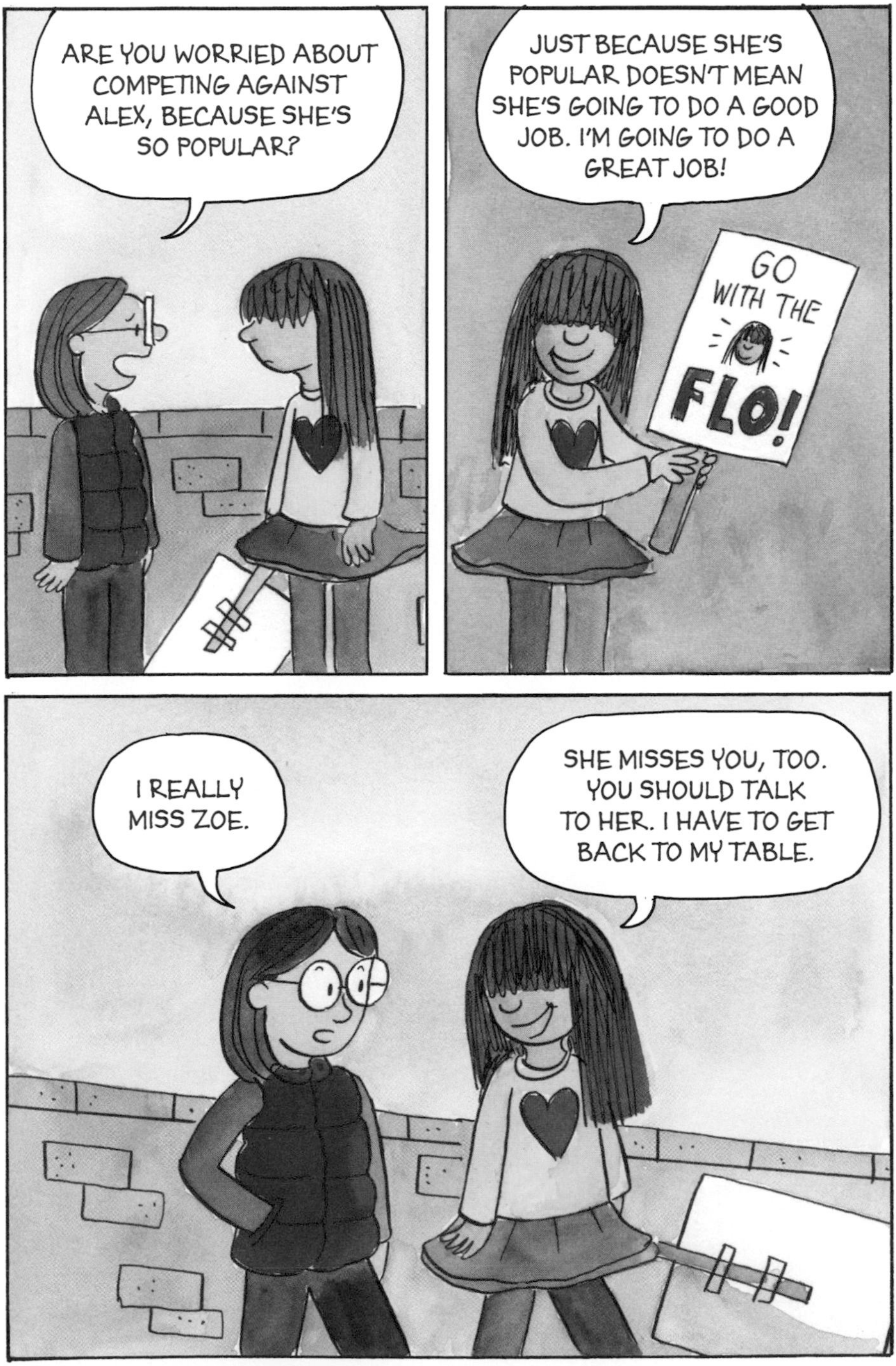
ARE YOU WORRIED ABOUT COMPETING AGAINST ALEX, BECAUSE SHE'S SO POPULAR?
JUST BECAUSE SHE'S POPULAR DOESN'T MEAN SHE'S GOING TO DO A GOOD JOB. I'M GOING TO DO A GREAT JOB!
GO WITH THE FLO!
I REALLY MISS ZOE.
SHE MISSES YOU, TOO. YOU SHOULD TALK TO HER. I HAVE TO GET BACK TO MY TABLE.

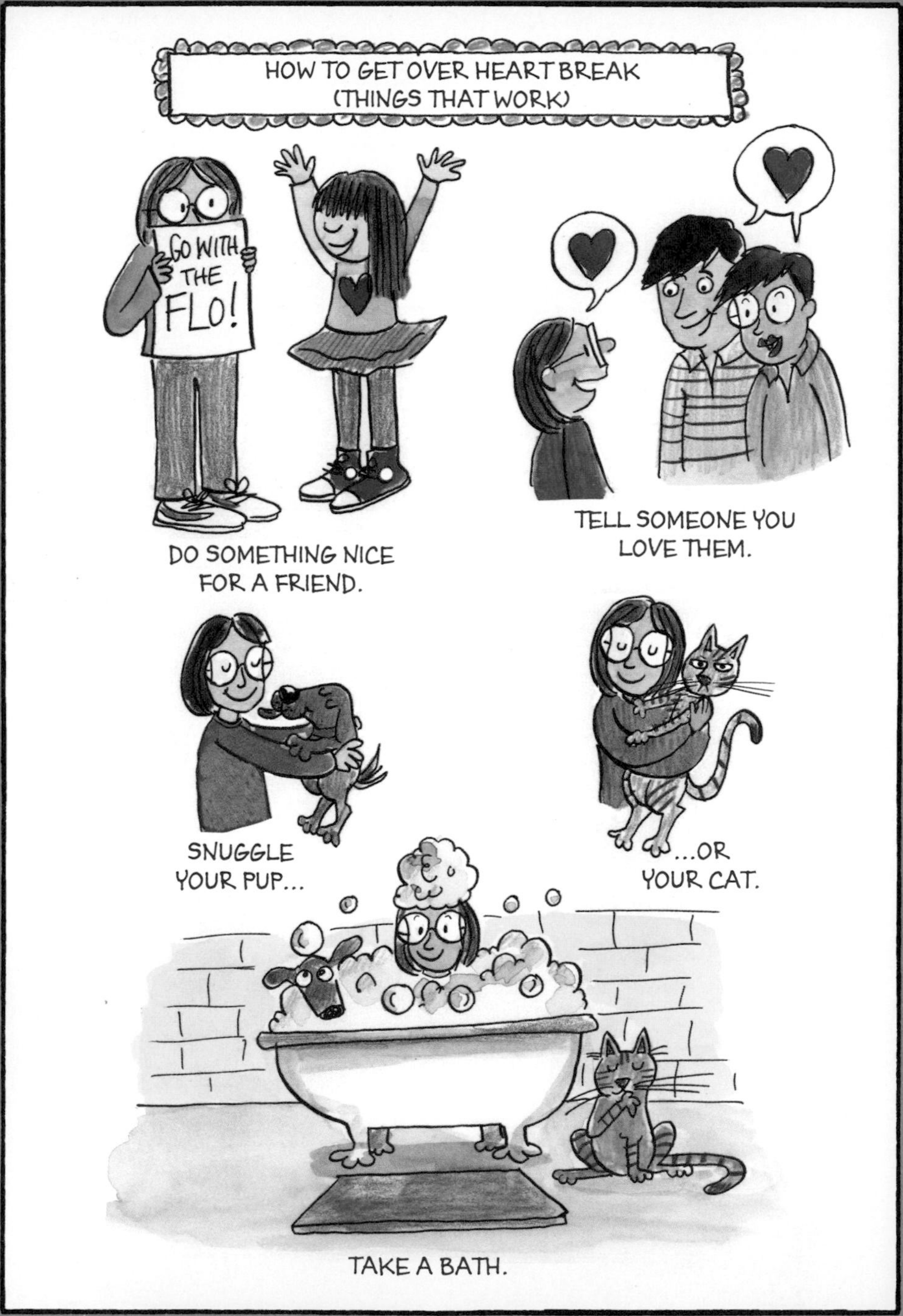
HOW TO GET OVER HEART BREAK
(THINGS THAT WORK)
GO WITH THE FLO!
DO SOMETHING NICE FOR A FRIEND.
TELL SOMEONE YOU LOVE THEM.
SNUGGLE YOUR PUP...
...OR YOUR CAT.
TAKE A BATH.

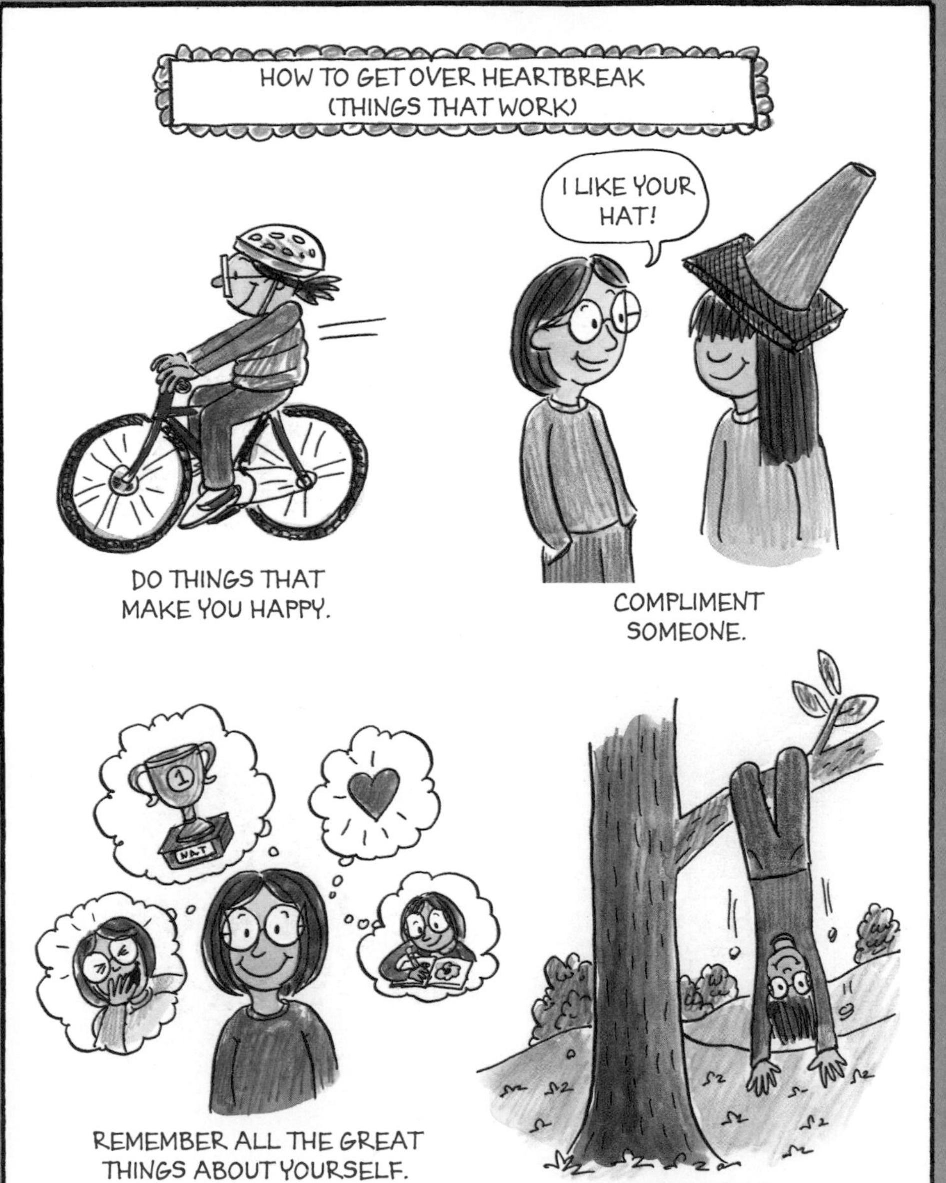
HOW TO GET OVER HEARTBREAK
(THINGS THAT WORK)
DO THINGS THAT MAKE YOU HAPPY.
I LIKE YOUR HAT!
COMPLIMENT SOMEONE.
REMEMBER ALL THE GREAT THINGS ABOUT YOURSELF.
DO SOMETHING FUN OUTSIDE.

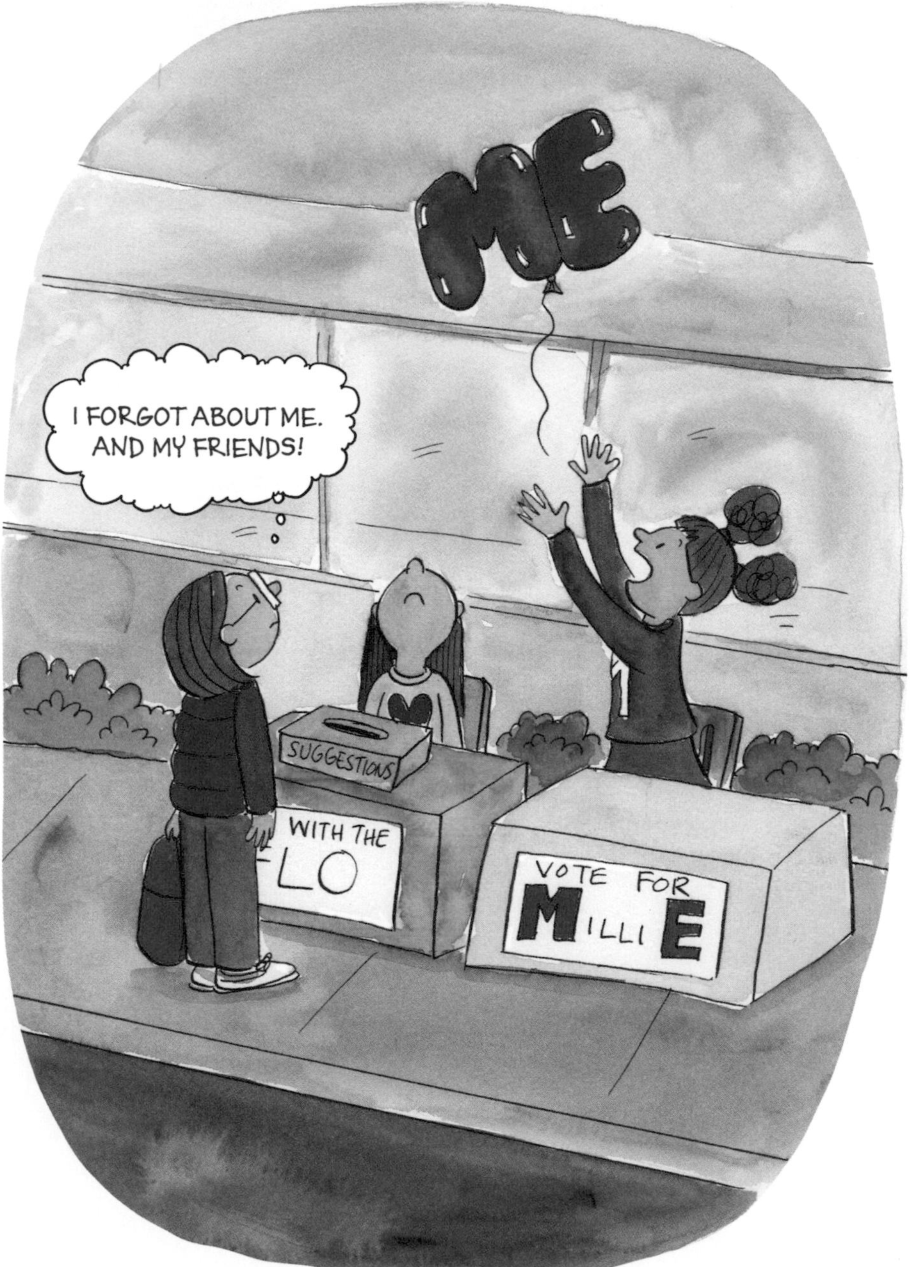
I FORGOT ABOUT ME.
AND MY FRIENDS!
SUGGESTIONS
WITH THE
LO
VOTE FOR
MILLIE

CHAPTER 12
FRIENDS

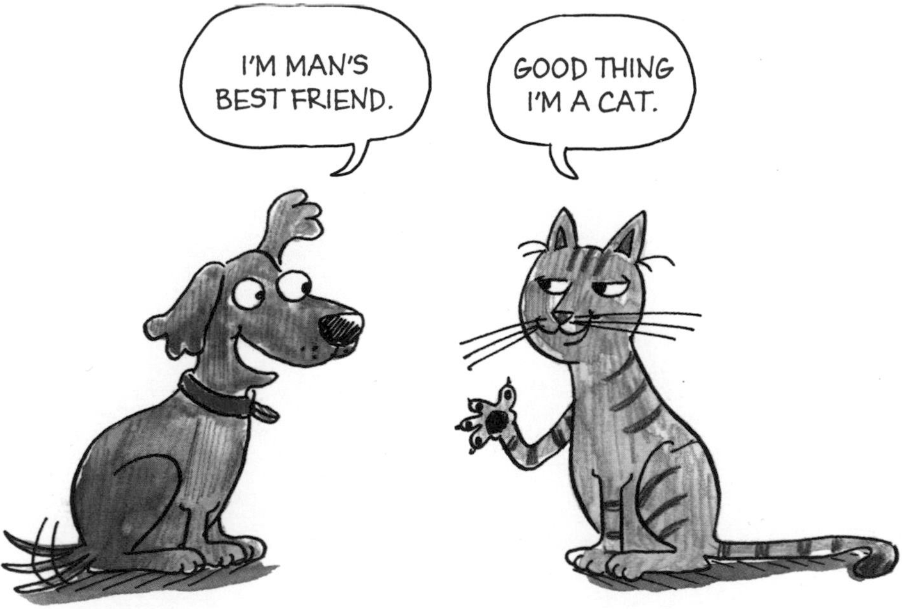

I'M MAN'S BEST FRIEND.
GOOD THING I'M A CAT.

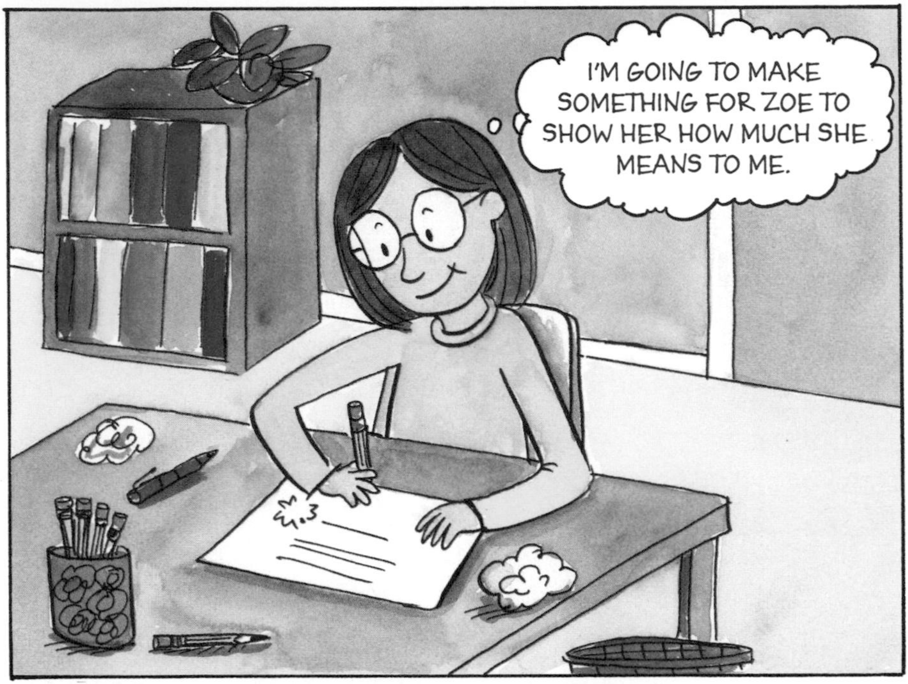
I'M GOING TO MAKE SOMETHING FOR ZOE TO SHOW HER HOW MUCH SHE MEANS TO ME.

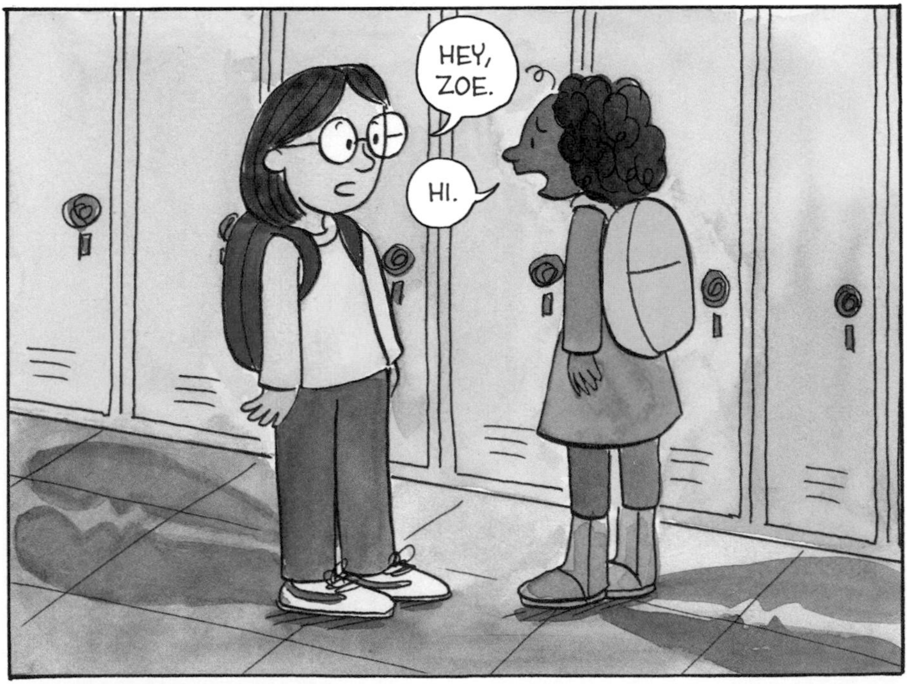
HEY, ZOE.
HI.

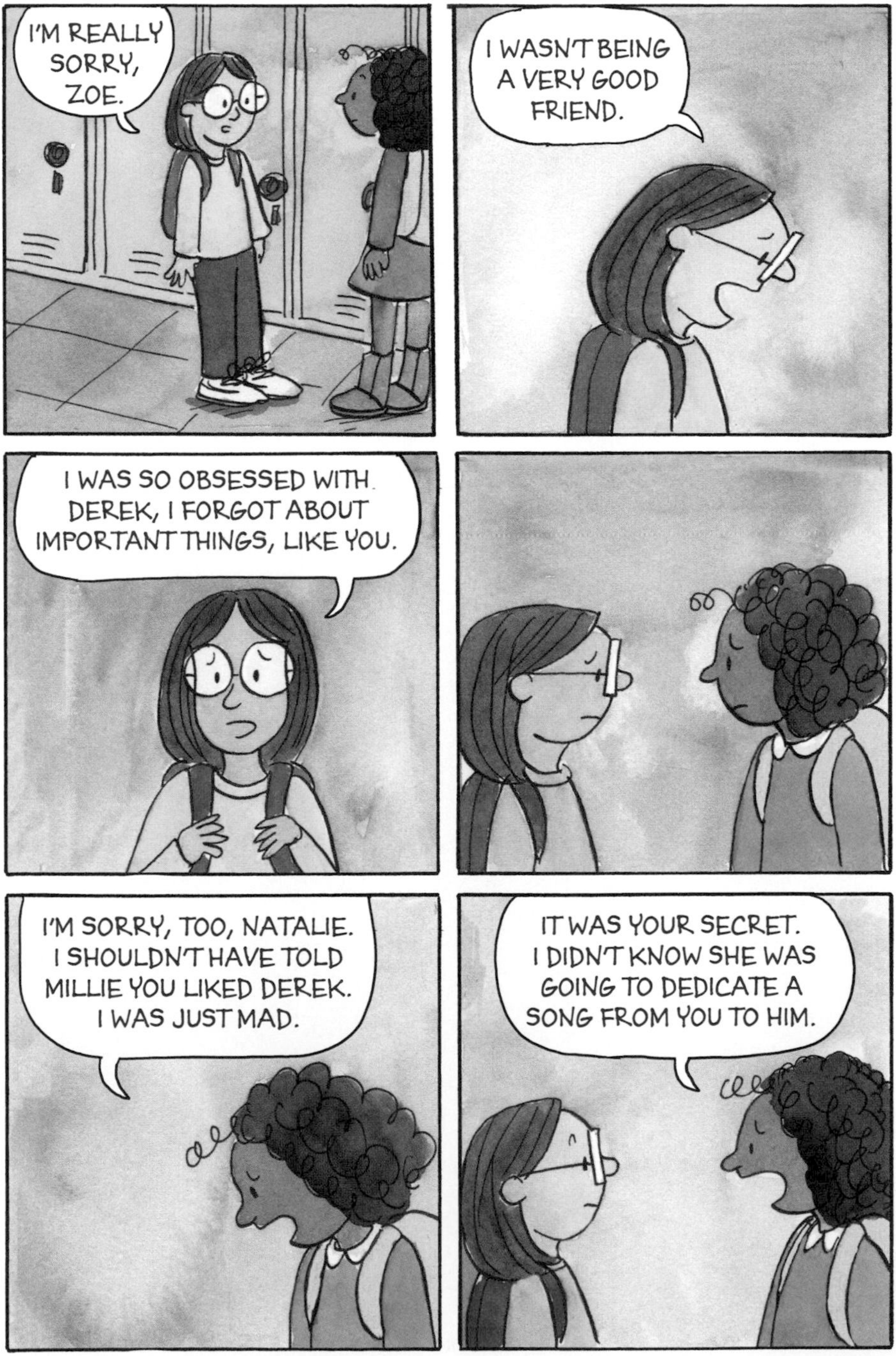
I'M REALLY SORRY, ZOE.
I WASN'T BEING A VERY GOOD FRIEND.
I WAS SO OBSESSED WITH DEREK, I FORGOT ABOUT IMPORTANT THINGS, LIKE YOU.
I'M SORRY, TOO, NATALIE. I SHOULDN'T HAVE TOLD MILLIE YOU LIKED DEREK. I WAS JUST MAD.
IT WAS YOUR SECRET. I DIDN'T KNOW SHE WAS GOING TO DEDICATE A SONG FROM YOU TO HIM.

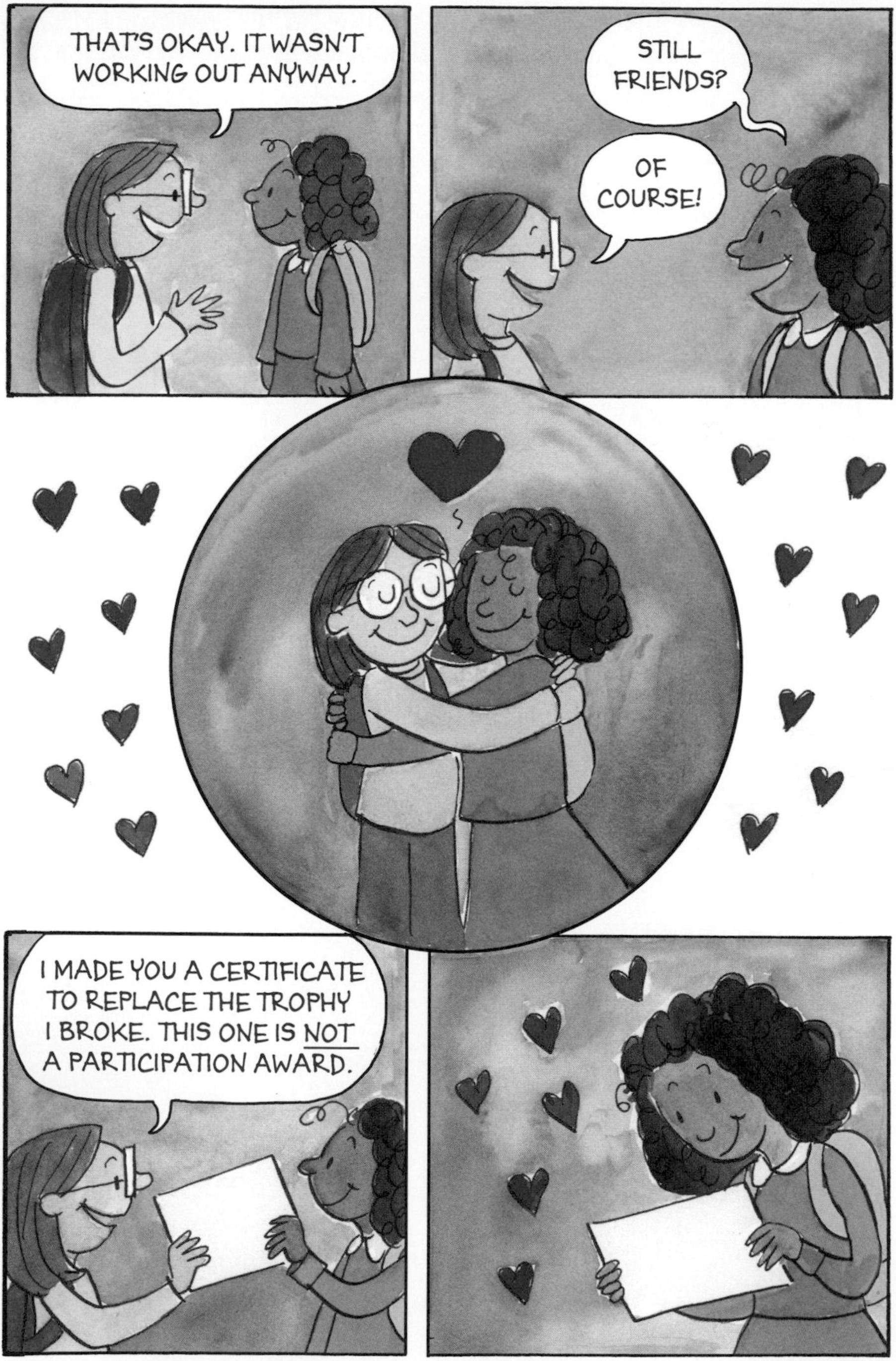
THAT'S OKAY. IT WASN'T WORKING OUT ANYWAY.
STILL FRIENDS?
OF COURSE!
I MADE YOU A CERTIFICATE TO REPLACE THE TROPHY I BROKE. THIS ONE IS NOT A PARTICIPATION AWARD.

CERTIFIED TRUE

YOU
ARE A PRIZE!

FOR: ZOE

- GREAT FRIEND
- AMAZING PERSON
- SMART
- FUNNY
- KIND

LOVE: NAT

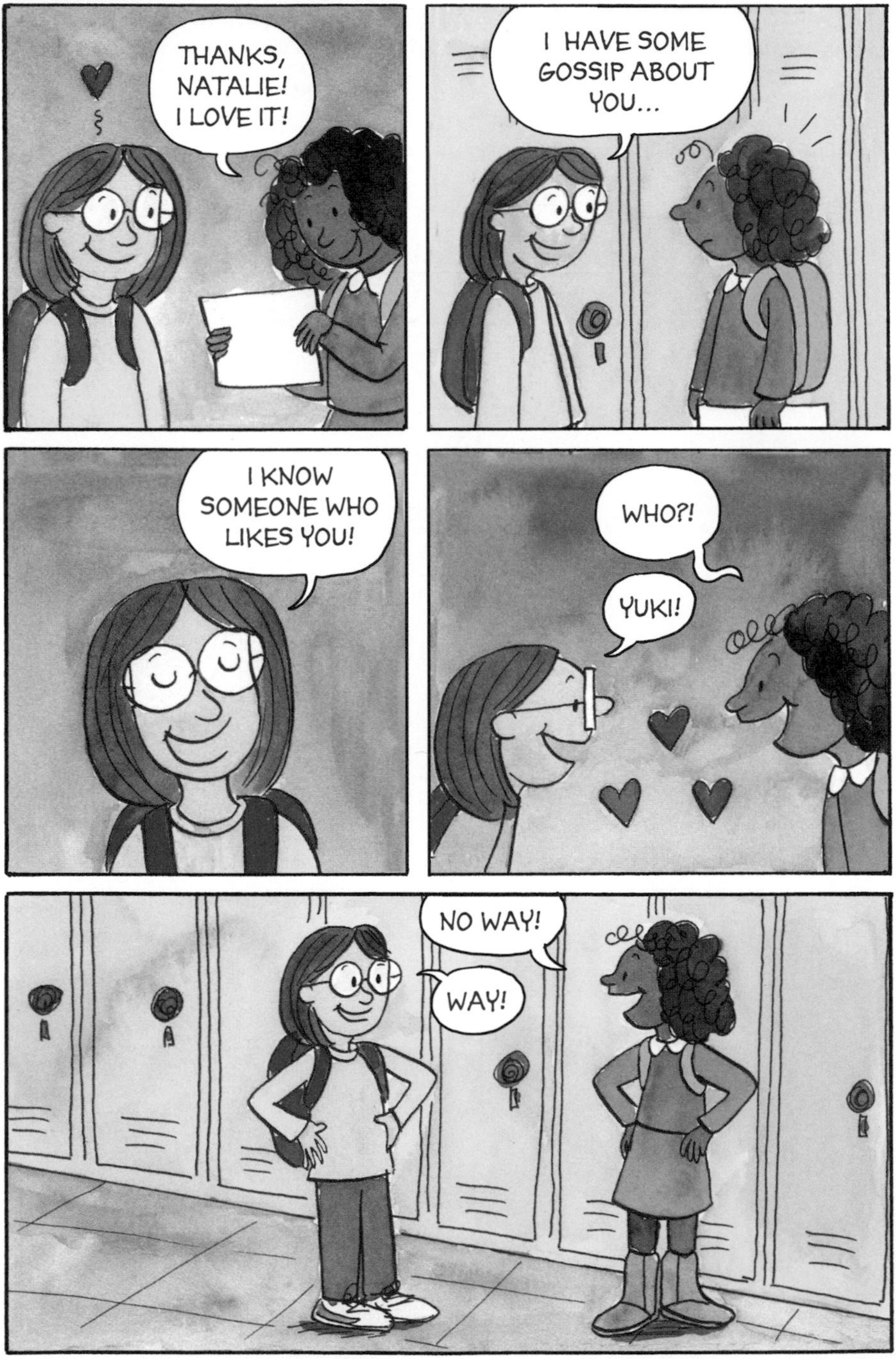
THANKS, NATALIE! I LOVE IT!
I HAVE SOME GOSSIP ABOUT YOU...
I KNOW SOMEONE WHO LIKES YOU!
WHO?!
YUKI!
NO WAY!
WAY!

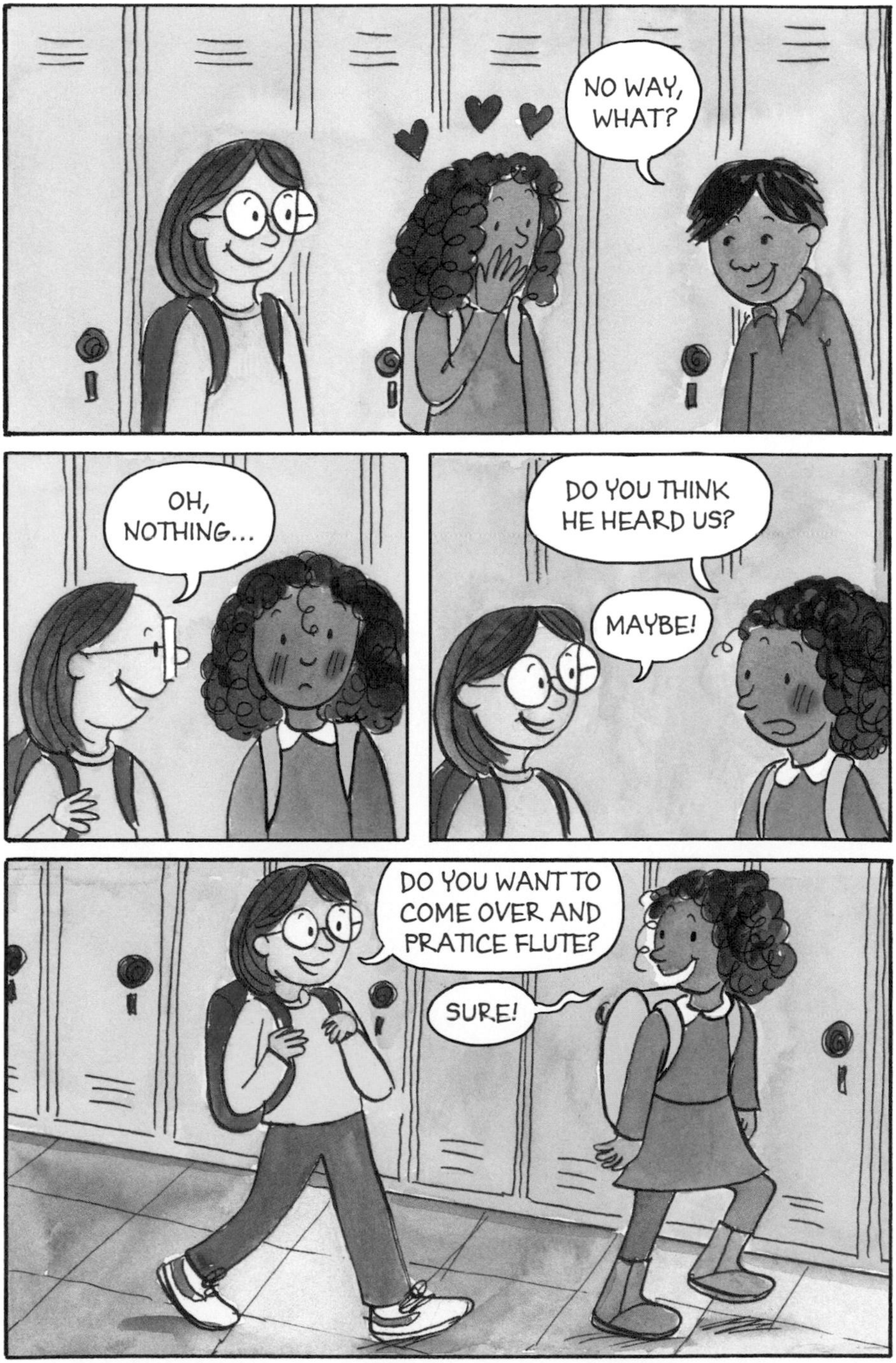
NO WAY, WHAT?
OH, NOTHING...
DO YOU THINK HE HEARD US?
MAYBE!
DO YOU WANT TO COME OVER AND PRATICE FLUTE?
SURE!

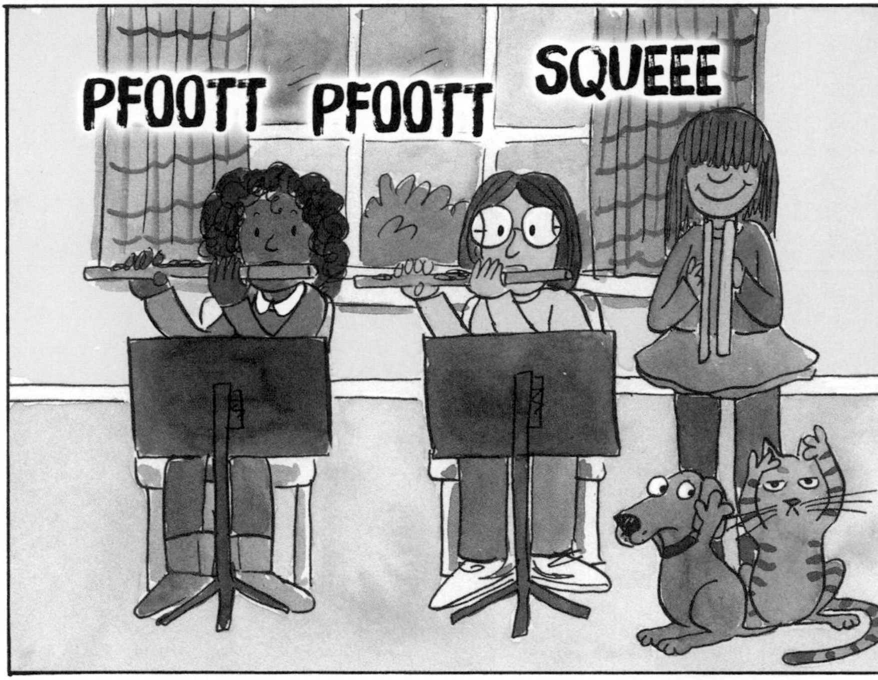
PFOOTT PFOOTT
SQUEEE

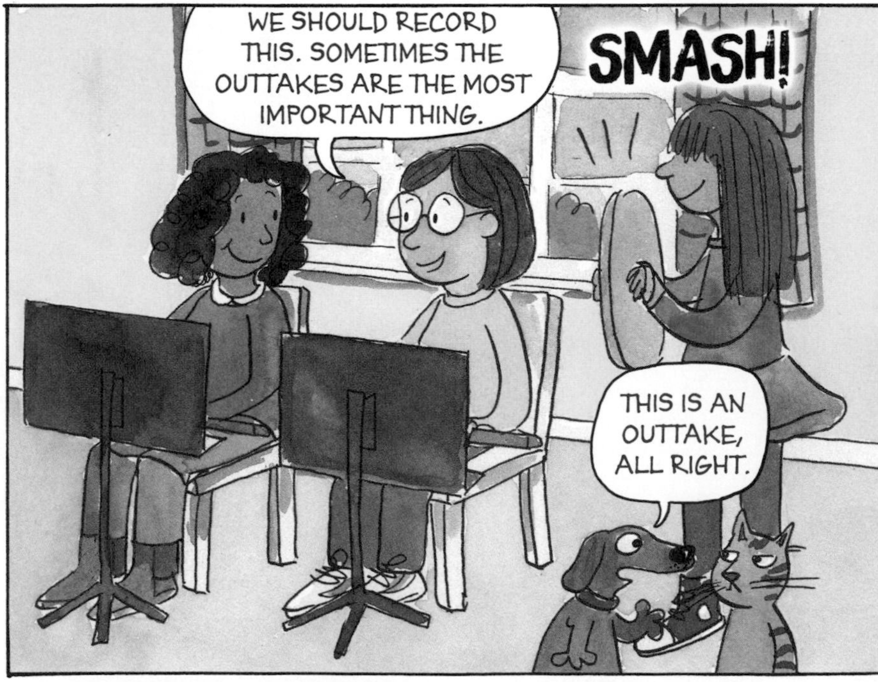
WE SHOULD RECORD THIS. SOMETIMES THE OUTTAKES ARE THE MOST IMPORTANT THING.
SMASH!
THIS IS AN OUTTAKE, ALL RIGHT.

CHAPTER 13
VOTE

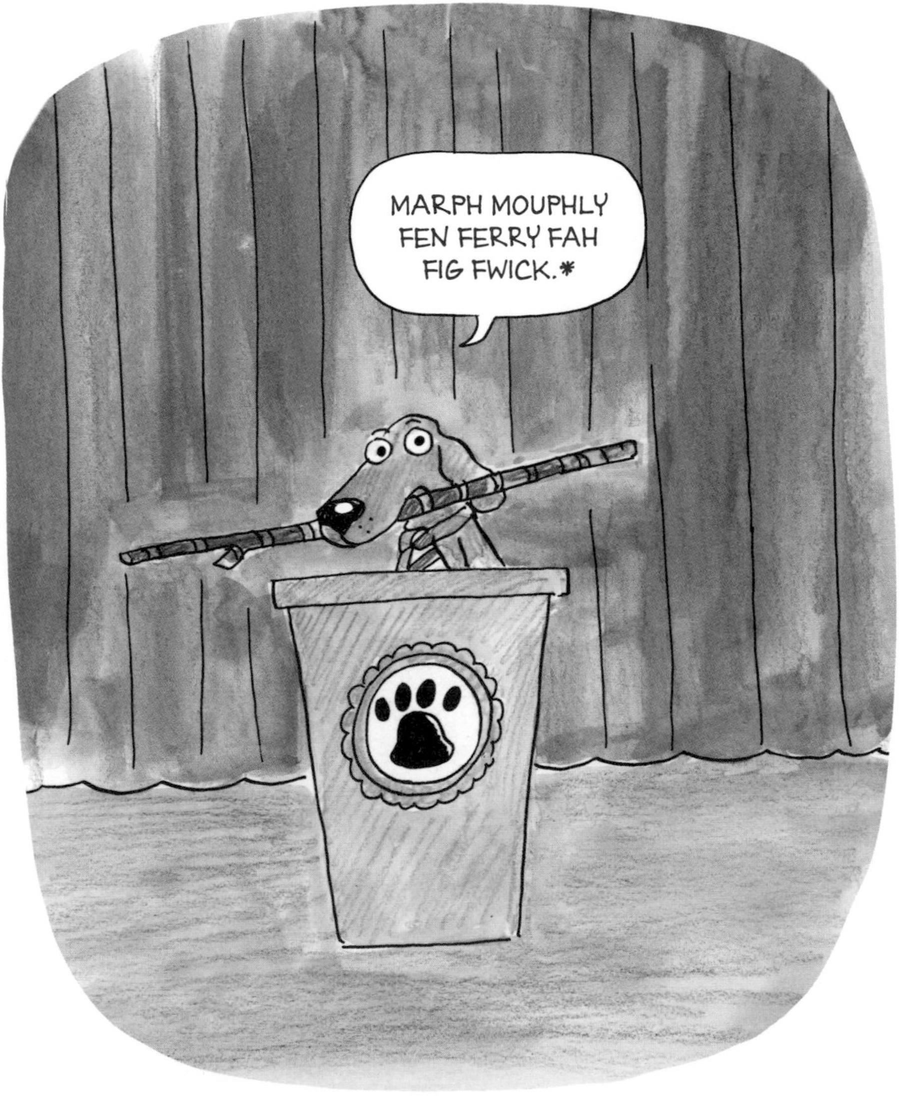
MARPH MOUPHLY FEN FERRY FAH FIG FWICK.*

* BARK LOUDLY AND CARRY A BIG STICK.

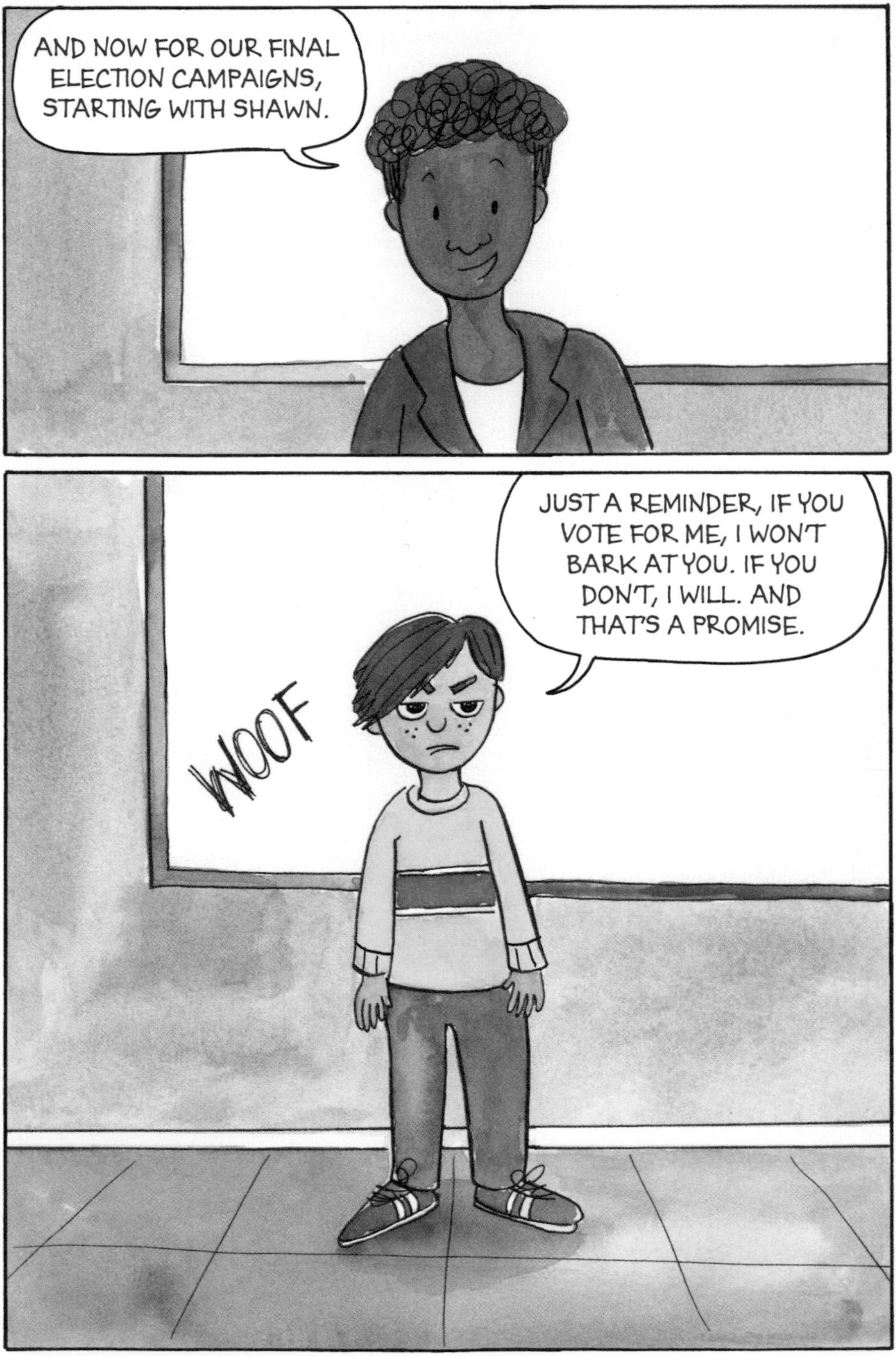
AND NOW FOR OUR FINAL ELECTION CAMPAIGNS, STARTING WITH SHAWN.
JUST A REMINDER, IF YOU VOTE FOR ME, I WON'T BARK AT YOU. IF YOU DON'T, I WILL. AND THAT'S A PROMISE.
WOOF

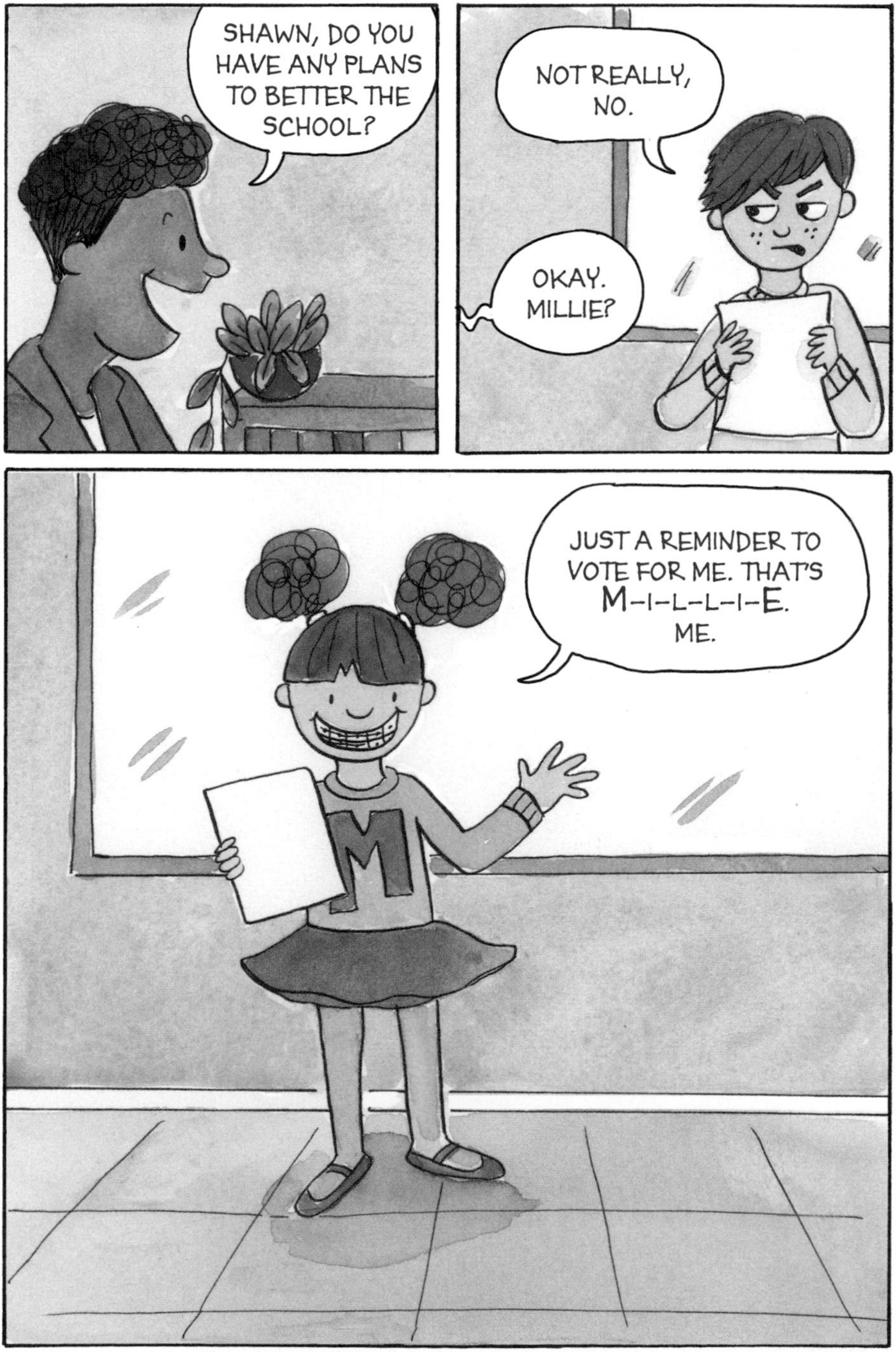
SHAWN, DO YOU HAVE ANY PLANS TO BETTER THE SCHOOL?
NOT REALLY, NO.
OKAY. MILLIE?
JUST A REMINDER TO VOTE FOR ME. THAT'S M-I-L-L-I-E. ME.

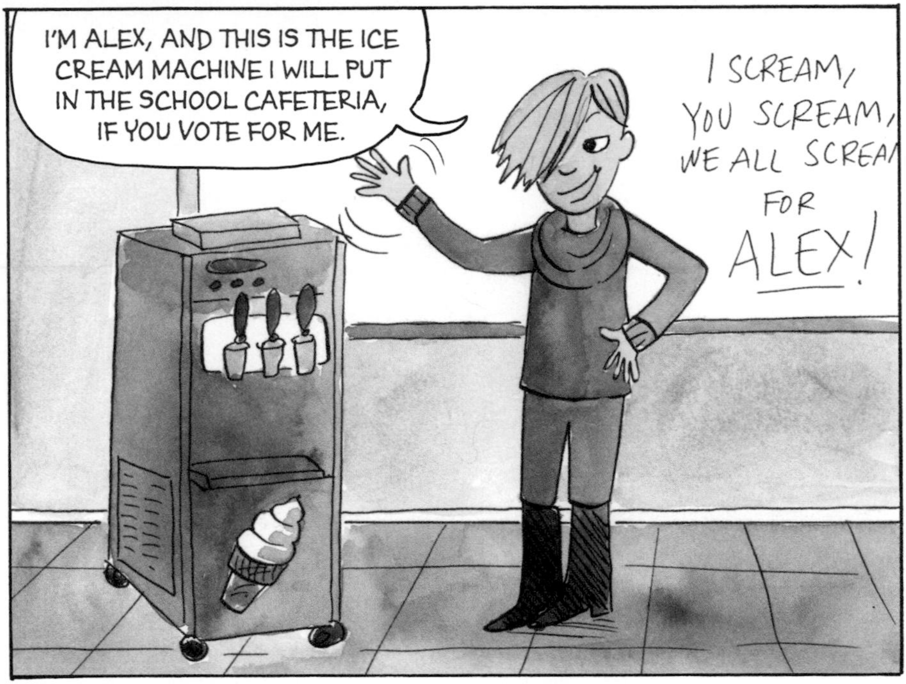
I'M ALEX, AND THIS IS THE ICE CREAM MACHINE I WILL PUT IN THE SCHOOL CAFETERIA, IF YOU VOTE FOR ME.
I SCREAM, YOU SCREAM, WE ALL SCREAM FOR ALEX!

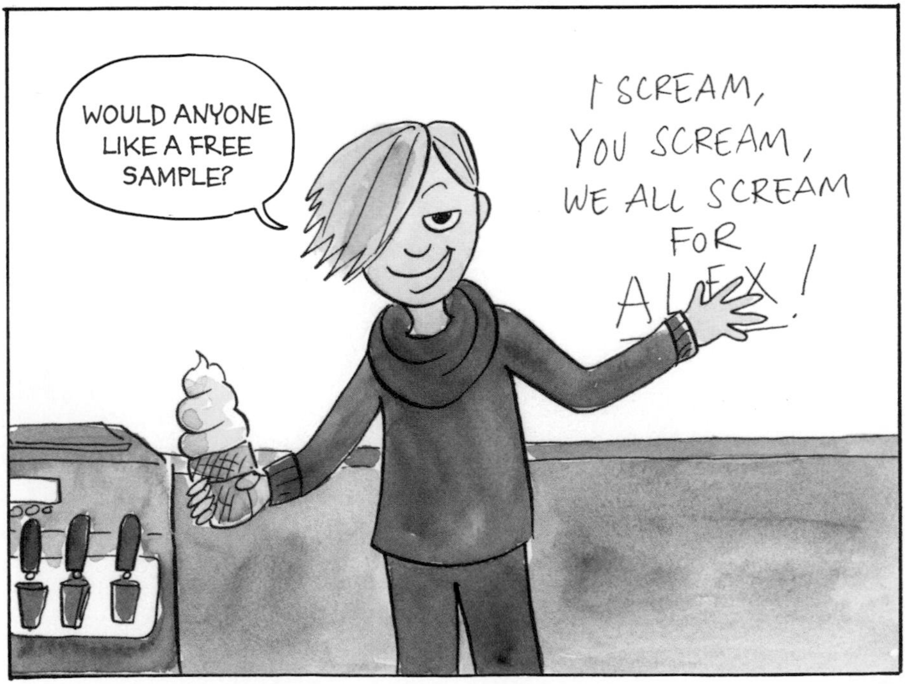
WOULD ANYONE LIKE A FREE SAMPLE?
I SCREAM, YOU SCREAM, WE ALL SCREAM FOR ALEX!

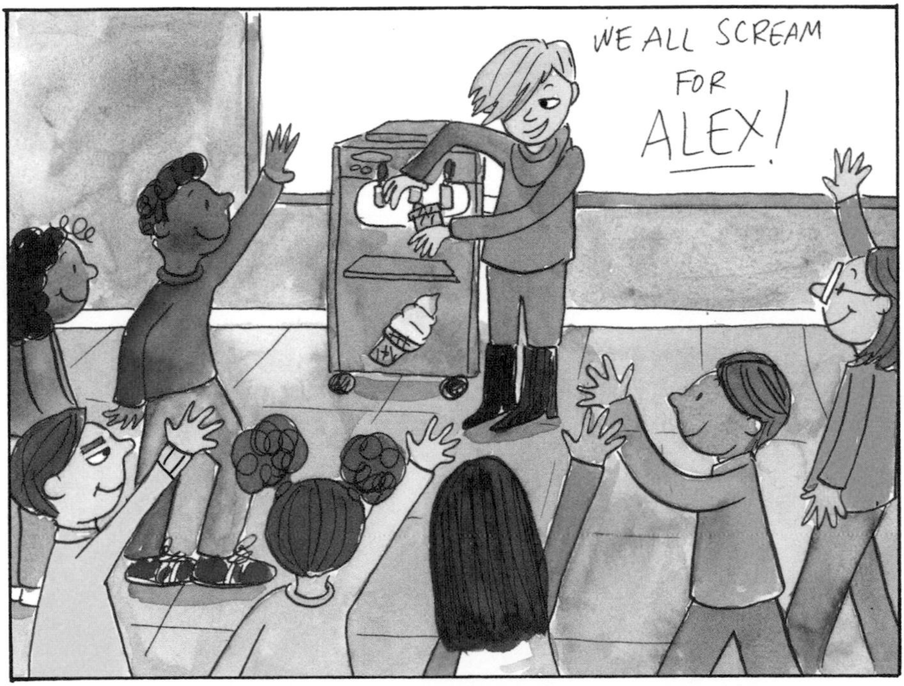
WE ALL SCREAM FOR ALEX!

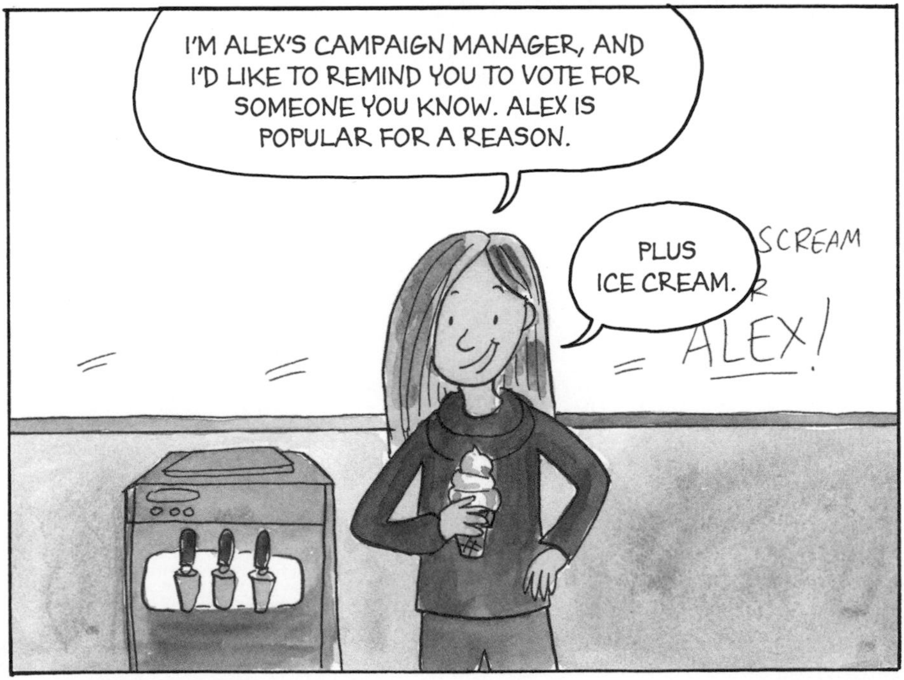
I'M ALEX'S CAMPAIGN MANAGER, AND I'D LIKE TO REMIND YOU TO VOTE FOR SOMEONE YOU KNOW. ALEX IS POPULAR FOR A REASON.
PLUS ICE CREAM.
SCREAM
ALEX!

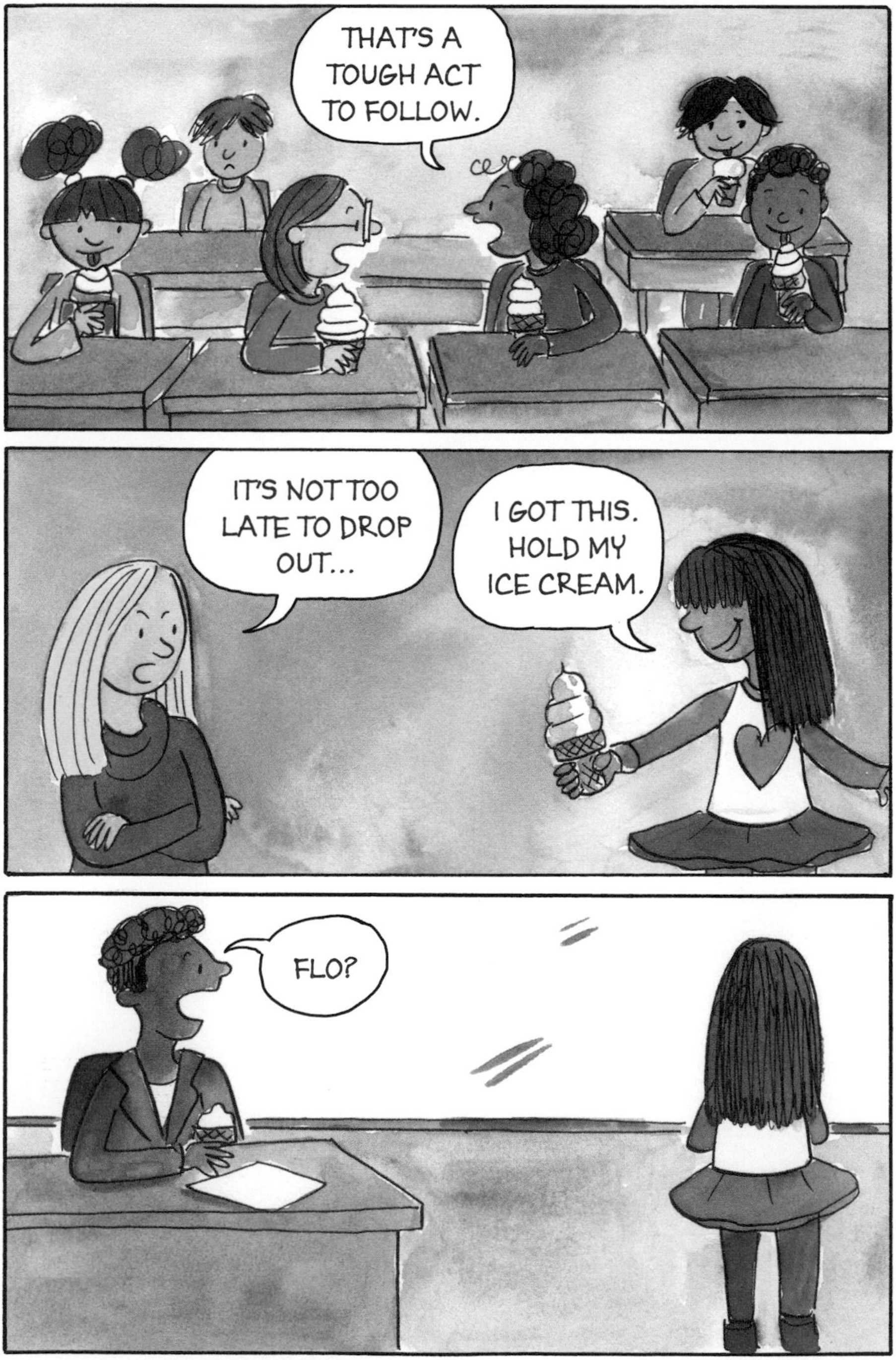
THAT'S A TOUGH ACT TO FOLLOW.
IT'S NOT TOO LATE TO DROP OUT...
I GOT THIS. HOLD MY ICE CREAM.
FLO?

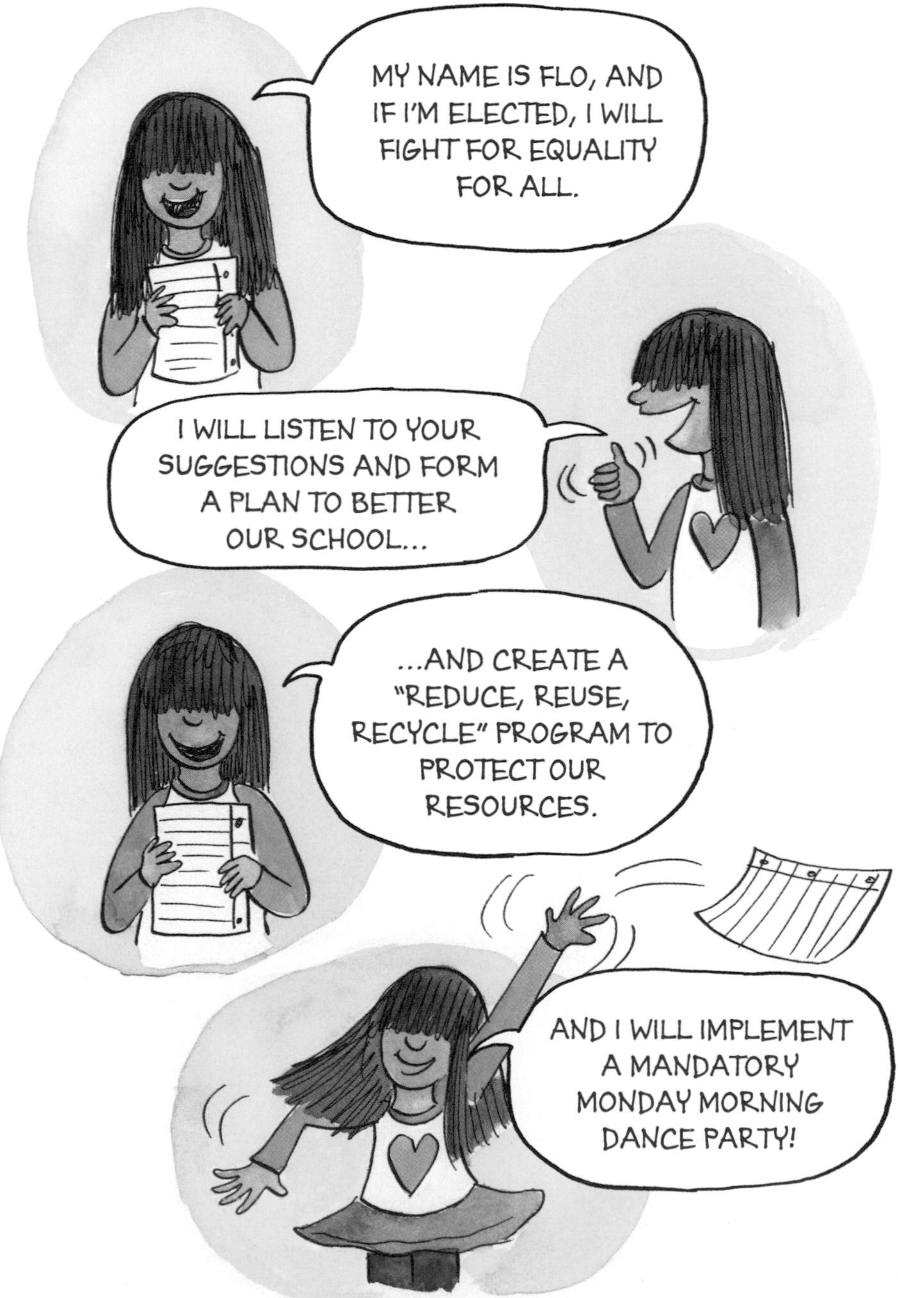
MY NAME IS FLO, AND IF I'M ELECTED, I WILL FIGHT FOR EQUALITY FOR ALL.
I WILL LISTEN TO YOUR SUGGESTIONS AND FORM A PLAN TO BETTER OUR SCHOOL...
...AND CREATE A "REDUCE, REUSE, RECYCLE" PROGRAM TO PROTECT OUR RESOURCES.
AND I WILL IMPLEMENT A MANDATORY MONDAY MORNING DANCE PARTY!

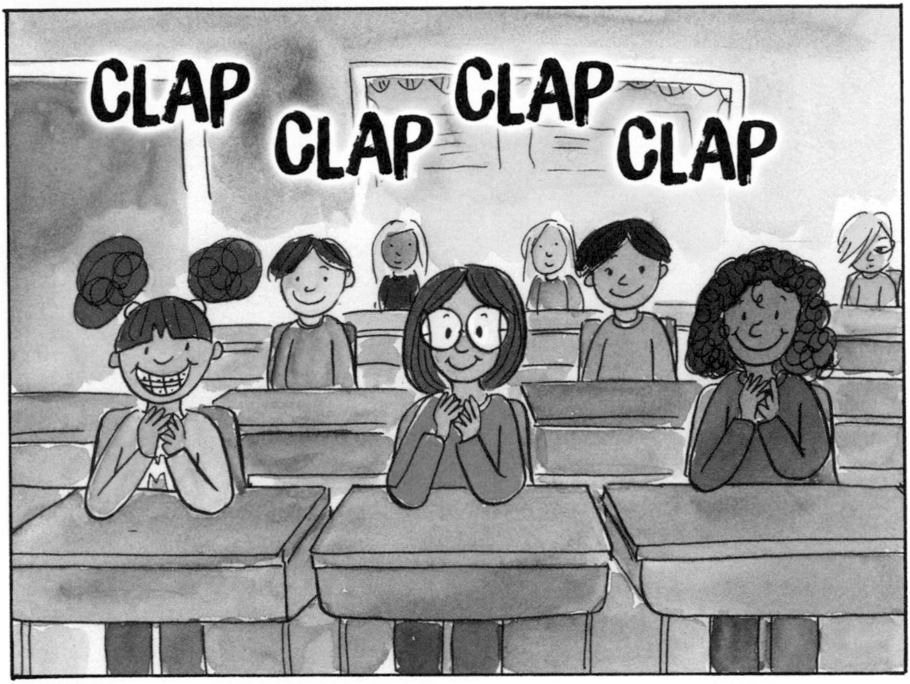
CLAP
CLAP
CLAP
CLAP

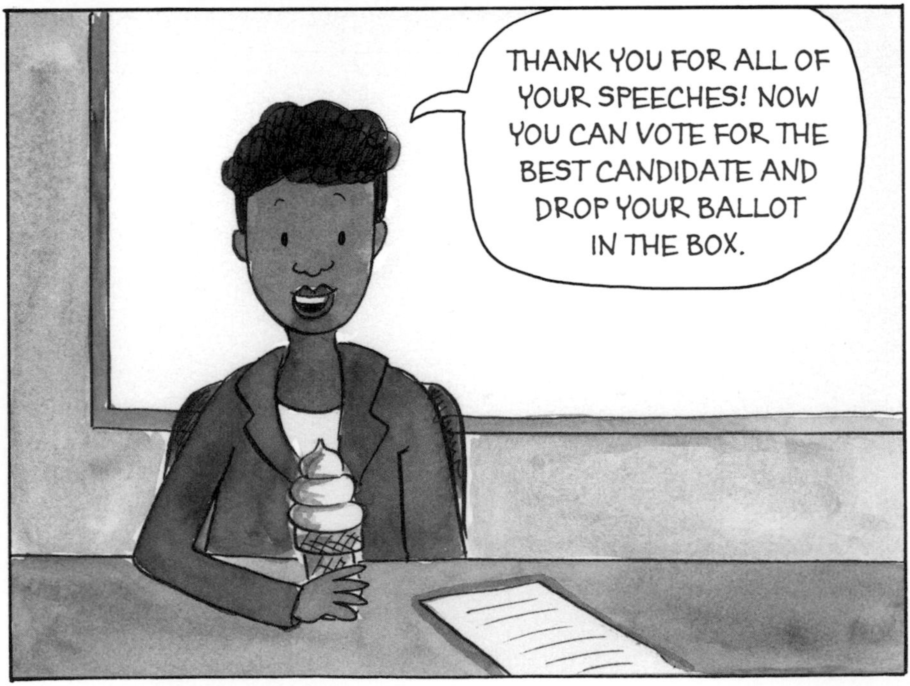
THANK YOU FOR ALL OF YOUR SPEECHES! NOW YOU CAN VOTE FOR THE BEST CANDIDATE AND DROP YOUR BALLOT IN THE BOX.

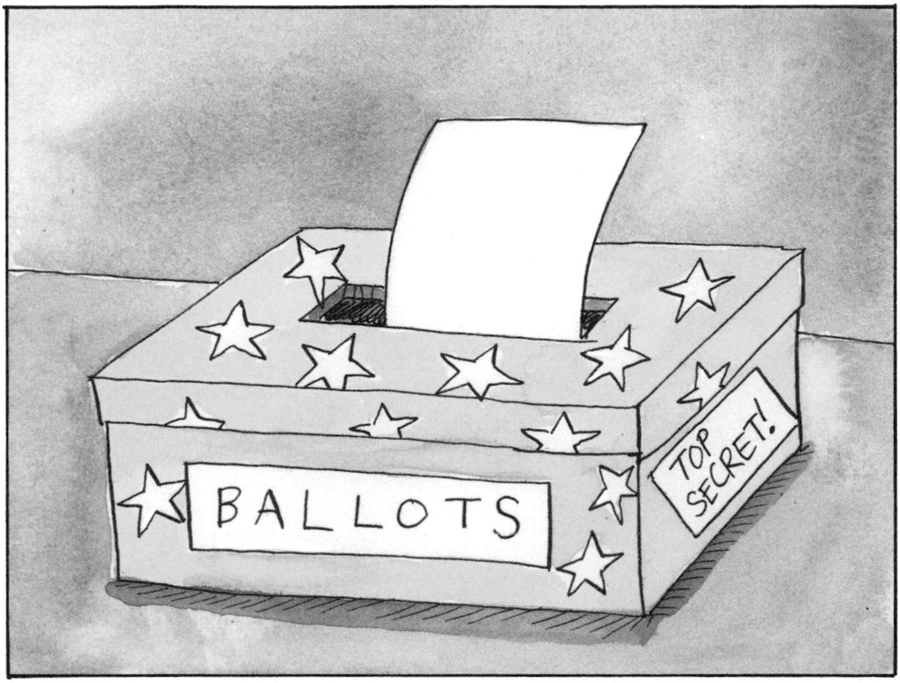
BALLOTS
TOP SECRET!

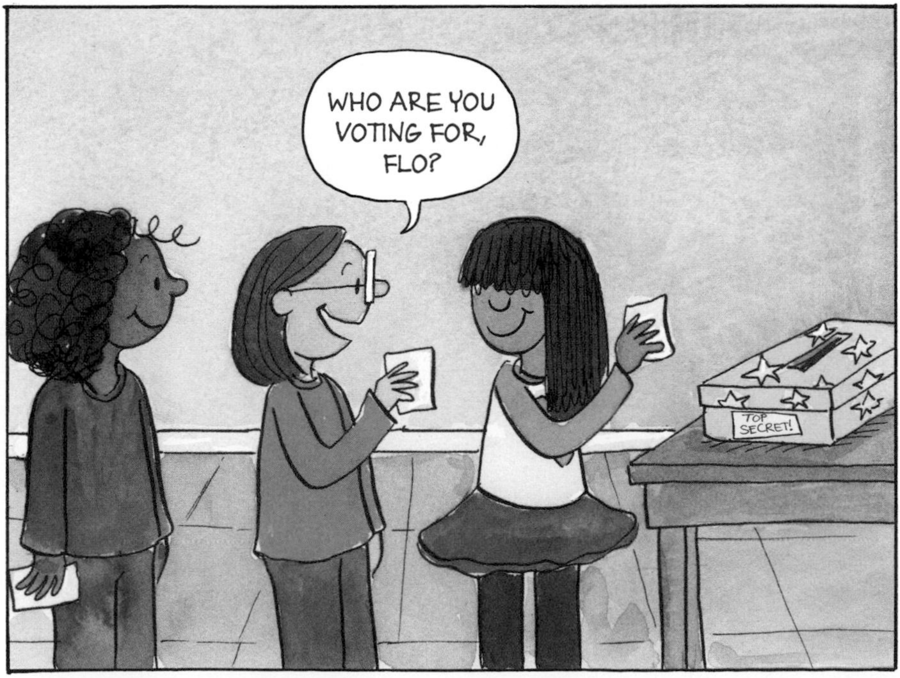
WHO ARE YOU VOTING FOR, FLO?
TOP SECRET!

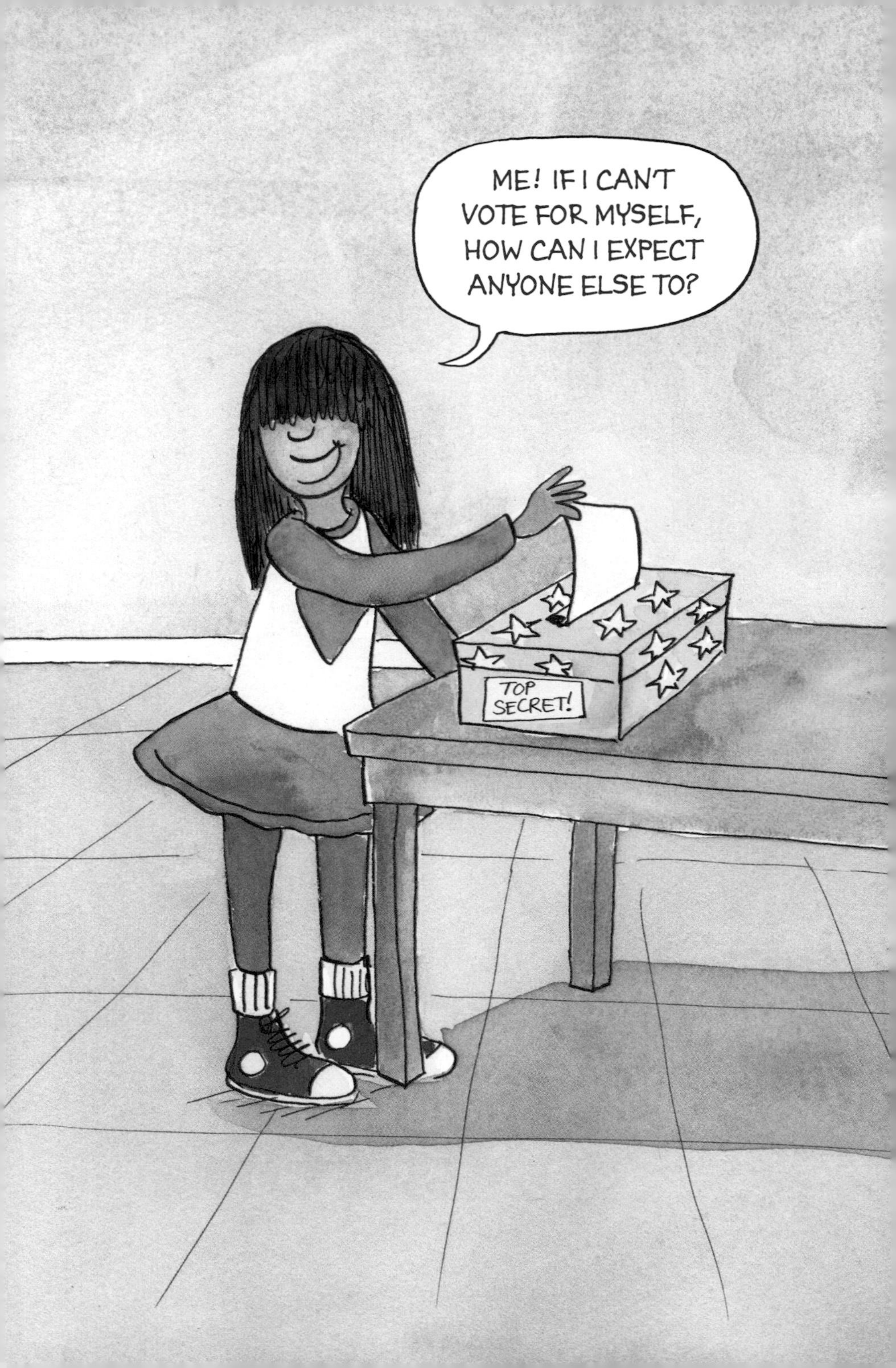
ME! IF I CAN'T VOTE FOR MYSELF, HOW CAN I EXPECT ANYONE ELSE TO?
TOP SECRET!

CHAPTER 14
RUBBER BAND

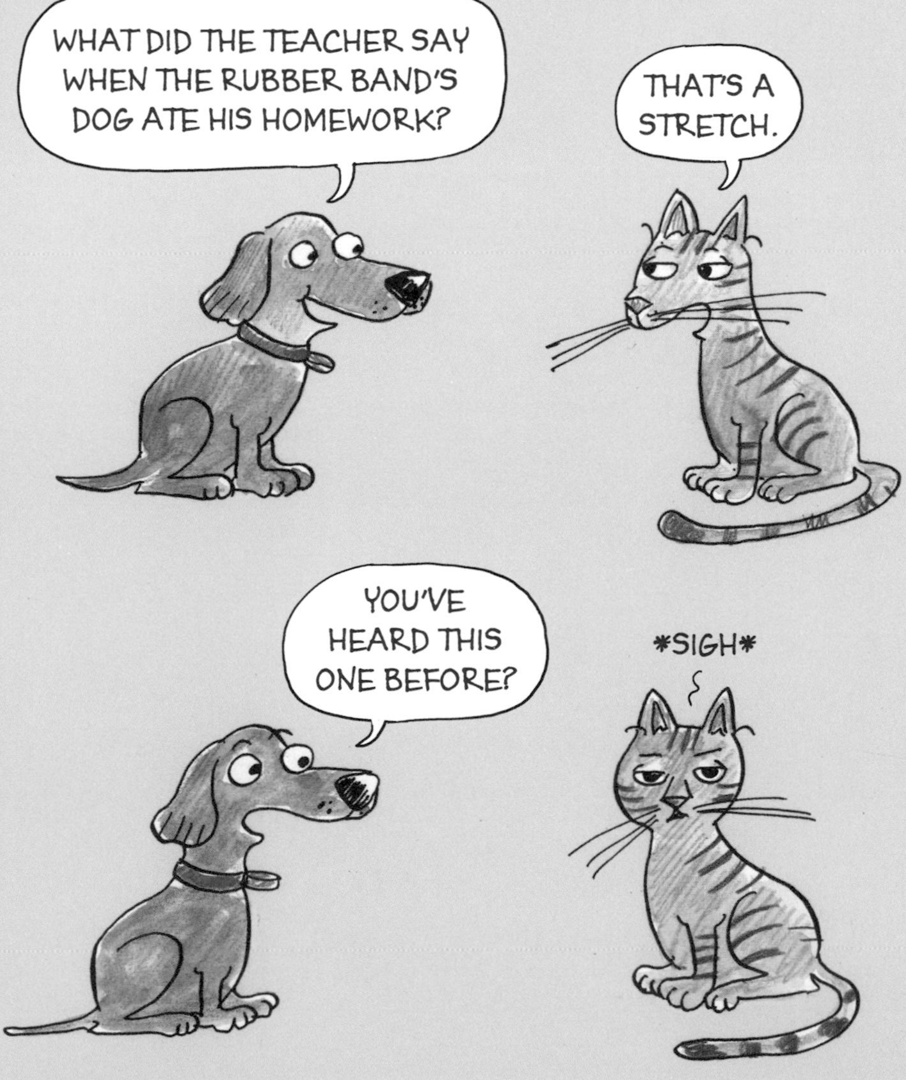
WHAT DID THE TEACHER SAY WHEN THE RUBBER BAND'S DOG ATE HIS HOMEWORK?
THAT'S A STRETCH.
YOU'VE HEARD THIS ONE BEFORE?
SIGH

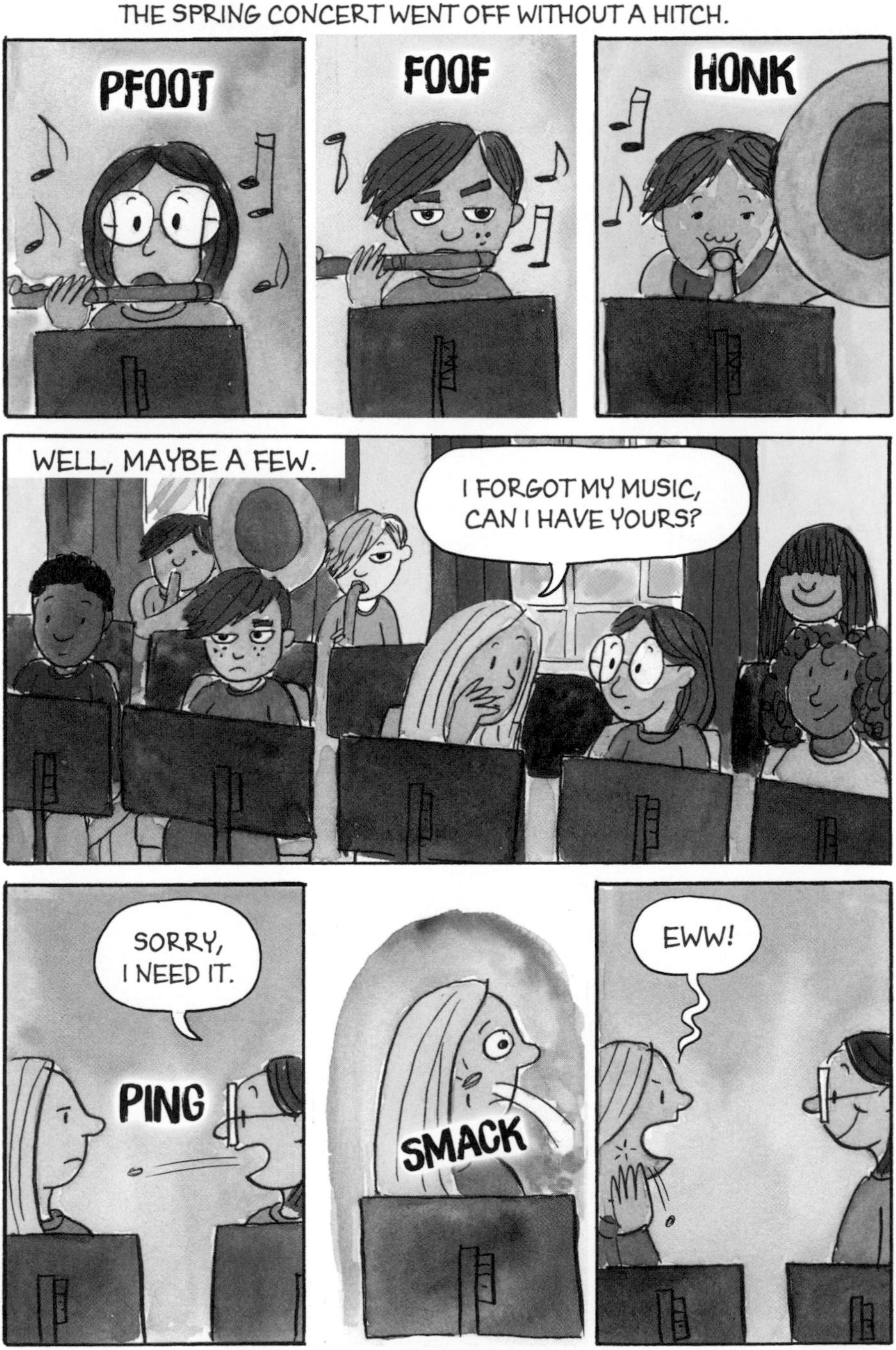
THE SPRING CONCERT WENT OFF WITHOUT A HITCH.
PFOOT
FOOF
HONK
WELL, MAYBE A FEW.
I FORGOT MY MUSIC, CAN I HAVE YOURS?
SORRY, I NEED IT.
PING
SMACK
EWW!

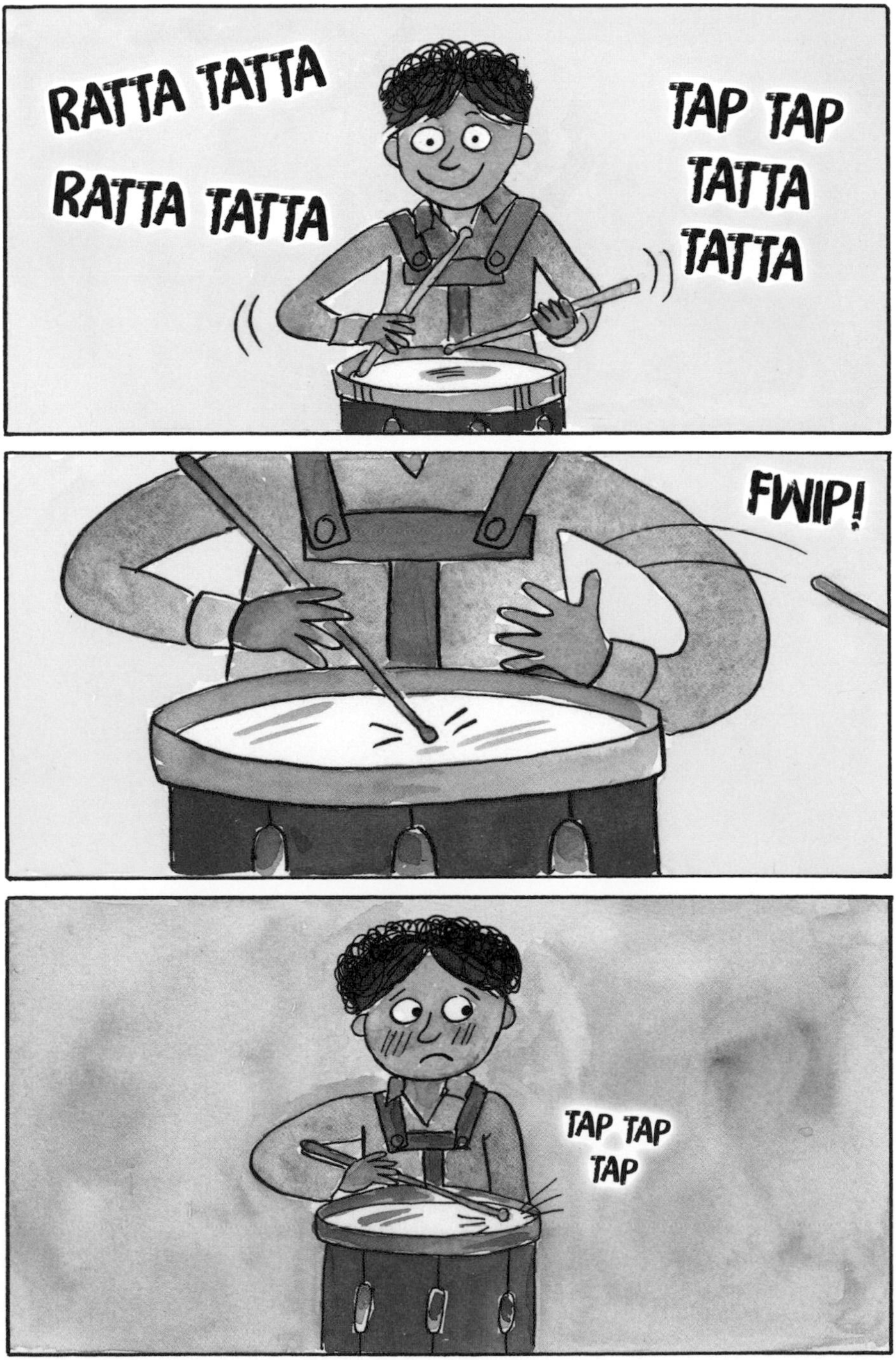
RATTA TATTA
RATTA TATTA
TAP TAP
TATTA
TATTA
FWIP!
TAP TAP
TAP

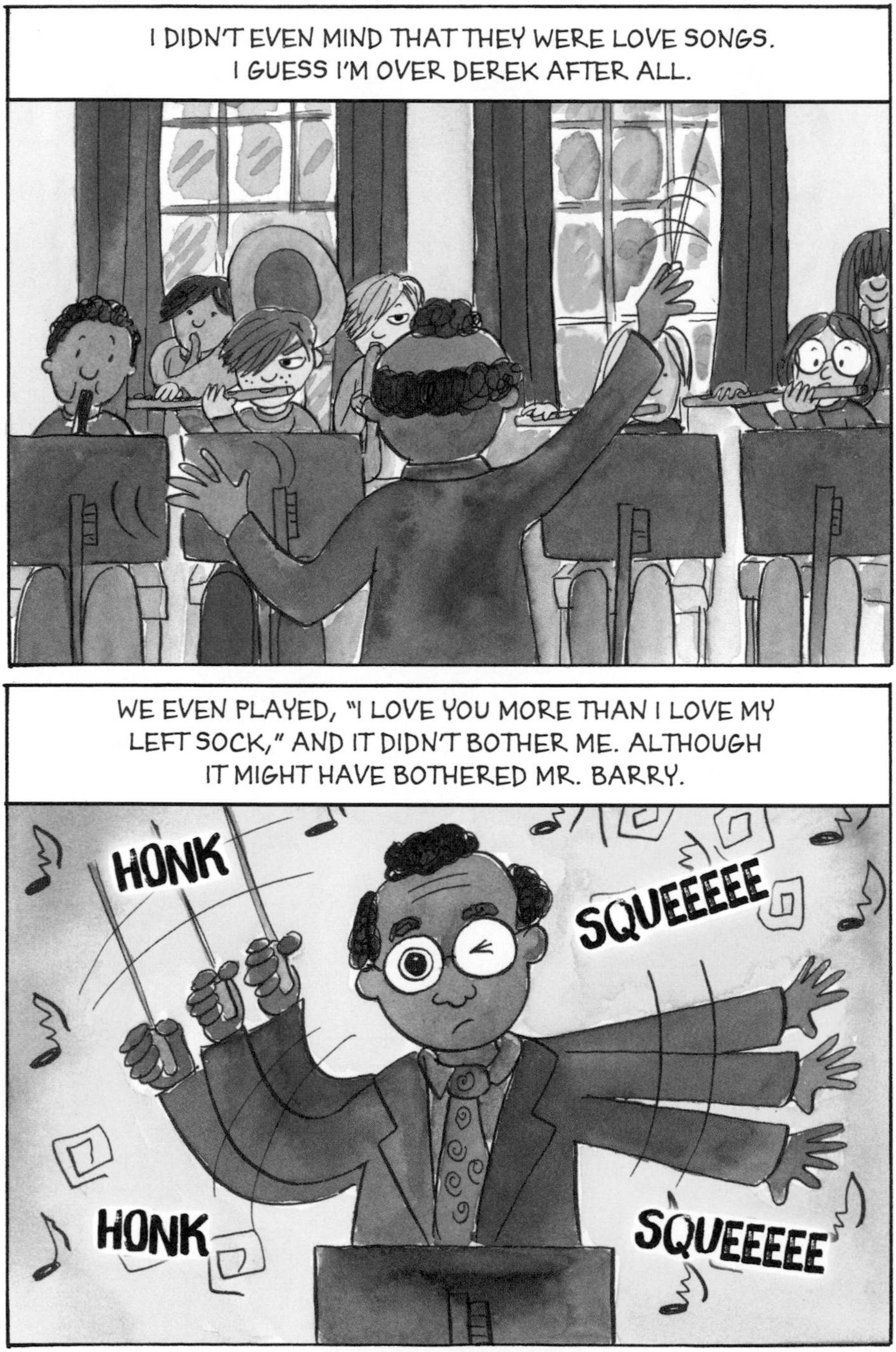
I DIDN'T EVEN MIND THAT THEY WERE LOVE SONGS. I GUESS I'M OVER DEREK AFTER ALL.
WE EVEN PLAYED, "I LOVE YOU MORE THAN I LOVE MY LEFT SOCK," AND IT DIDN'T BOTHER ME. ALTHOUGH IT MIGHT HAVE BOTHERED MR. BARRY.
HONK
SQUEEEEE
HONK
SQUEEEEE

MR. BARRY FIXED THE PROBLEM OF FLO MISSING HER CUE BY GIVING HER A SOLO.

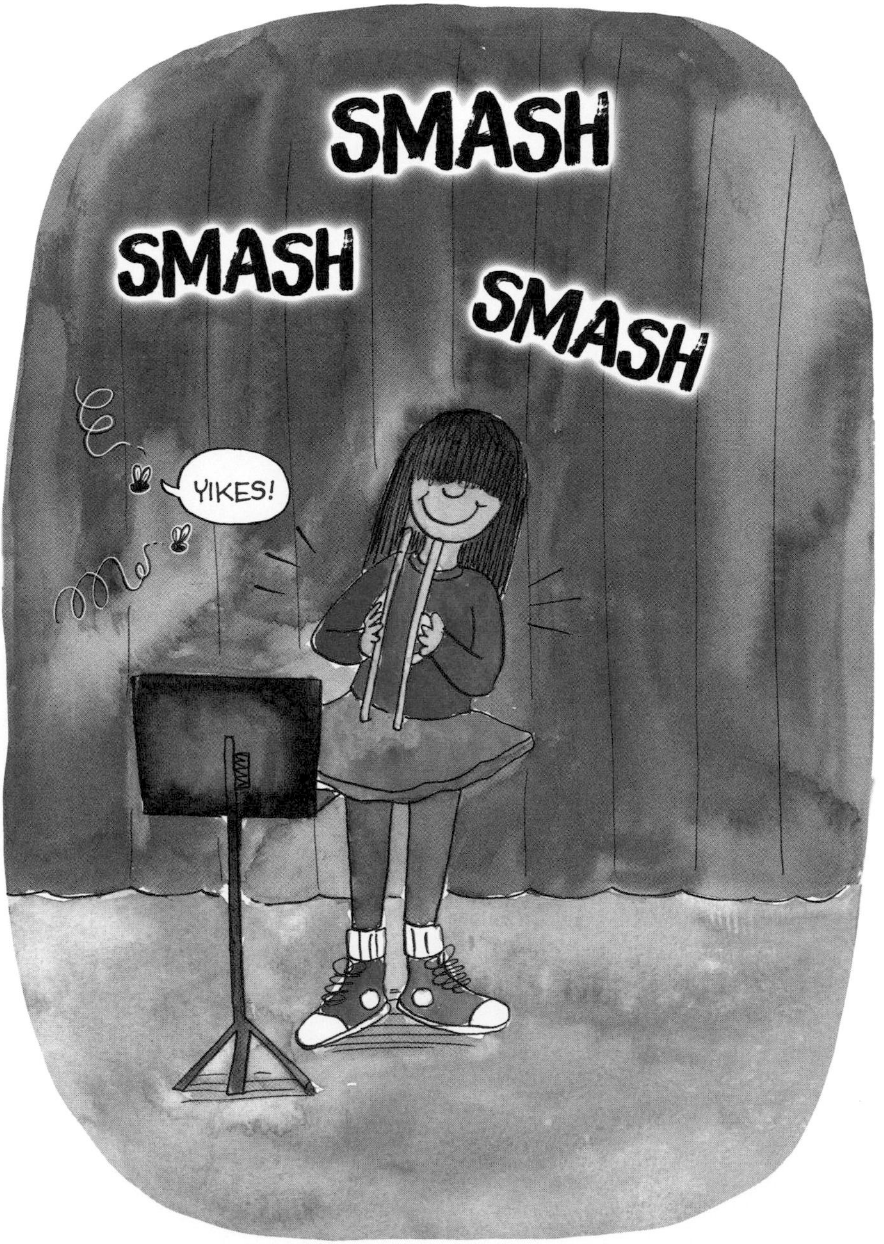
SMASH
SMASH
SMASH
YIKES!

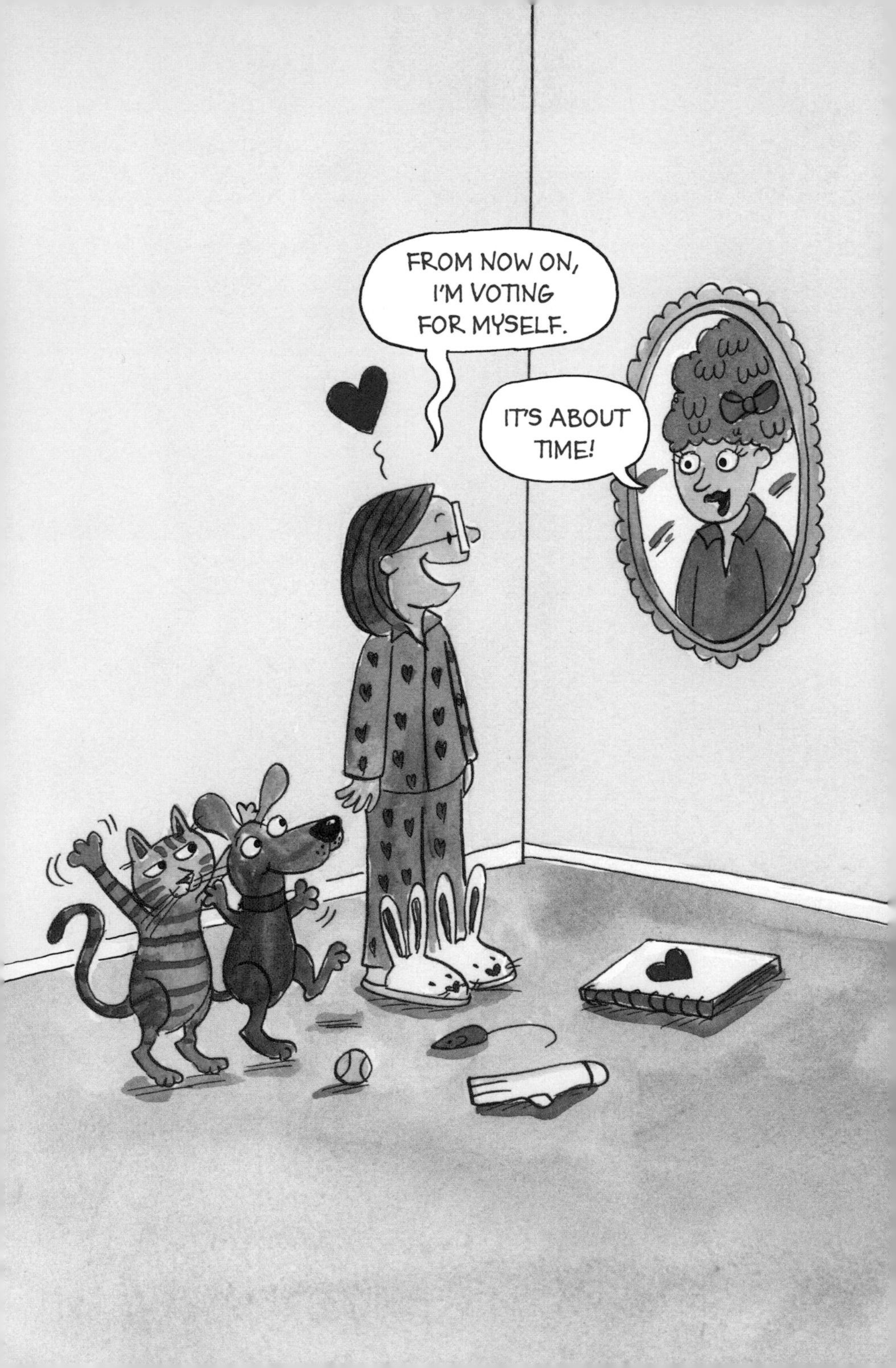
FROM NOW ON, I'M VOTING FOR MYSELF.
IT'S ABOUT TIME!

CHAPTER 15
ELECTION RESULTS

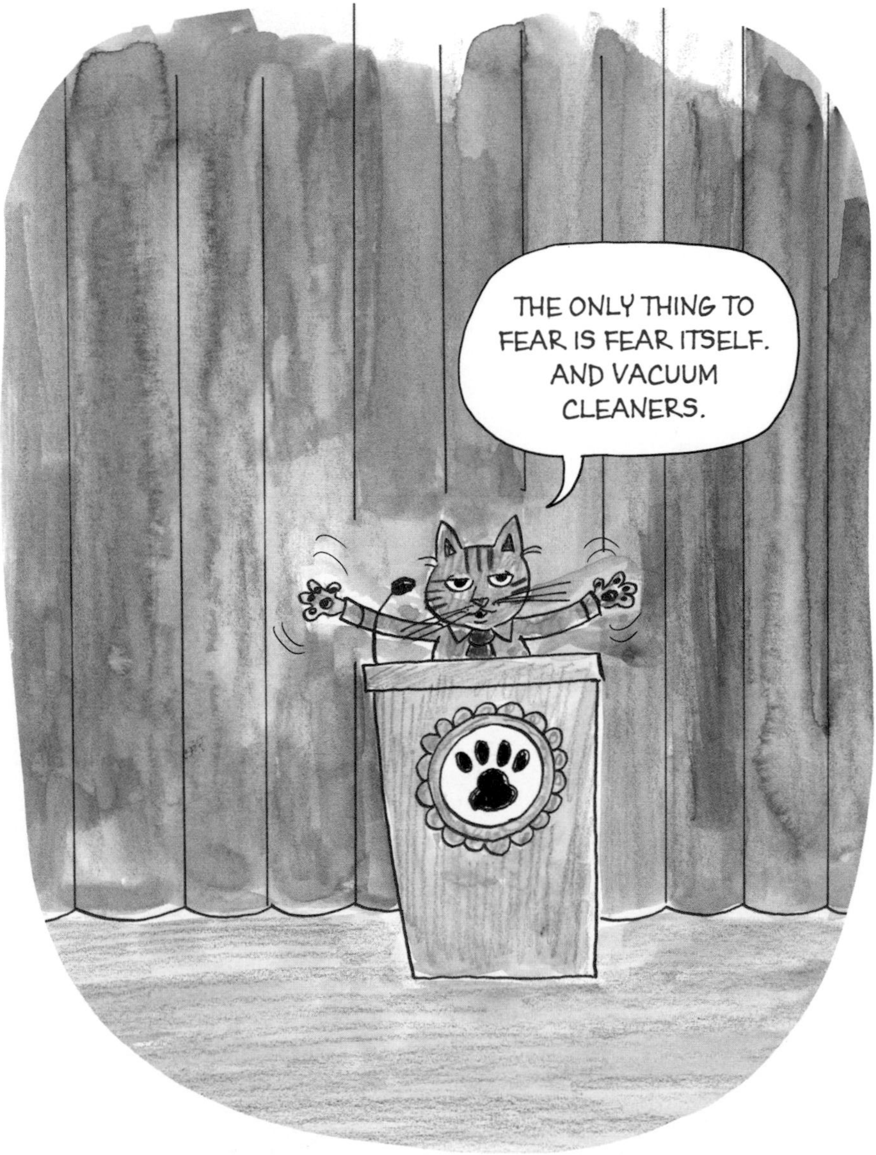
THE ONLY THING TO FEAR IS FEAR ITSELF. AND VACUUM CLEANERS.

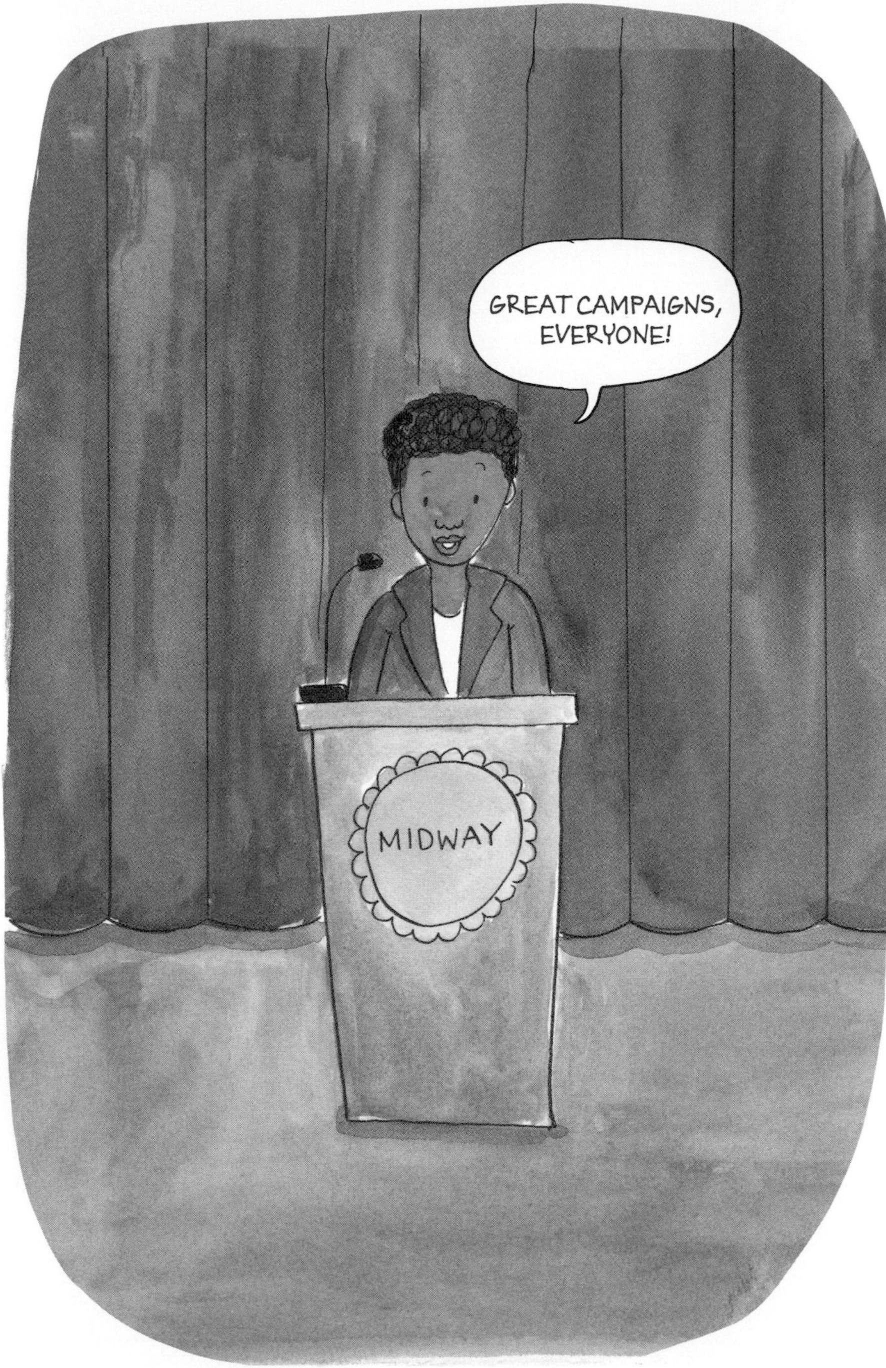
GREAT CAMPAIGNS, EVERYONE!
MIDWAY

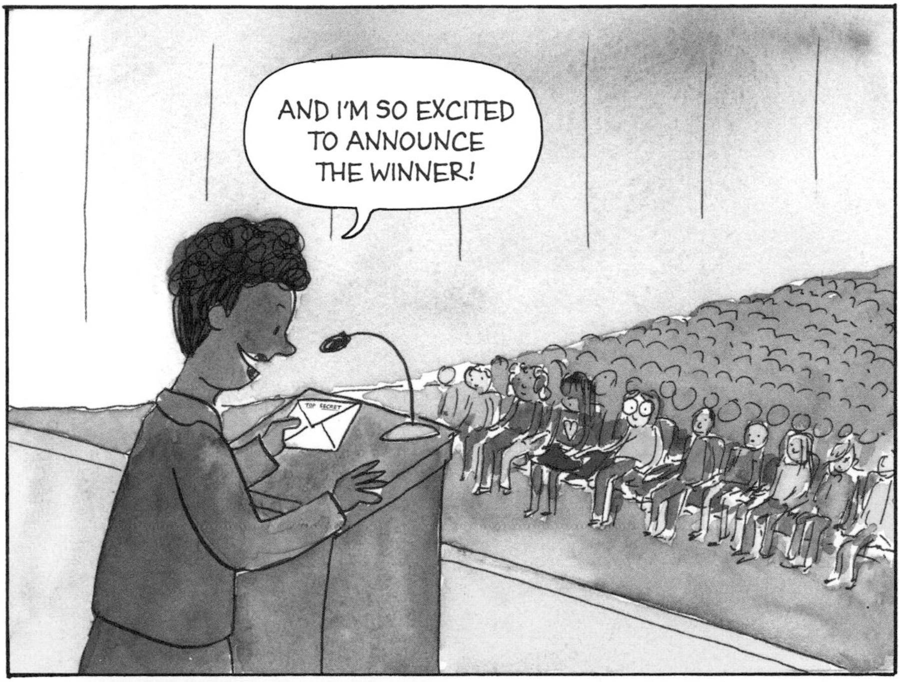
AND I'M SO EXCITED TO ANNOUNCE THE WINNER!
TOP SECRET

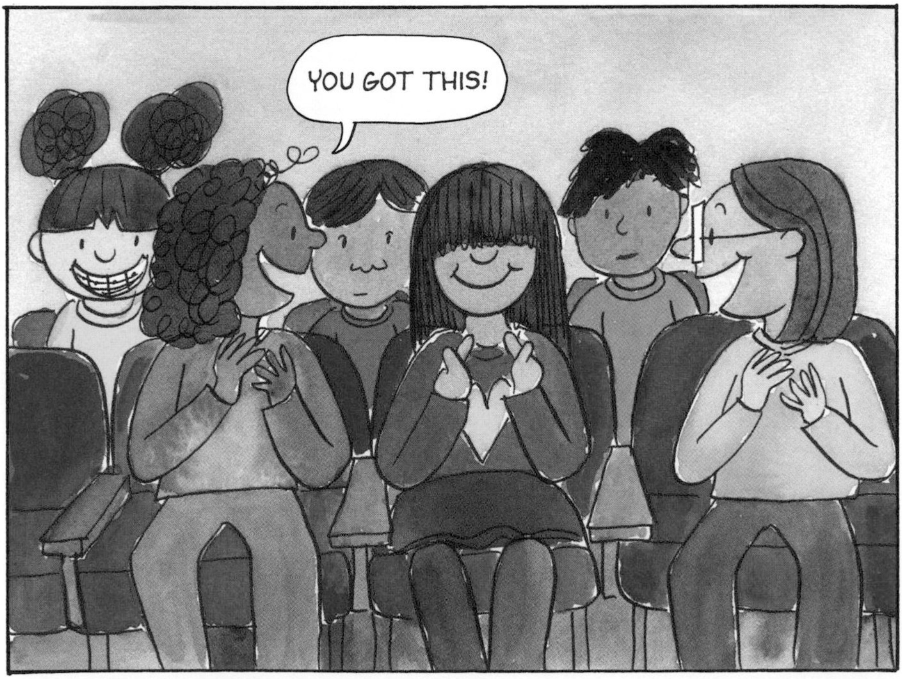
YOU GOT THIS!

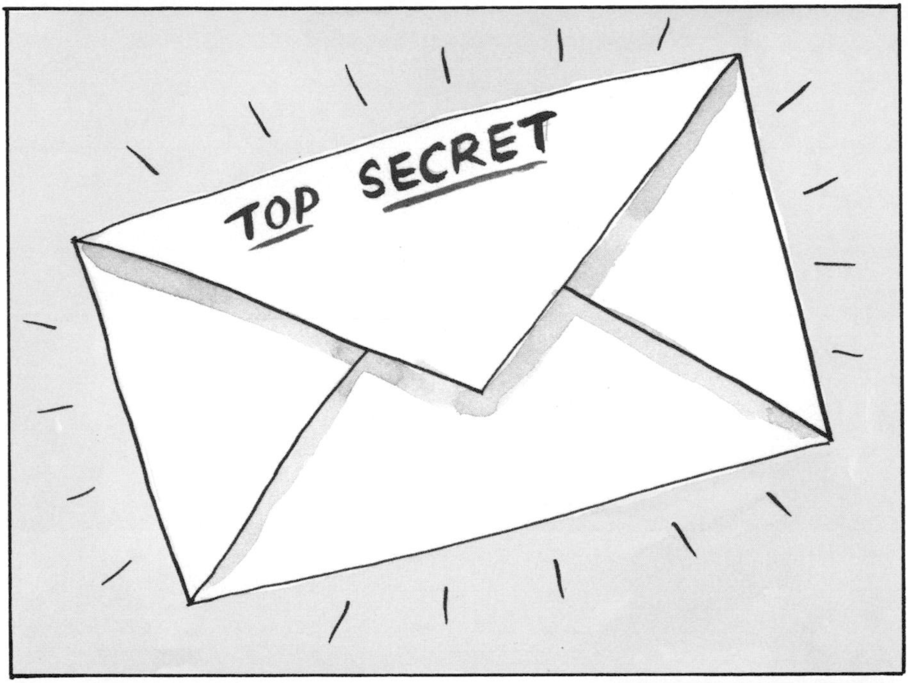
TOP SECRET

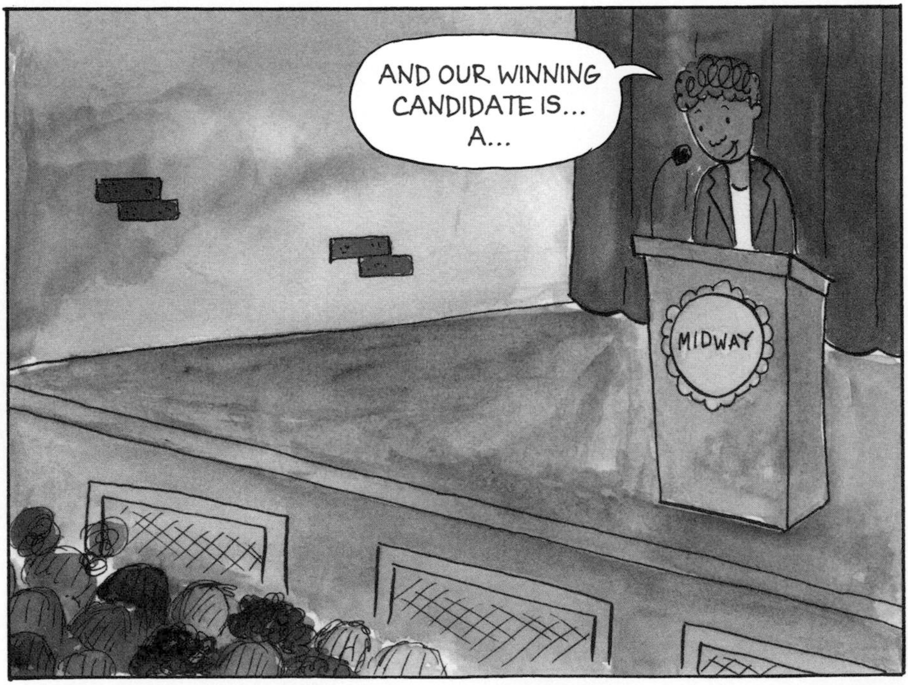
AND OUR WINNING CANDIDATE IS... A...
MIDWAY

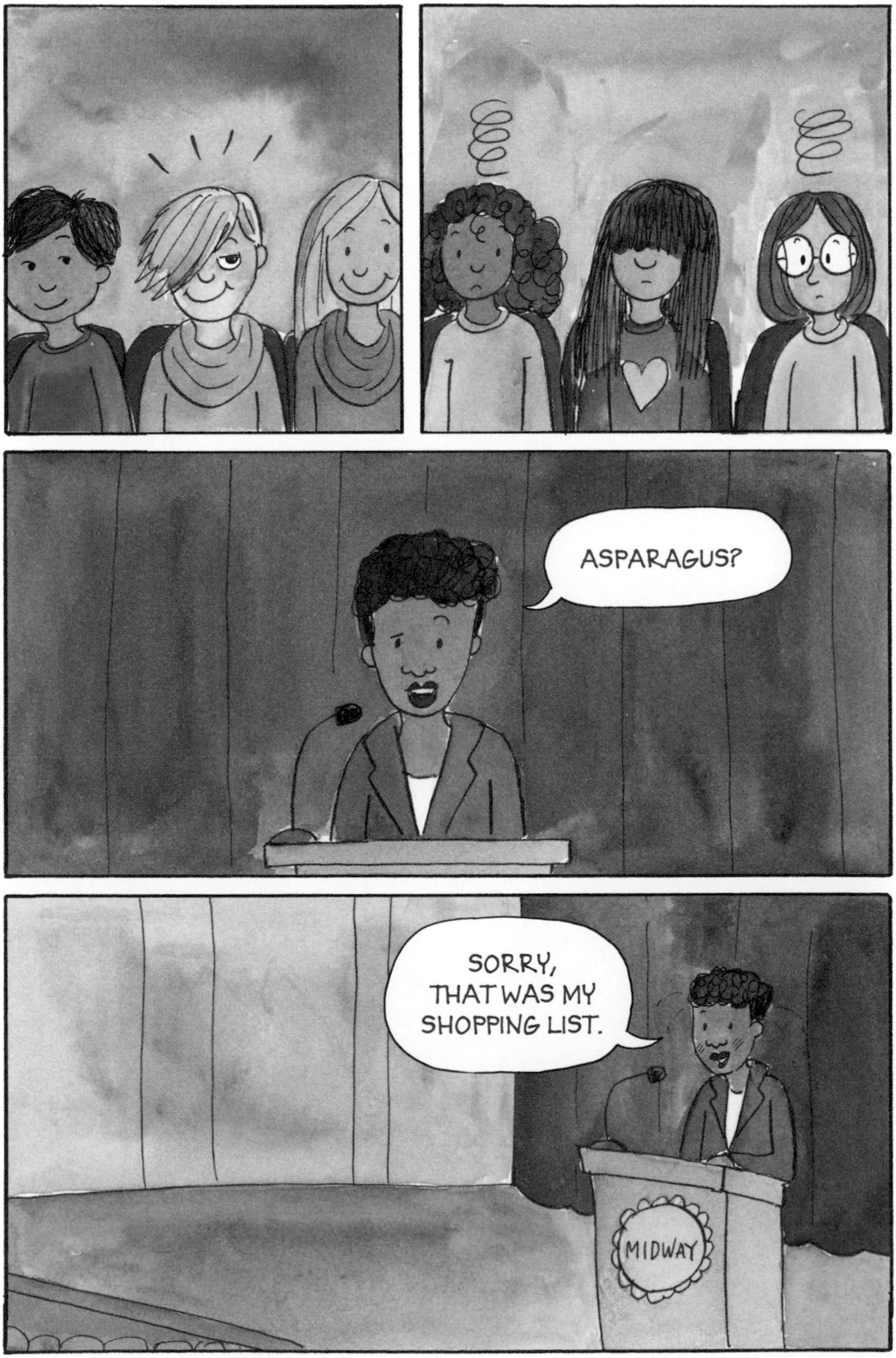
ASPARAGUS?
SORRY, THAT WAS MY SHOPPING LIST.
MIDWAY

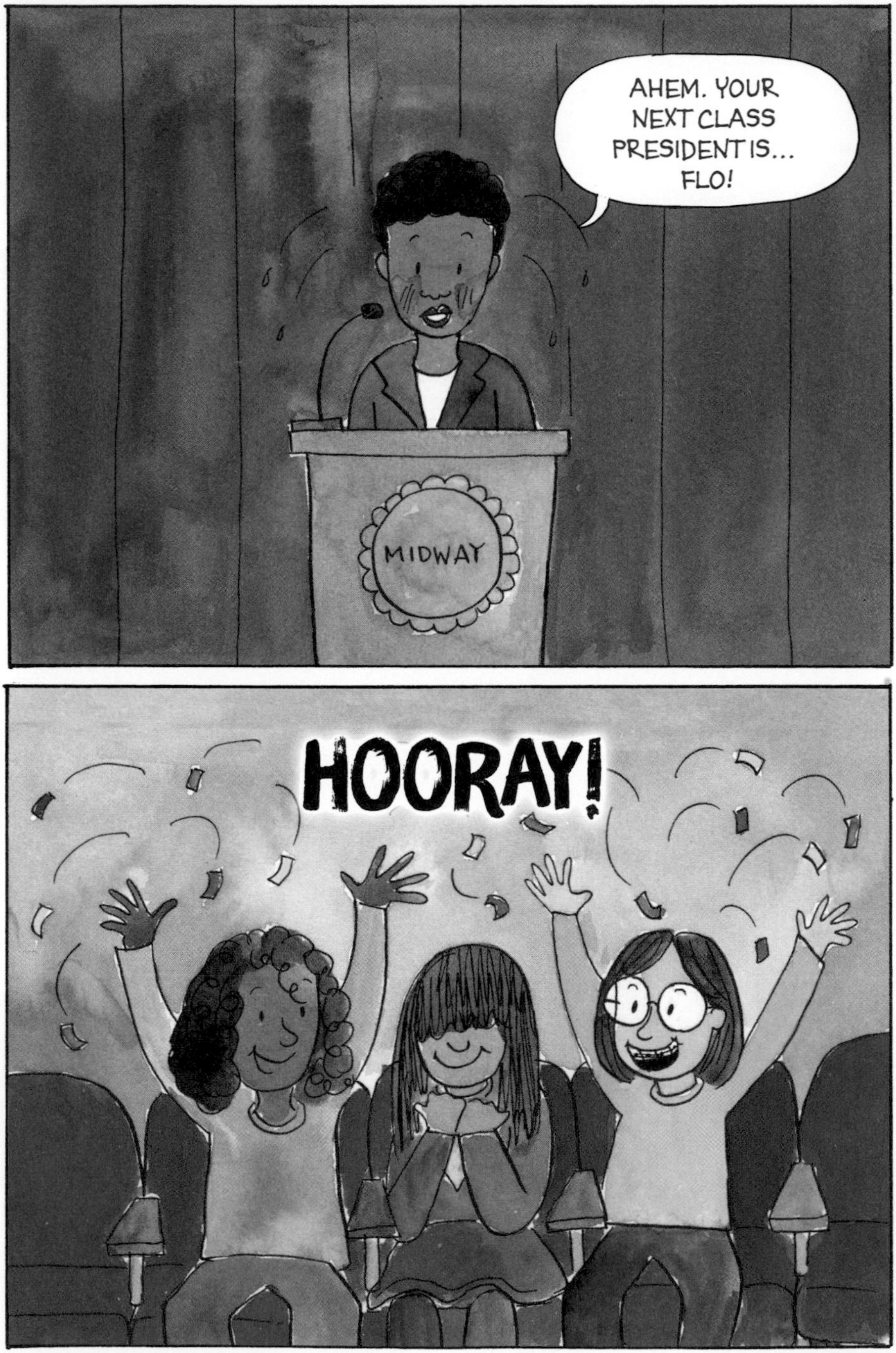
AHEM. YOUR NEXT CLASS PRESIDENT IS... FLO!
MIDWAY
HOORAY!

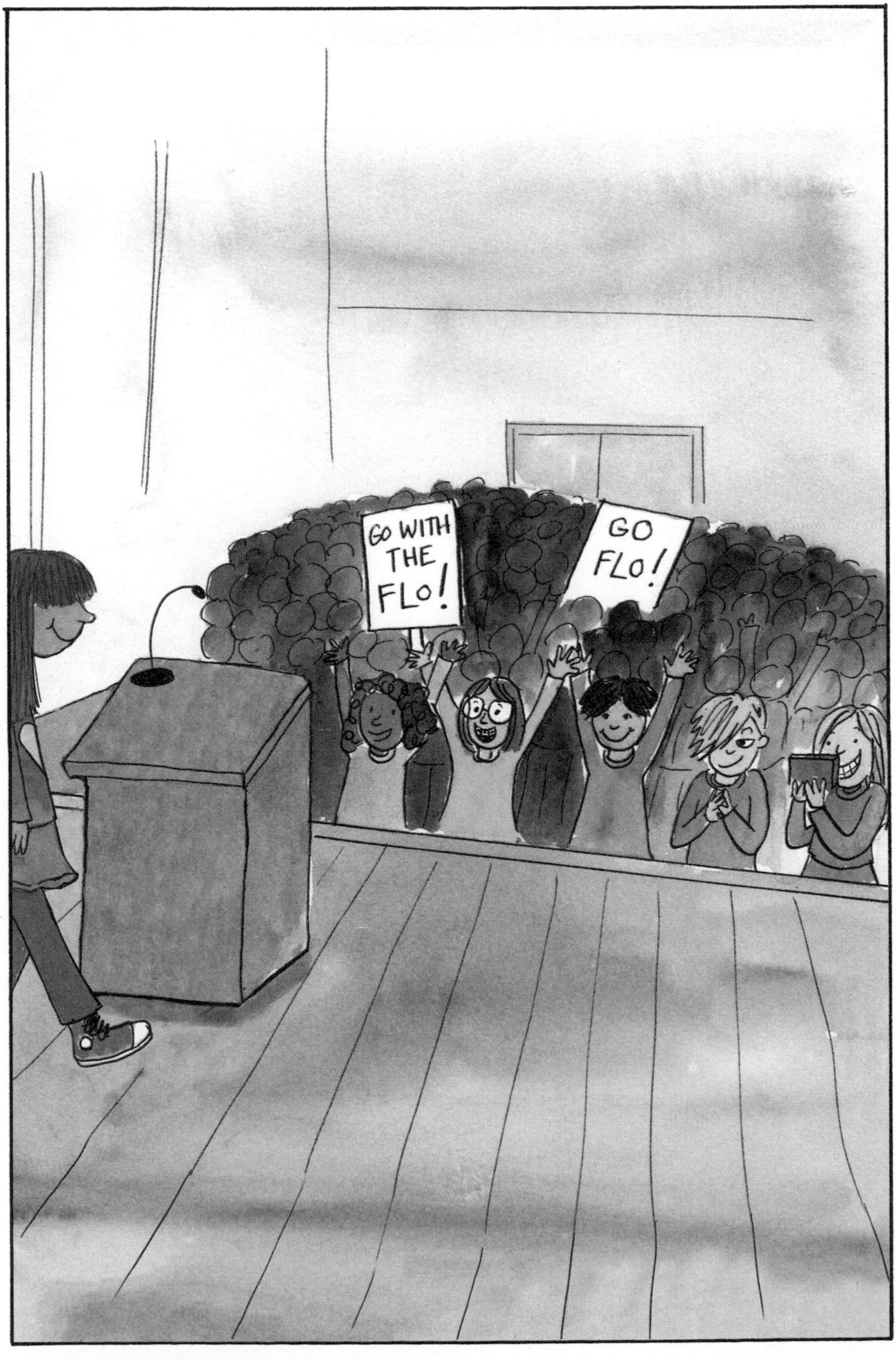
GO WITH THE FLO!
GO FLO!

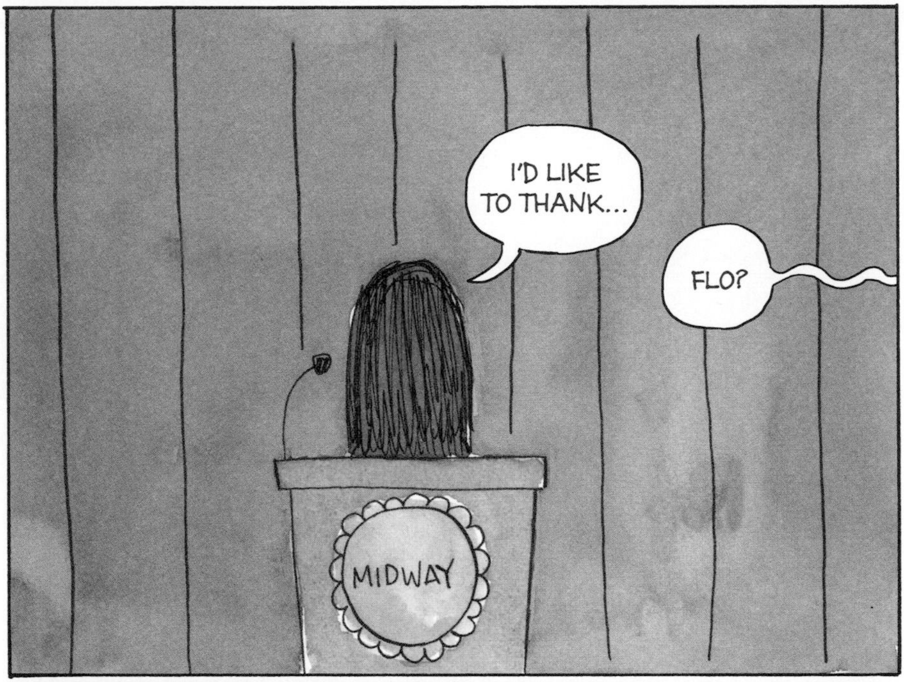
I'D LIKE
TO THANK...
FLO?

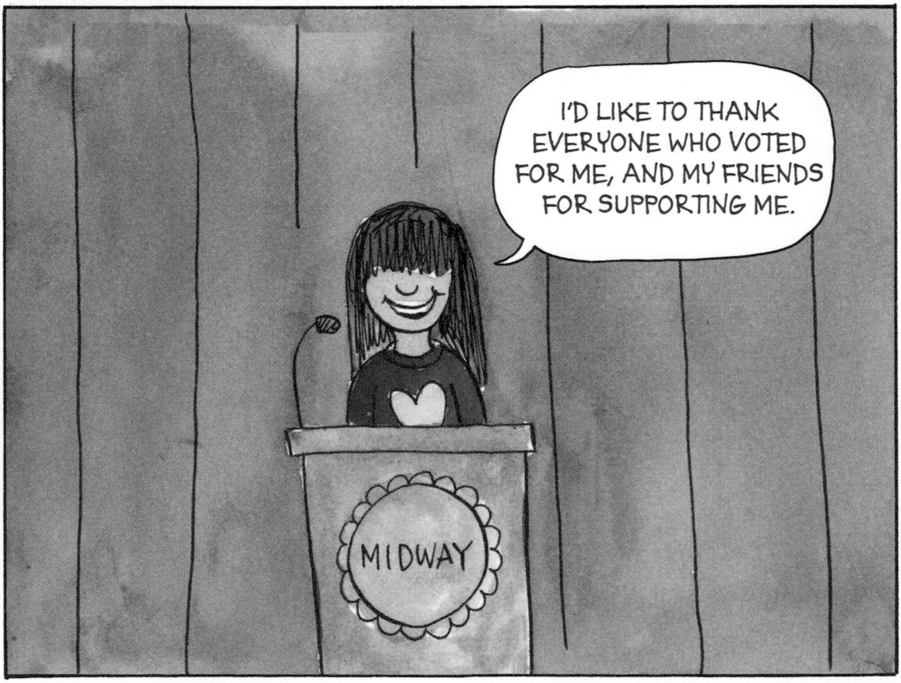
I'D LIKE TO THANK
EVERYONE WHO VOTED
FOR ME, AND MY FRIENDS
FOR SUPPORTING ME.
MIDWAY

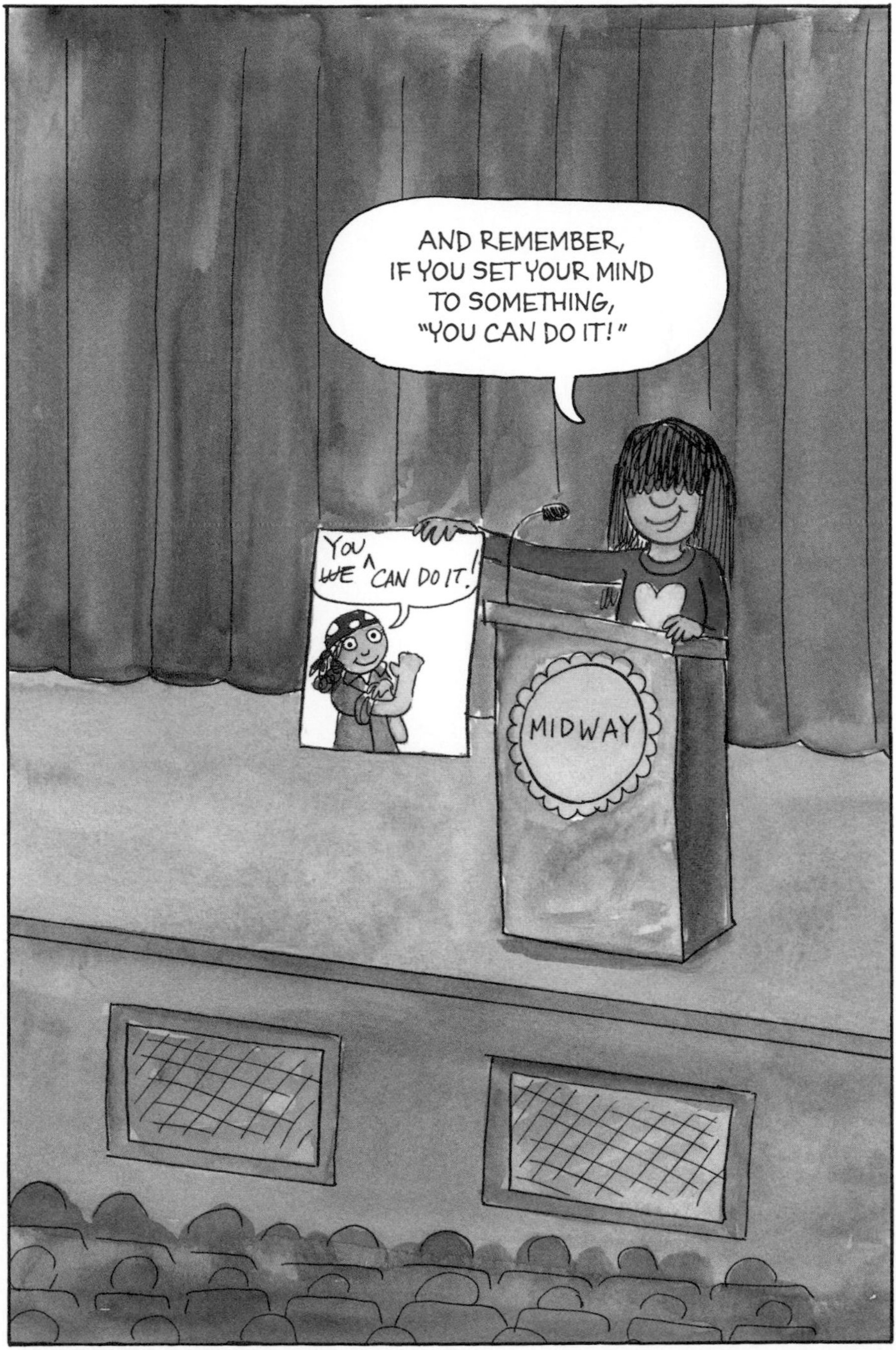
AND REMEMBER, IF YOU SET YOUR MIND TO SOMETHING, "YOU CAN DO IT!"
~~WE~~ YOU CAN DO IT!
MIDWAY

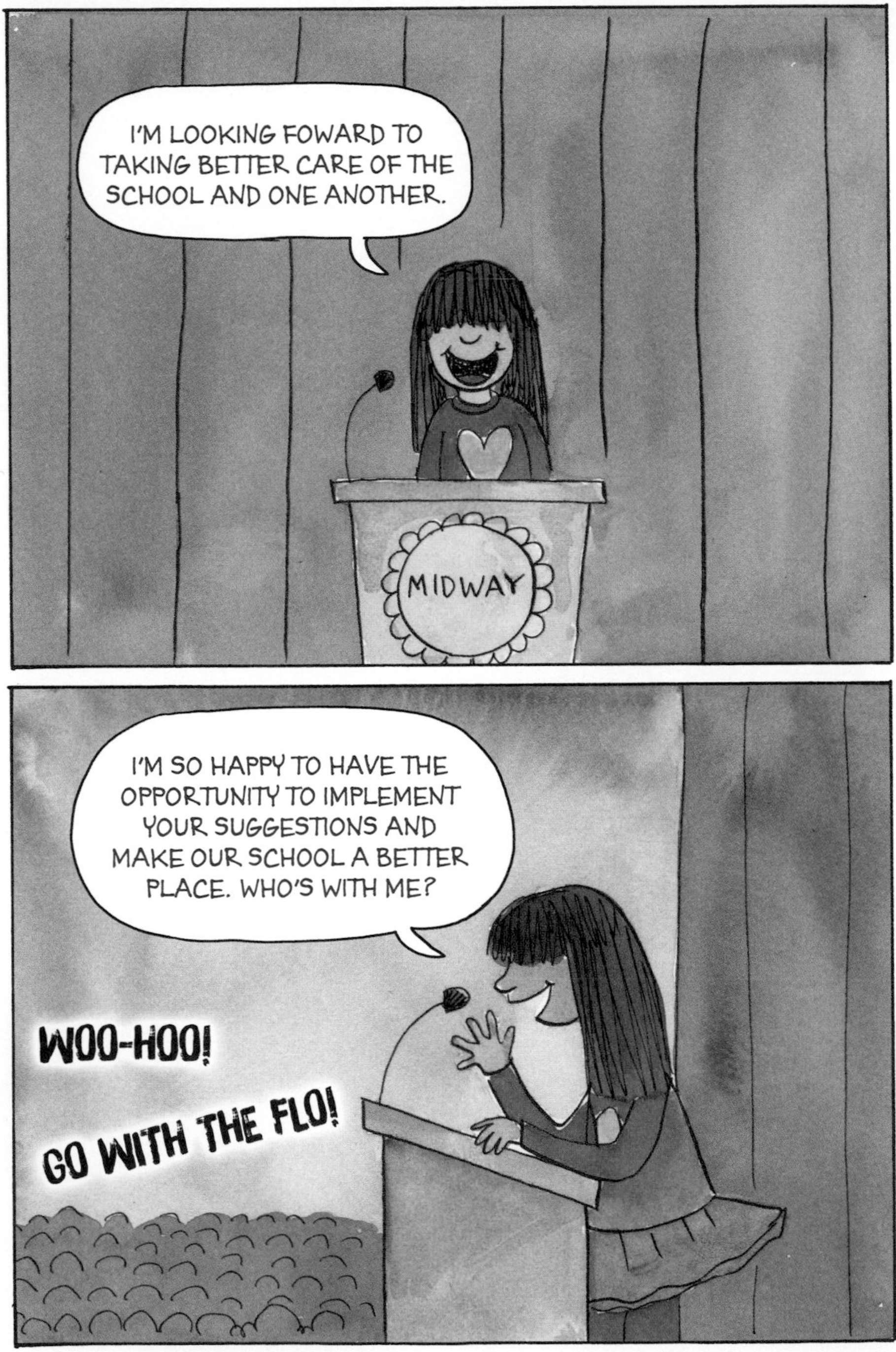
I'M LOOKING FOWARD TO TAKING BETTER CARE OF THE SCHOOL AND ONE ANOTHER.
MIDWAY
I'M SO HAPPY TO HAVE THE OPPORTUNITY TO IMPLEMENT YOUR SUGGESTIONS AND MAKE OUR SCHOOL A BETTER PLACE. WHO'S WITH ME?
WOO-HOO!
GO WITH THE FLO!

CHAPTER 16
PROMISES TOO

HOW TO MAKE A PROMISE:
PINKY SWEAR

I DON'T HAVE A PINKY.
ME NEITHER.

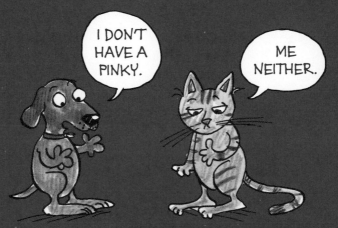

HOW TO BREAK A PROMISE:
CROSS YOUR FINGERS BEHIND YOUR BACK

AND I CAN'T CROSS MY FINGERS.
THAT'S OKAY. IT'S BETTER TO KEEP YOUR PROMISES.

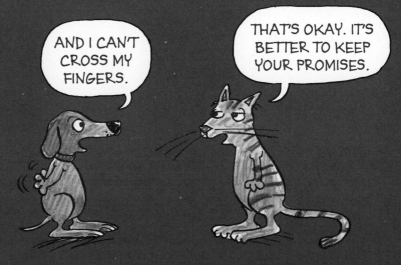

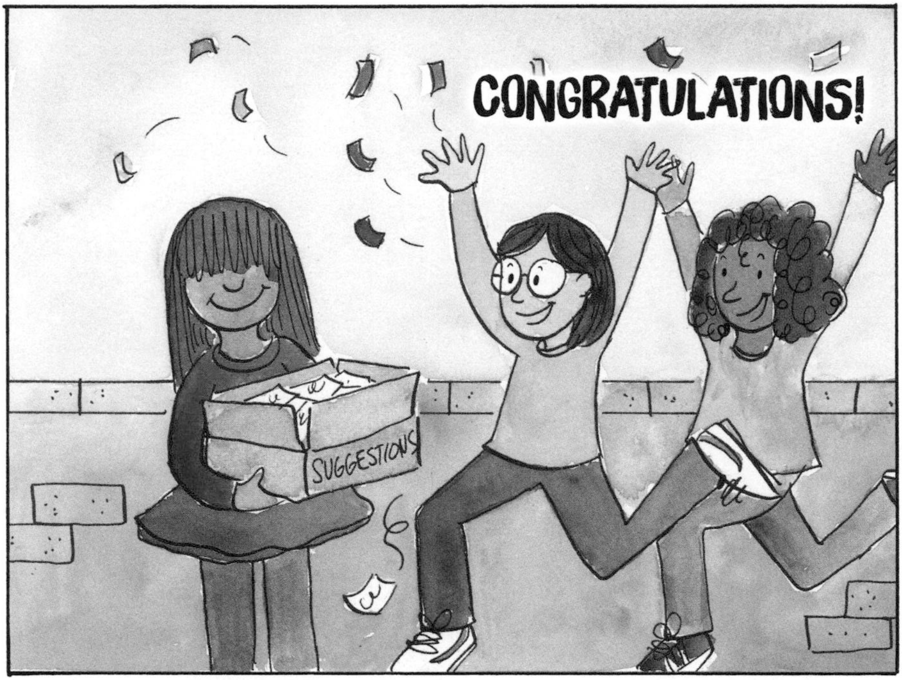
CONGRATULATIONS!
SUGGESTIONS

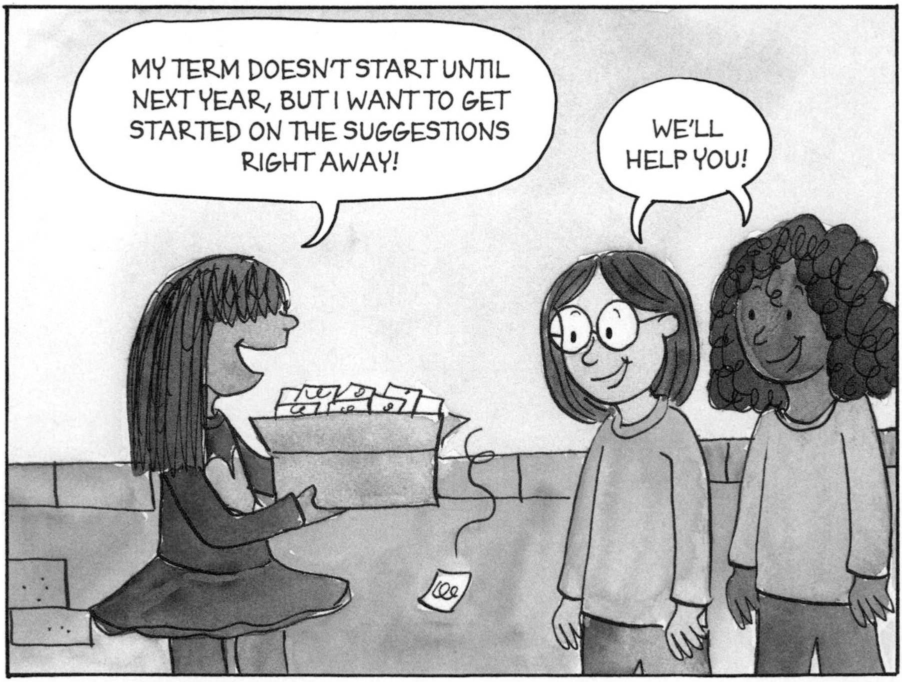
MY TERM DOESN'T START UNTIL NEXT YEAR, BUT I WANT TO GET STARTED ON THE SUGGESTIONS RIGHT AWAY!
WE'LL HELP YOU!

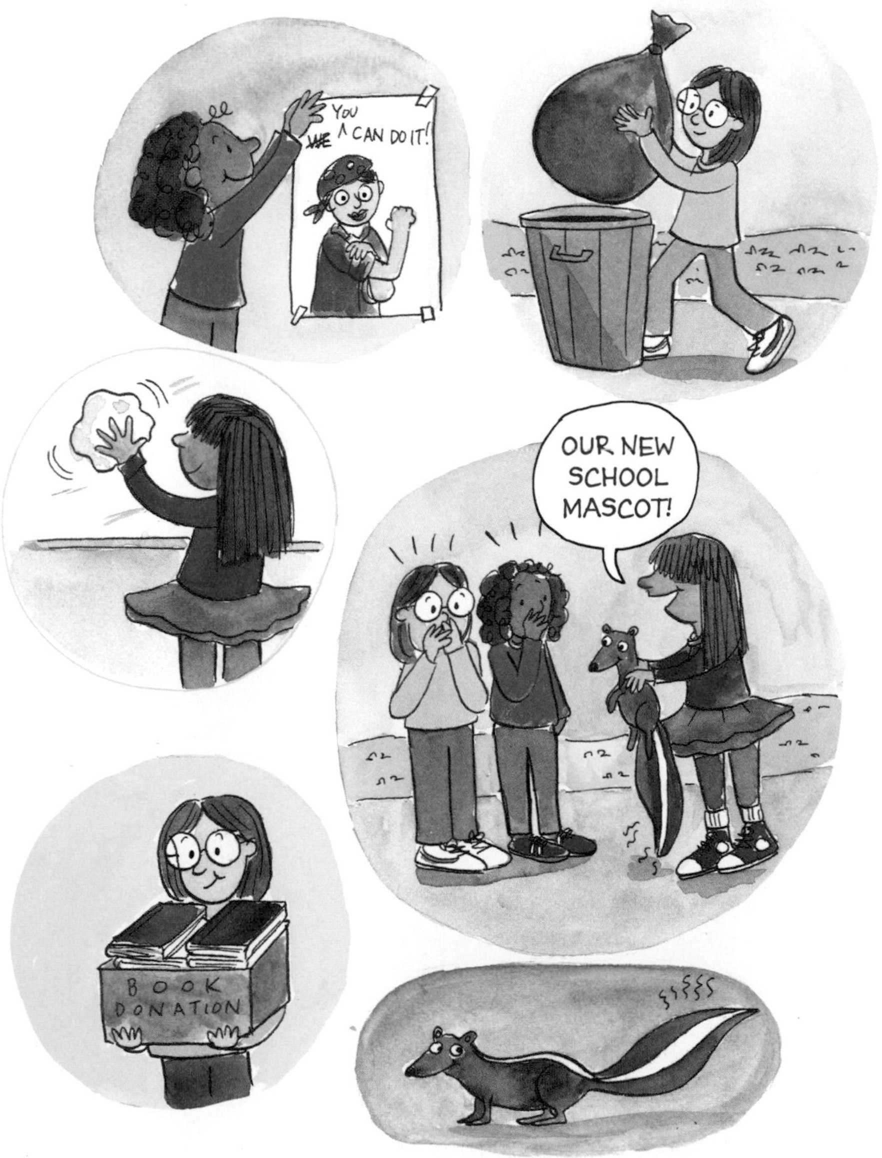
YOU
WE CAN DO IT!
OUR NEW SCHOOL MASCOT!
BOOK DONATION

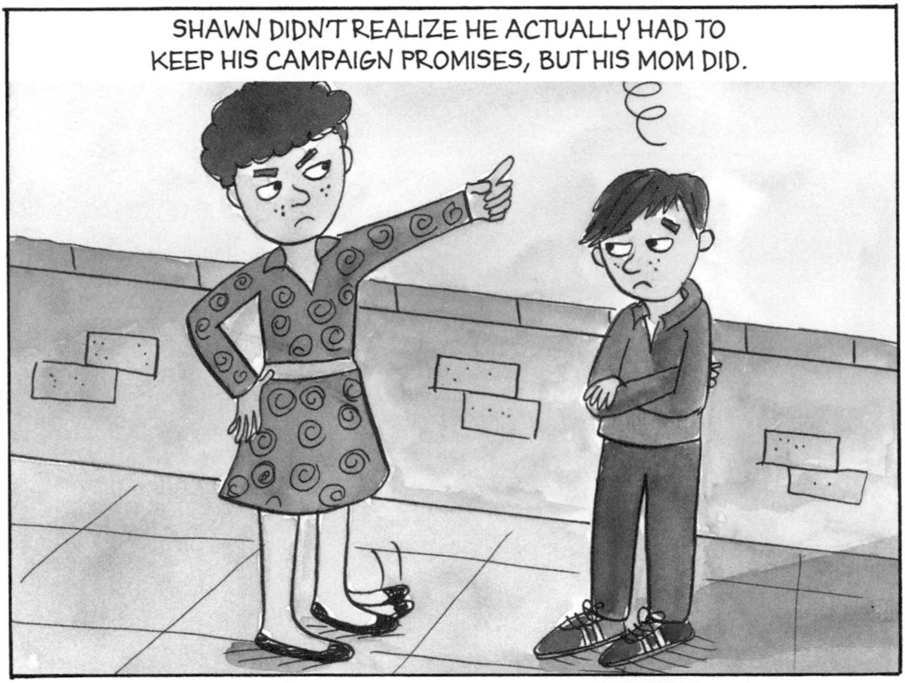
SHAWN DIDN'T REALIZE HE ACTUALLY HAD TO KEEP HIS CAMPAIGN PROMISES, BUT HIS MOM DID.

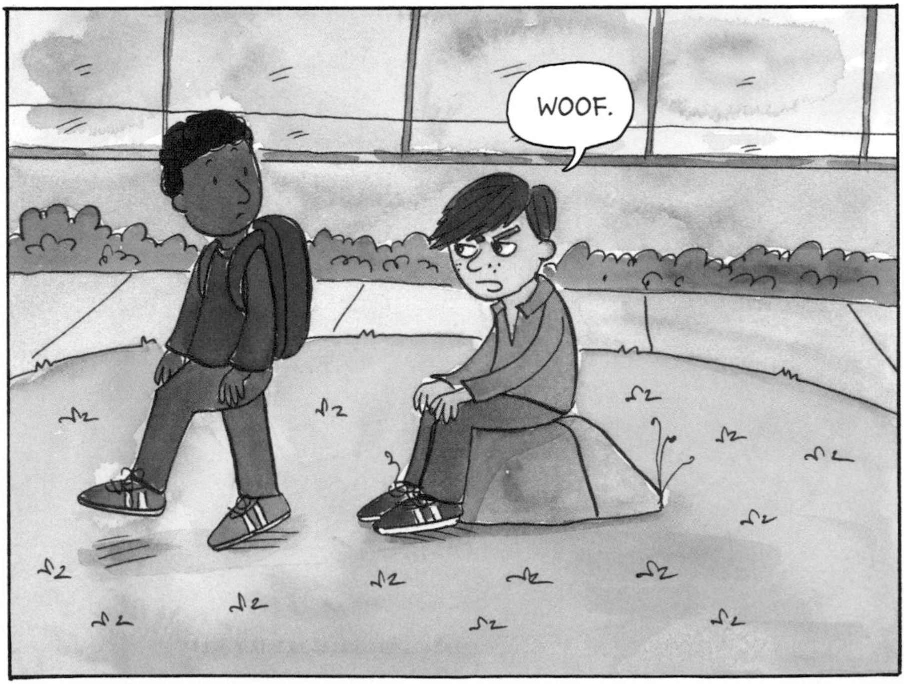
WOOF.

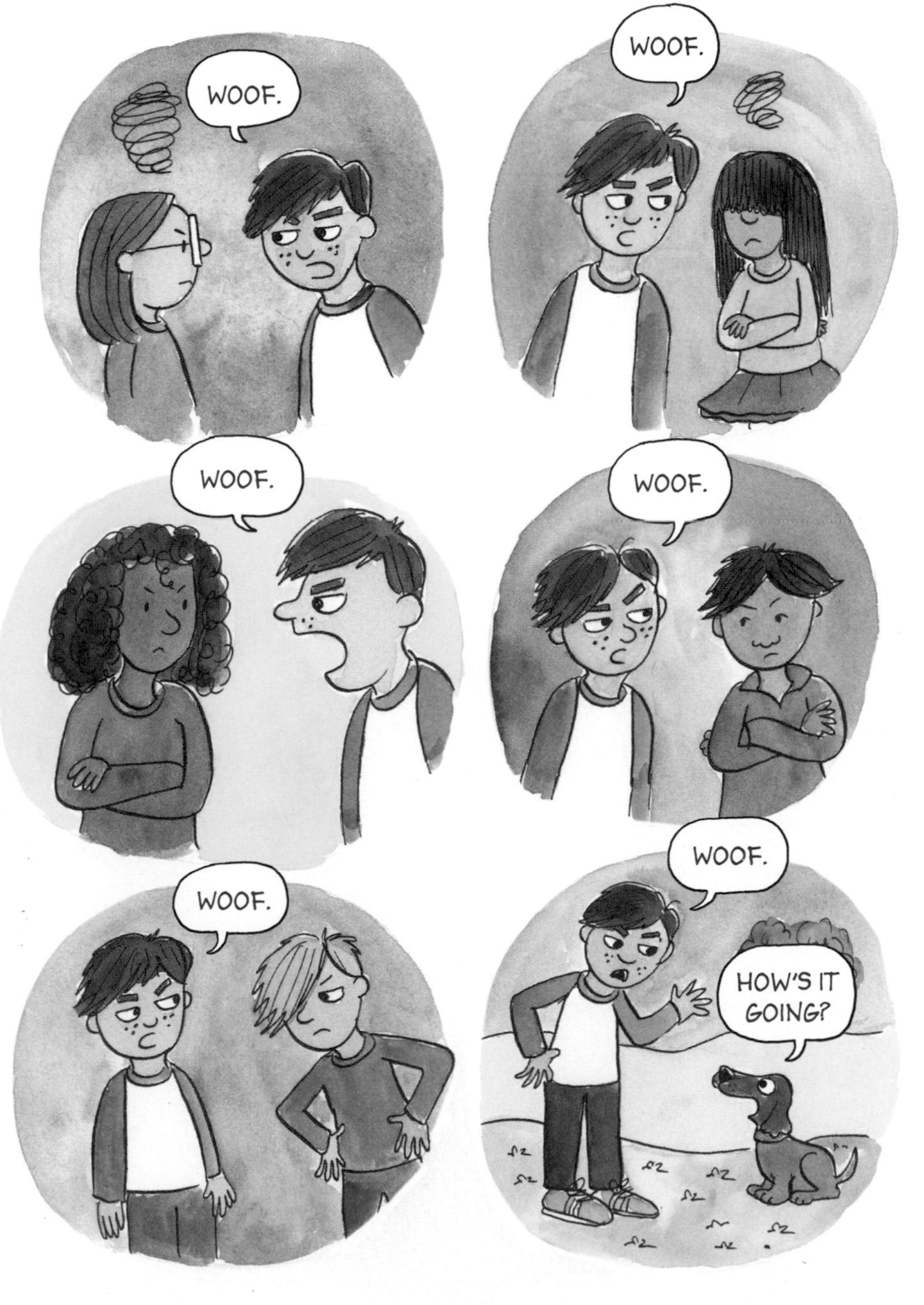
WOOF.
WOOF.
WOOF.
WOOF.
WOOF.
WOOF.
HOW'S IT GOING?

ALL THAT TIME HELPING FLO AND ZOE, I DIDN'T THINK ABOUT DEREK ONCE.

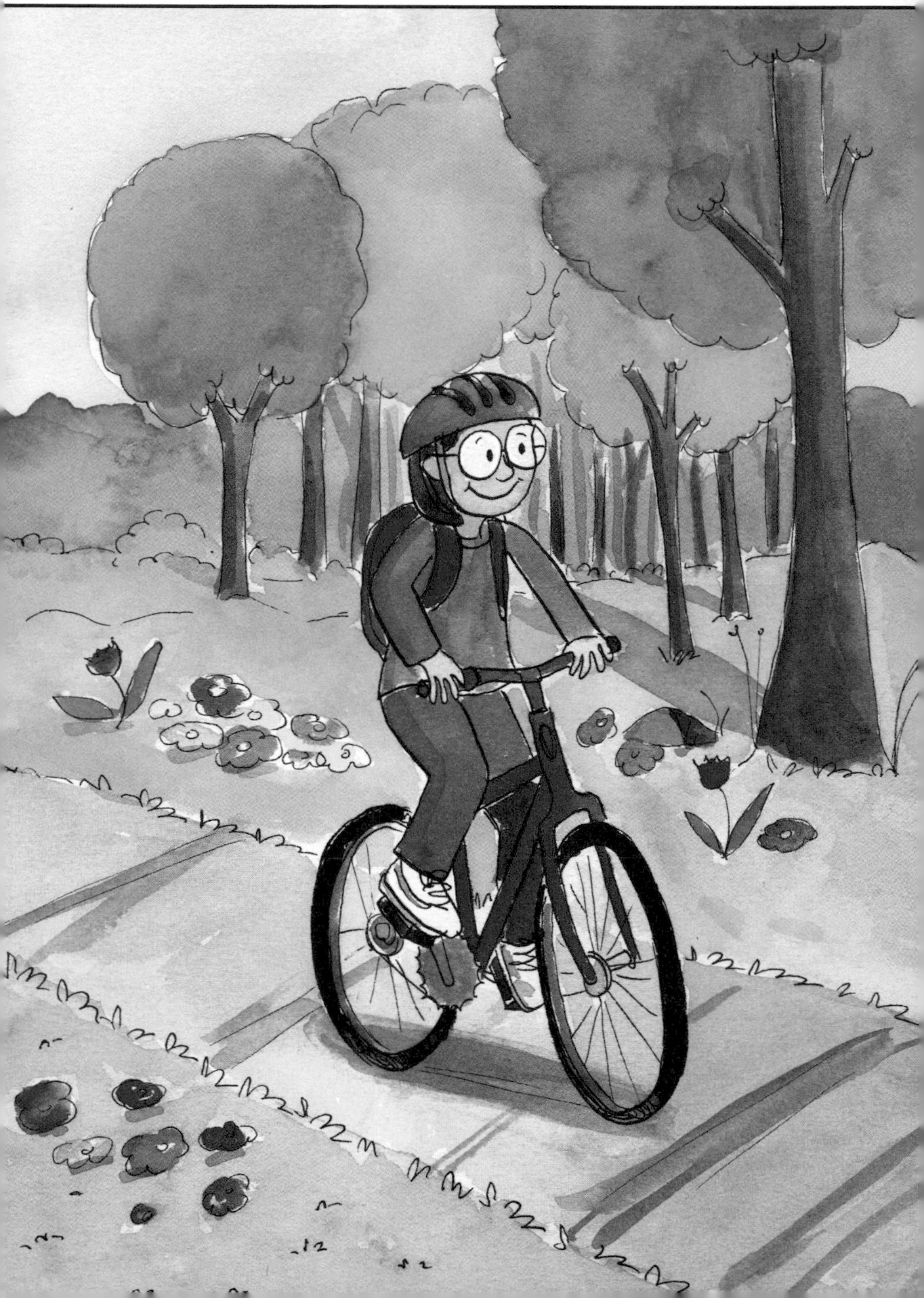

MY SKETCHBOOKS WERE FILLED WITH HEARTS AND DEREK'S NAME ALL OVER THE PLACE.

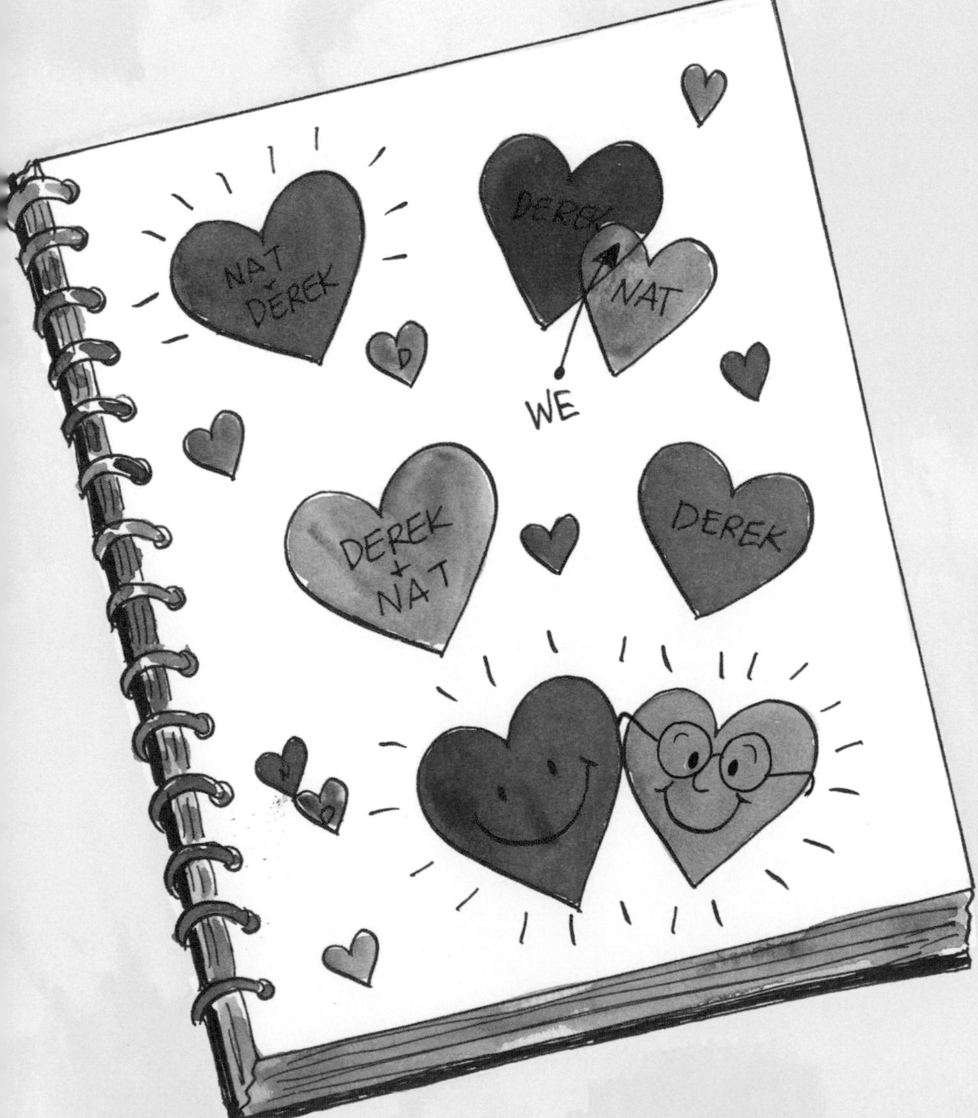
NAT + DEREK
DEREK
NAT
D
WE
DEREK + NAT
DEREK

AS I WAS WORKING ON MY ENGLISH ASSIGNMENT, I THOUGHT ABOUT MY OUTTAKES WITH DEREK.

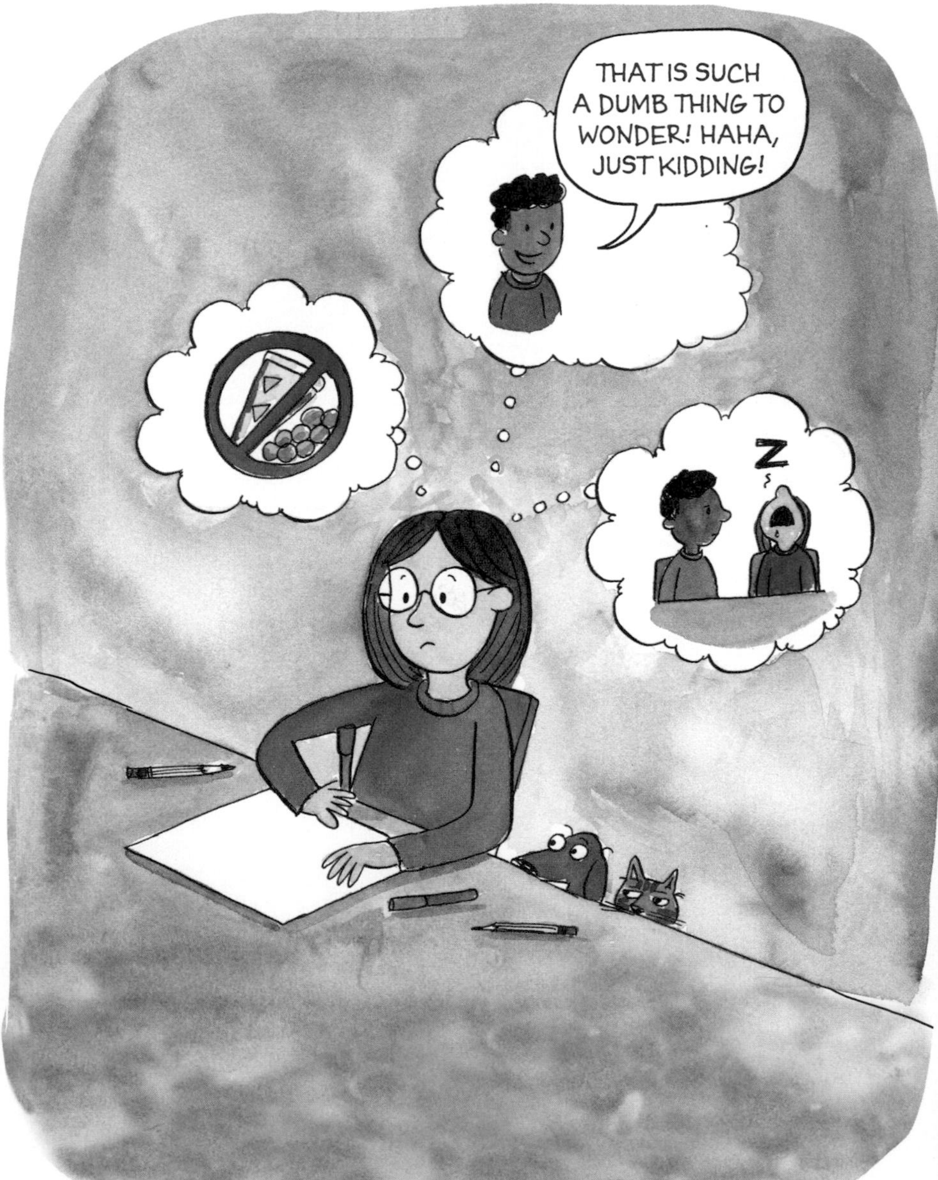
THAT IS SUCH A DUMB THING TO WONDER! HAHA, JUST KIDDING!
Z

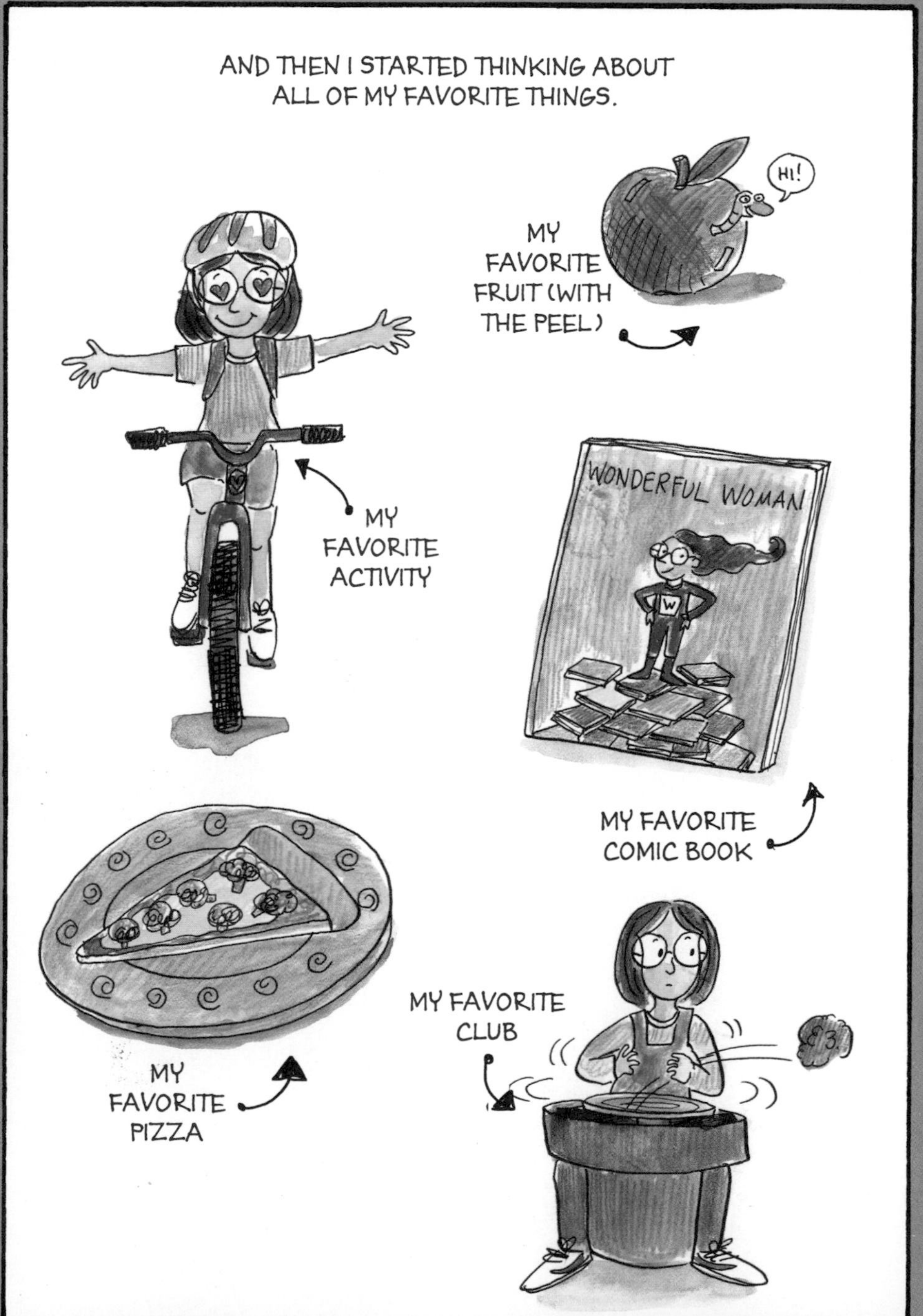
AND THEN I STARTED THINKING ABOUT ALL OF MY FAVORITE THINGS.
MY FAVORITE FRUIT (WITH THE PEEL)
HI!
MY FAVORITE ACTIVITY
WONDERFUL WOMAN
W
MY FAVORITE COMIC BOOK
MY FAVORITE PIZZA
MY FAVORITE CLUB

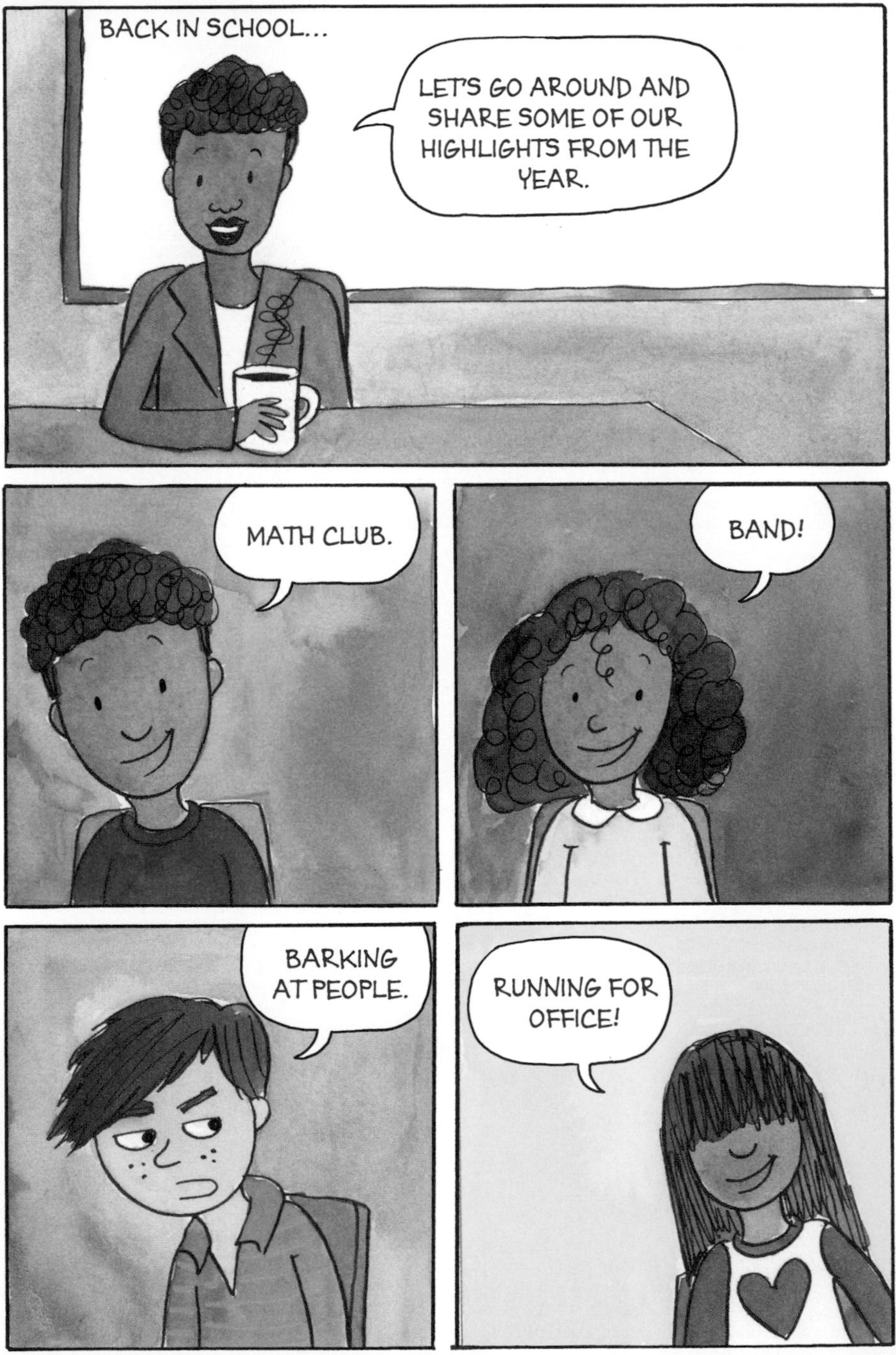
BACK IN SCHOOL...
LET'S GO AROUND AND SHARE SOME OF OUR HIGHLIGHTS FROM THE YEAR.
MATH CLUB.
BAND!
BARKING AT PEOPLE.
RUNNING FOR OFFICE!

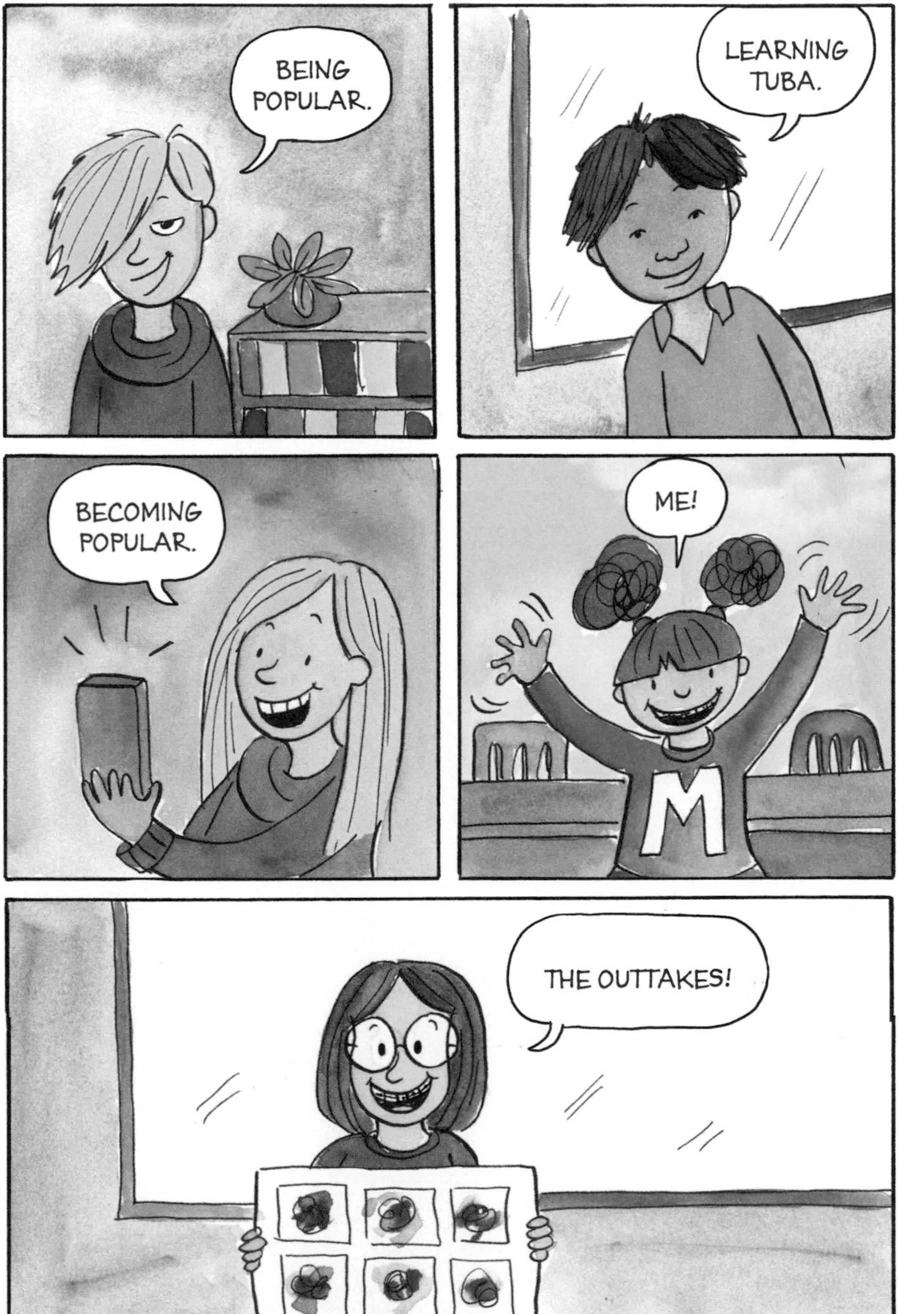
BEING POPULAR.
LEARNING TUBA.
BECOMING POPULAR.
ME!
M
THE OUTTAKES!

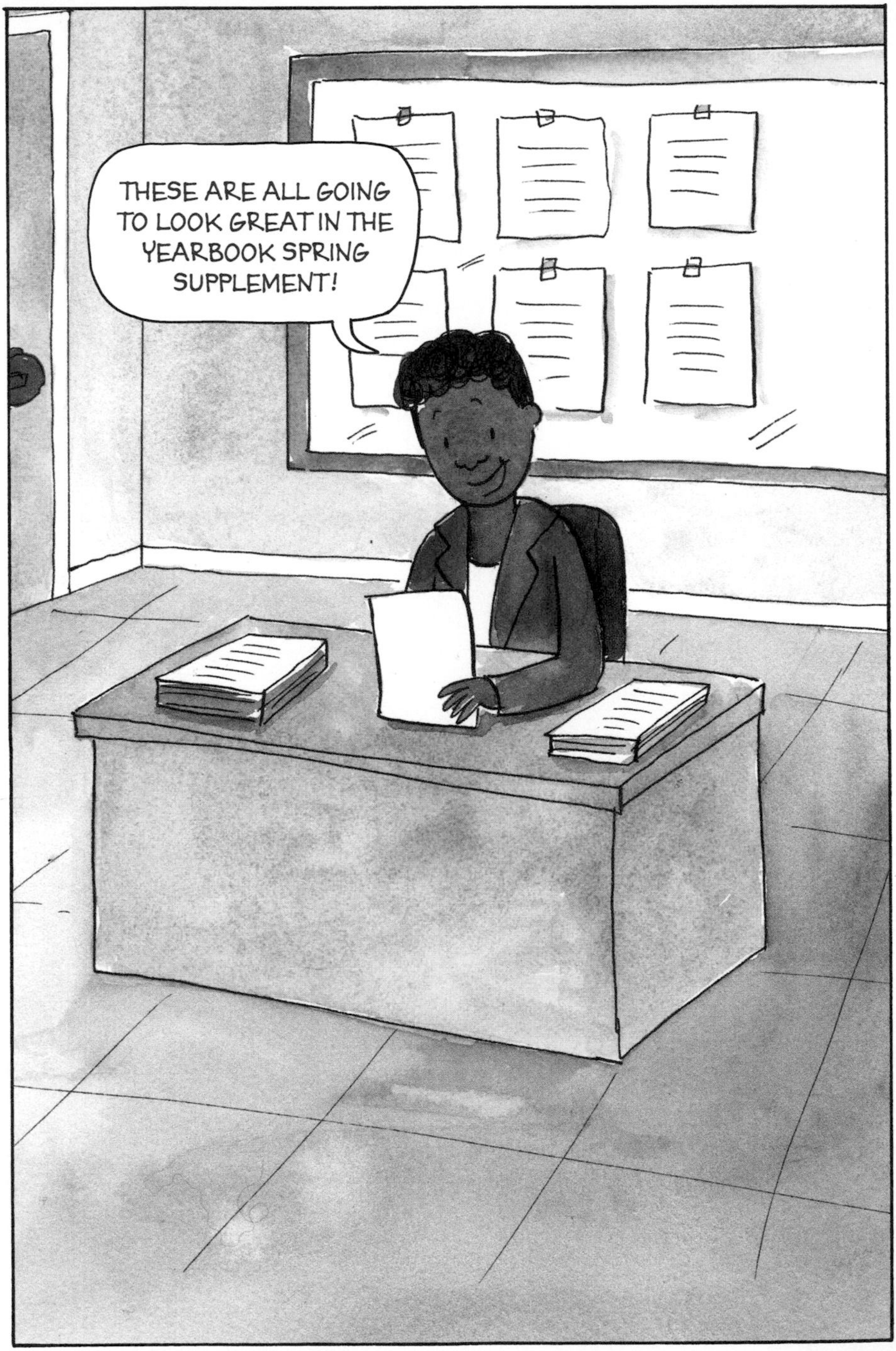
THESE ARE ALL GOING TO LOOK GREAT IN THE YEARBOOK SPRING SUPPLEMENT!

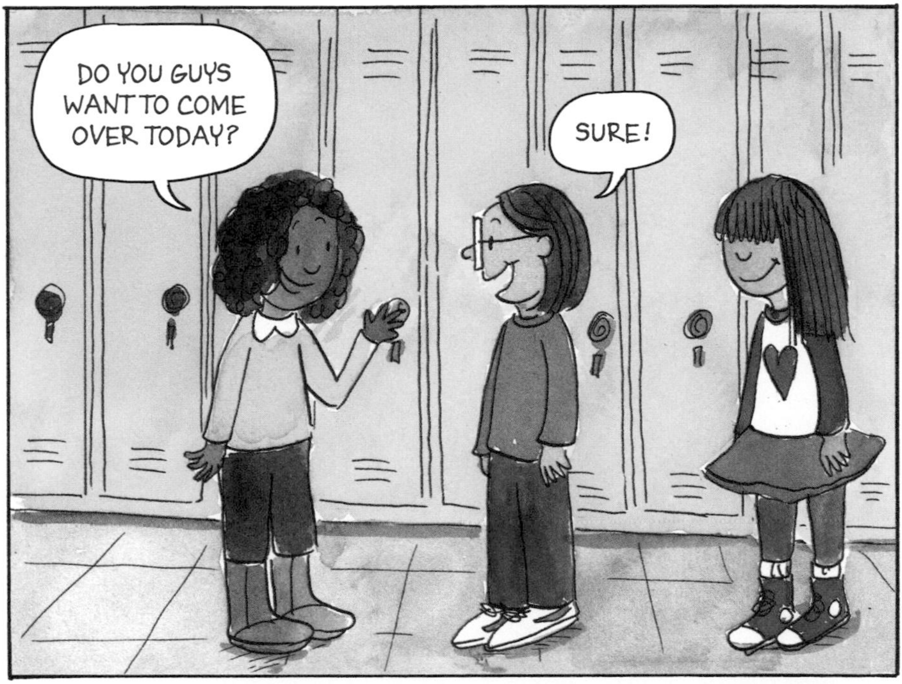
DO YOU GUYS WANT TO COME OVER TODAY?
SURE!

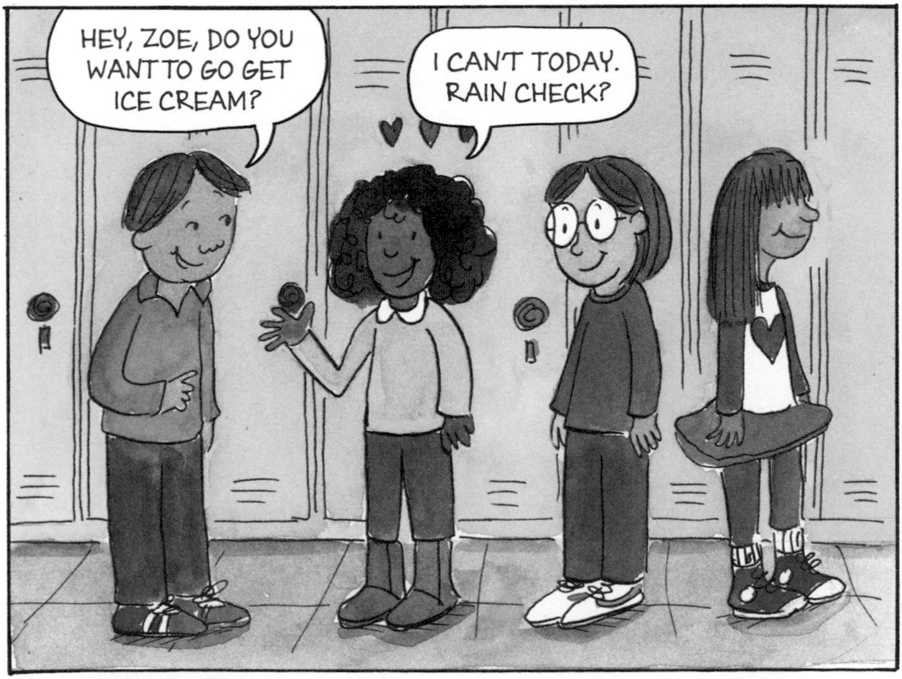
HEY, ZOE, DO YOU WANT TO GO GET ICE CREAM?
I CAN'T TODAY. RAIN CHECK?

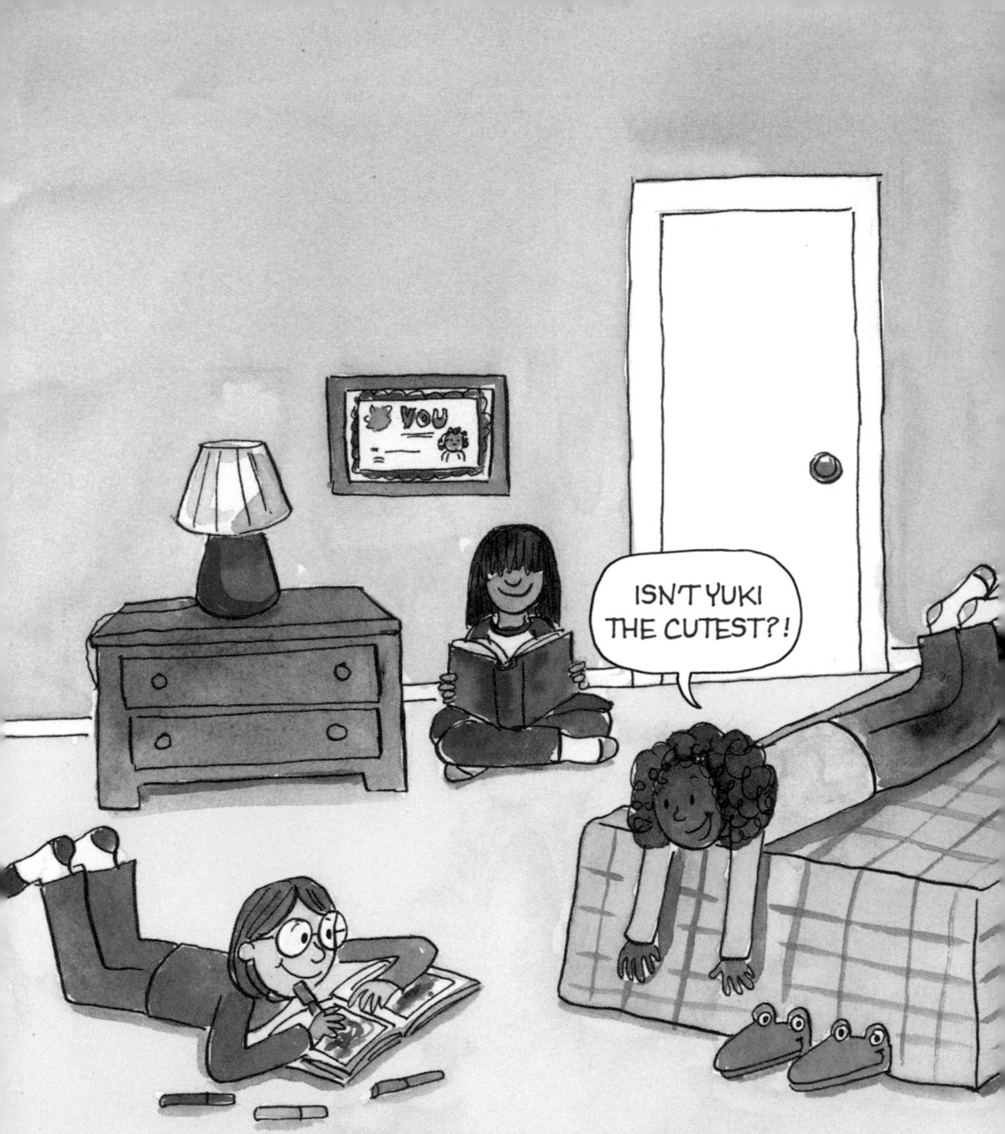
YOU
ISN'T YUKI THE CUTEST?!

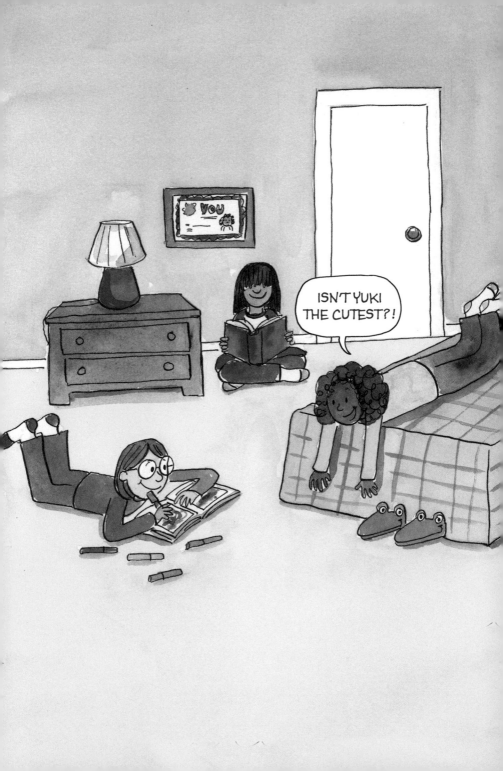

CHAPTER 17
YEARBOOK

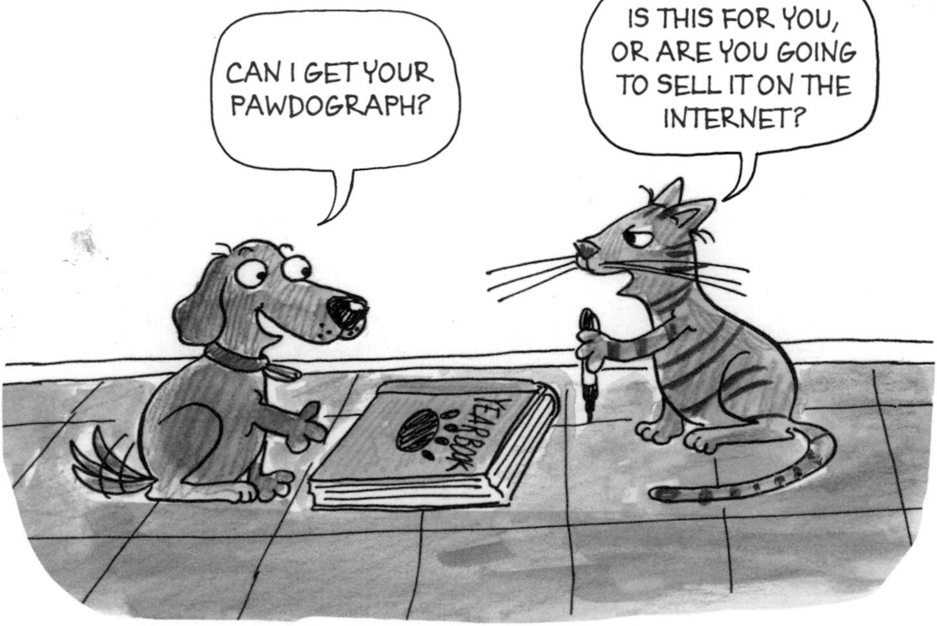
CAN I GET YOUR PAWDOGRAPH?
IS THIS FOR YOU, OR ARE YOU GOING TO SELL IT ON THE INTERNET?
YEARBOOK

A FEW WEEKS LATER WE GOT OUR YEARBOOKS.

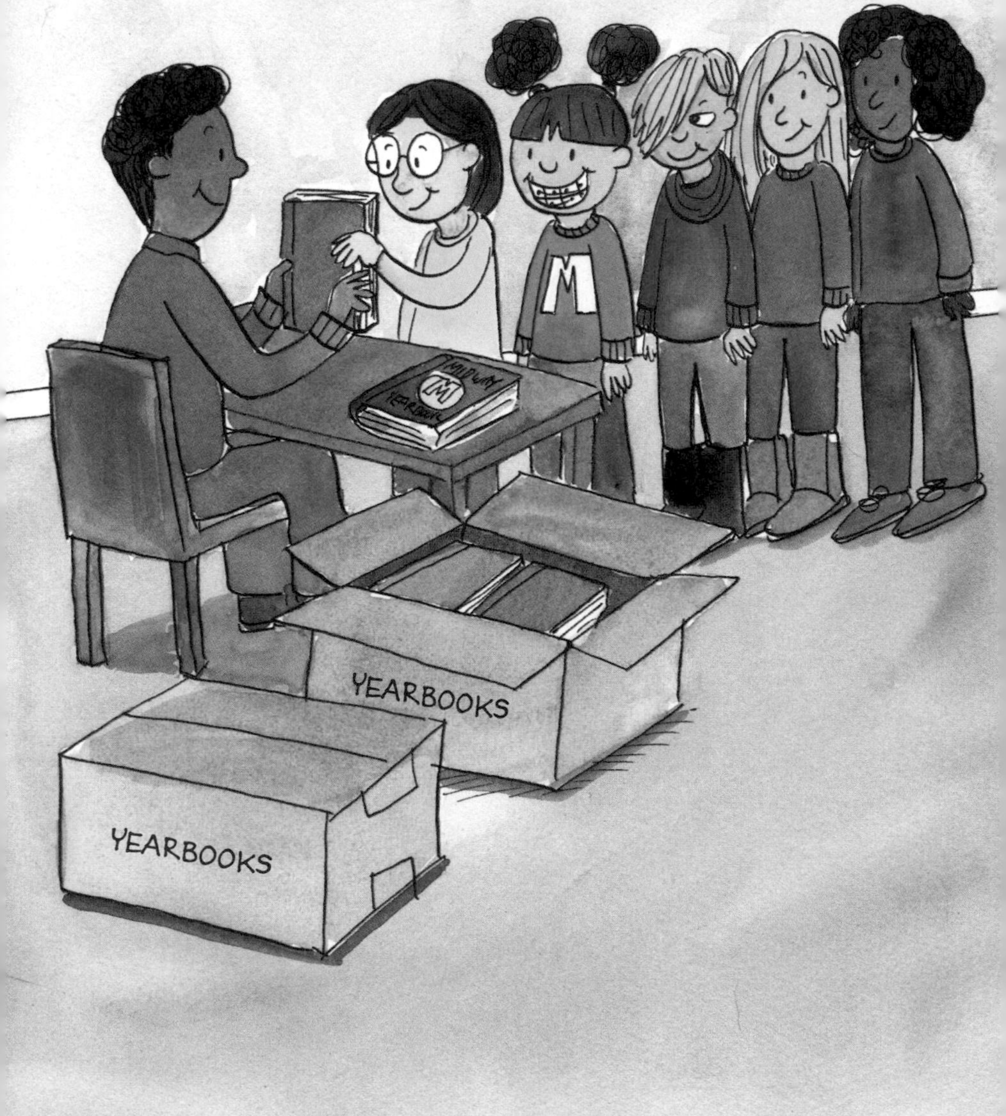
MIDWAY
M
YEARBOOK
M
YEARBOOKS
YEARBOOKS

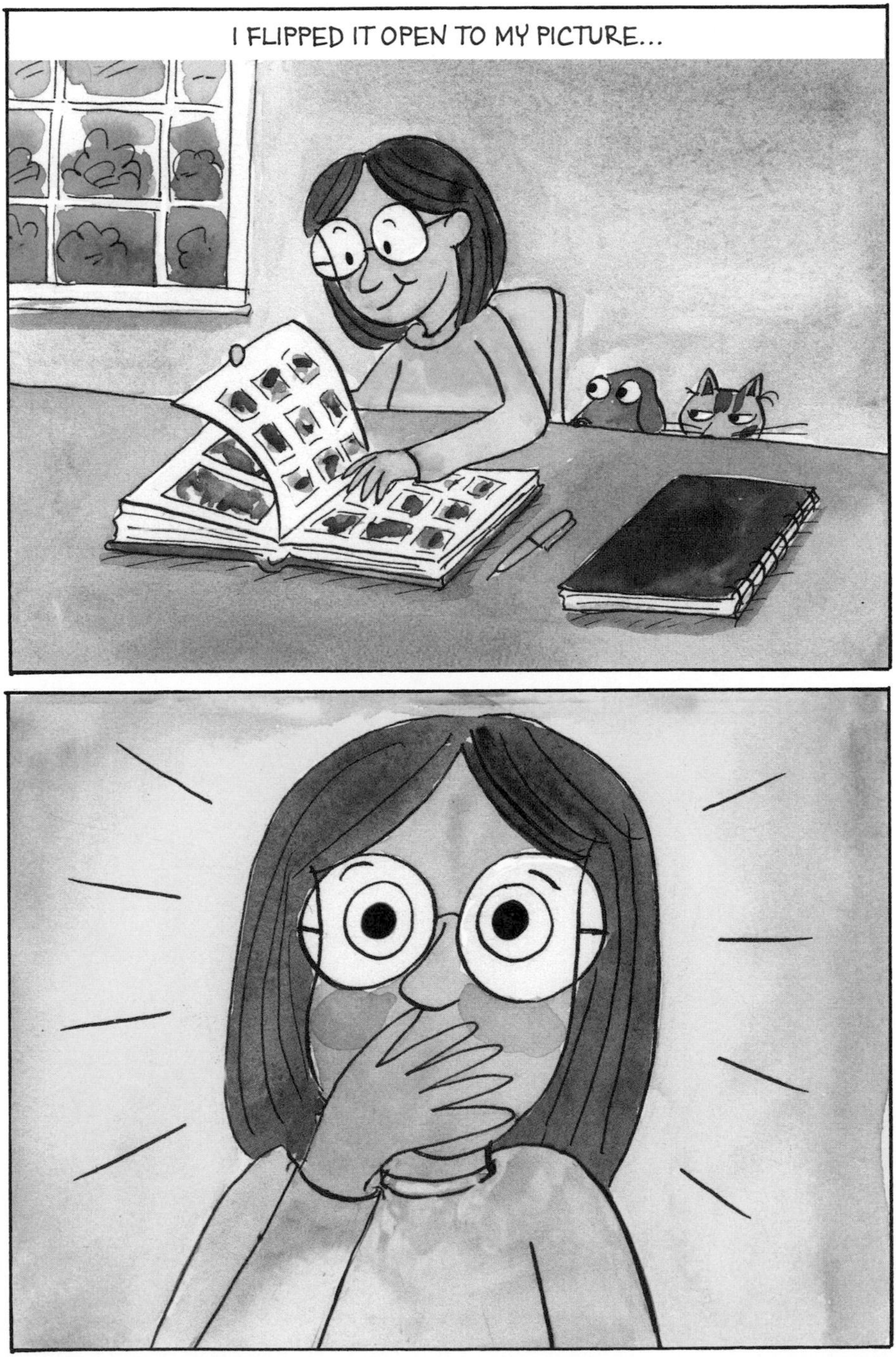
I FLIPPED IT OPEN TO MY PICTURE...

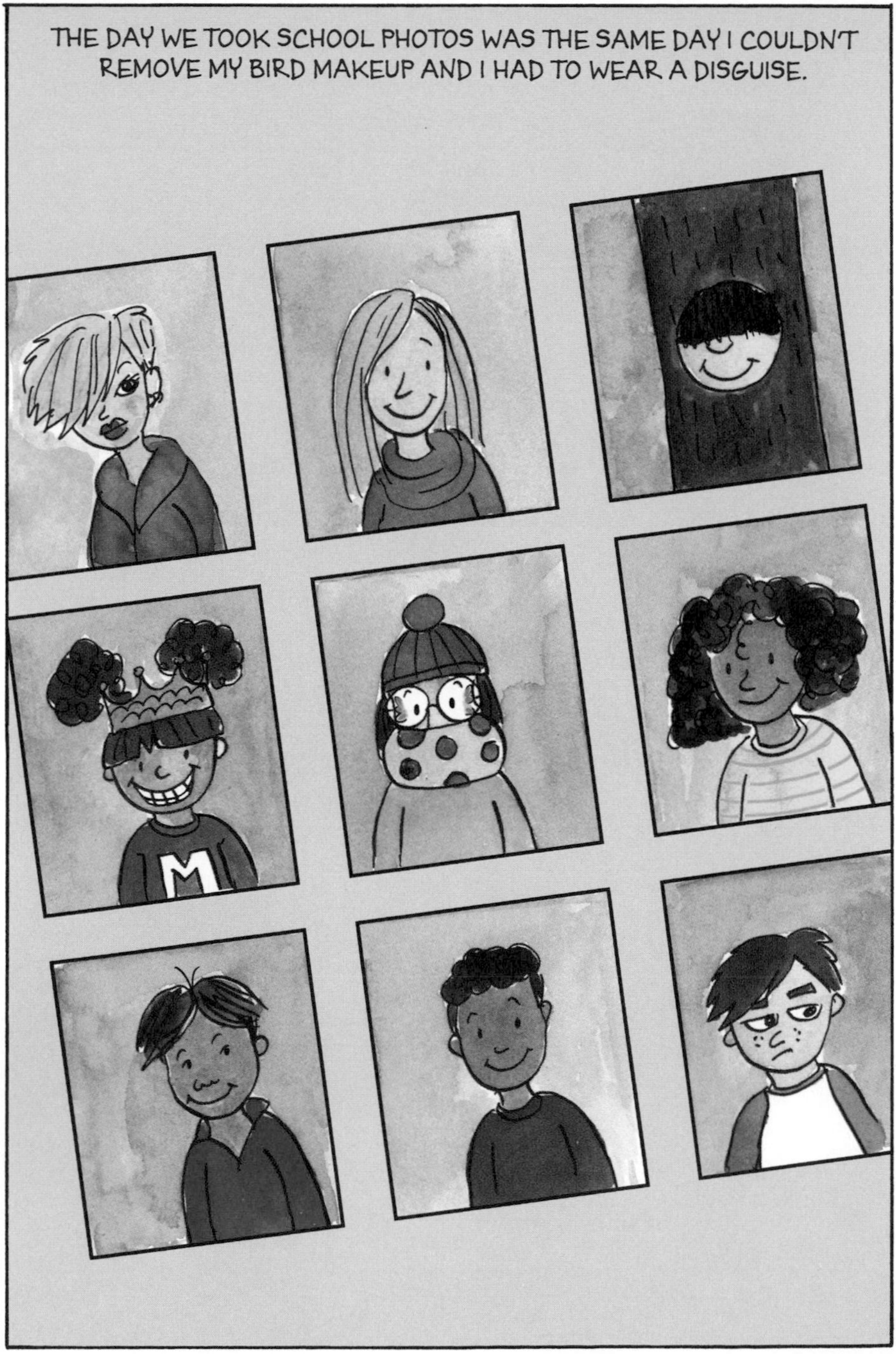
THE DAY WE TOOK SCHOOL PHOTOS WAS THE SAME DAY I COULDN'T REMOVE MY BIRD MAKEUP AND I HAD TO WEAR A DISGUISE.
M

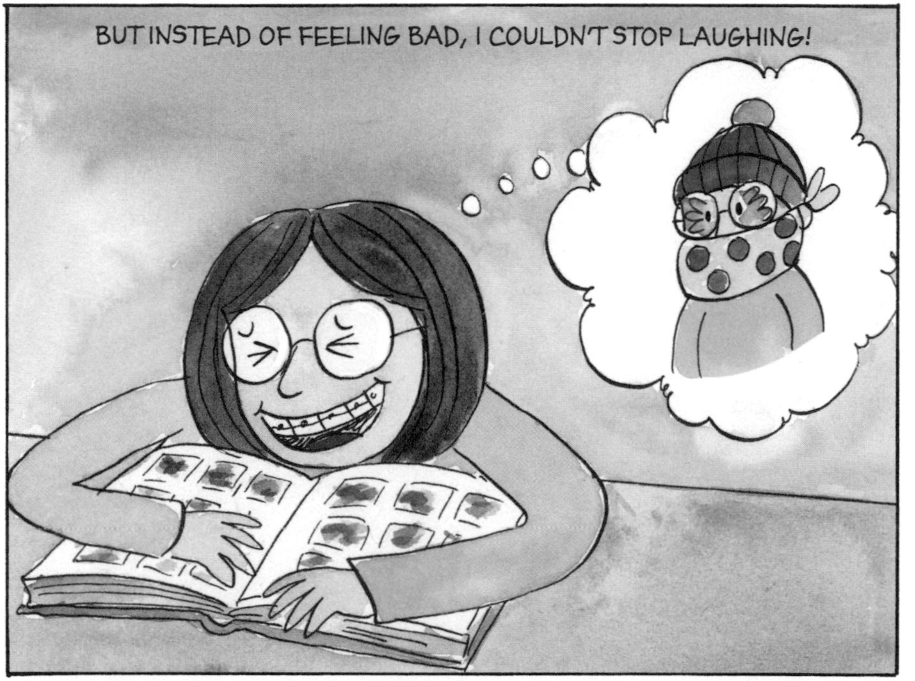
BUT INSTEAD OF FEELING BAD, I COULDN'T STOP LAUGHING!

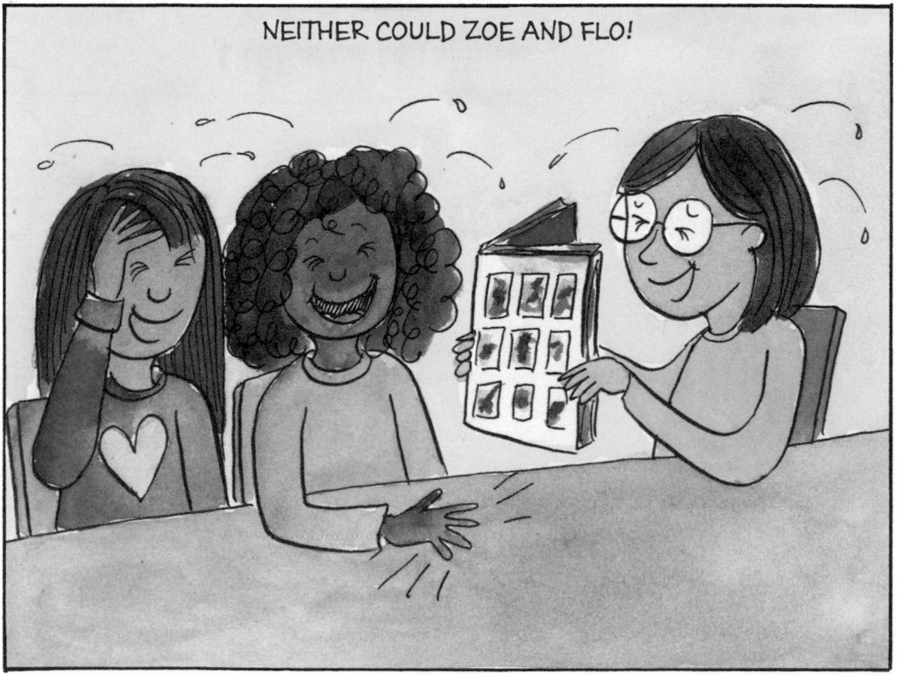
NEITHER COULD ZOE AND FLO!

I HAD SO MUCH FUN SIGNING EVERONE'S YEARBOOK AND MAKING BIRD JOKES.

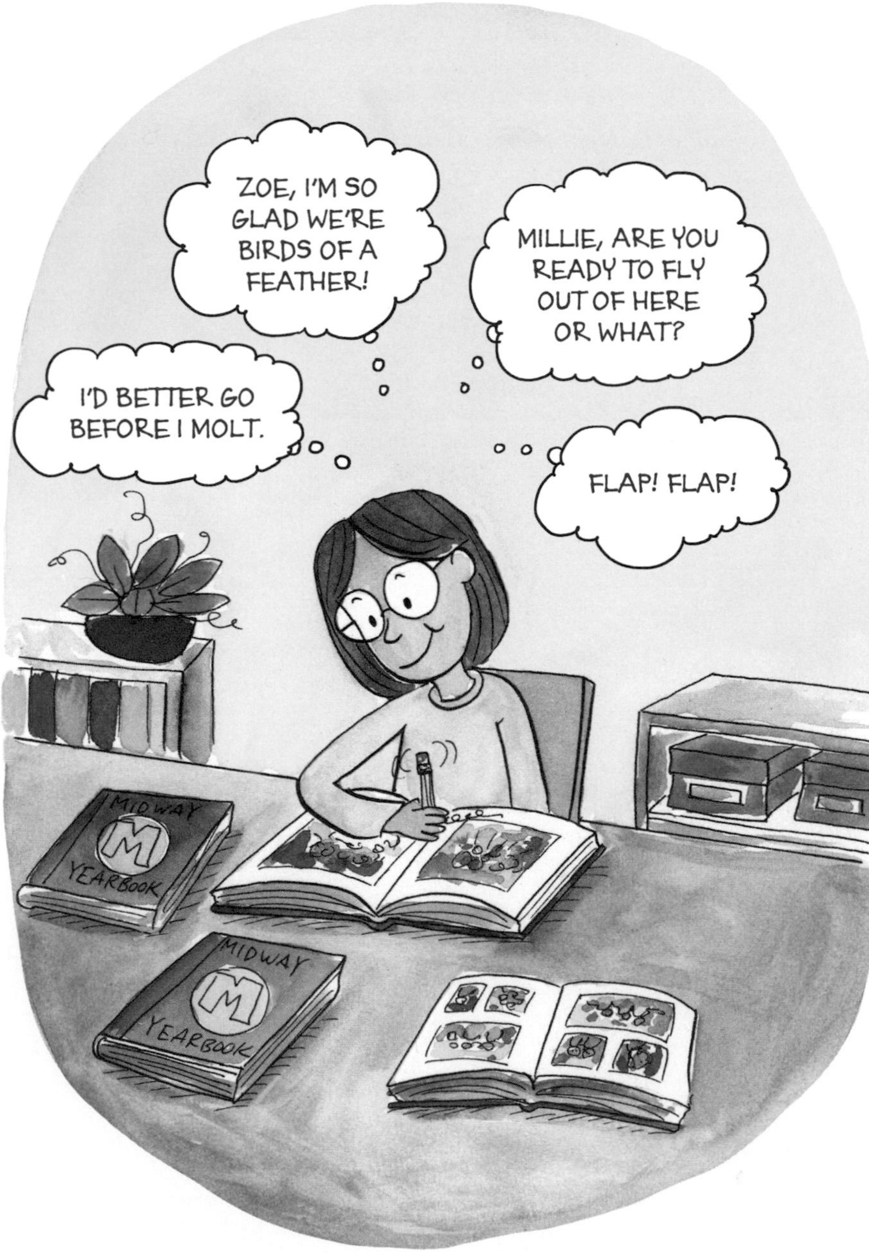
ZOE, I'M SO GLAD WE'RE BIRDS OF A FEATHER!
MILLIE, ARE YOU READY TO FLY OUT OF HERE OR WHAT?
I'D BETTER GO BEFORE I MOLT.
FLAP! FLAP!
MIDWAY
M
YEARBOOK
MIDWAY
M
YEARBOOK

AND IT WAS FUN TO READ WHAT EVERYONE WROTE TO ME.

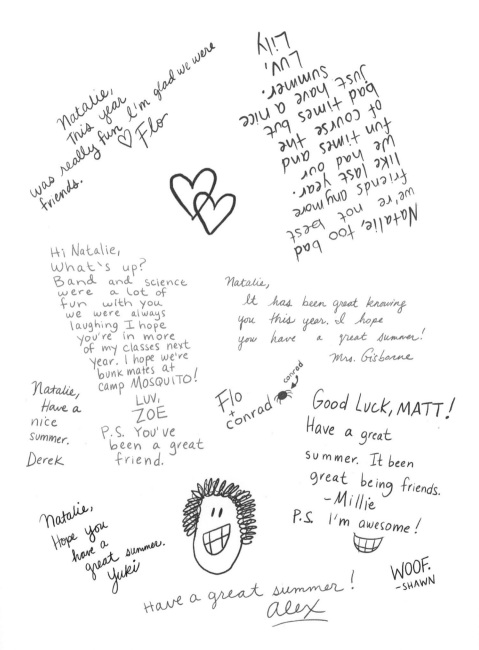

Natalie,
This year
was really fun I'm glad we were
friends. ♡ Flo

Natalie, too bad
we're not best
friends anymore
like last year.
We had our
fun times and
of course the
bad times but
just have a nice
summer.
LUV,
LiLy

Hi Natalie,
What's up?
Band and science
were a lot of
fun with you
we were always
laughing I hope
you're in more
of my classes next
year. I hope we're
bunk mates at
camp MOSQUITO!
LUV,
ZOE
P.S. You've
been a great
friend.

Natalie,
It has been great knowing
you this year. I hope
you have a great summer!
Mrs. Gisborne

Natalie,
Have a
nice
summer.

Derek

Flo
+
conrad
conrad

Good Luck, MATT!
Have a great
summer. It been
great being friends.
-Millie
P.S. I'm awesome!

Natalie,
Hope you
have a
great summer.
Yuki

Have a great summer!
alex

WOOF.
-SHAWN

WHO'S WHO AT MIDWAY MIDDLE SCHOOL

LILY AND ALEX
MOST LIKELY TO
TAKE A SELFIE

YUKI
MOST LIKEY TO HAVE
A COMEDY SPECIAL

FLO
MOST LIKELY TO TALK
TO A HOUSEPLANT

DEREK
MOST LIKELY TO FIX
YOUR LAPTOP

WHO'S WHO AT MIDWAY MIDDLE SCHOOL

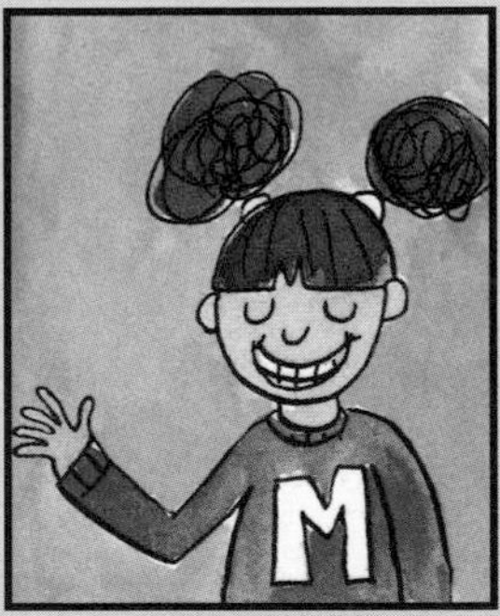

MILLIE
MOST LIKELY TO TALK
A LOT BUT SAY A LITTLE

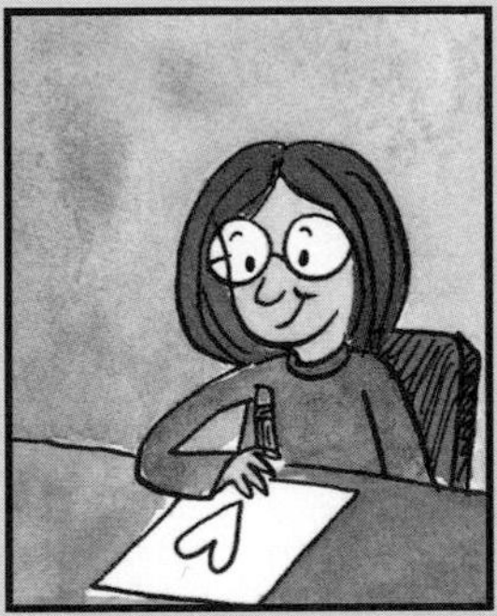

NATALIE
MOST LIKELY TO
DRAW HER WAY OUT
OF A CORNER

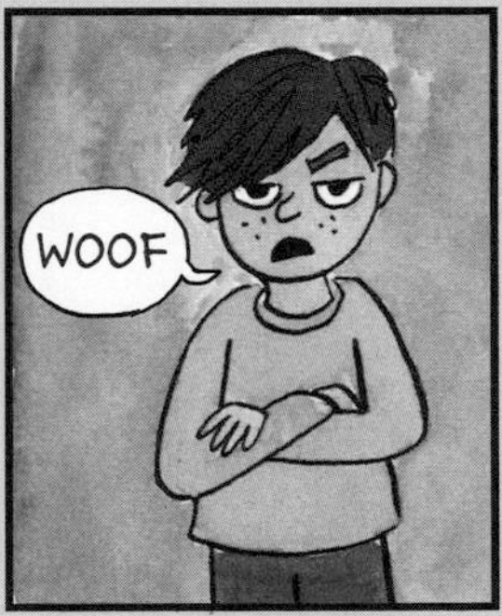
WOOF

SHAWN
MOST LIKELY
TO BARK

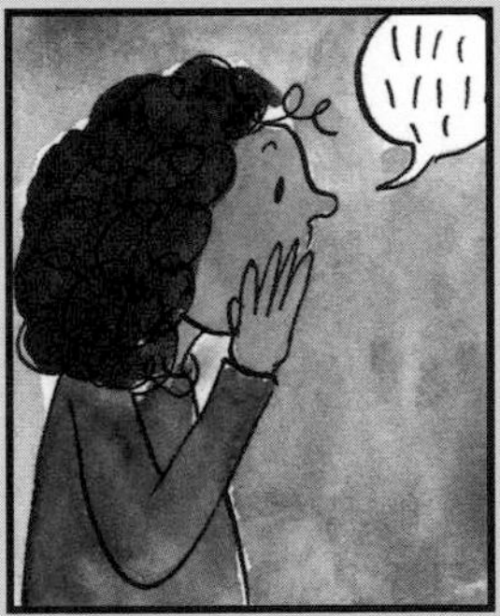

ZOE
MOST LIKELY TO
BE A REPORTER

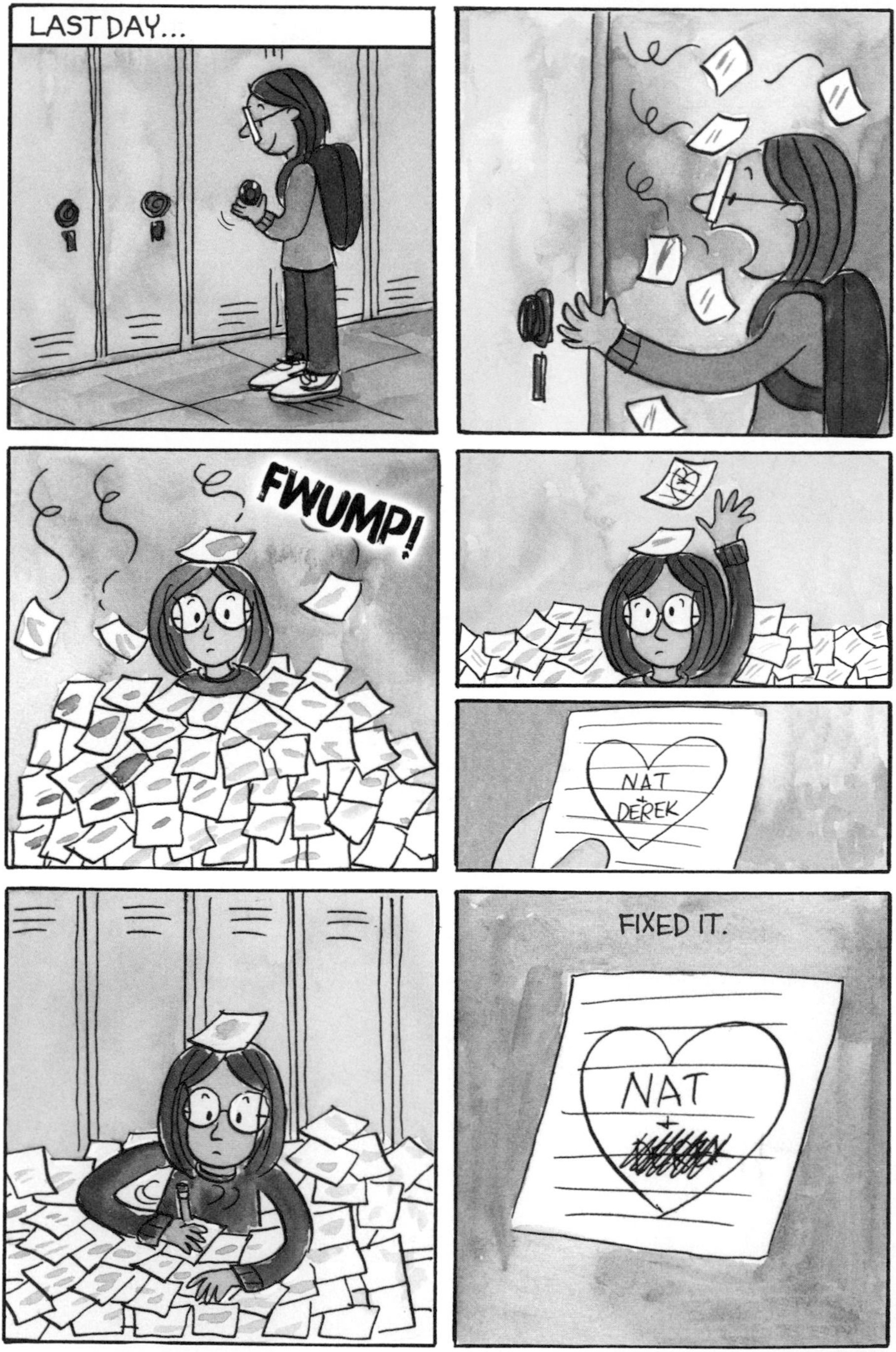
LAST DAY...
FWUMP!
NAT
+
DEREK
FIXED IT.
NAT
+

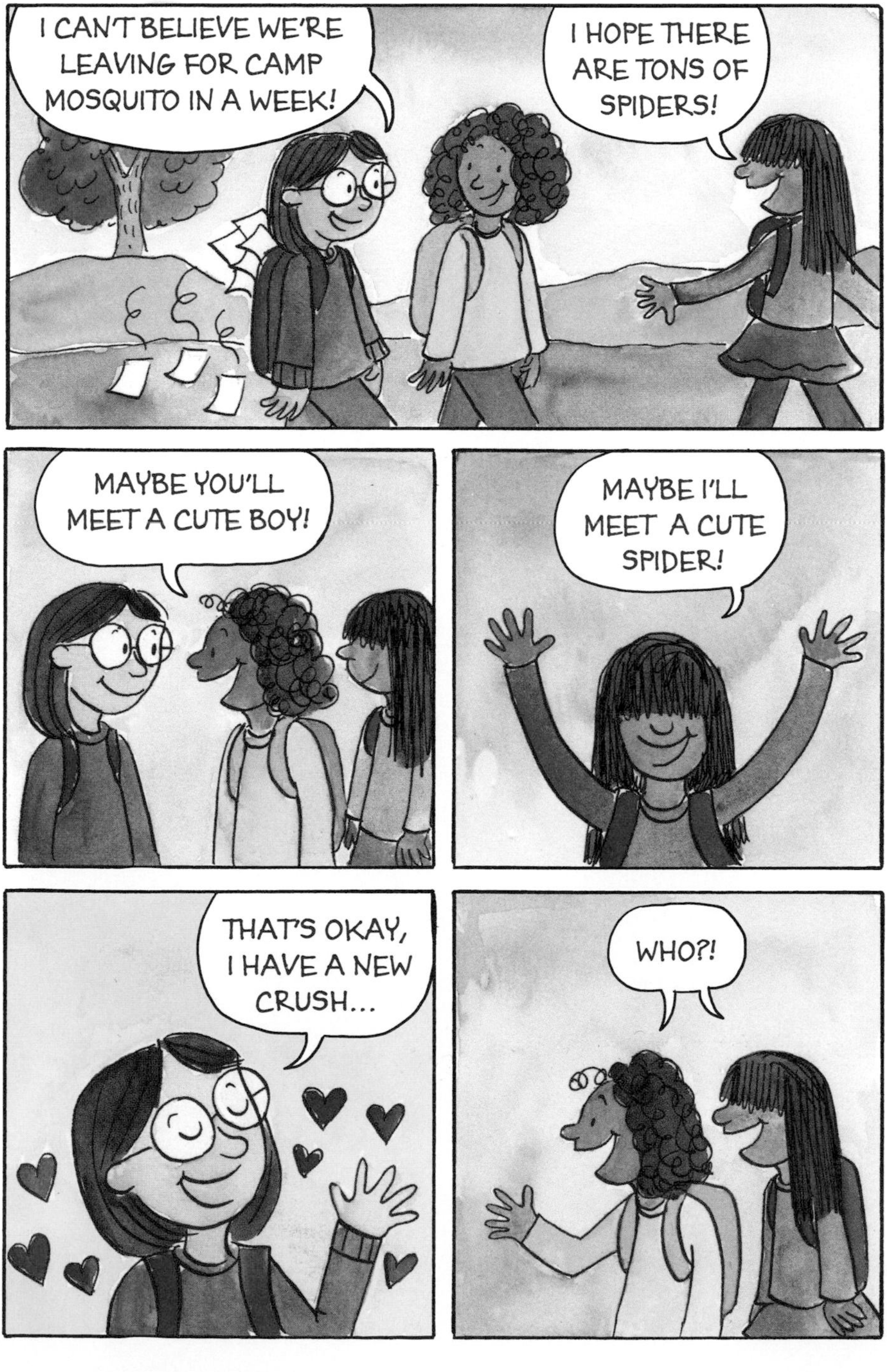
I CAN'T BELIEVE WE'RE LEAVING FOR CAMP MOSQUITO IN A WEEK!
I HOPE THERE ARE TONS OF SPIDERS!
MAYBE YOU'LL MEET A CUTE BOY!
MAYBE I'LL MEET A CUTE SPIDER!
THAT'S OKAY, I HAVE A NEW CRUSH...
WHO?!

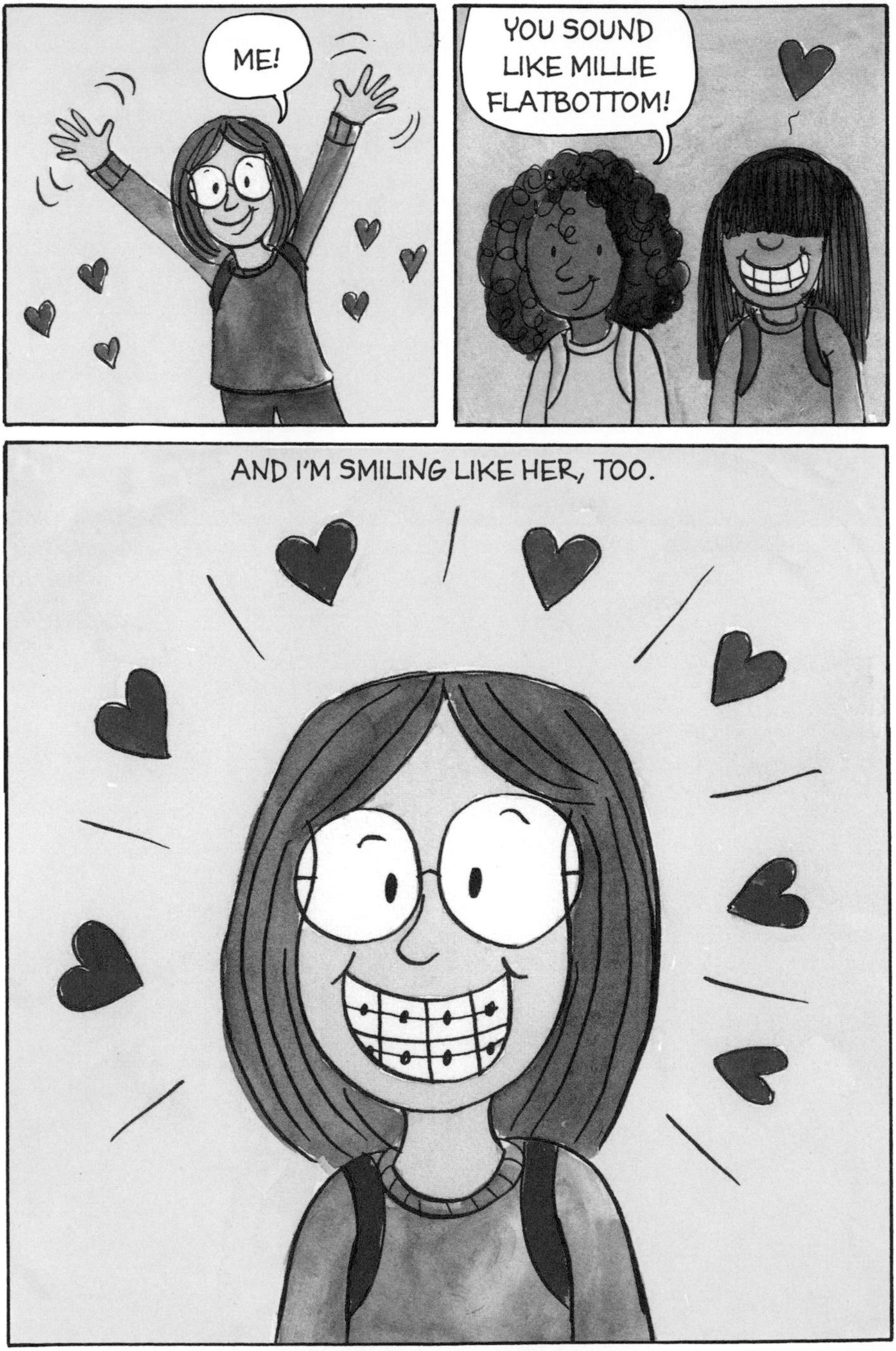
ME!
YOU SOUND LIKE MILLIE FLATBOTTOM!
AND I'M SMILING LIKE HER, TOO.

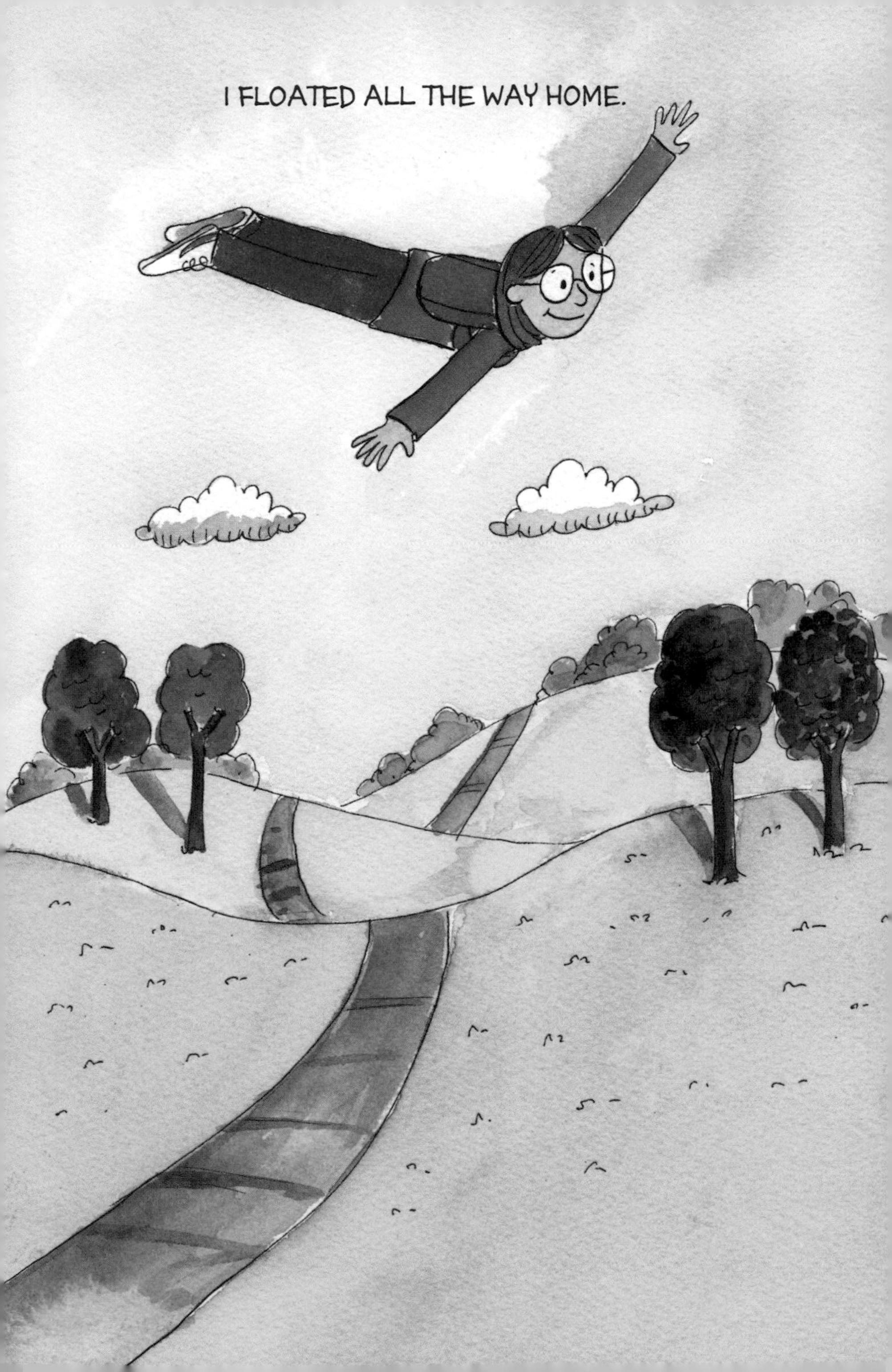
I FLOATED ALL THE WAY HOME.

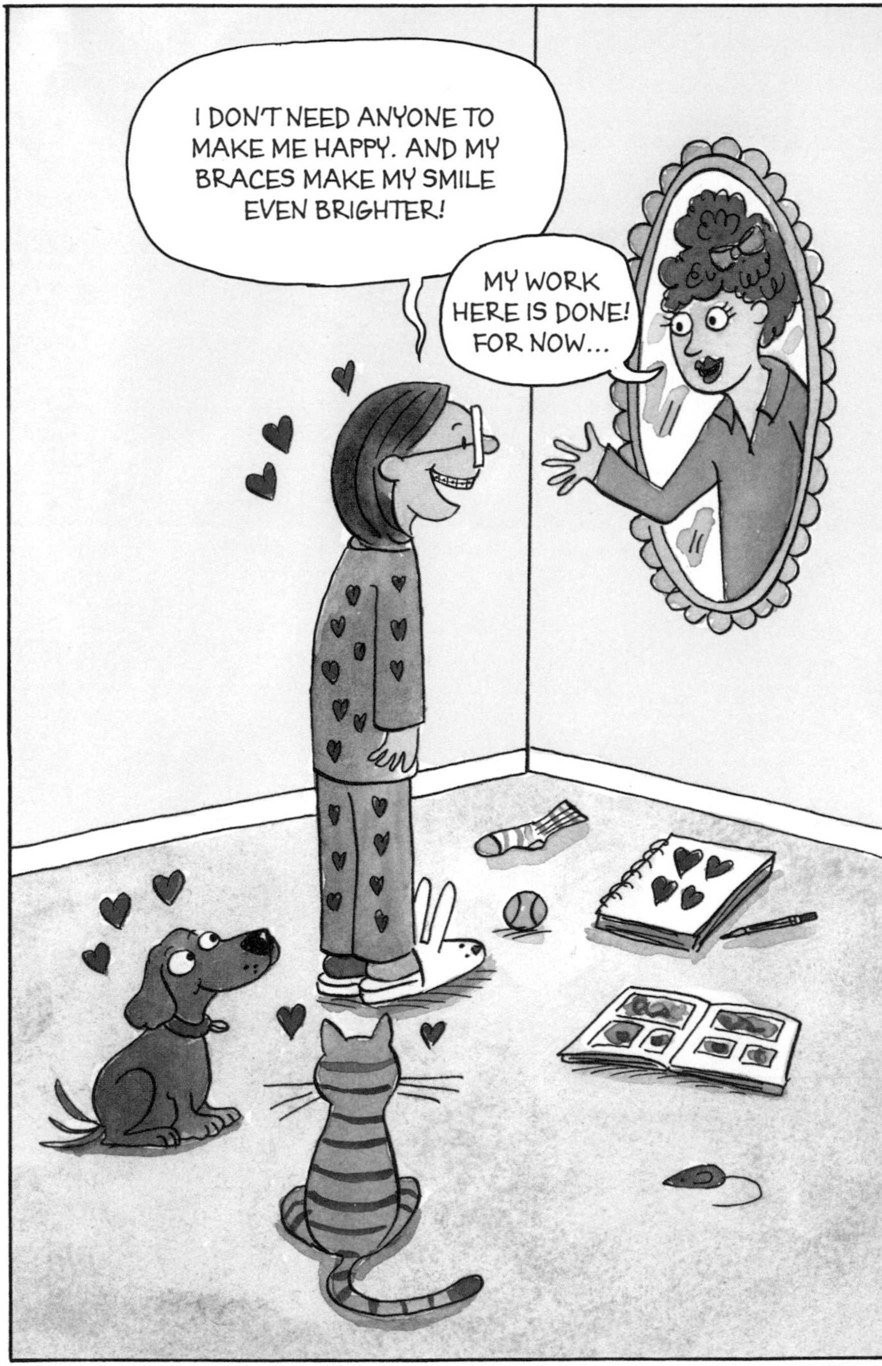
I DON'T NEED ANYONE TO MAKE ME HAPPY. AND MY BRACES MAKE MY SMILE EVEN BRIGHTER!
MY WORK HERE IS DONE! FOR NOW...

THE OUTTAKES

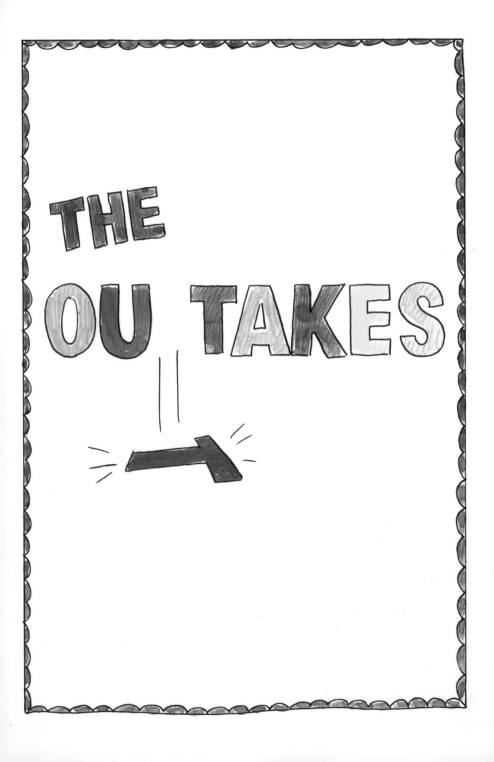

DEREK'S HOMERUN KICKBALL KICK

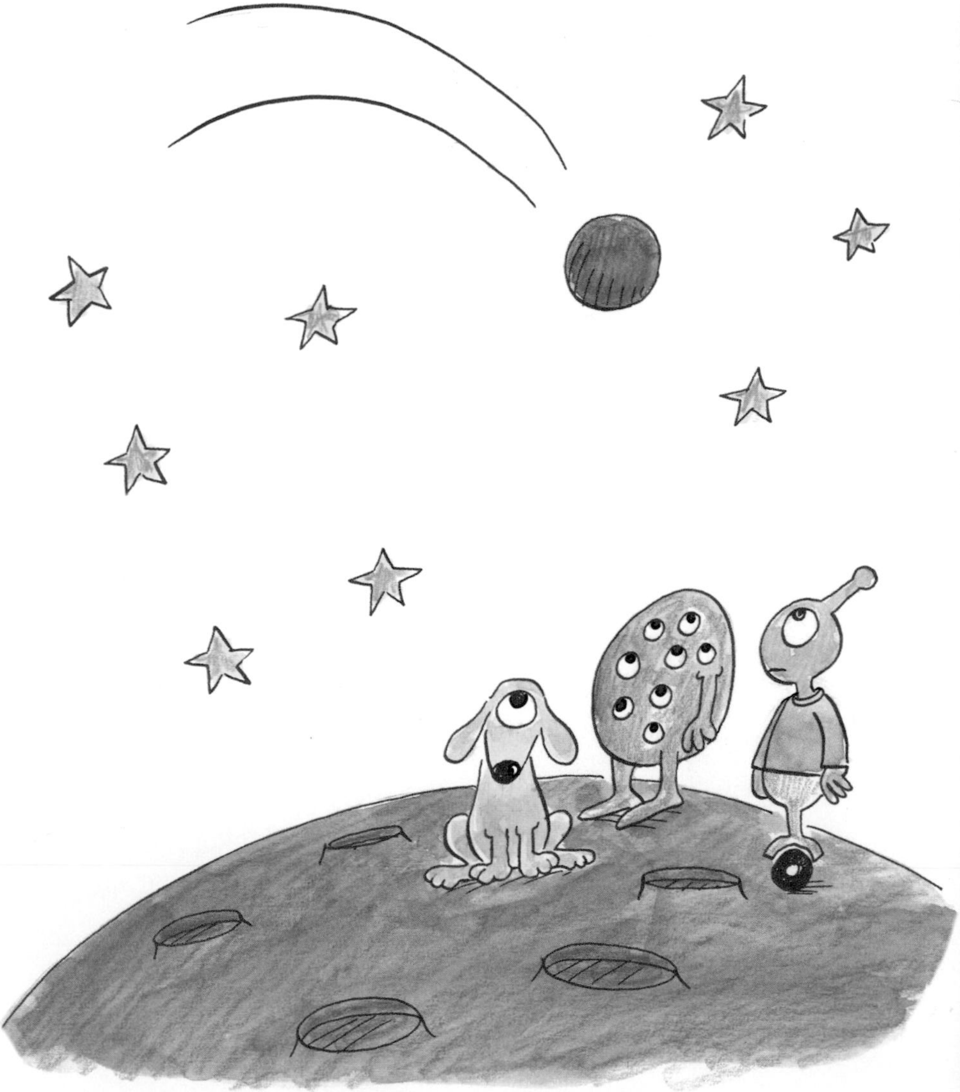

EVEN MORE LUNCHROOM UTENSILS

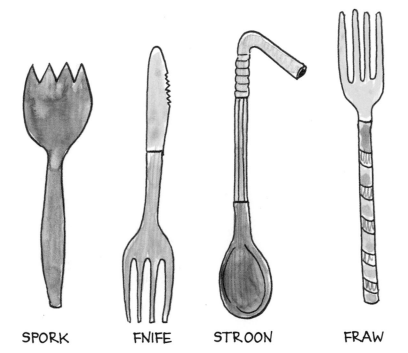

SPORK   FNIFE   STROON   FRAW

FLO'S SOLO

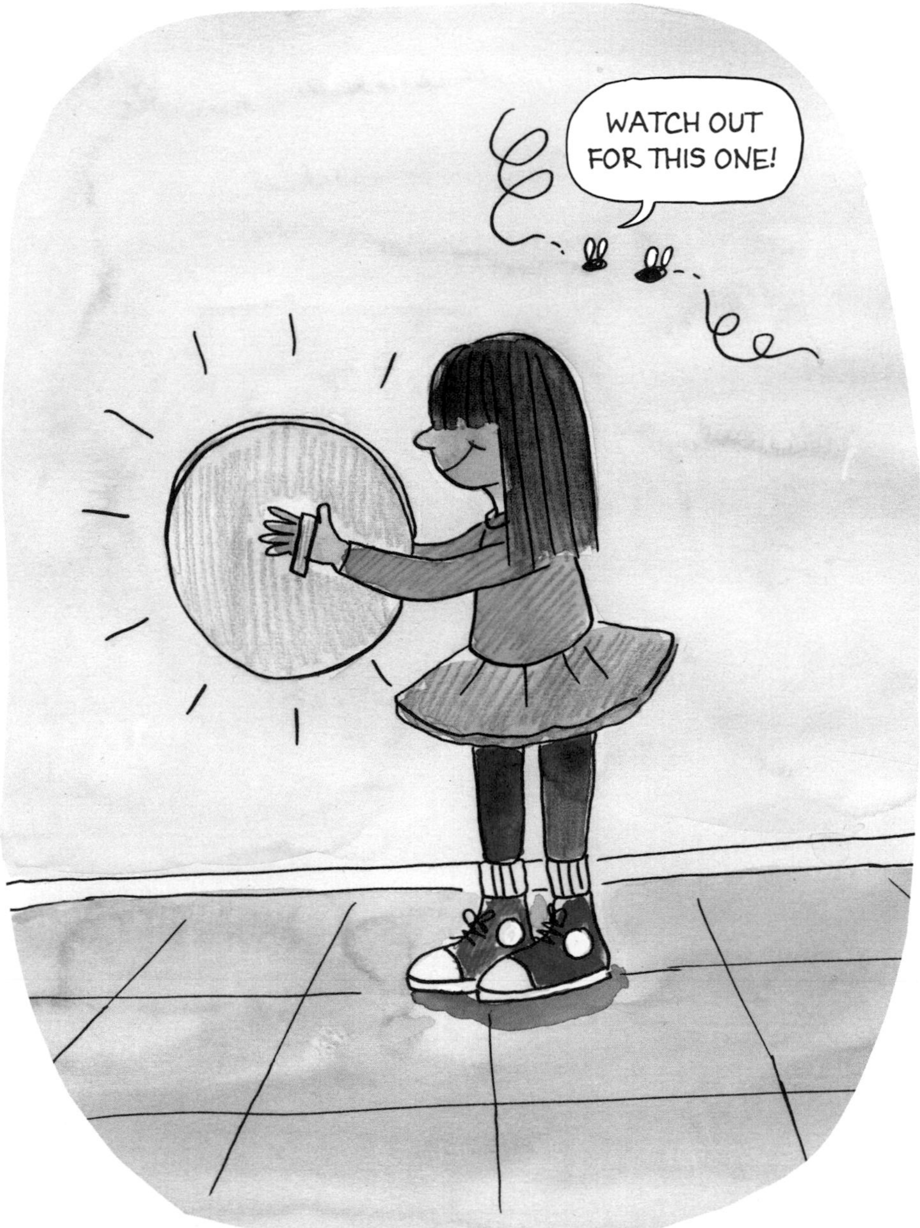

WATCH OUT FOR THIS ONE!

MR. BARRY'S CLOSET

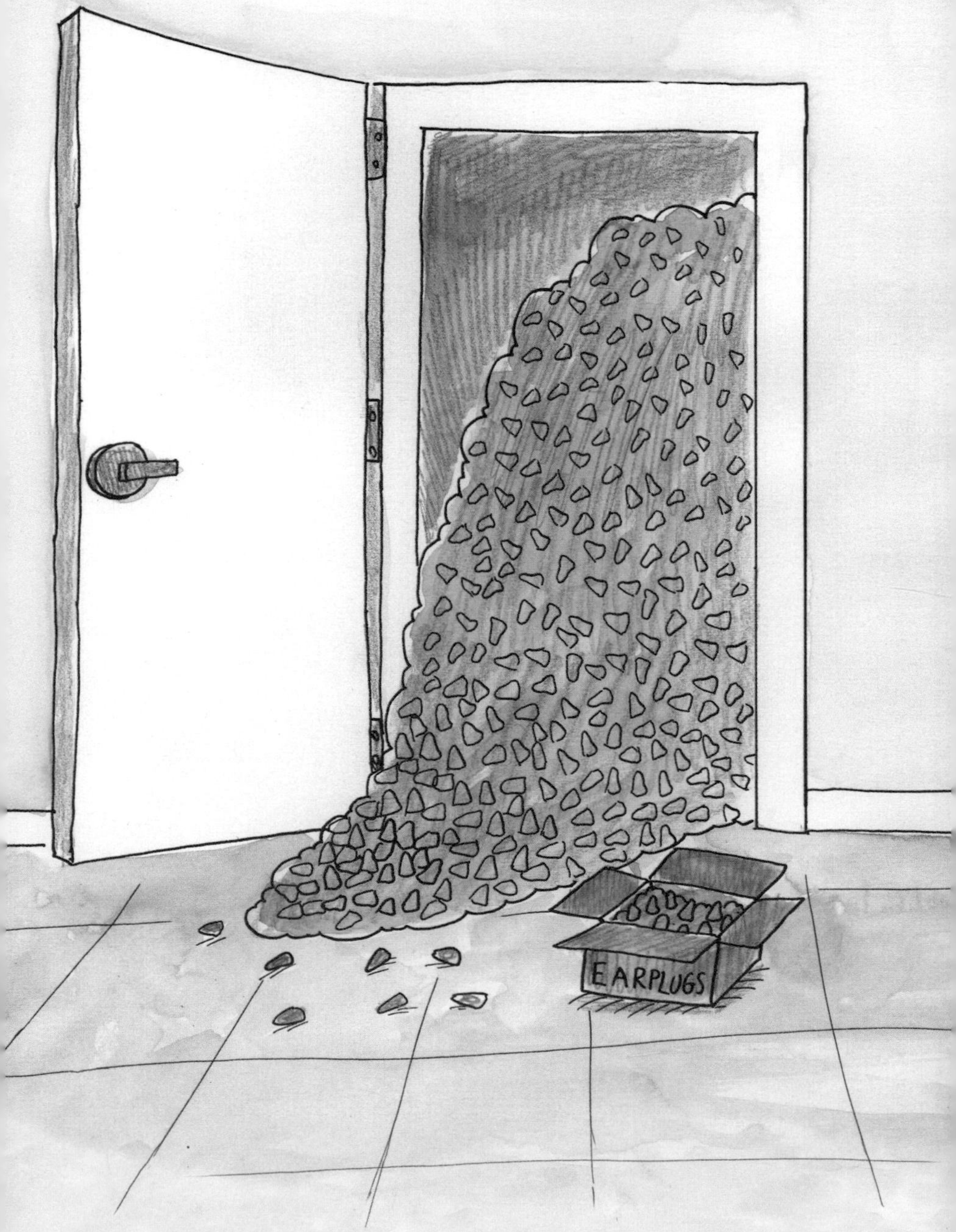
EARPLUGS

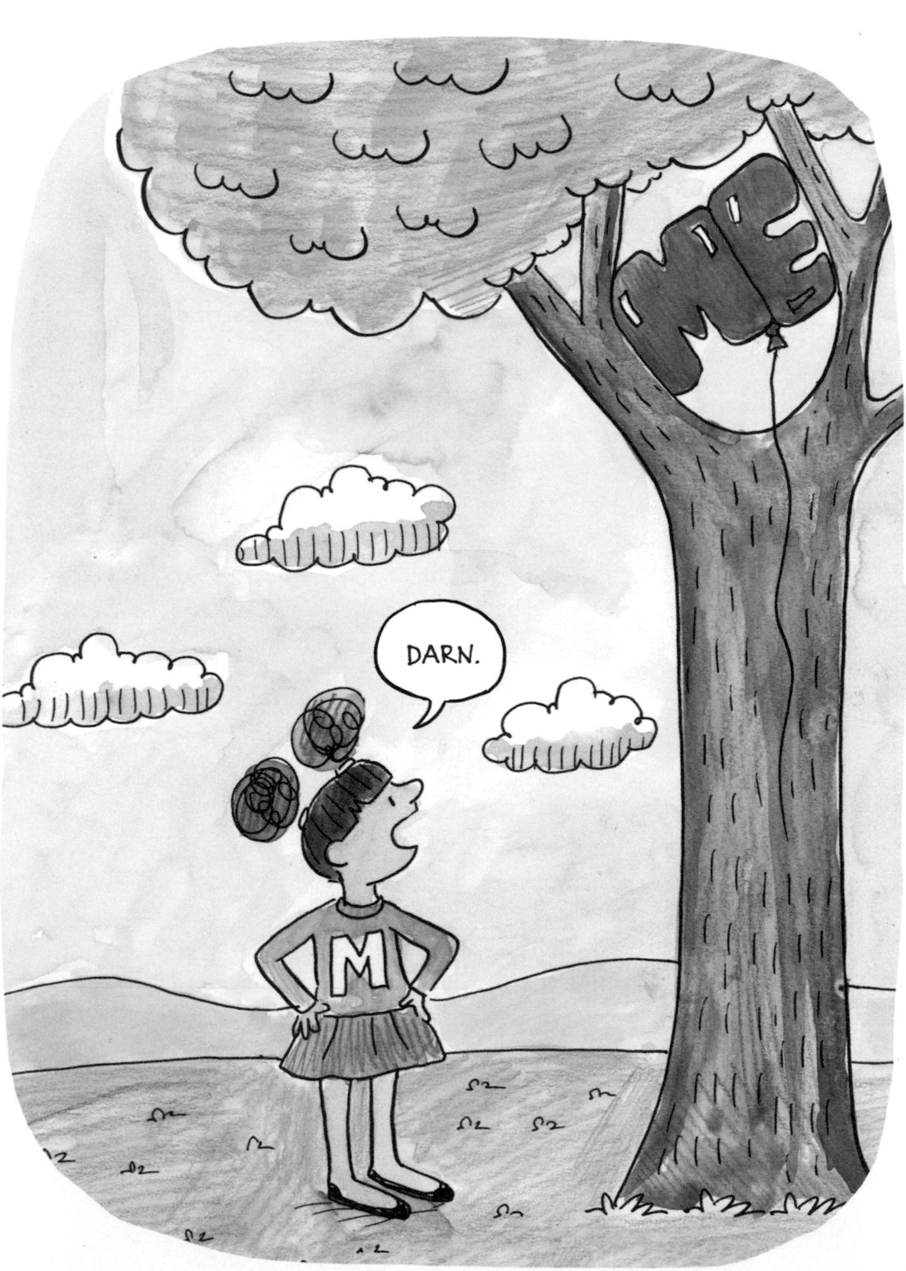
DARN.
M

MY UNSUCCESSFUL JUMPSHOT

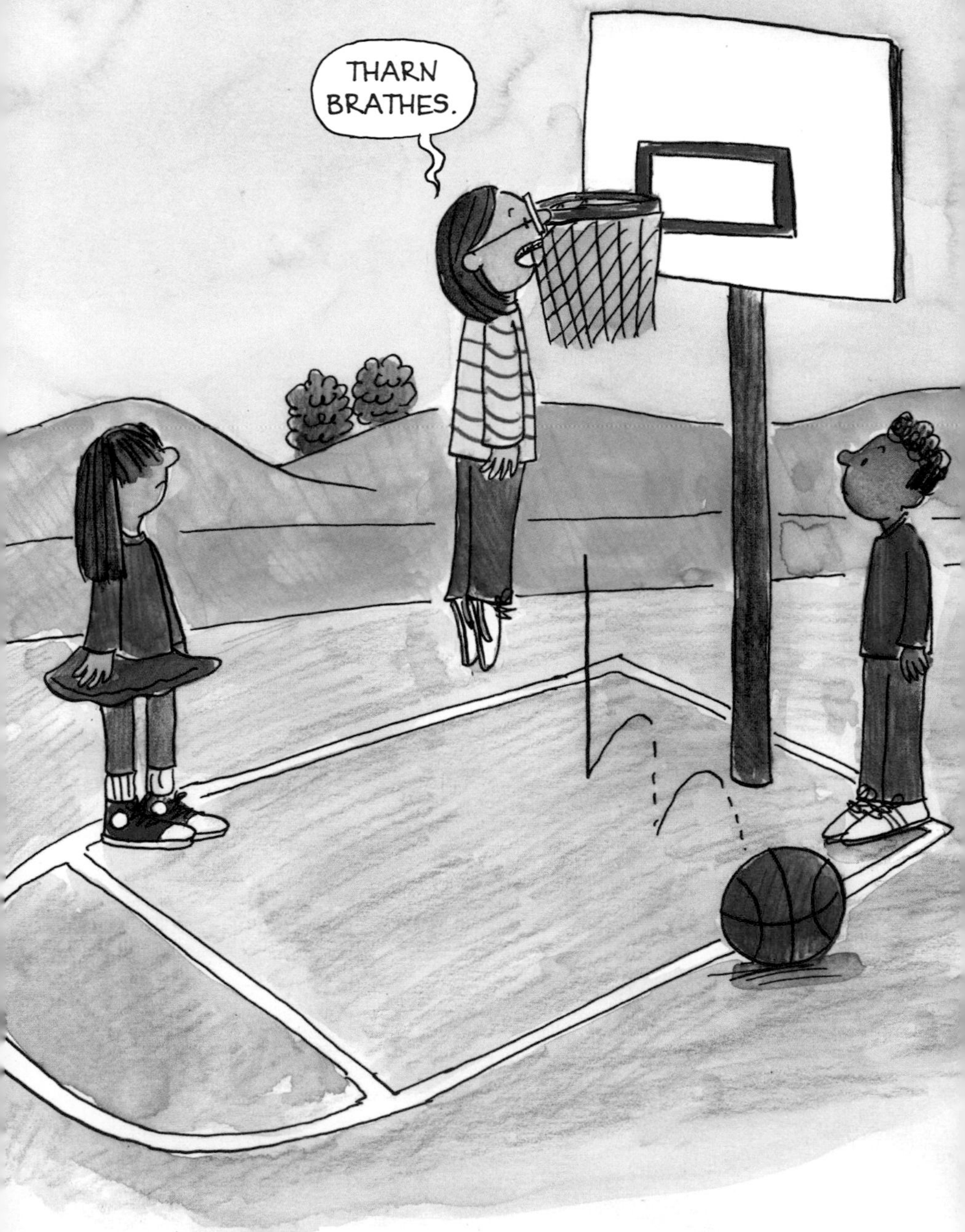
THARN BRATHES.

FLO'S SUGGESTION BOX

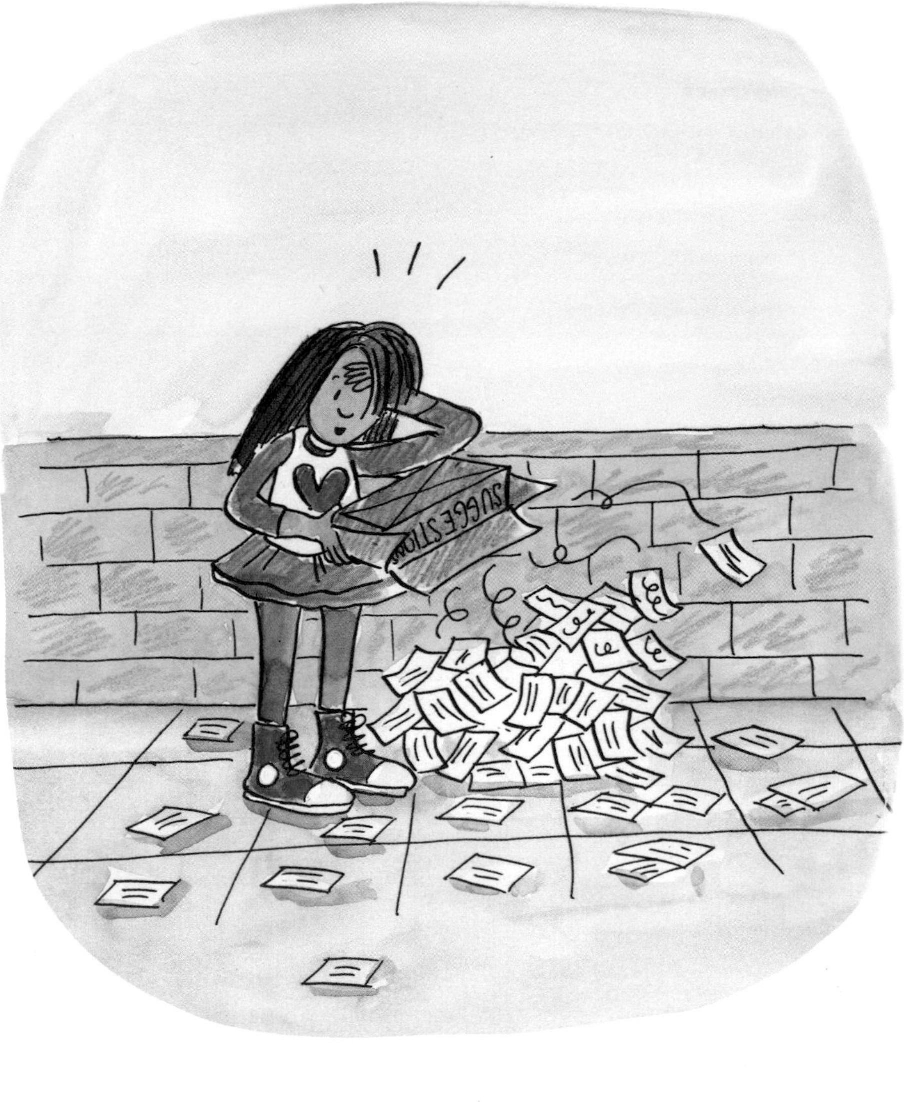
SUGGESTIONS

YUKI'S TUBA PRACTICE

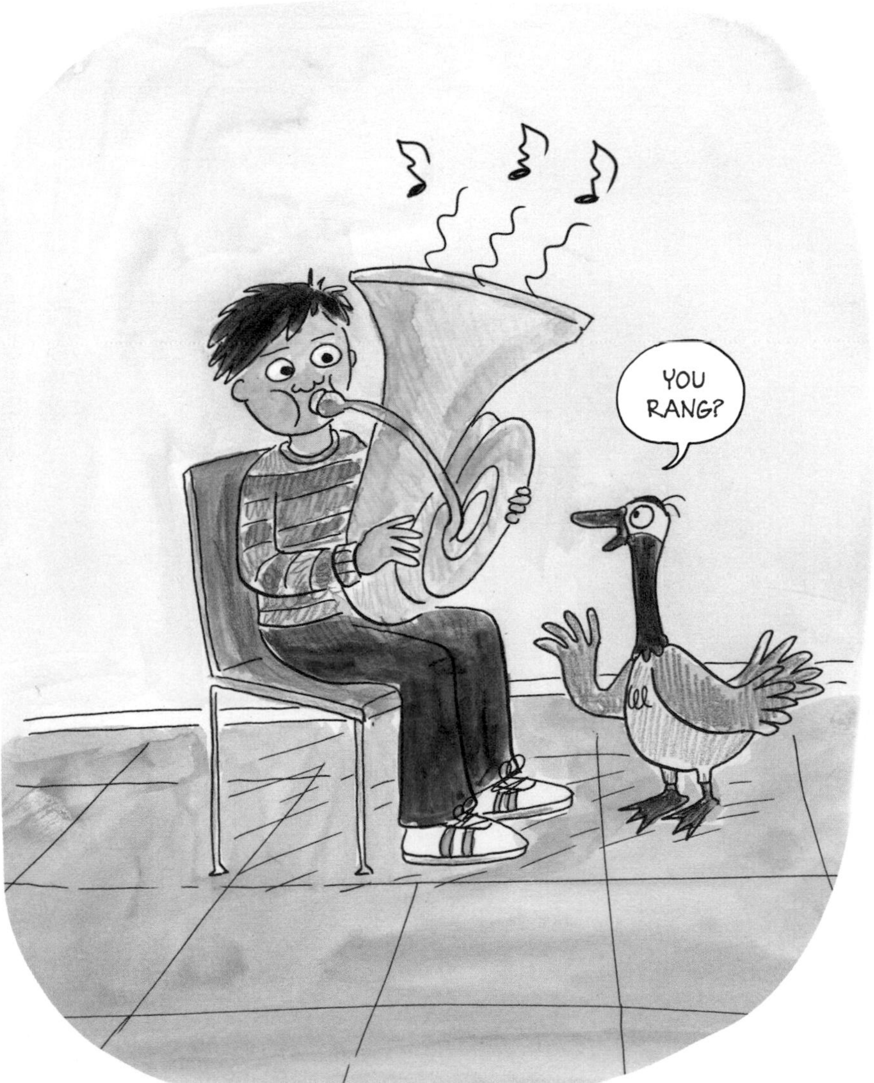
YOU RANG?

SHAWN BARKING

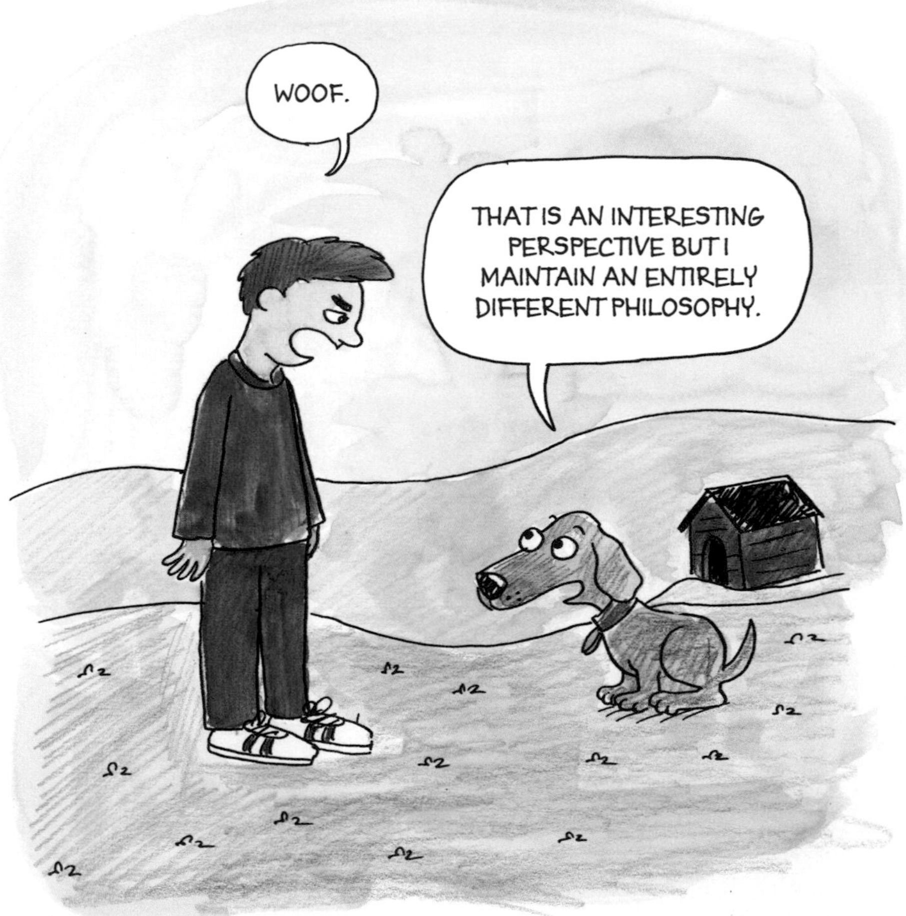
WOOF.
THAT IS AN INTERESTING PERSPECTIVE BUT I MAINTAIN AN ENTIRELY DIFFERENT PHILOSOPHY.

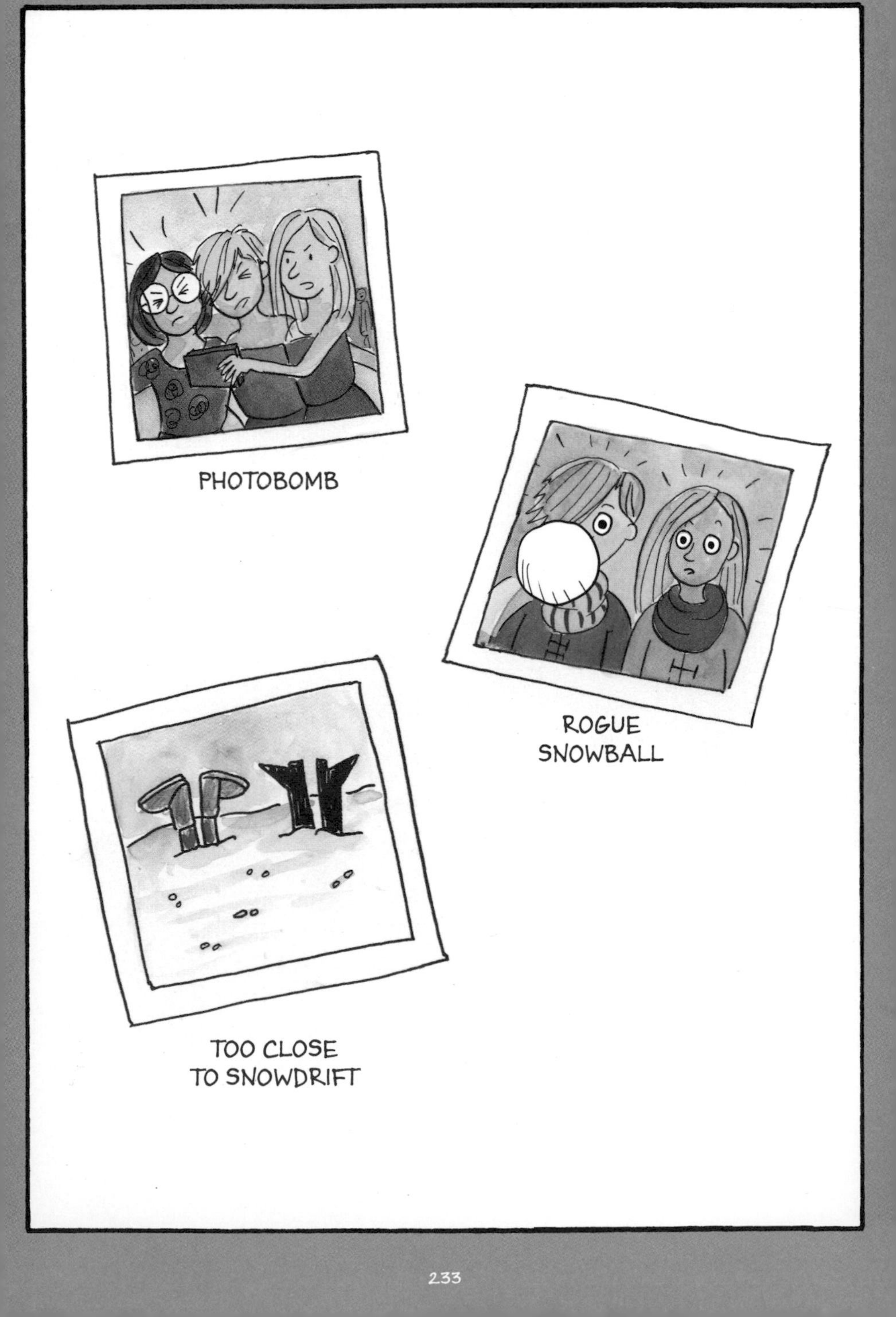
PHOTOBOMB
ROGUE SNOWBALL
TOO CLOSE TO SNOWDRIFT

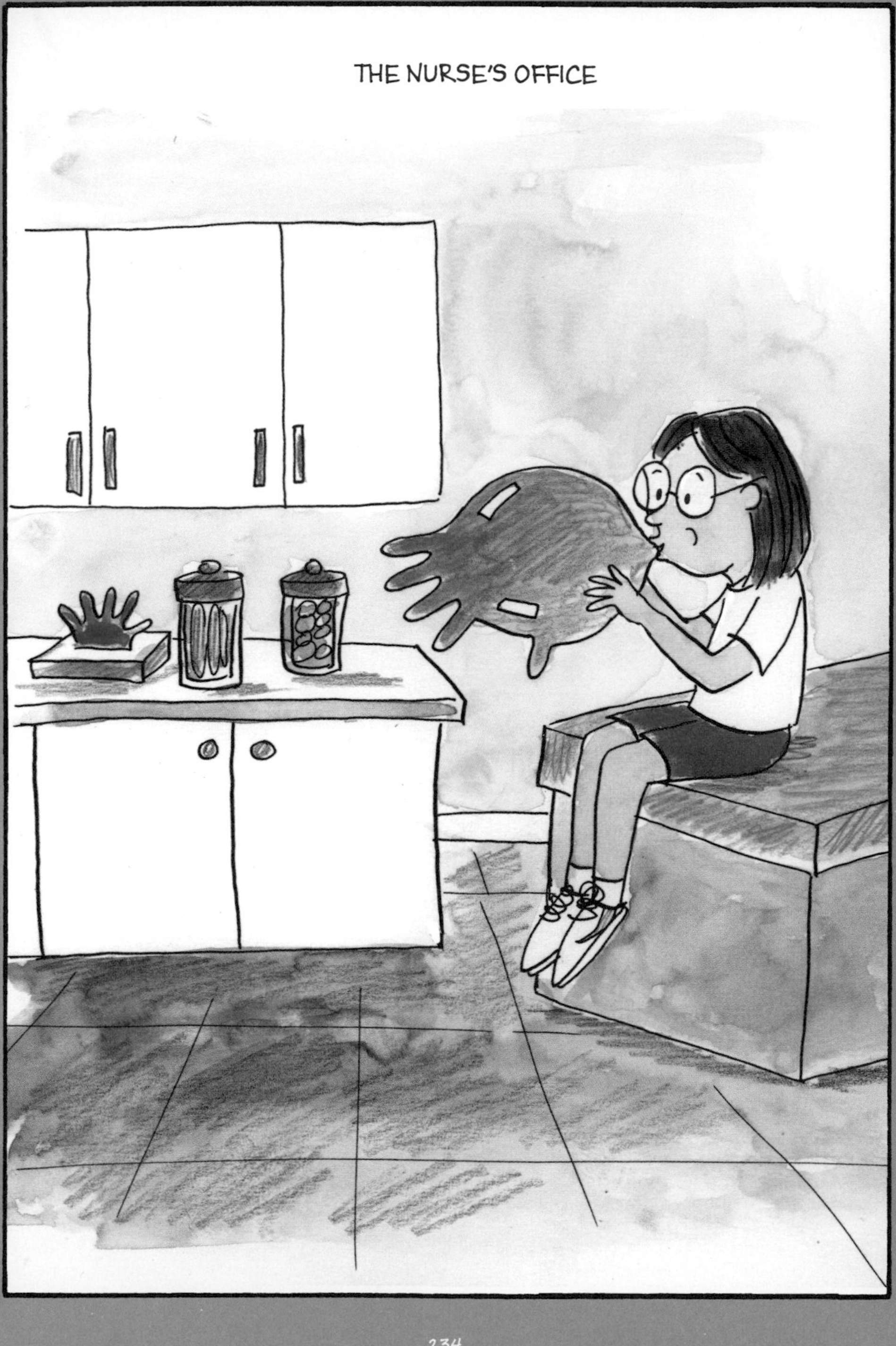
THE NURSE'S OFFICE

THE END

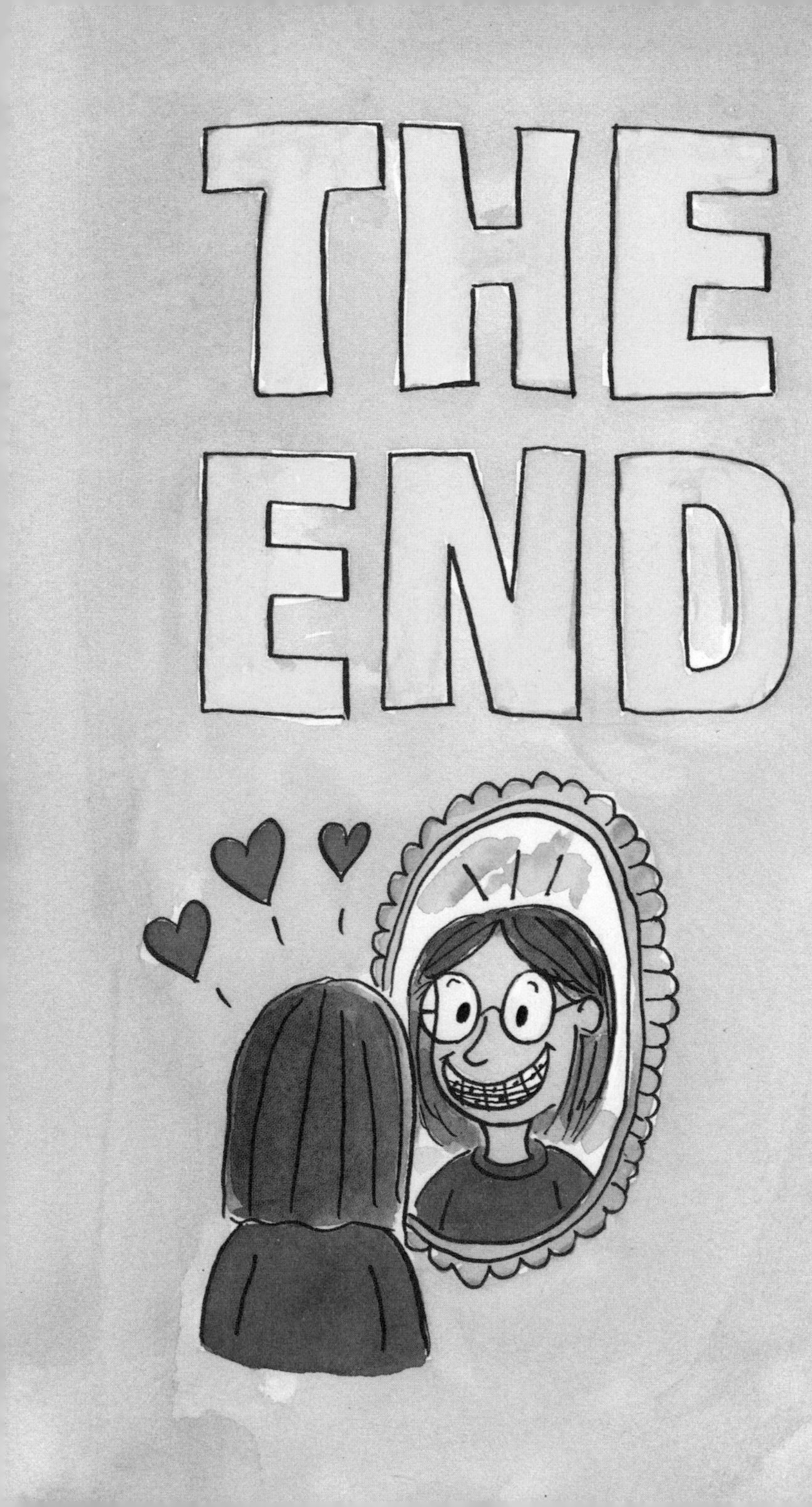

MARIA SCRIVAN is an award-winning cartoonist, illustrator, and author based in Stamford, Connecticut. Her debut graphic novel, *Nat Enough*, released to great acclaim, and her laugh-out-loud syndicated comic, *Half Full*, appears daily in newspapers nationwide and on gocomics.com. Maria licenses her work for greeting cards, and her cartoons have also appeared in *MAD Magazine*, *Parade*, and many other publications. Visit Maria online at mariascrivan.com.